The House Of Dreams-Come-True

by

Margaret Pedler

Double 9 BOOKS

The House Of Dreams-Come-True
by Margaret Pedler

ISBN: 978-93-62765-41-3

Published by

DOUBLE 9 BOOKS

2/13-B, Ansari Road
Daryaganj, New Delhi – 110002
info@double9books.com
www.double9books.com
Tel. 011-40042856

ABOUT THE AUTHOR

Margaret Pedler was a celebrated British novelist renowned for her captivating romantic fiction. Initially, Pedler pursued her passion for music, studying piano and singing at the prestigious Royal Academy of Music. Her musical talent extended beyond performance; she also composed numerous songs, crafting both the music and lyrics for her compositions. However, it was in the realm of literature that Pedler found her true calling. From 1917 to 1947, she dedicated herself to writing, producing an impressive oeuvre of 28 novels. These works quickly garnered widespread acclaim and solidified Pedler's reputation as a best-selling author. Pedler's novels were characterized by their enchanting narratives, richly drawn characters, and compelling romantic themes, captivating readers with their emotional depth and evocative storytelling. Her ability to craft tales of love and longing resonated deeply with audiences, establishing her as a beloved figure in the world of romantic fiction. Throughout her prolific career, Margaret Pedler's novels continued to enchant readers, leaving an indelible mark on the literary landscape. Even decades after her passing, her works remain cherished by readers around the world, a testament to her enduring legacy as a master storyteller of romance.

CONTENTS

It's a strange road leads to the House of Dreams,
To the House of Dreams-Come-True,
Its hills are steep and its valleys deep,
And salt with tears the Wayfarers weep,
The Wayfarers—I and you.

But there's sure a way to the House of Dreams,
To the House of Dreams-Come-True.
We shall find it yet, ere the sun has set,
If we fare straight on, come fine, come wet,
Wayfarers—I and you.
Margaret Pedler.

CHAPTER I
THE WANDER-FEVER

THE great spaces of the hall seemed to slope away into impenetrable gloom; velvet darkness deepening imperceptibly into sable density of panelled wall; huge, smoke-blackened beams, stretching wide arms across the roof, showing only as a dim lattice-work of ebony, fretting the shadowy twilight overhead.

At the furthermost end, like a giant golden eye winking sleepily through the dark, smouldered a fire of logs, and near this, in the luminous circle of its warmth, a man and woman were seated at a table lit by tall wax candles in branched candlesticks. With its twinkling points of light, and the fire's red glow quivering across its shining surface, the table gleamed out like a jewel in a sombre setting—a vivid splash of light in the grey immensity of dusk-enfolded hall.

Dinner was evidently just over, for the candlelight shone softly on satin-skinned fruit, while wonderful gold-veined glass flecked the dark pool of polished mahogany with delicate lines and ripples of opalescent colour.

A silence had fallen on the two who had been dining. They had been gay enough together throughout the course of the meal, but, now that the servants had brought coffee and withdrawn, it seemed as though the stillness—that queer, ghostly, memory-haunted stillness which lurks in the dim, disused recesses of a place—had crept out from the four corners of the hall and were stealing upon them, little by little, as the tide encroaches on the shore, till it had lapped them round in a curious atmosphere of oppression.

The woman acknowledged it by a restless twist of her slim shoulders. She was quite young—not more than twenty—and as she glanced half-enquiringly at the man seated opposite her there was sufficiency of likeness between the two to warrant the assumption that they were father and daughter.

In each there was the same intelligent, wide brow, the same straight nose with sensitively cut nostrils—though a smaller and daintier affair in the feminine edition, and barred across the top by a little string of golden freckles—and, above all, the same determined, pointed chin with the contradictory cleft in it that charmed away its obstinacy.

But here the likeness ended. It was from someone other than the dark-browed man with his dreaming, poet's eyes—which were neither purple nor grey, but a mixture of the two—that Jean Peterson had inherited her beech-leaf brown hair, tinged with warm red where the light glinted on it, and her vivid hazel eyes—eyes that were sometimes golden like the heart of a topaz and sometimes clear and still and brown like the waters of some quiet pool cradled among the rocks of a moorland stream.

They were like that now—clear and wide-open, with a certain pensive, half-humorous questioning in them.

"Well?" she said, at last breaking the long silence. "What is it?"

The man looked across at her, smiling a little.

"Why should it be—anything?" he demanded.

She laughed amusedly.

"Oh, Glyn dear"—she never made use of the conventional address of "father." Glyn Peterson would have disliked it intensely if she had—"Oh, Glyn dear, I haven't been your daughter for the last twenty years without learning to divine when you are cudgelling your brains as to the prettiest method of introducing a disagreeable topic."

Peterson grinned a little. He tossed the end of his cigarette into the fire and lit a fresh one before replying.

"On this occasion," he observed at last, slowly, "the topic is not necessarily a disagreeable one. Jean"—his quizzical glance raked her face suddenly—"how would you like to go to England?"

"To England?"

Her tone held the same incredulous excitement that anyone unexpectedly invited to week-end at El Dorado might be expected to evince.

"*England!* Glyn, do you really mean to take me there at last?"

"You'd like to go then?" A keen observer might have noticed a shade of relief pass over Peterson's face.

"Like it? It's the one thing above all others that I've longed for. It seems so ridiculous to be an Englishwoman and yet never once to have set foot in England."

The man's eyes clouded.

"You're not—entirely—English," he said in a low voice. Jean knew from what memory the quick correction sprang. Her mother, the beautiful opera singer who had been the one romance of Glyn Peterson's life, had been of French extraction.

"I know," she returned soberly. "Yet I think I'm mostly conscious of being English. I believe it's just the very fact that I know Paris—Rome—Vienna—so well, and nothing at all about England, that makes me feel more absolutely English than anything else."

A spark of amusement lit itself in Peterson's eyes.

"How truly feminine!" he commented drily.

Jean nodded.

"I'm afraid it's rather illogical of me."

Her father blew a thin stream of smoke into the air.

"Thank God for it!" he replied lightly. "It's the cussed contradictoriness of your sex that makes it so enchanting. If women were logical they would be as obvious and boring as the average man."

He relapsed into a dreaming silence. Jean broke it rather hesitatingly.

"You've never suggested taking me to England before."

His face darkened suddenly. It was an extraordinarily expressive face—expressive as a child's, reflecting every shade of his constant changes of mood.

"There's no sense of adventure about England," he said shortly. "It's a dull corner of the world—bristling with the proprieties."

Jean realised how very completely, from his own point of view, he had answered her. Romance, beauty, the sheer delight of utter freedom from the conventions were as the breath of his nostrils to Glyn Peterson.

Born to the purple, as it were, of an old English county family, he had stifled in the conventional atmosphere of his upbringing. There had been moments of wild rebellion, bitter outbursts against the established order of things, but these had been sedulously checked and discouraged by his father, a man of iron will, who took himself and his position intensely seriously.

Ultimately, Glyn had come to accept with more or less philosophy the fact of his heirship to old estates and old traditions, with their inevitable responsibilities and claims, and he was just preparing to fulfill his parents' wishes by marrying, suitably and conventionally, when Jacqueline Mavory, the beautiful half-French opera singer, had flashed into his horizon.

In a moment the world was transformed. Artist soul called to artist soul; the romantic vein in the man, so long checked and thwarted, suddenly asserted itself irresistibly, and the very day before that appointed for his wedding, he and Jacqueline ran away together in search of happiness.

And they had found it. The "County" had been shocked; Glyn's father, unbending descendant of the old Scottish Covenanters, his whole creed outraged, had broken under the blow; but the runaway lovers had found what they sought.

At Beirnfels, a beautiful old schloss on the eastern border of Austria, remote from the world and surrounded by forest-clad hills, Glyn Peterson and Jacqueline had lived a romantically happy existence, roaming the world whenever the wander-fever seized them, but always returning to Schloss Beirnfels, where Peterson had contrived a background of almost exotic richness for the adored woman who had flung her career to the winds in order to become his wife.

The birth of Jean, two years after their marriage, had been frankly regarded by both of them as an inconvenience. It interrupted their idyll. They were so essentially lovers that no third—not even a third born of love's consummation—could be other than superfluous.

They had proceeded to shift the new responsibility with characteristic lightheartedness. A small army of nursemaids and governesses was engaged, and later, when Jean was old enough, she was despatched to one of the best Continental schools, whilst her parents continued their customary happy-go-lucky existence uninterruptedly. During the holidays she shared their wanderings, and Egypt and the southern coast of Europe became familiar places to her.

At the age of seventeen, Jean came home to live at Beirnfels, thenceforward regarding her unpractical parents with a species of kindly tolerance and amusement. The three of them had lived quite happily together, though Jean had remained always the odd man out; but she had accepted the fact with a certain humorous philosophy which robbed it of half its sting.

Then, two years later, Jacqueline had developed rapid consumption, and though Glyn hurried her away to Montavan, in the Swiss Alps, there had been no combating the disease, and the romance of a great love had closed down suddenly into the grey shadows of death.

Peterson had been like a man demented. For a time he had disappeared, and no one ever knew, either then or later, how he had first faced the grim tragedy which had overtaken him.

Jean had patiently awaited his return to Beirnfels. When at last he came, he told her that it was the most beautiful thing which could have happened—that Jacqueline should, have died in the zenith of their love.

"We never knew the downward swing of the pendulum," he explained. "And when we meet again it will be as young lovers who have never grown tired. I shall always remember Jacqueline as still perfectly beautiful— never insulted by old age. And when she thinks of me—well, I'm still a 'personable' fellow, as they say— —"

"My dear Glyn, you're still a boy! You've never grown up," Jean made answer. To her he seemed a sort of Peter Pan among men.

She had been amazed—although in a sense relieved—to find how swiftly he had rallied. It seemed almost as though his intense loathing of the onset of old age and decay, of that slow cooling of passion and gradual decline of faculties which age inevitably brings, had served to reconcile him to the loss of the woman he had worshipped whilst yet there had been no dimming of her physical perfection, no blunting of the fine edge of their love.

It was easily comprehensible that to two such temperamental, joy-loving beings as Glyn and Jacqueline, England, with her neutral-tinted skies and strictness of convention, had made little appeal, and Jean could with difficulty harmonise the suddenly projected visit to England with her knowledge of her father's idiosyncrasies.

It was just possible of course, since all which had meant happiness to him lay buried in a little mountain cemetery in Switzerland, that it no longer mattered to Peterson where he sojourned. One place might be as good—or as bad—as another.

Rather diffidently Jean voiced her doubts, recalling him from the reverie into which he had fallen.

"I go to England?" he exclaimed. "God forbid! No, you would go without me."

"Without you?"

Peterson sprang up and began pacing restlessly to and fro.

"Yes, without me. I'm going away. I—I can't stay here any longer. I've tried, Jean, for your sake"—he looked across at her with a kind of appeal in his eyes—"but I can't stand it. I must move on—get away somewhere by myself. Beirnfels—without her——"

He broke off abruptly and stood still, staring down into the heart of the fire. Then he added in a wrung voice:

"It will be a year ago... to-morrow."

Jean was silent. Never before had he let her see the raw wound in his soul. Latterly she had divined a growing restlessness in him, sensed the return of the wander-fever which sometimes obsessed him, but she had not realised that it was pain—sheer, intolerable pain—which was this time driving him forth from the place that had held his happiness.

He had appeared so little changed after Jacqueline's death, so much the wayward, essentially lovable and unpractical creature of former times, still able to find supreme delight in a sunset, or an exquisite picture, or a wild ride across the purple hills, that Jean had sometimes marvelled, how easily he seemed able to forget.

And, after all, he had not forgotten—had never been able to forget!

The gay, debonair side which he had shown the world—that same rather selfish, beauty-loving, charming personality she had always known—had been only a shell, a husk hiding a hurt that had never healed—that never would find healing in this world.

Jean felt herself submerged beneath a wave of self-reproach that she could have thus crudely accepted Glyn's attitude at its face value. But it was useless to give expression to her penitence. She could find no words which might not wound, and while she was still dully trying to readjust her mind to this new aspect of things, her father's voice broke across her thoughts— smooth, polished, with just its usual inflection of whimsical amusement, rather as though the world were a good sort of joke in which he found himself constrained to take part.

"I've made the most paternal arrangements for your welfare in my absence, Jean. I want to discuss them with you. You see, I couldn't take you with me—I don't know in the least where I'm going or where I shall fetch up. That's the charm of it"—his face kindling. "And it wouldn't be right or proper for me to drag a young woman of your age—and attractions—half over the world with me."

By which Jean, not in the least deceived by his air of conscious rectitude, comprehended that he didn't want to be bothered with her. He was bidding for freedom, untrammelled by any petticoats.

"So I've written to my old pal, Lady Anne Brennan," pursued Peterson, "asking if you may stay with her for a little. You would have a delightful time. She was quite the most charming woman I knew in England."

"That must be rather more than twenty years ago," observed Jean drily. "She may have altered a good deal."

Peterson frowned. He hated to have objections raised to any plan that particularly appealed to him.

"Rubbish! Why should she change? Anne was not the sort of woman to change."

Jean was perfectly aware that her father hadn't the least wish to "discuss" his proposals with her, as he had said. What he really wanted was to tell her about them and for her to approve and endorse them with enthusiasm—which is more or less what a man usually wants when he suggests discussing plans with his womankind.

So, recognising that he had all his arrangements cut and dried, Jean philosophically accepted the fact and prepared to fall in with them.

"And has Lady Anne signified her readiness to take me in for an indefinite period?" she enquired.

"I haven't had her answer yet. But I have no doubt at all what form it will take. It will be a splendid opportunity for you, altogether. You know, Jean"—pictorially—"you ought really to see the 'stately homes of England.' Why, they're—they're your birthright!"

Jean reflected humorously that this point of view had only occurred to him now that it chanced to coincide so admirably with his own wishes. Hitherto the "stately homes of England" had been relegated to a quite unimportant position in the background and Jean's attention focussed more directly upon the unpleasing vagaries of the British climate.

"I should like to go to England," was all she said. Peterson smiled at her radiantly—the smile of a child who has got its own way with much less difficulty than it had anticipated.

"You shall go," he promised her. "You'll adore Staple. It's quite a typical old English manor—lawns and terraces all complete, even down to the last detail of a yew hedge."

"Staple? Is that the Brennans' place?"

"God bless my soul, no! The Tormarins acquired it when they came pushing over to England with the Conqueror, I imagine. Anne married twice, you know. Her first husband, Tormarin, led her a dog's life, and after his death she married Claude Brennan—son of a junior branch of the Brennans. Now she is a widow for the second time."

"And are there any children?"

"Two sons. The elder is the son of the first marriage and is the owner of Staple, of course. The younger one is the child of the second marriage. I believe that since Brennan's death they all three live very comfortably together at Staple—at least, they did ten years ago when I last heard from Anne. That was not long after Brennan died."

Jean wrinkled her brows.

"Rather a confusing household to be suddenly pitchforked into," she commented.

"But not dull!" submitted Peterson triumphantly. "And dullness is, after all, the biggest bugbear of existence."

As if suddenly stabbed by the palpable pose of his own remark, the light died out of his face and he looked round the great dim ball with a restless, eager glance, as though trying to impress the picture of it on his memory.

"Beirnfels—my 'House of Dreams-Come-True,'" he muttered to himself.

He had named it thus in those first glowing days when love had transfigured the grim old border castle, turning it into a place of magic visions and consummated hopes. The whimsical name took its origin from a little song which Jacqueline had been wont to sing to him, her glorious voice investing the simple words with a passionate belief and triumph.

> It's a strange road leads to the House of Dreams,
> To the House of Dreams-Come-True,
> Its hills are steep and its valleys deep,
> And salt with tears the Wayfarers weep,
> The Wayfarers—I and you.

But there's sure a way to the House of Dreams,
To the House of Dreams-Come-True.
We shall find it yet, ere the sun has set.
If we fare straight on, come fine, come wet,
Wayfarers—I and you.

Peterson's eyes rested curiously on his daughter's face. There was something mystic, almost visionary, in their quiet, absent gaze.

"One day, Jean," he said, "when you meet the only man who matters, Beirnfels shall be yours—the house where *your* dreams shall come true. It's a house of ghosts now—a dead house. But some day you and the man you love will make it live again."

CHAPTER II
MADAME DE VARIGNY

JEAN was standing looking out from the window of her room in the hotel at Montavan. In the distance, the great white peaks of the Alps strained upwards, piercing the mass of drifting cloud, whilst below lay a world sheeted in snow, the long reach of dazzling purity broken only where the pine-woods etched black trunks against the whiteness and the steely gleam of a frozen lake showed like a broad blade drawn from a white velvet scabbard.

It had been part of Peterson's expressed programme that, before going their separate ways, he and Jean should make a brief stay at Montavan, there to await Lady Anne Brennan's answer to his letter. Jean had divined in this determination an excuse, covering his need to take farewell of that grave on the lonely mountain-side before he set out upon the solitary journey which could not fail to hold poignant memories of other, former wanderings—wanderings invested with the exquisite joy of sharing each adventure with a beloved fellow-wayfarer.

Instinctively though Jean had recognised the desire at the back of Glyn's decision to stop at Montavan, she was scrupulously careful not to let him guess her recognition. She took her cue from his own demeanour, which was outwardly that of a man merely travelling for pleasure, and she listened with a grim sense of amusement when poor Monsieur Vautrinot, the *maître d'hôtel*, recognising Peterson as a former client, sympathetically recalled the sad circumstances of his previous visit and was roundly snubbed for his pains.

To Jean the loss of her mother had meant far less than it would have done to a girl in more commonplace circumstances. It was true that Jacqueline had shown herself all that was kindhearted and generous in her genuine wish to compass the girl's happiness, and that Jean had been frankly fond of her and attracted by her, but in no sense of the words had there been any interpretation of a maternal or filial relationship. As Jean herself, to the huge entertainment of her parents, had on one occasion summed up the situation:

"Of course I know I'm a quite superfluous third at Beirnfels, but, all the same, you two really do make the most perfect host and hostess, and you try awfully hard not to let me feel *de trop*."

But, despite the fact that Jacqueline had represented little more to her daughter than a brilliant and delightful personality with whom circumstances happened to have brought her into contact, Jean was conscious of a sudden thrill of pain as her glance travelled across the wide stretches of snow and came at last to rest on the little burial ground which lay half hidden beneath the shoulder of a hill. She was moved by an immense consciousness of loss—not just the mere sense of bereavement which the circumstances would naturally have engendered, but something more absolute—a sense of all the exquisite maternal element which she had missed in the woman who was dead.

And then came recognition of the uselessness of such regret. Nothing could have made Jacqueline other than she was—one of the world's great lovers. Mated to the man she loved, she asked nothing more of Nature, nor had she herself anything more to give. And the same reasoning, though perhaps in a less degree, could be applied to Peterson's own attitude of detachment towards his daughter; although Jean was intuitively aware that she had come to mean much more to him since her mother's death, even though it might be, perhaps, only because she represented a tangible link with his past happiness.

Thrusting aside the oppression of thought conjured up by her glimpse of that quiet God's Acre, set high up among the hills, she turned abruptly from the window and made her way downstairs to the hotel vestibule.

Here she discovered that Peterson had been claimed by some acquaintances. The encounter was obviously not of his own choosing, for, to Jean's experienced eye, his face bore the slightly restive expression common to it when circumstances had momentarily got the better of him.

His companions were a somewhat elaborate little Frenchman of fifty or thereabouts, with an unmistakable air of breeding about him, and a stately-looking woman some fifteen years younger, whose warm brunette colouring and swift, mobile gesture proclaimed her of Latin blood. All three were conversing in French.

"*Ah! La voici qui vient!*," Peterson turned as Jean approached, his quick exclamation tinctured with relief. Still in French, which both he and Jean spoke as fluently and with as little accent as English, he continued rapidly: "Jean, let me present you to Madame la Comtesse de Varigny."

The girl found herself looking straight into a pair of eyes of that peculiarly opaque, dense brown common to Southern races. They were heavily fringed with long black lashes, giving them a fictitiously soft and disarming expression, yet Jean was vaguely conscious that their real expression held something secret and implacable, almost repellant, an impression strengthened by the virile, strongly-marked black brows that lay so close above them.

For the rest, Madame de Varigny was undeniably a beautiful woman, her blue-black, rather coarse hair framing an oval face, extraordinarily attractive in contour, with somewhat high cheek bones and a clever, flexible mouth.

Jean's first instinctive feeling was one of distaste. In spite of her knowledge that Varigny was one of the oldest names in France, the Countess struck her as partaking a little of the adventuress—of the type of woman of no particular birth who has climbed by her wits—and she wondered what position she had occupied prior to her marriage.

She was sharply recalled from her thoughts to find that Madame de Varigny was introducing the little middle-aged Frenchman to her as her husband, and immediately she spoke Jean felt her suspicions melting away beneath the warm, caressing cadences of an unusually beautiful voice. Such a voice was a straight passport to the heart. It seemed to clothe even the prosaic little Count in an almost romantic atmosphere of tender charm, an effect which he speedily dispelled by giving Jean a full, true, and particular account of the various pulmonary symptoms which annually induced him to seek the high, dry air of Montavan.

"It is as an insurance of good health that I come," he informed Jean gravely.

"Oh, yes, we are not here merely for pleasure—*comme ces autres*" —- Madame de Varigny gestured smilingly towards a merry party of men and girls who had just come in from luging and were stamping the snow from off their feet amid gay little outbursts of chaff and laughter. "We are here just as last year, when we first made the acquaintance of Monsieur Peterson"—the suddenly muted quality of her voice implied just the right amount of sympathetic recollection—"so that *mon pauvre mari* may assure himself of yet another year of health."

The faintly ironical gleam in her eyes convinced Jean that, as she had shrewdly begun to suspect, the little Count was a *malade imaginaire*, and once she found herself wondering what could be the circumstances responsible for the union of two such dissimilar personalities as the high-bred, hypochondriacal little Count and the rather splendid-looking but almost certainly plebeian-born woman who was his wife.

She intended, later on, to ask her father if he could supply the key to the riddle, but he had contrived to drift off during the course of her conversation with the Varignys, and, when at last she found herself free to join him, he had disappeared altogether.

She thought it very probable that he had gone out to watch the progress of a ski-ing match to which he had referred with some enthusiasm earlier in the day, and she smiled a little at the characteristic way in which he had extricated himself, at her expense, from the inconvenience of his unexpected recontre with the Varignys.

But, two hours later, she realised that once again his superficial air of animation had deceived her. From her window she saw him coming along the frozen track that led from the hillside cemetery, and for a moment she hardly recognised her father in that suddenly shrank, huddled figure of a man, stumbling down the path, his head thrust forward and sunken on his breast.

Her first imperative instinct was to go and meet him. Her whole being ached with the longing to let him feel the warm rush of her sympathy, to assure him that he was not utterly alone. But she checked the impulse, recognising that he had no use for any sympathy or love which she could give.

She had never really been anything other than exterior to his life, outside his happiness, and now she felt intuitively that he would wish her to remain equally outside the temple of his grief.

He was the type of man who would bitterly resent the knowledge that any eyes had seen him at a moment of such utter, pitiable self-revelation, and it was the measure of her understanding that Jean waited quietly till he should choose to come to her.

"When he came, he had more or less regained his customary poise, though he still looked strained and shaken. He addressed her abruptly.

"I've decided to go straight on to Marseilles and sail by the next boat, Jean. There's one I can catch if I start at once."

"At once?" she exclaimed, taken aback. "You don't mean—to-day?"

He nodded.

"Yes, this very evening. I find I can get down to Montreux in time for the night mail." Then, answering her unspoken thought: "You'll be quite all right. You will be certain to hear from Lady Anne in a day or two, and, meanwhile, I'll ask Madame de Varigny to play chaperon. She'll be delighted"—with a flash of the ironical humour that was never long absent from him.

"Who was she before she married the Count?" queried Jean.

"I can't tell you. She is very reticent about her antecedents—probably with good reason"—smiling grimly. "But she is a big and beautiful person, and our little Count is obviously quite happy in his choice."

"She is rather a fascinating woman," commented Jean.

"Yes—but preferable as a friend rather than an enemy. I don't know anything about her, but I wouldn't mind wagering that she has a dash of Corsican blood in her. Anyway, she will look after you all right till Anne Brennan writes."

"And if no letter comes?" suggested Jean. "Or supposing Lady Anne can't have me? We're rather taking things for granted, you know."

His face clouded, but cleared again almost instantly.

"She *will* have you. Anne would never refuse a request of mine. If not, you must come on to me, and I'll make other arrangements,"—vaguely. "I'll let the next boat go, and stay in Paris till I hear from you. But I can't wait here any longer."

He paused, then broke out hurriedly:

"I ought never to have come to this place. It's haunted. I know you'll understand—you always do understand, I think, you quiet child—why I must go."

And Jean, looking with the clear eyes of unhurt youth into the handsome, grief-ravaged face, was suddenly conscious of a shrinking fear of that mysterious force called love, which can make, and so swiftly, terribly unmake the lives of men and women.

CHAPTER III
THE STRANGER ON THE ICE

"AND this friend of your father's? You have not heard from her yet?"

Jean and Madame de Varigny were breakfasting together the morning after Peterson's departure.

"No. I hoped a letter might have come for me by this morning's post. But I'm afraid I shall be on your hands a day or two longer" — smiling.

"But it is a pleasure!" Madame de Varigny reassured her warmly. "My husband and I are here for another week yet. After that we go on to St. Moritz. He is suddenly discontented with Montavan. If, by any chance, you have not then heard from Lady—Lady—I forget the name——"

"Lady Anne Brennan," supplied Jean.

A curiously concentrated expression seemed to flit for an instant across Madame de Varigny's face, but she continued smoothly:

"*Mais, oui*—Lady Brennan. *Eh bien*, if you have not heard from her by the time we leave for St. Moritz, you must come with us. It would add greatly to our pleasure."

"It's very good of you," replied Jean. She felt frankly grateful for the suggestion, realising that if, by any mischance, the letter should be delayed till then, Madame de Varigny's offer would considerably smooth her path. In spite of Glyn's decision that she must join him in Paris, should Lady Anne's invitation fail to materialise, she was well aware that he would not greet her appearance on the scene with any enthusiasm.

"I suppose" — the Countess was speaking again — "I suppose Brennan is a very frequent—a common name in England?"

The question was put quite casually, more as though for the sake of making conversation than anything else, yet Madame de Varigny seemed to await the answer with a curious anxiety.

"Oh, no," Jean replied readily enough, "I don't think it is a common name. Lady Anne married into a junior branch of the family, I believe," she added.

"That would not be considered a very good match for a peer's daughter, surely?" hazarded the Countess. "A junior branch? I suppose there was a romantic love-affair of some kind behind it?"

"It was Lady Anne's second marriage. Her first husband was a Tormarin—one of the oldest families in England." Jean spoke rather stiffly. There was something jarring about the pertinacious catechism.

Madame de Varigny's lips trembled as she put her next question, and not even the dusky fringe of lashes could quite soften the sudden tense gleam in her eyes.

"Tor—ma—rin!" She pronounced the name with a French inflection, evidently finding the unusual English word a little beyond her powers. "What a curious name! That, I am sure, must be uncommon. And this Lady Anne—she has children—sons? No?"

"Oh, yes. She has two sons."

"Indeed?" Madame de Varigny looked interested. "And what are the sons called?"

Jean regarded her with mild surprise. Apparently the subject of nomenclature had a peculiar fascination for her.

"I really forget. My father did once tell me, but I don't recollect what he said."

A perceptible shade of disappointment passed over the other's face, then, as though realising that she had exhibited a rather uncalled-for curiosity, she said deprecatingly:

"I fear I seem intrusive. But I am so interested in your future—I have taken a great fancy to you, mademoiselle. That must be my excuse." She rose from the table, adding smilingly: "At least you will not find it dull, since Lady Anne has two sons. They will he companions for you."

Jean rose, too, and together they passed out of the *salle à manger*.

"And what do you propose to do with yourself to-day?" asked the Countess, pausing in the hall. "My husband and I are going for a sleigh drive. Would you care to come with us? We should he delighted."

Jean shook her head.

"It's very kind of you. But I should really like to try my luck on the ice. I haven't skated for some years, and as I feel a trifle shaky about beginning again, Monsieur Griolet, who directs the sports, has promised to coach me up a bit some time this morning."

"*Bon!*" Madame de Varigny nodded pleasantly. "You will be well occupied while we are away. Au revoir, then, till our return. Perhaps we shall walk down to the rink later to witness your progress under Monsieur Groilet's instruction."

She smiled mischievously, the smile irradiating her face with a sudden charm. Jean felt as though, for a moment, she had glimpsed the woman the Countess might have been but for some happening in her life which had soured and embittered it, setting that strange implacability within the liquid depths of her soft, southern eyes.

She was still speculating on Madame de Varigny's curious personality as she made her way along the beaten track that led towards the rink, and then, as a sudden turn of the way brought the sheet of ice suddenly into full view, all thoughts concerning the bunch of contradictions that goes to make up individual character were swept out of her mind.

In the glory of the morning sunlight the stretch of frozen water gleamed like a shield of burnished silver, whilst on its further side rose great pine-woods, mysteriously dark and silent, climbing the steeply rising ground towards the mountains.

There were a number of people skating, and Jean discovered Monsieur Griolet in the distance, supervising the practice of a pretty American girl who was cutting figures with an ease and exquisite balance of lithe body that hardly seemed to stand in need of the instructions he poured forth so volubly. Probably, Jean decided, the American had entered for some match and was being coached up to concert pitch accordingly.

She stood for a little time watching with interest the varied performances of the skaters. Bands of light-hearted young folk, indulging in the sport just for the sheer enjoyment of it, sped gaily by, broken snatches of their talk and laughter drifting back to her as they passed, whilst groups of more accomplished skaters performed intricate evolutions with an earnestness and intensity of purpose almost worthy of a better cause.

Jean felt herself a little stranded and forlorn. She would have liked someone to share her enthusiasm for the marvels achieved by the figure-skaters—and to laugh with her a little at their deadly seriousness and at the scraps of heated argument anent the various schools of technique which came to her, borne on the still, clear air.

Presently her attention was attracted by the solitary figure of a man who swept past her in the course of making a complete circle of the rink. He skimmed the ice with the free assurance of an expert, and as he passed, Jean caught a fleeting glimpse of a supple, sinewy figure, and of a lean, dark face, down-bent, with a cap crammed low on to the somewhat scowling brows.

There was something curiously distinctive about the man. Brief as was her vision of him, it possessed an odd definiteness—a vividness of impression that was rather startling.

He flashed by, his arms folded across his chest, moving with long, rhythmic strokes which soon carried him to the further side of the rink. Jean's eyes followed him interestedly. He was unmistakably an Englishman, and he seemed to be as solitary as herself, but, unlike her, he appeared indifferent to the fact, absorbed in his own thoughts which, to judge by the sullen, brooding expression of his face, were not particularly pleasant ones.

Soon she lost sight of him amid the scattered groups of smoothly gliding figures. The scene reminded her of a cinema show. People darted suddenly into the picture, materialising in full detail in the space of a moment, then rushed out of it again, dwindling into insignificant black dots which merged themselves into the continuously shifting throng beyond.

At last she bent her steps towards the lower end of the rink, by common consent reserved for beginners in the art of skating. She had not skated for several years, owing to a severe strain which had left her with a weak ankle, and she felt somewhat nervous about starting again.

Rather slowly she fastened on her skates and ventured tentatively on to the ice. For a few minutes she suffered from a devastating feeling that her legs didn't belong to her, and wished heartily that she had never quitted the safe security of the bank, but before long her confidence returned, and with it that flexible ease of balance which, once acquired, is never really lost.

In a short time she was thoroughly enjoying the rapid, effortless motion, and felt herself equal to steering a safe course beyond the narrow limits of the "Mugs' Corner"—as that portion of the ice allotted to novices was unkindly dubbed.

She struck out for the middle of the rink, gradually increasing her speed and revelling in the sting of the keen, cold air against her face. Then, all at once, it seemed as though the solid surface gave way beneath her foot. She lurched forward, flung violently off her balance, and in the same moment the sharp clink of metal upon ice betrayed the cause. One of her skates, insecurely fastened, had come off.

She staggered wildly, and in another instant would have fallen had not someone, swift as a shadow, glided suddenly abreast of her and, slipping a supporting arm round her waist, skated smoothly beside her, little by little slackening their mutual pace until Jean, on one blade all this time, could stop without danger of falling.

As they glided to a standstill, she turned to offer her thanks and found herself looking straight into the lean, dark face of the Englishman who had passed her when she had been watching the skaters.

He lifted his cap, and as he stood for a moment bare-headed beside her, she noticed with a curious little shock—half surprised, half appreciative—that on the left temple his dark brown hair was streaked with a single pure white lock, as though a finger had been laid upon the hair and bleached it where it lay. It conferred a certain air of distinction—an added value of contrast—just as the sharp black shadow in a neutral-tinted picture gives sudden significance to the whole conception.

The stranger was regarding Jean with a flicker of amusement in his grey eyes.

"That was a near thing!" he observed.

Evidently he judged her to be a Frenchwoman, for he spoke in French—very fluently, but with an unmistakable English accent. Instinctively Jean, who all her life had been as frequently called upon to converse in French as English, responded in the same language.

She was breathing rather quickly, a little shaken by the suddenness of the incident, and his face took on a shade of concern.

"You're not hurt, I hope? Did you twist your ankle?"

"No—oh, no," she smiled up at him. "I can't have fastened my skate on properly, and when it shot off like that I'm afraid I rather lost my head. You see," she added explanatorily, "I haven't skated for some years. And I was never very proficient."

"I see," he said gravely. "It was a little rash of you to start again quite alone, wasn't it?"

"I suppose it was. However, as you luckily happened to be there to save me from the consequences, no harm is done. Thank you so much."

There was a note of dismissal in her voice, but apparently he failed to notice it, for he held out his hands to her crosswise, saying:

"Let me help you to the bank, and then I'll retrieve your errant skate for you."

He so evidently expected her to comply with his suggestion that, almost without her own volition, she found herself moving with him towards the edge of the rink, her hands grasped in a close, steady clasp, and a moment later she was scrambling up the bank. Once more on level ground, she made a movement to withdraw her hands.

"I can manage quite well now," she said rather nervously. There was something in that strong, firm grip of his which sent a curious tremor of consciousness through her.

He made no answer, but released her instantly, and in her anxiety to show him how well she could manage she hurried on, struck the tip of the skate she was still wearing against a little hummock of frozen snow, and all but fell. He caught her as she stumbled.

"I think." he remarked drily, "you would do well to sacrifice your independence till your feet are on more equal terms with one another."

Jean laughed ruefully.

"I think I should," she agreed meekly.

He led her to where the prone trunk of a tree offered a seat of sorts, then went in search of the missing skate. Returning in a few moments, he knelt beside her and fastened it on—securely this time—to the slender foot she extended towards him.

"You're much too incompetent to be out on the ice alone," he remarked as he buckled the last strap.

A faint flush of annoyance rose in Jean's cheeks at the uncompromising frankness of the observation.

"What are your friends thinking of to let you do such a thing?" he pursued, blandly ignoring her mute indignation.

"I have no friends here. I am—my own mistress," she replied rather tartly.

He was still kneeling in the snow in front of her. Now he sat back on his heels and subjected her face to a sharp, swift scrutiny. Almost, she thought, she detected a sudden veiled suspicion in the keen glance.

"You're not the sort of girl to be knocking about—alone—at a hotel," he said at last, as though satisfied.

"How do you know what I'm like?" she retorted quickly, "You are hardly qualified to judge."

"*Pardon, mademoiselle*, I do not know what you are—but I do know very certainly what you are not. And"—smiling a little—"I think we have just had ocular demonstration of the fact that you're not accustomed to fending for yourself."

There was something singularly attractive about his smile. It lightened his whole face, contradicting the settled gravity that seemed habitual to it, and Jean found herself smiling back in response.

"Well, as a matter of fact, I'm not," she admitted. "I came here with my father, and he was—was suddenly called away. I am going on to stay with friends."

"This is my last day here," he remarked with sudden irrelevance. "I am off first thing to-morrow morning."

"You're not stopping at the hotel, are you?"

He shook his head.

"No. I'm staying at a friend's chalet a little way beyond it. *Mais, voyons, mademoiselle,* you will catch cold sitting there. Are you too frightened to try the ice again?"

He seemed to assume that her next essay would be made in his company. Jean spoke a little hurriedly.

"Oh, no, I was supposed to have a lesson with Monsieur Griolet this morning. He is an instructor," she explained. "But he was engaged coaching someone else when I came out."

"And which is this Monsieur Griolet? Can you see him?"

Jean's glance ranged over the scattered figures on the rink.

"Yes. There he is."

His eyes followed the direction indicated.

"He seems to be well occupied at the moment," he commented. "Suppose—would you allow me to act as coach instead?"

She hesitated. This stranger appeared to be uncompromisingly progressive in his tendencies.

"I'm perfectly capable," he added curtly.

"I'm sure of that. But——"

His eyes twinkled. "But it would not be quite *comme il faut?* Is that it?"

"Well, it wouldn't, would it?" she retaliated.

His face grew suddenly grave, and she noticed that when in repose there were deep, straight lines on either side of his mouth—lines that are usually only furrowed by severe suffering, either mental or physical.

"Mademoiselle," he said quietly. "To-day, it seems, we are two very lonely people. Couldn't we forget what is *comme il faut* for once? We shall probably never meet again. We know nothing of each other—just 'ships that pass in the night.' Let us keep one another company—take this one day together."

He drew a step nearer to her.

"Will you?" he said. "Will you?"

He was looking down at her with eyes that were curiously bright and compelling. There was a tense note in his voice which once again sent that disconcerting tremor of consciousness tingling through her blood.

She knew that his proposal was impertinent, unconventional, even regarded from the standpoint of the modern broad interpretation of the word convention, and that by every law of Mrs. Grundy she ought to snub him soundly for his presumption and retrace her steps to the hotel with all the dignity at her command.

But she did none of these things. Instead, she stood hesitating, alternately flushing and paling beneath the oddly concentrated gaze he bent on her.

"I swear it shall bind you to nothing," he pursued urgently. "Not even to recognising me in the street should our ways ever chance to cross again. Though that is hardly likely to occur"—with a shrug—"seeing that mademoiselle is French and that I am rarely out of England. It will be just one day that we shall have shared together out of the whole of life, and after that the 'darkness again and a silence.'.... I can promise you the 'silence'!" he added with a sudden harsh inflection.

It was that bitter note which won the day. In some subtle, subconscious way Jean sensed the pain which lay at the back of it. She answered impulsively:

"Very well. It shall be as you wish."

A rarely sweet smile curved the man's grave lips.

"Thank you," he said simply.

CHAPTER IV
THE STOLEN DAY

"ENCORE *une fois!* Bravo! That went better!" Monsieur Griolet's understudy had amply justified his claim to capability. After a morning's tuition at his hands, Jean found her prowess in the art of skating considerably enhanced. She was even beginning to master the mysteries of "cross-cuts" and "rocking turns," and a somewhat attenuated figure eight lay freshly scored on the ice to her credit.

"You are really a wonderful instructor," she acknowledged, surveying the graven witness to her progress with considerable satisfaction.

Her self-appointed teacher smiled.

"There is something to be said for the pupil, also," he replied. "But now"—glancing at his watch—"I vote we call a halt for lunch."

"Lunch!" Jean's glance measured the distance to the hotel with some dismay.

"But not lunch at the hotel," interposed her companion quickly.

Jean regarded him with curiosity.

"Where then, monsieur?"

"Up there!" he pointed towards the pine-woods. "Above the woods there is a hut of sorts—erected as a shelter in case of sudden storms for people coming up from the lower valley to Montavan and beyond. It's a rough little shanty, but it would serve very well as a temporary salle à manger. It isn't a long climb," he added persuasively. "Are you too tired to take it on after your recent exertion?"

"Not in the least. But are you expecting a wayside refuge of that description to be miraculously endowed with a well-furnished larder?"

"No. But I think my knapsack can make good the deficiency." he replied composedly.

Jean looked at him with dancing eyes. Having once yielded to the day's unconventional adventure, she had surrendered herself whole-heartedly to the enjoyment of it.

She made one reservation, however. Some instinct of self-protection prevented her from enlightening her companion as to her partly English nationality. There was no real necessity for it, seeing that he spoke French with the utmost fluency, and his assumption that she was a Frenchwoman seemed in some way to limit the feeling of intimacy, conferring on her, as it were, a little of the freedom of an incognito.

"*A la bonne heure!*" she exclaimed gaily. "So you invite me to share your lunch, *monsieur le professeur?*"

"I've invited you to share my day, haven't I?" he replied, smiling.

They steered for the bank, and when he had helped off her skates and removed his own, slinging them over his arm, they started off along the steep white track which wound its way upwards through the pine-woods.

As they left the bright sunlight that still glittered on the snowy slopes behind them, it seemed as though they plunged suddenly into another world—a still, mysterious, twilit place, where the snow underfoot muffled the sound of their steps and the long shadows of the pines barred their path with sinister, distorted shapes.

Jean, always sensitive to her surroundings, shivered a little.

"It's rather eerie, isn't it?" she said. "It's just as if someone had suddenly turned the lights out."

"Quite a nice bit of symbolism," he returned enigmatically.

"How? I don't think I understand."

He laughed a little.

"How should you? You're young. Fate doesn't come along and snuff out the lights for you when you are—what shall we say? Eighteen?"

"You're two years out," replied Jean composedly.

"As much? Then let's hope you'll have so much the longer to wait before Madame Destiny comes round with her snuffers."

He spoke with a kind of bitter humour, the backwash, surely, of some storm through which he must have passed. Jean looked across at him with a vague trouble in her face.

"Then, do you think"—she spoke uncertainly—"do you believe it is inevitable that she will come—sooner or later?"

"I hope not—to you," he said gently. "But she comes to most of us."

She longed to put another question, but there was a note of finality in his voice—a kind of "thus far shalt thou come and no further"—that warned her to probe no deeper. Whatever it was of bitterness that lay in the Englishman's past, he had no intention of sharing the knowledge with his chance companion of a day. He seemed to have become absorbed once more in his own thoughts, and for a time they tramped along together in silence.

The ascent steepened perceptibly, and Jean, light and active as she was, found it hard work to keep pace with the man's steady, swinging stride. Apparently his thoughts engrossed him to the exclusion of everything else, for he appeared to have utterly forgotten her existence. It was only when a slip of her foot on the beaten surface of the snow wrung a quick exclamation from her that he paused, wheeling round in consternation.

"I beg your pardon! I'm walking you off your legs! Why on earth didn't you stop me?"

There was something irresistibly boyish about the quick apology. Jean laughed, a little breathless from the swift climb uphill.

"You seemed so bent on getting to the top in the least possible time," she replied demurely, "that I didn't like to disappoint you."

"I'm afraid I make a poor sort of guide," he admitted. "I was thinking of something else. You must forgive me."

They resumed their climb more leisurely. The trees were thinning a bit now, and ahead, between the tall, straight trunks winged with drooping, snow-laden branches, they could catch glimpses of the white world beyond.

Presently they came out above the pine-wood on to the edge of a broad plateau and Jean uttered an exclamation of delight, gazing spell-bound at the scene thus suddenly unfolded.

Behind them, in the pine-ringed valley, a frozen reach of water gleamed like a dull sheet of metal, whilst before them, far above, stretched the great chain of mountains, pinnacle after pinnacle, capped with snow, thrusting up into the cloud-swept sky. Through rifts in the cloud—almost, it seemed, torn in the breast of heaven by those towering peaks—the sunlight slanted in long shafts, chequering the snows with shimmering patches of pale gold.

"It was worth the climb, then?"

The Englishman, his gaze on Jean's rapt face, broke the silence abruptly. She turned to him, radiant-eyed.

"It's so beautiful that it makes one's heart ache!" she exclaimed, laying her hand on her breast with the little foreign turn of gesture she derived from her French ancestry.

She said no more, but remained very still, drinking in the sheer loveliness of the scene.

The man regarded her quietly as she stood there silhouetted against the skyline, her slim, brown-clad figure striking a warm note amid the chill Alpine whites and greys. Her face was slightly tilted, and as the sunshine glinted on her hair and eyes, waking the russet lights that slumbered in them, there was something vividly arresting about her—a splendour of ardent youth which brought a somewhat wistful expression into the rather weary eyes of the man watching her.

His thought travelled hack to the brief snatch of conversation evoked by the sudden gloom of the pine-woods. Surely, for once, Fate would lay aside her snuffers and let this young, eager life pass by unshadowed!

Even as the thought took shape in his mind, Jean turned to him again, her face still radiant, "Thank you for bringing me up here," she said simply. "It has been perfect."

She stretched out her hand, and he took it and held it in his for a moment.

"I'm glad you've liked it," he answered quietly. "It will always be a part of our day together—the day we stole from *les convenances*"—he smiled whimsically. "And now, if you can bring yourself back to more prosaic matters, I suggest we have lunch. Scenery, however fine, isn't exactly calculated to sustain life."

"Most material person!" She laughed up at him. "I suppose you think a ham sandwich worth all the scenery in the world?"

"I'll admit to a preference for the sandwich at the moment," he acknowledged. "Come, now, confess! Aren't you hungry, too?"

"Starving! This air makes me feel as if I'd never had anything to eat in my life before!"

"Well, then, come and inspect my *salle à manger*."

The proposed refuge proved to be a roughly constructed little hut— hardly more than a shed provided with a door and thick-paned window, its only furniture a wooden bench and table. But that it had served its purpose as a kind of "travellers' rest" was proved by the fragments of appreciation, both in prose and verse, that were to be found inscribed in a species of "Visitors' Book" which lay on the table, carefully preserved from damp in a strong metal box. Jean amused herself by perusing the various contributions to its pages while the Englishman unpacked the contents of his knapsack.

The lunch that followed was a merry little meal, the two conversing with a happy intimacy and freedom from reserve based on the reassuring knowledge that they would, in all probability, never meet again. Afterwards, they bent their energies to concerting a suitable inscription for insertion in the "Visitors' Book," squabbling like a couple of children over the particular form it should take.

So absorbed were they in the discussion that they failed to notice the perceptible cooling of the temperature. The sun no longer warmed the roofing of the hut, and there was a desolate note in the sudden gusts of wind which shook the door at frequent intervals as though trying to attract the attention of those within. Presently a louder rattle than usual, coincident with a chance pause in the conversation, roused them effectually.

The Englishman's keen glance flashed to the little window, through which was visible a dancing, whirling blur of white.

"Great Scott!" he exclaimed in good round English. "It's snowing like the very dickens!"

In two strides he had reached the door, and, throwing it open, peered out. A draught of icy air rushed into the hut, accompanied by a flurry of fine snow driven on the wind.

When he turned back, his face had assumed a sudden look of gravity.

"We must go at once," he said, speaking in French again and apparently unconscious of his momentary lapse into his native tongue. "If we don't, we shan't be able to get back at all. The snow drifts quickly in the valley. Half an hour more of this and we shouldn't be able to get through."

Jean thrust the Visitors' Book back into its box, and began hastily repacking her companion's, knapsack, but he stopped her almost roughly.

"Never mind that. Fasten that fur thing closer round your throat and come on. There's no taking chances in a blizzard like this. Don't you understand?"—almost roughly. "If we waste time we may have to spend the night here."

Impelled by the sudden urgency of his tones, Jean followed him swiftly out of the hut, and the wind, as though baulked by her haste, snatched the door from her grasp and drove it to with a menacing thud behind them.

CHAPTER V
AMONG THE SNOWS

AS Jean stepped outside the hut it seemed as though she had walked straight into the heart of the storm. The bitter, ice-laden blast that bore down from the mountains caught away her breath, the fine driving flakes, crystal-hard, whipped her face, almost blinding her with the fury of their onslaught, whilst her feet slipped and slid on the newly fallen snow as she trudged along beside the Englishman.

"This is a good preparation for a dance!" she gasped breathlessly, forcing her chilled lips to a smile.

"For a dance? What dance?"

"There's a fancy dress ball at the hotel to-night. There won't be—much of me—left to dance, will there?"

The Englishman laughed suddenly.

"My chief concern is to get you back to the hotel—alive," he observed grimly.

Jean looked at him quickly.

"Is it as bad as that?" she asked more soberly.

"No. At least I hope not. I didn't mean to frighten you"—hastily. "Only it seemed a trifle incongruous to be contemplating a dance when we may be struggling through several feet of snow in half an hour."

The fierce gusts of wind, lashing the snow about them in bewildering eddies, made conversation difficult, and they pushed on in a silence broken only by an occasional word of encouragement from the Englishman.

"All right?" he queried once, as Jean paused, battered and spent with the fury of the storm.

She nodded speechlessly. She had no breath left to answer, but once again her lips curved in a plucky little smile. A fresh onslaught of the wind forced them onwards, and she staggered a little as it blustered by.

"Here," he said quickly. "Take my arm. It will be better when we get into the pine-wood. The trees there will give us some protection."

They struggled forward again, arm in arm. The swirling snow had blotted out the distant mountains; lowering storm-filled clouds made a grey twilight of the day, through which they could just discern ahead the vague, formless darkness of the pine-wood.

Another ten minutes walking brought them to it, only to find that the blunted edge of the storm was almost counterbalanced by the added difficulties of the surrounding gloom. High up overhead they could hear the ominous creak and swing of great branches shaken like toys in the wind, and now and again the sharper crack of some limb wrenched violently from its parent trunk. Once there came the echoing crash of a tree torn up bodily and flung to earth.

"It's worse here," declared Jean, "I think" —with a nervous laugh—"I think I'd rather die in the open!"

"It might be preferable. Only you're not going to die at all, if I can help it," the Englishman returned composedly.

But, cool though he appeared, he experienced a thrill of keen anxiety as they emerged from the pine-wood and his quick eyes scanned the dangerously rapid drifting of the snow.

The wind was racing down the valley now, driving the snow before it and piling it up, inch by inch, foot by foot, against the steep ground which skirted the sheet of ice where they had been skating but a few hours before.

Through the pitiless beating of the snow Jean strove to read her companion's face. It was grim and set, the lean jaw thrust out a little and the grey eyes tense and concentrated.

"Can we get through?" she asked, raising her voice so that it might carry against the wind.

"If we can get through the drifted snow between here and the track on the left, we're all right," answered the man.

"The wind's slanting across the valley and there'll be no drifts on the further side. I wish I'd got a bit of rope with me."

He felt in his pockets, finally producing the rolled-up strap of a suit-case.

"That's all I have," he said discontentedly.

"What's it for?"

"It's to go round your waist. I don't want to lose you"—smiling briefly—"if you should stumble into deep snow."

"Deep snow? But it's only been snowing an hour or so!" she objected.

"Evidently you don't know what a blizzard can accomplish in the way of drifting during the course of an 'hour or so.' I do."

Deftly he fastened the strap round her waist, and, taking the loose end, gave it a double turn about his wrist before gripping it firmly in his hand.

"Now, keep close behind me. Regard me"—laughing shortly—"as a snow-plough. And if I go down deep rather suddenly, throw your weight backward as much as you can."

He moved forward, advancing cautiously. He was badly handicapped by the lack of even a stick with which to gauge the depth of drifting snow in front of him, and he tested each step before trusting his full weight to the delusive, innocent-looking surface.

Jean went forward steadily beside him, a little to the rear. The snow was everywhere considerably more than ankle-deep, and at each step she could feel that the slope of the ground increased and with it the depth of the drift through which they toiled.

The cold was intense. The icy fingers of the snow about her feet seemed to creep upward and upward till her whole body felt numbed and dead, and as she stumbled along in the Englishman's wake, buffeted and beaten by the storm, her feet ached as if leaden weights were attached to them.

But she struggled on pluckily. The man in front of her was taking the brunt of the hardship, cutting a path for her, as it were, with his own body as he forged ahead, and she was determined not to add to his work by putting any weight on the strap which bound them together.

All at once he gave a sharp exclamation and pulled up abruptly.

"It's getting much deeper," he called out, turning back to her. "You'll never get through, hampered with your skirts. I'm going to carry you."

Jean shook her head, and shouted back:

"*You* wouldn't get through, handicapped like that. No, let's push on as we are. I'll manage somehow."

A glint of something like admiration flickered in his eyes.

"Game little devil!" he muttered. But the wind caught up the words, and Jean did not hear them. He raised his voice again, releasing the strap from his wrist as he spoke.

"You'll do what I tell you. It's only a matter of getting through this bit of drift, and we'll be out of the worst of it. Put your arms round my neck." Then, as she hesitated: "Do you hear? Put your arms round my neck— *quick!*"

The dominant ring in his voice impelled her. Obediently she clasped her arms about his neck as he stooped, and the next moment she felt herself swung upward, almost as easily as a child, and firmly held in the embrace of arms like steel.

For a few yards he made good progress, thrusting his way through the yielding snow. But the task of carrying a young woman of average height and weight is no light one, even to a strong man and without the added difficulty of plunging through snow that yields treacherously at every step, and Jean could guess the strain entailed upon him by the double burden.

"Oh, do put me down!" she urged him. "I'm sure I can walk it—really I am."

He halted for a moment.

"Look down!" he said. "Think you could travel in that?"

The snow was up to his knees, above them whenever the ground hollowed suddenly.

"But you?" she protested unhappily. "You'll—you'll simply kill yourself!"

"Small loss if I do! But as that would hardly help you out of your difficulties, I've no intention of giving up the ghost just at present."

He started on again, pressing forward slowly and determinedly, but it was only with great difficulty and exertion that he was able to make headway. Jean, her cheek against the rough tweed of his coat, could hear the labouring beats of his heart as the depth of the snow increased.

"How much further?" she whispered.

"Not far," he answered briefly, husbanding his breath.

A few more steps. They were both silent now. Jean's eyes sought his face. It was ashen, and even in that bitter cold beads of sweat were running down it; he was nearing the end of his tether. She could bear it no longer. She stirred restlessly in his arms.

"Put me down," she cried imploringly. "*Please* put me down."

But he shook his head.

"Keep still, can't you?" he muttered between his teeth. She felt his arms tighten round her.

The next moment he stumbled heavily against some surface root or boulder, concealed beneath the snow, and pitched forward, and in the same instant Jean felt herself sinking down, down into a soft bed of something that yielded resistlessly to her weight. Then came a violent jerk and jar, as though she had been seized suddenly round the waist, and the sensation of sinking ceased abruptly.

She lay quite still where she had fallen and, looking upwards, found herself staring straight into the eyes of the Englishman. He was lying flat on his face, on ground a little above the snow-filled hollow into which his fall had flung her, his hand grasping the strap which was fastened round her body. He had caught the flying end of it as they fell, and thus saved her from sinking into seven or eight feet of snow.

"Are you hurt?"

His voice came to her roughened with fierce anxiety.

"No. I'm not hurt. Only don't leave go of your end of the strap!"

"Thank God!" she heard him mutter. Then, aloud, reassuringly: "I've got my end of it all right. How, can you catch hold of the strap and raise yourself a little so that I can reach you?"

Jean obeyed. A minute later she felt his arms about her shoulders, underneath her armpits, and then very slowly, but with a sure strength that took from her all sense of fear, he drew her safely up beside him on to the high ground.

Eor a moment they both rested quietly, recovering their breath. The Englishman seemed glad of the respite, and Jean noticed with concern the rather drawn look of his face. She thought he must be more played out than he cared to acknowledge.

Across the silence of sheer fatigue their eyes met—Jean's filled with a wistful solicitude as unconscious and candid as a child's, the man's curiously brilliant and inscrutable—and in a moment the silence had become something other, different, charged with emotional significance, the revealing silence which falls suddenly between a man and woman.

At last:

"This is what comes of stealing a day from Mrs. Grundy," commented the man drily.

And the tension was broken.

He sprang up, as though, anxious to maintain the recovered atmosphere of the commonplace.

"Come! Having shot her bolt and tried ineffectually to down you in a ditch, I expect the old lady will let us get home safely now. We're through the worst. There are no more drifts between here and the hotel."

It was true. Anything that might have spelt danger was past, and it only remained to follow the beaten track up to the hotel, though even so, with the wind and snow driving in their faces, it took them a good half-hour to accomplish the task.

Monsieur and Madame de Varigny, a distracted *maître d'hôtel*, and a little crowd of interested and sympathetic visitors welcomed their arrival.

"*Mon dieu, mademoiselle!* But we rejoice to see you back!" exclaimed Madame de Varigny. "We ourselves are only newly returned—and that, with difficulty, through this terrible storm—and we arrive to find that none knows where you are!"

"Me, I made sure that mademoiselle had accompanied *Madame la Comtesse*." asseverated Monsieur Vautrinot, nervously anxious to exculpate himself from any charge of carelessness.

"We were just going to organise a search-party," added the little Count. "I, myself"—stoutly—"should have joined in the search."

Weary as she was, Jean could hardly refrain from smiling at the idea of the diminutive Count in the rôle of gallant preserver. He would have been considerably less well-qualified even than herself to cope with the drifting snow through which the sheer, dogged strength of the Englishman had brought her safely.

Instinctively she turned with the intention of effecting an introduction between the latter and the Varignys, only to find that he had disappeared. He had taken the opportunity presented by the little ferment of excitement which had greeted her safe return to slip away.

She felt oddly disconcerted. And yet, she reflected, it was so like him— so like the conception of him which she had formed, at least—to evade both her thanks and the enthusiasm with which a recital of the afternoon's adventure Would have been received.

CHAPTER VI
THE MAGIC MOMENT

JEAN, surprisingly revived by a hot bath and a hot drink, and comfortably tucked up beside the fire in her room, was recounting the day's adventure to Madame de Varigny.

It was a somewhat expurgated version of the affair that she outlined—thoughtfully calculated to allay the natural apprehensions of a temporary chaperon—in which the unknown Englishman figured innocuously as merely having come to her assistance when, in the course of her afternoon's tramp, she had been overtaken by the blizzard. Of the stolen day, snatched from under Mrs. Grundy's enquiring nose, Jean preserved a discreet silence.

"I don't know who he could be," she pursued. "I've never seen him on the ice before; I should certainly have recognised him if I had. He was a lean, brown man, very English-looking—that sort of cold-tub-every-morning effect, you know. Oh! And he had one perfectly white lock of hair that was distinctly attractive. It looked"—descriptively—"as though someone had dabbed a powdered finger on his hair—just in the right place."

Madame de Varigny's eyes narrowed, and a quick ejaculation escaped her. It was something more than a mere exclamation connoting interest; it held a definitely individual note, as though it sprang from some sudden access of personal feeling.

Jean, hearing it, looked up in some surprise, and the other, meeting her questioning glance, rushed hastily into speech.

"A lock of white hair? But how *chic!*

"It should not"—thoughtfully—"be difficult to discover the identity of anyone with so distinctive a characteristic."

"He is not staying in the hotel, at all events," said Jean. "He told me he was at a friend's chalet."

"And he did not enlighten you as to his name? Gave you no hint?"

Madame de Varigny spoke with an assumption of indifference, but there was an undertone of suppressed eagerness in her liquid voice.

Jean shook her head, smiling a little to herself. It had been part of the charm of that brief companionship that neither of the two comrades knew any of the everyday, commonplace details concerning the other.

"Perhaps you will see him again at the rink to-morrow," suggested Madame de Varigny, still with that note of restrained eagerness in her tones. "The snow is not deep except where it has drifted; they will clear the ice in the morning."

Jean was silent. She was not altogether sure that she wanted to see him again. As it stood, robbed of all the commonplace circumstances of convention, the incident held a certain glamour of whimsical romance which could not but appeal to the daughter of Glyn Peterson. Nicely rounded off, as, for instance, by the unknown Englishman's prosaically calling at the hotel the next day to enquire whether she had suffered any ill effects, it would lose all the thrill of adventure. It was the suggestion of incompleteness which flavoured the entire episode so piquantly.

No, on the whole, Jean rather hoped that she would not meet the Englishman again—at least, not yet. Some day, perhaps, it might be rather nice if chance brought them together once more. There would be a certain element of romantic fitness about it, should that happen.

"I don't think I am likely to see him again," she said quietly, replying to Madame de Varigny's suggestion. "He told me he was going away to-morrow."

Had it been conceivable, Jean would have said that a flash of disappointment crossed the Countess's face. But there seemed no possible reason why the movements of an unknown Englishman should cause her any excitement of feeling whatever, pleasant or otherwise. The only feasible explanation was that odd little streak of inquisitiveness concerning other people's affairs which appeared to be characteristic of her and which she had before evinced concerning the circumstances of Lady Anne Brennan.

Whatever curiosity she may have felt, however, on this occasion Madame de Varigny refrained from giving expression to it. Apparently dismissing the subject of the Englishman's identity from her mind, she switched the conversation into a fresh channel.

"It is unfortunate that you should have met with such a contretemps to-day. You will not feel disposed to dance this evening, after so much fatigue," she observed commiseratingly.

But Jean scouted the notion. With the incomparable resiliency of youth, she felt quite equal to dancing all night if needs be.

"Mais tout au contraire!" she exclaimed. "I'm practically recovered — at least, I shall be after another half-hour's lazing by this glorious fire. I wonder what heaven-sent inspiration induced Monsieur Vautrinot to install a real English fire-place in this room? It's delicious."

The Countess rose, shrugging her expressive shoulders.

"You are wonderful — you English! If it had been I who had experienced your adventure to-day, I should be fit for nothing. As to dancing the same evening — *ma foi, non! Voyons,* I shall leave you to rest a little."

She nodded smilingly and left the room. Once in the corridor outside, however, the smile vanished as though it had been wiped off her face by an unseen hand. Her curving lips settled into a hard, inflexible line, and the soft, disarming dark eyes grew suddenly sombre and brooding.

She passed swiftly along to her own suite. It was empty. The little Count was downstairs, agreeably occupied in comparing symptoms with a fellow health crank he had discovered.

With a quick sigh of relief at his absence she flung herself into a chair and lit a cigarette, smoking rapidly and exhaling the smoke in quick, nervous jerks. The long, pliant fingers which held the cigarette were not quite steady.

"Tout va bien!" she muttered restlessly. "All goes well! *Assurément,* his punishment will come." She bent her head. *"Que Dieu le veuille!"* she whispered passionately.

Jean took a final and not altogether displeased survey of herself in the mirror before descending to the big *salle* where the fancy-dress ball was to be held. She had had her dinner served to her in her room so that she might rest the longer, and now, as there came wafted to her ears the preliminary grunts and squeals and snatches of melody of the hotel orchestra in process of tuning up, she was conscious of a pleasant glow of anticipation.

There was nothing strikingly original about the conception of her costume. It represented "Autumn," and had been designed for a fancy-dress ball of more than a year ago — before the death of Jacqueline had suddenly shuttered down all gaiety and mirth at Beirnfels. But, simple as it was, it had been carried out by an artist in colour, and the filmy diaphanous layers of brown and orange and scarlet, one over the other, zoned with a girdle of autumn-tinted leaves, served to emphasise the russet of beech-leaf hair and the topaz-gold of hazel eyes.

Madame de Varigny's glance swept the girl with approval as they entered the great *salle* together.

"But it is charming, your costume! *Regarde*, Henri"—turning to the Count, who, as a swashbuckling d'Artagnan, was getting into difficulties with his sword. "Has it not distinction—this costume *d'automne?*"

The Count retrieved himself and, hitching his sword once more into position, poured forth an unembarrassed stream of Gallic compliment.

Madame de Varigny herself was looking supremely handsome as Cleopatra. Jean reflected that her eyes,—slumberous and profound, with their dusky frame of lashes and that strange implacability she always sensed in them—might very well have been the eyes of the Egyptian queen herself.

The *salle* was filling up rapidly. Jean, who did not anticipate dancing overmuch, as she had made but few acquaintances in the hotel, watched the colourful, shifting scene with interest. There was the usual miscellany of a masquerade—Pierrots jostling against Kings and Cossacks, Marie Antoinettes flaunting their jewels before the eyes of demure-faced nuns, with here and there an occasional costume of outstanding originality or merit of design.

Contrary to her expectations, however, Jean soon found herself with more partners than she had dances to bestow, and, newly emancipated from the rigour of her year's mourning, she threw herself into the enjoyment of the moment with all the long repressed enthusiasm of her youth.

It was nearing the small hours when at last she found herself alone for a few minutes. In the exhilaration of rapid movement she had completely forgotten the earlier fatigues of the day, but now she was beginning to feel conscious of the strain which the morning's skating, followed by that long, exhausting struggle through the blizzard, had imposed upon even young bones and muscles. Close at hand was a deserted alcove, curtained off from the remainder of the *salle*, and here Jean found temporary sanctuary, subsiding thankfully on to a big cushioned divan.

The sound of the orchestra came to her ears pleasantly dulled by the heavy folds of the screening curtain. Vaguely she could feel the rhythmic pulsing, the sense of movement, in the *salle* beyond. It was all very soothing and reposeful, and she leaned her head against a fat, pink satin cushion and dosed, at the back of her mind the faintly disturbing thought that she was cutting a Roman senator's dance.

Presently she stirred a little, hazily aware of some disquiet that was pushing itself into her consciousness. The discomfort grew, crystallising at last into the feeling that she was no longer alone. Eor a moment, physically unwilling to be disturbed, she tried to disregard it, but it persisted, and, as though to strengthen it, the recollection of the defrauded senator came back to her with increased insistence.

Broad awake at last, she opened her eyes. Someone—the senator presumably—was standing at the entrance to the little alcove, and she rushed into conscience-stricken speech.

"Oh, have I cut your dance? I'm so sorry——"

She broke off abruptly, realising as she spoke that the intruder was not, after all, the senator come to claim his dance, but a stranger wearing a black mask and domino. She was sure she had not seen him before amongst the dancers in the *salle*, and for a moment she stared at him bewildered and even a little frightened. Vague stories she had heard of a "hold-up" by masked men at some fancy-dress ball recalled themselves disagreeably to her memory, and her pulse quickened its beat perceptibly.

Then, quite suddenly, she knew who it was. It did not need even the evidence of that lock of *poudré* hair above the mask he wore, just visible in the dim light of the recess, to tell her. She knew. And with the knowledge came a sudden, disturbing sense of shy tumult.

She half-rose from the divan.

"You?" she stammered nervously. "Is it you?"

He whipped off his mask.

"Who else? Did this deceive you?"—dangling the strip of velvet from his finger, and regarding her with quizzical grey eyes. "I've been hunting for you everywhere. I'd almost made up my mind that you had gone to bed like a good little girl. And then my patron saint—or was it the special devil told off to look after me, I wonder?—prompted me to look in here. *Et vous voilà, mademoiselle!* How are you feeling after your exploits in the snow?"

He spoke very rapidly, in a light half-mocking tone that seemed to Joan to make the happenings of the afternoon unreal and remote. His eyes were very bright, almost defiant in their expression—holding a suggestion of recklessness, as though he were embarked upon something of which his inmost self refused to approve but which he was nevertheless determined to carry through.

"So you *did* 'call to enquire,' after all!"

As she spoke, Jean's mouth curled up at the corners in an involuntary little smile of amused recollection.

"So I did call after all?" He looked puzzled—not unnaturally, since he had no clue to her thoughts. "What do you mean? I came"—he went on lightly—"because I wanted the rest of the day which you promised to share with me. The proceedings were cut short rather abruptly this afternoon."

"But how did you get here?" she asked. "And—and why did you disappear so suddenly after we got back to the hotel this afternoon?"

"I got here by the aid of a pair of excellent skis and the light of the moon; the snow ceased some hours ago and the surface is hardening nicely. I disappeared because, as I told you, if you gave me this one day, it should bind you to nothing—not even to introducing me to your friends."

"I should have had to present you as *Monsieur l'Inconnu*," remarked Jean without thinking.

"Yes." He met her glance with smiling eyes, but he did not volunteer his name.

He had made no comment, uttered no word beyond the bald affirmative, yet somehow Jean felt as though she had committed an indiscretion and he had snubbed her for it. The blood rushed into her cheeks, staining them scarlet.

"I beg your pardon," she said stiffly.

Again that glint of ironical amusement in his eyes.

"For what, mademoiselle?"

She was conscious of a rising indignation at his attitude. She could not understand it; he seemed to have completely changed from the man of a few hours ago. Then he had proved himself so good a comrade, been so entirely delightful in his thought and care of her, whereas now he appeared bent on wilfully misunderstanding her, putting her in a false position just for his own amusement.

"You know perfectly well what I meant," she answered, a tremor born of anger and wounded feeling in her voice. "You thought I was inquisitive— trying to find out your name——"

"Well"—humorously—"you were, weren't you?" Then, as her lip quivered sensitively, "Ah! Forgive me for teasing you! And"—more earnestly—"forgive me for not telling you my name. It is better—much better—that you should not know. Remember, we can only have this one day together; we're just 'ships that pass.'" He paused, then added: "Mine's only a battered old hulk—a derelict vessel—and derelicts are best forgotten."

There was an undercurrent of deep sadness in his voice, the steadfast, submissive sadness of a man who has long ago substituted endurance for revolt.

"Remember, we can only have this one day together." The quiet utterance of the words stung Jean into a realisation of their significance, and suddenly she was conscious that the knowledge that this unknown Englishman was going away—going out of her life as abruptly as he had come into it—filled her with a quite disproportionate sense of regret. She found herself unexpectedly up against the recognition of the fact that she would miss him—that she would like to see him again.

"Then—you want me to forget?" she asked rather wistfully.

Her eyes fell away from him as she spoke.

"Yes," he returned gravely. "Just that. I want you to forget."

"And—and you?" The words seemed dragged from her without her own volition.

"I? Oh"—he laughed a little—"I'm afraid I'm inconsistent. I'm going to ask you to give me something I can remember. That'll even matters up, if you forget and I—remember."

"What do you want me to give you?"

He made a sudden step towards her.

"I want you to dance with me—just once. Will you?"—intently.

He waited for her reply, his keen, compelling glance fixed on her face. Then, as though he read his answer there, he stepped to her side and held out his arm.

"Come," he said.

Almost as if she were in a dream, Jean laid her hand lightly on his sleeve and he pulled aside the portière for her to pass through. Then, putting his arm about her, he swung her out on to the smooth floor of the *salle*.

They danced almost in silence. Somehow the customary small-change of ballroom conversation would have seemed irrelevant and apart. This dance—the Englishman had implied as much—was in the nature of a farewell. It was the end of their stolen day.

The band was playing *Valse Triste*, that unearthly, infinitely sad vision of Sibelius', and the music seemed to hold all the strange, breathless ecstacy, the regret and foreboding of approaching end of which this first, and last, dance was compact.

It was over at last. The three final chords of the *Valse*—inexorable Death knocking at the door—dropped into silence, and with the end of the dance uprose the eager hum of gay young voices, as the couples drifted out from the *salle* in search of the buffet or of secluded corners in which to "sit out" the interval, according as the spirit moved them.

Jean and her partner, making their way through the throng, encountered Madame de Varigny on the arm of a handsome Bedouin Arab. For the fraction of a second her eyes rested curiously on Jean's partner, and a gleam of something that seemed like triumph flickered across her face. But it was gone in an instant, and, murmuring some commonplace to Jean, she passed on.

"Who was that?"

The Englishman rapped out the question harshly, and Jean was struck by an unaccustomed note in his voice. It held apprehension, distaste; she could not quite analyse the quality.

"The Cleopatra, do you mean?" she said. "That was my chaperon, the Comtesse de Varigny. Why do you ask?" He gave a short, relieved laugh.

"No particular reason," he returned with some constraint "She reminded me—extraordinarily—of someone I used to know, that's all. Even the timbre of her voice was similar. It startled me for a moment."

He dismissed the matter with apparent indifference, and led Jean again into the same little alcove in which he had found her. They stood together silently in the dim, rose-hued twilight diffused by the shaded lamp above.

"Well," he said at last, slowly, reluctantly. "So this is really the end of our stolen day."

Jean's hands, hanging loosely clasped in front of her, suddenly tightened their grip of each other. She felt herself struggling in the press of new and incomprehensible emotions. A voice within her was crying out rebelliously: "Why? Why must it be the end? Why not—other days?" Pride alone kept her silent. It was his choice, his decision, that they were not to meet again, and if he could so composedly define the limits of their acquaintance, she was far too sensitively proud to utter a word of protest. After all, he was only the comrade of a day. How—why should it matter to her whether he stayed or went?

"I always believe"—the Englishman was speaking again, his eyes bent on hers—"I always believe that, no matter how sad or tragic people's lives may be, God invariably gives them one magic moment—so that they may believe in heaven.... I have had mine to-day."

"Don't you—believe in heaven?"

He laid his hands lightly on her shoulders.

"I do now. I believe... in a heaven that is out of my reach."

His hands slipped upward from her shoulders, cupping her face, and for a moment he held her so, staring down at her with grave, inscrutable eyes. Then, stooping his head, he kissed her lips.

"Good-bye, little comrade," he said unevenly. "Thank you for my magic moment."

He turned away sharply. She heard his step, followed by the quick, jarring rattle of brass rings jerked violently along the curtain-pole, and a moment later he was gone. With a dull sense of finality she watched the heavy folds of the portière swing sullenly back into their place.

CHAPTER VII
WHICH DEALS WITH REFLECTIONS

THE dawn of a new day possesses a curious potency of readjustment. It is as though Dame Nature, like some autocratic old nurse, wakes us up and washes and dresses our minds afresh for us each morning, so that they come to the renewed consideration of the affairs of life freed from the influences and emotions which were clogging their pores when we went asleep. Not infrequently, in the course of this species of mental ablution, a good deal of the glamour which invested the doings of the previous day gets scrubbed off, and a new and not altogether pleasing aspect of affairs presents itself.

This was somewhat Jean's experience when she woke on the morning following that of the fancy-dress ball. Looking back upon the events of the previous day, it seemed to her newly-tubbed, matutinal mind almost incredible that they should have occurred. It was like a dream—life itself tricked out in fancy dress.

Stripped of the glamour of romance and adventure with which the unknown Englishman had contrived to clothe it, the whole episode of their day together presented itself as disagreeably open to criticism, and the memory of that final scene in the alcove sent the blood flying into her cheeks. She asked herself in mute amazement how it was possible that such a thing should have happened to her,—to "our chaste Diana," as her father used laughingly to call her in recognition of the instinctive little air of aloofness with which she had been wont to keep men at a distance.

Of course, the Englishman had taken her by surprise, but Jean was too honest, even in her dealings with herself, to shelter behind this excuse.

She knew that she had yielded to his kiss—and knew, too, that the bare memory of it sent her heart throbbing in an inexplicable tumult of emotion.

The stolen day, that day embarked upon so unconcernedly, in a gay spirit of adventure, had flamed up at its ending into something altogether different from the light-hearted companionship with which it had begun.

Then her conscience, recreated and vigorous from its morning toilet, presented another facet of the affair for her inspection. With officious detail it marshalled the whole series of events before her, dwelling particularly on the fact that, with hut very slight demur, she had consented to abrogate the accepted conventions of her class—conventions designed to safeguard people from just such consequences as had ensued—and winding up triumphantly with the corollary that although, like most men in similar circumstances, the Englishman had not scrupled to avail himself of the advantages the occasion offered, he had probably, none the less, thought rather cheaply of her for permitting him to do so.

This reflection stung her pride—exactly as Conscience had intended it should, without doubt. Last night there had seemed to her no question about the quality of that farewell in the little screened-off alcove. There had been nothing common or "cheap" about it. The gathering incidents of the whole day, the fight through the storm, the prelude of *Valse Triste*, all seemed to have led her by imperceptible degrees to a point where she and the Englishman could kiss at parting without shame. And now, with the morning, the delicate rainbow veiling woven by romance was rudely torn asunder, and the word "cheap" dinned in her ears like the clapper of a bell.

The appearance of her *premier dejeuner* came as a web come distraction from her thoughts, and with the consumption of *café au lait* and the crisp little rolls, hot from the oven, accompanying it, the whole matter began to assume a less heinous aspect. After all, argued Jean's weak human nature, the unconventionality of the affair had been considerably tempered by the fact that the Englishman had practically saved her life during the course of the day. Alone, she would undoubtedly have foundered in the drifting snow; and when a man has rescued you from an early and unpleasantly chilly grave, it certainly sets the acquaintance between you, however short its duration, on a new and more intimate plane.

"Good-bye, little comrade; thank you for my magic moment."

The words, and the manner of their utterance, came back to Jean, bringing with them a warm and comforting reassurance. The man who had thus spoken had not thought her cheap; he was too fine in his perceptions to have misunderstood like that. She felt suddenly certain of it. And the pendulum of self-respect swung back into its place once more.

Presently she caught herself wondering whether she would see him again before she left Montavan. True, he had told her he was going away the next day. But had he actually gone? Somewhere within her lurked a fugitive, half-formed hope that he might have altered his intention.

She tried to brush the thought aside, refusing to recognise it and determinedly maintaining that it mattered nothing to her whether he stayed or went. Nevertheless, throughout the whole day—in the morning when she made a pretence of enjoying the skating on the rink, and again in the afternoon when she walked through the pine-woods with the Varignys—she was subconsciously alert for any glimpse of the lean, supple figure which a single day had sufficed to make so acutely familiar.

But by evening she was driven into accepting the fact that he had quitted the mountains, and of a sudden Montavan ceased to interest her; the magic that had disguised it yesterday was gone. It had become merely a dull little village where she was awaiting Lady Anne Brennan's answer to her father's letter, and she grew restlessly impatient for that answer to arrive.

It came at last, during the afternoon of the following day, in the form of a telegram: *"Delighted to welcome you. Letter follows."*

The letter followed in due course, two days later, the tardiness of its arrival accounted for by the fact that the writer had been moving about from place to place, and that Peterson's own letter, after pursuing her for days, had only just caught up with her.

"I cannot tell you," wrote Lady Anne in her squarish, characteristic hand, "how delighted I shall be to have the daughter of Glyn and Jacqueline with me for a time. Although Glyn with a grown-up daughter sounds quite improbable; he never really grew up himself. So you must come and convince me that the unexpected has happened."

Jean liked the warm-hearted, unconventional tone of the letter, and the knowledge that she would so soon be leaving Montavan filled her with a sense of relief.

During the four days which had elapsed since the Englishman's departure her restlessness had grown on her. Montavan had become too vividly reminiscent of the hours which they had shared together for her peace of mind. She wanted to forget that stolen day—thrust it away into the background of her thoughts.

Unfortunately for the success of her efforts in this direction, the element of the unknown which surrounded the Englishman, quite apart from anything else, would have tended to keep him in the forefront of her mind. It was only now, surveying their acquaintance in retrospect, that she fully realised how complete had been his reticence. True his figure dominated her thoughts, but it was a figure devoid of any background of home, or friends, or profession. He might be a king or a crossing-sweeper, for all she knew to the contrary—only that neither the members of the one nor the other profession are usually addicted to sojourning at Swiss chalets and forming promiscuous friendships on the ice.

There were moments when she felt that she detested this man from nowhere who had contrived to break through her feminine guard of aloofness merely to gratify his whim to spend a day in her company.

But there were other moments when the memory of that stolen day glowed and pulsed like some rare gem against the even, grey monotony of all the days that had preceded it—and of those which must come after. She could not have analysed, even to herself, the emotions it had wakened in her. They were too complex, too fluctuating.

As she packed her trunks in preparation for an early start the following day, Jean recalled with satisfaction the genuine ring of welcome which had sounded through the letter that had come from England. Until she had received it, she had been the prey of an increasing diffidence with regard to suddenly billeting herself for an indefinite period upon even such an old friend of her father's as Lady Anne—a timidity Peterson himself had certainly not shared when he penned his request.

"Give my little girl house-room, will you, Anne?" he had written with that candid and charming simplicity which had made and kept for him a host of friends through all the vicissitudes of his varied and irresponsible career. "I am off once more on a wander-year, and I can't be tripped up by a petticoat—certainly not my own daughter's—at every yard. This isn't quite as cynical as it sounds. You'll understand, I know. Frankly, a man whose life, to all intents and purposes, is ended, is not fit company for youth and beauty standing palpitating on the edge of the world. By the way, did I tell you that Jean is rather beautiful? I forget. Let her see England—that little corner where you live, down Devonshire way, always means England to my mind. And let her learn to love Englishwomen—if there are any more there like you."

And, having accomplished this characteristic, if somewhat; sketchy provision for his daughter's welfare, Peterson had gone cheerfully on his way, convinced that he had done all that was paternally encumbent on him.

Madame de Varigny was voluble in her regrets at the prospect of losing her "*chère Mademoiselle Peterson*," yet in spite of her protestations of dismay Jean was conscious of an impression that the Countess derived some kind of satisfaction from the imminence of her departure.

She could not reconcile the contradiction, and it worried her a little. She believed—quite justly—that Madame de Varigny had conceived a real affection for her, and, as far as she herself was concerned, she had considerably revised her first impressions of the other, finding more to like in her than she had anticipated, noticeably a genuine warmth and fervour of nature, and a certain kind-hearted capacity for interesting herself in other people.

And, liking her so much better than she had at first conceived possible, Jean resented the sudden recurrence of her original distrust produced by the suggestion of insincerity which she thought she detected in the Countess's expressions of regret.

On the face of it the thing seemed absurd. She could imagine no conceivable reason why her departure should give Madame de Varigny any particular cause for complacency, which only made the more perplexing her impression that this was the actual feeling underlying the latter's cordial interest in her projected visit to England.

On the morning of her departure, Jean's mind was too preoccupied with the small details attendant upon starting off on a journey dwell upon the matter. But, as she shook bands with Madame de Varigny for the last time, the recollection surged over her afresh, and she was strongly conscious that beneath the other woman's pleasant, *"Adieu, mademoiselle! Bon voyage!"* something stirred that was less pleasant—even inimical—just as some slimy and repulsive form of life may stir amid the ooze at the bottom of a sunlit stream.

CHAPTER VIII
THE MAN FROM MONTAVAN

JEAN arrived in London with a good three hours to spare before the South-Western express, by which she proposed to travel to Devonshire, was due to leave Waterloo Station. She elected, therefore, to occupy the time by touring round the great, unknown city of her dreams in a taxicab, and spent a beatific hour glimpsing the Abbey and the Houses of Parliament, and the old, grey, misty river that Londoners love, and skirmishing in and out of the shops in Regent Street and Bond Street with her hands full of absurd, expensive, unnecessary purchases only bought because this was London and she felt she just simply *must* have something English at once, and winding up with a spin through Hyde Park—which didn't impress her very favourably in its winter aspect of leafless trees and barren stretches of sodden grass.

Then she drove to a hotel, and, her luggage deposited there to await her departure, her thoughts turned very naturally towards lunch. Her scamper round London in the crisp, clear, frosty air had converted the recollection of her early morning coffee and roll into something extremely nebulous and unsupporting, and it was with the healthy appetite of an eager young mind in an eager young body that she faced the several courses of the table d'hote.

She glanced about her with interest, the little snatches of English conversation which drifted to her from other near-by tables giving her a patriotic thrill of pure delight. These were typically English people lunching in a typically English hotel, and she, hitherto a stranger to her own mother-country, was doing likewise. The knowledge filled her with ridiculous satisfaction.

Nor were English people—at home in their own country—anything like as dull and dowdy as Glyn Peterson's sweeping criticisms had led her to expect. The men were immensely well-groomed and clean-looking. She liked the "morning-tub" appearance they all had; it reminded her of the Englishman at Montavan. Apparently it was a British characteristic.

The women, too, filled her with a species of vicarious pride. They were so well turned-out, with a slim, long limbed grace of figure she found admirable, and with splendid natural complexions—skins like rose and ivory.

Two of them were drifting into the room together now, with a superbly cool assurance of manner—rather as though they had bought the hotel—which brought the sleek head-waiter automatically to their side, bowing and obsequious.

Somewhat to Jean's satisfaction he convoyed them to the table next her own, and she was pleasantly conscious, as they passed her, of a provocative whisper of silk and of the faint fragrance of violets subtly permeating the atmosphere.

Conscious that perhaps she had been manifesting her interest a little too openly, she turned her attention to a magazine she had bought en route from Dover and was soon absorbed in the inevitable happy-ever-after conclusion of the story she had been reading.

"Lady Anne? Oh, she lives at Staple now. Didn't you know?"

The speaker's voice was clear and resonant, with the peculiar carrying quality which has replaced in the modern Englishwoman of the upper classes that excellent thing in woman which was the proud boast of an earlier generation.

The conjunction of the familiar words "Lady Anne" and "Staple" struck sharply on Jean's ears, and almost instinctively she looked up.

As she stirred, one of the women glanced indifferently in her direction, then placidly resumed her conversation with her companion.

"It was just after the smash-up," she pursued glibly. "Blaise Tormarin rushed off abroad for a time, and the news of Nesta's death came while he was away. Poor Lady Anne had to write and tell him of it."

"Rather ghastly!" commented the other woman. "I never heard the whole story of the affair. I was in Paris, then, and it was all over—barring the general gossip, of course!—by the time I returned. I tried to pump it out of Lady Anne once, but she was as close as an oyster."

Both women talked without lowering their voices in the slightest degree, and with that complete indifference to the proximity of a stranger sometimes exhibited by a certain arrogant type.

Jean, realising that it was her father's friends who were under discussion, and finding herself forced into the position of an unwilling auditor, felt wretchedly uncomfortable. She wished fervently that she could in some way arrest the conversation. Yet it was clearly as impossible for her to lean forward and say: "You are talking about the people I am on my way to visit," as it would have been for her to put her fingers in her ears. So far nothing had been said to which she could actually object. Her feeling was chiefly the offspring of a supersensitive fear that she might learn from the lips of these two gossiping women, one of whom was apparently intimately acquainted with the private history of the Tormarin family, some little fact or detail which Lady Anne might not care for her future guest to know. Apart from this fear, it would hardly have been compatible with human nature—certainly not feminine human nature—if she had not felt pricked to considerable personal interest in the topic under discussion.

"Oh, it was a fool business," the first woman rejoined, settling down to supply the details of the story with an air of rapacious satisfaction which reminded Jean of nothing so much as of a dog with a bone. "Nesta Freyne was a typical Italian—though her father was English, I believe—all blazing, passionate eyes and blazing, passionate emotion, you know; then there was another man—and there was Blaise Tormarin! You can imagine the consequences for yourself. Blaise has his full share of the Tormarin temper—and a Tormarin in a temper is like a devil with the bit between his teeth. There were violent quarrels and finally the girl bolted, presumably with the other man. Then, later, Lady Anne heard that she had died abroad somewhere. The funny thing is that it seemed to cut Tormarin up rather badly. He's gloomed about the world ever since, so I suppose he must have been pretty deeply in love with her before the crash came. I never saw her, but I've been told she was diabolically pretty."

The other woman laughed, dismissing the tragedy of the little tale with a shallow tinkle of mirth.

"Oh, well, I've only met Blaise Tormarin once, but I should say he was not the type to relish being thrown over for another man!" She peered short-sightedly at the grilled fish on her plate, poking at it discontentedly with her fork. "I never think they cook their fish decently here, do you?" she complained.

And, with that, both women shelved the affairs of Blaise Tormarin and concentrated upon the variety of culinary sins from which even expensive hotel chefs are not necessarily exempt.

Jean had no time to bestow upon the information which had been thus thrust upon her until she had effected the transport of herself and her belongings from the hotel to Waterloo Station, but when this had been satisfactorily accomplished and she found herself comfortably settled in a corner seat of the Plymouth express, her thoughts reverted to her newly acquired knowledge.

It added a bit of definite outline to the very slight and shadowy picture she had been able to form of her future environment—a picture roughly sketched in her mind from the few hints dropped by her father.

She wondered a little why Glyn should have omitted all mention of Blaise Tormarin's love affair and its unhappy sequel, but a moment's reflection supplied the explanation. Peterson had admitted that it was ten years since he had heard from Lady Anne; presumably, then, the circumstances just recounted in Jean's hearing had occurred during those years.

Jean felt that the additional knowledge she had gained rather detracted from the prospective pleasure of her visit to Staple. Judging from the comments which she had overheard, her host was likely to prove a somewhat morose and gloomy individual, soured by his unfortunate experience of feminine fidelity.

Thence her thoughts vaulted wildly ahead. Most probably, as a direct consequence, he was a woman-hater and, if so, it was more than possible that he would regard her presence at Staple as an unwarrantable intrusion.

A decided qualm assailed her, deepening quickly into a settled conviction—Jean was nothing if not thorough!—that the real explanation of the delay in Lady Anne's response to Glyn's letter had lain in Blaise Tormarin's objection to the invasion of his home by a strange young woman—an objection Lady Anne had had to overcome, or decide to ignore, before she could answer Glyn's request in the affirmative.

The idea that she might be an unwelcome guest at Staple filled Jean with lively consternation, and by the time she had accomplished the necessary change of train at Exeter, and found herself being trundled along on the leisurely branch line which conducted her to her ultimate destination, she had succeeded in working herself up into a condition that almost verged upon panic.

"Coombe *Ea*-vie! *Coombe* Eavie!"

The sing-song intonation of a depressed-looking porter, first rising from a low note to a higher, then descending in contrary motion abruptly from high to low, was punctuated by the sharper, clipped pronouncement of the stationmaster as he bustled up the length of the platform declaiming: "'Meavie! 'Meavie! 'Meavie!" with a maddeningly insistent repetition that reminded one of a cuckoo in June.

Apparently both stationmaster and porter were too much absorbed in the frenzied strophe and antistrophe effect they were producing to observe that any passenger, handicapped by luggage, contemplated descending from the train—unexpected arrivals were of rare occurrence at Coombe

Eavie—and Jean therefore hastened to transfer herself and her hand-baggage to the platform unassisted. A minute later the train ambled on its way again, leaving the stationmaster and the depressed porter grouped in astonished admiration before the numerous trunks and suit-cases, labelled "Peterson," which the luggage van of the departing train had vomited forth.

To the bucolic mind, such an unwonted accumulation argued a passenger of quite superlative importance, and with one accord the combined glances of the station staff raked the diminutive platform, to discover Jean standing somewhat forlornly in the middle, of it, surrounded by the smaller fry of her luggage. The stationmaster hurried forward immediately to do the honours, and Jean addressed him eagerly.

"I want a *fiacre*—cab"—correcting herself hastily—"to take me to Staple Manor."

The man shook his head.

"There are no cabs here, miss," he informed her regretfully. "Anyone that wants to be met orders Wonnacott's wagonette in advance." Then, seeing Jean's face lengthen, he continued hastily: "But if they're expecting you up at Staple, miss, they'll be sure to send one of the cars to meet you. There!"—triumphantly, as the chug-chug of an approaching motor came to them clearly on the crisp, cold air—"that'll be it, for certain."

Followed the sound of a car braking to a standstill in the road outside the station, and almost immediately a masculine figure appeared advancing rapidly from the lower end of the platform.

Even through the dusk of the winter's afternoon Jean was struck by something curiously familiar in the man's easy, swinging stride. A surge of memories came flooding over her, and she felt her breath catch in her throat at the sudden possibility which flashed into her mind. For an instant she was in doubt—the thing seemed so amazingly improbable. Then, touching his hat, the stationmaster moved respectfully aside, and she found herself face to face with the unknown Englishman from Montavan.

She gazed at him speechlessly, and for a moment he, too, seemed taken aback. His eyes met hers in a startled, leaping glance of recognition and something more, something that set her pulses racing unsteadily.

"*Little comrade!*" She could have sworn the words escaped him. Then, almost in the same instant, she saw the old, rather weary gravity replace the sudden fire that had blazed up in the man's eyes, quenching its light.

"So—*you* are Miss Peterson!"

There was no pleasure, no welcome in his tones; rather, an undercurrent of ironical vexation as though Fate had played some scurvy trick upon him.

"Yes." The brief monosyllable came baldly in reply; she hardly knew how to answer him, how to meet his mood. Then, hastily calling up her reserves, she went on lightly: "You don't seem very pleased to see me. Shall I go away again?"

His mouth relaxed into a grim smile.

"This isn't Clapham Junction," he answered tersely. "There won't be a train till ten o'clock to-night."

A glint of humour danced in Jean's eyes.

"In that case," she returned gravely, "what do you advise?"

"I don't advise," he replied promptly. "I apologise. Please forgive such an ungracious reception, Miss Peterson—but you must acknowledge it was something in the nature of a surprise to find that you were—you!"

Jean laughed.

"It's given you an unfair advantage, too," she replied. "I still haven't penetrated your incognito—but I suppose you are Mr. Brennan?"

"No. Nick Brennan's my half-brother. I'm Blaise Tormarin, and, as my mother was unable to meet you herself, I came instead. Shall we go? I'll give the station-master instructions about your baggage."

So the unknown Englishman of Montavan was the man of whom the two women at the neighbouring lunch table in the hotel had been gossiping—the central figure of that most tragic love-affair! Jean thought she could discern, now, the origin of some of those embittered comments he had let fall when they were together in the mountains.

In silence she followed him out of the little wayside station to where the big head-lamps of a stationary car shed a blaze of light on the roadway, and presently they were slipping smoothly along between the high hedges which flanked the road on either hand.

CHAPTER IX
THE MASTER OF STAPLE

IT was too dark to distinguish details as the big car flew-along, but Jean found herself yielding instinctively to the still, mysterious charm of the country-side at even.

A slender young moon drifted like a curled petal in the dusky blue of the calm sky, its pale light faintly outlining the tops of the trees and the dim, gracious curves of distant hills, and touching the mist that filled the valleys to a nebulous, pearly glimmer, so that to Jean's eager eyes the foot of the hills seemed laved by some phantom sea of faery.

She felt no inclination to talk. The smooth rhythm of the pulsing car, the chill sweetness of the evening air against her face, the shadowy, half-revealed landscape all combined to lull her into a mood of tranquil appreciation, aloof and restful after the fatigue of her journey and the shock of her unexpected meeting with the Englishman from Montavan. She knew that later she would have to take up the thread of things again, adjust her mind to the day's surprising developments, but just for the moment she was content to let everything else slide and simply enjoy this first exquisite revelation of twilit Devon.

For a long time they drove in silence, Tormarin seeming no more disposed to talk than she herself.

Presently, however, he slowed the car down and, half-turning in his seat, addressed her abruptly.

"This is somewhat in the nature of an anti-climax," he remarked, the comment quite evidently springing from the thoughts which had been absorbing him.

He spoke curtly, as though he resented the march of events.

Jean felt herself jolted suddenly out of the placid reverie into which she had fallen.

"Yes. It is odd we should meet again so soon," she assented hurriedly.

"The silence has been broken—after all! You may be sure, Miss Peterson, it was by no will of mine."

Jean smiled under cover of the darkness.

"You're not very complimentary," she returned. "I'm sorry our meeting seems to afford you so little satisfaction." There was a ripple of laughter in her tones.

"It's not that." As he spoke, he slackened speed until the car was barely moving. "You know it's not that," he continued, his voice tense. "But, all the same, I'm going to ask you to—forget Montavan."

Jean's heart gave a violent throb, and the laughter went suddenly out of her voice as she repeated blankly:

"To forget Montavan?"

"Please. I said—and did—a few mad things that day we spent together. It was to be an uncounted day, you know, and—oh, well, the air of the Alps is heady! I want you to forgive me—and to blot out all remembrance of it."

He seemed to speak with some effort, yet each word was uttered deliberately, searing its way into her consciousness like red-hot iron.

The curt, difficultly spoken sentences could only signify one thing—that he had meant nothing, not even good, honest comradeship, that day at Montavan. He had merely been amusing himself with a girl whom he never expected to meet again, and now that circumstances had so unexpectedly brought them together he was clearly anxious that she should be under no misapprehension in the matter.

Jean's pride writhed beneath the insult of it. It was as though he feared she might make some claim upon his regard and had hastened to warn her, almost in so many words, not to set a fictitious value upon anything that had occurred between them. The glamour was indeed torn from her stolen day on the mountains! The whole memory of it, above all the memory of that pulsing moment of farewell, would henceforth be soiled and vulgarised—converted into a rather sordid little episode which she would gladly have blotted out from amongst the concrete happenings of life.

The feminine instinct against self-betrayal whipped her into quick speech.

"I've no wish to forget that you practically saved my life," she said. "I shall always" —lightly— "feel very much obliged for that."

"You exaggerate my share in the matter," he replied carelessly. "You would have extricated yourself from your difficulties without my assistance, I have no doubt. Or, more truly" —with a short laugh— "you would never have got into them."

He said no more, but let out the car and they shot forward into the gathering dusk. Presently they approached a pair of massive iron gates admitting to the manor drive, and as these were opened in response to a shrill hoot from Tormarin's horn the car swung round into an avenue of elms, the bare boughs, interlacing overhead, making a black network against the moonlit sky.

Still in silence they approached the house, its dim grey bulk, looming indeterminately through the evening mist, studded here and there with a glowing shield of orange from come unshaded window, and almost before Tormarin had pulled up the car, the front door flew open and a wide riband of light streamed out from the hall behind.

Jean was conscious of two or three figures grouped in the open doorway, dark against the welcoming blaze of light, then one of them detached itself from the group and hastened forward with outstretched hands.

"Here you are at last!"

For an instant Jean hesitated, doubtful as to whether the speaker could be Lady Anne. The voice which addressed her was so amazingly young—clear and full of vitality like the voice of a girl. Then the light flickered on to hair as white as if it had been powdered, and she realized that this surprisingly young voice must belong to her hostess.

"I was so sorry I could not meet you at the station myself," continued Lady Anne, leading the way into the house. "But a tiresome visitor turned up—one of those people who never know when it's time to go—and I simply couldn't get away without forcibly ejecting her."

In the fuller light of the hall, Jean discerned in Lady Anne's appearance something of that same quality of inherent youth apparent in her voice. The keen, humorous grey eyes beneath their black, arched brows were alertly vivacious, and the quite white hair served to enhance, rather than otherwise, the rose-leaf texture of her skin. Many a much younger woman had envied Lady Anne her complexion; it was so obviously genuine, owing nothing at all to art.

"And now"—Jean felt herself pulled gently into the light—"let me have a good look at you. Oh, yes!"—Lady Anne laughed amusedly—"You're Glyn Peterson's daughter right enough—you have just his chin with that delicious little cleft in it. But your eyes and hair are Jacqueline's." She leaned forward a little and kissed Jean warmly. "My dear, you're very welcome at Staple. There is nothing I could have wished more than to have you here—except that you could have prevailed upon Glyn to bring you himself."

"When you have quite finished going into the ancestral details of Miss Peterson's features, madonna, perhaps you will present me."

Lady Anne laughed good-humouredly.

"Oh, this is my pushful younger son, Jean. (I'm certainly going to call you Jean without asking whether I may!) You've already made acquaintance with Blaise. This is Nick."

Nick Brennan was as unlike his half-brother as he could possibly be — tall, and fair, and blue-eyed, with a perfectly charming smile and an air of not having a care in the world. Jean concluded he must resemble closely the dead Claude Brennan, since, except for a certain family similarity in cut of feature, he bore little resemblance to his mother.

"Blaise has had an hour's start of me in getting into your good graces, Miss Peterson," he said, shaking hands. "I consider it very unfair, but of course I had to be content—as usual—with the younger son's portion."

Jean liked him at once. His merry, lazy blue eyes smiled friendship at her, and she felt sure they should get on together. She could not imagine Nick "glooming" about the world, as one of the women at the hotel had declared his half-brother did.

It occurred to her that it would simplify matters if both he and Lady Anne were made aware at once of her former meeting with Blaise, so she took the opportunity offered by Nick's speech.

"He's had more than that," she said gaily. "Mr. Tor-marin and I had already met before—at Montavan."

"At Montavan?" Lady Anne gave vent to an ejaculation of amused impatience. "If we had only known! Blaise could have accompanied you back and saved you all the bothersome details of the journey. But we had no idea where he was. He went off in his usual way"—smiling a shade ruefully—"merely condescending to inform his yearning family that he was going abroad for a few weeks." Then, as Tormarin, having surrendered the car to a chauffeur, joined the group in the hall, she turned to him and continued with a faint note of expostulation in her voice: "You never told us you had already met Miss Peterson, Blaise."

"I didn't know it myself till I found her marooned on the platform at Coombe Eavie," he returned. His eyes, meeting Jean's, flickered with brief amusement as he added nonchalantly: "I did not catch Miss Peterson's name when we met at Montavan."

"No, we were not formally introduced," supplemented Jean. "But Mr. Tormarin was obliging enough to pull me out of an eight-foot deep snowdrift up in the mountains, so we allowed that to count instead."

"What luck!" exclaimed Nick with fervour.

"Yes, it was rather," agreed Jean. "To be smothered in a snowdrift isn't exactly the form of extinction I should choose."

"Oh, I meant luck for Blaise," explained Nick. "Opportunities of playing knight-errant are few and far between nowadays"—regretfully.

They all laughed, and then Lady Anne carried Jean off upstairs.

Here she found that a charming bedroom, with a sitting-room connecting, had been allotted her—"so that you'll have a den of your own to take refuge in when you're tired of us," as Lady Anne explained.

Jean felt touched by the kindly thought. It takes the understanding hostess to admit frankly that a guest may sometimes crave for the solitude of her own company—and to see that she can get it.

The rooms which were to constitute Jean's personal domain were delightfully decorated, old-world tapestries and some beautiful old prints striking just the right note in conjunction with the waxen-smooth mahogany of Chippendale. From the bedroom, where a maid was already busying herself unstrapping the traveller's manifold boxes, there opened off a white-tiled bathroom frankly and hygienically modern, and here Jean was soon splashing joyfully. By the time she had finished her bath and dressed for dinner she felt as though the fatigue of the journey had slipped from her like an outworn garment.

The atmosphere at dinner was charmingly informal, and presently, when the meal was at an end, the party of four adjourned into the hall for coffee. As Jean's eyes roved round the old-fashioned, raftered place, she was conscious of a little intimate thrill of pleasure. With its walls panelled in Jacobean oak, and its open hearth where a roaring fire of logs sent blue and green flames leaping up into the chimney's cavernous mouth, it reminded her of the great dining-hall at Beirnfels. But here there was a pleasant air of English cosiness, and it was obvious that at Staple the hall had been adopted as a living-room and furnished with an eye to comfort. There were wide, cushioned window-seats, and round the hearth clustered deep, inviting chairs, while everywhere were the little, pleasant, home-like evidences—an open book flung down here, a piece of unfinished needlework there—of daily use and occupation.

Nick at once established himself at Jean's side, kindly informing her that now that his inner man was satisfied he was prepared to make himself agreeable. Upon which Lady Anne apologised for his manners and Nick interrupted her, volubly pointing out that the fault, if any (which he denied), was entirely hers, since she had been responsible both for his upbringing and inherited tendencies. They both talked at once, wrangling together with huge zest and enjoyment, and it was easily apparent that the two were very close friends indeed.

Blaise took no part in the stream of chatter and nonsense which ensued, but stood a little apart, his shoulder propped against the chimney-piece, drinking his coffee in silence.

Jean's glance wandered reflectively from one brother to the other. They presented a striking contrast—the stern, dark-browed face of the elder man, with its bitter-looking mouth and that strange white streak lying like some, ghostly finger-mark across his dark hair, and the bubbling, blue-eyed charm of the younger. The difference between them was as definite as the difference between sunlight and shadow.

Nick was full of plans for Jean's entertainment, suggestions for boating and tennis occupying a prominent position in the programme he sketched out.

"It's really quite jolly paddling about on our lake," he rattled on. "The stream that feeds it hails from Dartmoor, of course. All Devonshire streams do, I believe—at least, you'll never hear of one that doesn't, the Moor being our proudest possession. Besides, people always believe that your water supply must be of crystalline purity if you just casually mention that its source is a Dartmoor spring. So of course, we all swear to the Dartmoor origin of our domestic waterworks. It sounds well—even if not always strictly true."

"Miss Peterson must find it a trifle difficult to follow your train of thought," commented Blaise a little sharply. "A moment ago you were discussing boating, and now it sounds as though you'll shortly involve yourself—and us—in a disquisition upon hygiene."

Nick smiled placidly.

"My enthusiasm got away with me a bit," he admitted with unruffled calm. "But I haven't the least doubt that Miss Peterson will like to know these few reassuring particulars. However——" And he forthwith returned enthusiastically to the prospects of tennis and kindred pastimes.

Once again Blaise broke in ungraciously. It seemed as though, for some reason, Nick's flow of light-hearted nonsense and the dozen different plans he was proposing for Jean's future divertisement, irritated him.

"Your suggestions seem to me remarkably inept, Nick," he observed scathingly, "seeing that at present it is midwinter and the lake frozen over about a foot deep. Quite conceivably, by the time that tennis and boating become practicable, Miss Peterson may not be here. She may get tired of us long before the summer comes," he added quickly, as though in a belated endeavour to explain away the suggestion of inhospitality which might easily be inferred from his previous sentence.

But if the hasty addition were intended to reassure Jean, it failed of its purpose. The idea that her coming to Staple was not particularly acceptable to its master had already taken possession, of her. Originally the consequence of the conversation she had overheard at the hotel, Tormarin's reluctantly given welcome when he met her at Coombe Eavie Station had served to increase her feeling of embarrassment And now, this last speech, though so hastily qualified, convinced her that her advent was regarded by her host in anything but a pleasurable light.

"Yes, I don't think you must count on me for the tennis season, Mr. Brennan," she said quickly, "I don't propose to billet myself on you indefinitely, you know."

"Oh, but I hope you do, my dear," Lady Anne interposed with a simple sincerity there was no doubting. "You must certainly stay with us till your father comes home, and" —with a smile— "unless Glyn has altered considerably, I imagine Beirnfels will not see him again under a year."

"But I couldn't possibly foist myself on to you for a year!" exclaimed Jean. "That would be a sheer imposition."

Lady Anne smiled across at her.

"My dear," she said, "I've never had a daughter—only these two great, unmanageable sons—and I'm just longing to play at having one. You're not going to disappoint me, I hope?"

There was something irresistibly winning in Lady Anne's way of putting the matter, and Jean jumped up and kissed her impulsively.

"I should hate to!" she answered warmly.

But she evaded giving a direct promise; there must be a clearer understanding between herself and Tormarin before she could accept Lady Anne's hospitality as frankly and fully as it was offered.

The opportunity for this clearer understanding came with the entry of Baines, the butler, who brought the information that a favourite young setter of Nick's had been taken ill and that the stableman feared the dog had distemper.

Nick sprang up, his concern showing in his face.

"I'll come out and have a look at him," he said quickly.

"I'll come with you," added Lady Anne.

She slipped her hand through his arm, and they hurried off to the stables, leaving Blaise and Jean alone together.

For a moment neither spoke. Blaise, smoking a cigarette, remained staring sombrely into the fire. Apparently he did not regard it as incumbent on him to make conversation, and Jean felt miserably nervous about broaching the subject of her visit. At last, however, fear lest Lady Anne and Nick should return before she could do so drove her into speech.

"Mr. Tormarin," she said quietly—so quietly that none would have guessed the flurry of shyness which underlay her cool little voice—"I am very sorry my presence here is so unwelcome to you. I'm afraid you will have to put up with me for a week or two, but I promise you I will try to make other arrangements as soon as I can."

He turned towards her abruptly.

"May I ask what you mean?" he demanded. It was evident from the haughty, almost arrogant tone of his voice that something had aroused his anger, though whether it was the irritation consequent upon her presence there, or because he chose to take her speech as censuring his attitude, Jean was unable to determine. His eyes were stormy and inwardly she quailed a little beneath their glance; outwardly, however, she retained her composure.

"I think my meaning is perfectly clear," she returned with spirit. "Even at the station you made it quite evident that my appearance came upon you in the light of an unpleasant surprise. And—from what you said just now to Mr. Brennan—it is obvious you hope my visit will not be a long one."

If she had anticipated spurring him into an impulsive disclaimer, she was disappointed.

"I am sorry I have failed so lamentably in my duties as host," he said coldly.

The apology, uttered with such an entire lack of ardour, served to emphasise the offence for which it professed to ask pardon. Jean's face whitened. She would hardly have felt more hurt and astonished if he had struck her.

"I—I——" she began. Then stopped, finding her voice unsteady.

But he had heard the break in the low, shaken tones, and in a moment his mood of intolerant anger vanished.

"Forgive me," he said remorsefully—and there was genuine contrition in his voice now. "I'm a cross-grained fellow, Miss Peterson; you'll find that out before you've been here many days. But never think that you are unwelcome at Staple."

"Then why—I don't understand you," she stammered. She found his sudden changes of humour bewildering.

He smiled down at her, that rare, strangely sweet smile of his which when it came always seemed to transform his face, obliterating the harsh sternness of its lines.

"Perhaps I don't quite understand, either," he said gently. "Only I know it would have been better if you had never come to Staple."

"Then—you wish I hadn't come?"

"Yes,"—slowly. "I think I do wish that."

She looked at him a little wistfully.

"Is that why you were angry—because I've come here? Lady Anne and—and Mr. Brennan seemed quite pleased," she added as though in protest.

"No doubt. Nick, lucky devil, has no need to economise in magic moments."

She felt her cheeks flush under the look he bent upon her, but she forced herself to meet it.

"And—and you?" she questioned very low.

"I have"—briefly.

It was long before sleep visited Jean that night The events of the day marched processionally through her mind, and her thoughts persisted in clustering round the baffling, incomprehensible personality of Blaise Tormarin.

His extreme bitterness of speech she ascribed to the unfortunate episode that lay in his past. But she could find no reason for his strange, expressed wish to disregard their former meeting at Montavan—to wipe out, as it were, all recollection of it.

That he did not dislike her she felt sure; and a woman rarely makes a mistake over a man's personal attitude towards her. But for some reason, it seemed to her, he was *afraid* to let himself like her! It was as though he were anxious to bolt and bar the door against any possibility of friendship between them. From whichever way she looked at it, she could find no key to the mystery of his behaviour. It was inexplicable.

Only one thing emerged from the confusion of thought; the lost glamour of that night at Montavan had returned—returned with fresh impulse and persuasiveness. And when at last she fell asleep, it was with the beseeching, soul-haunting melody of *Valse Triste* crying in her ears.

CHAPTER X
OTHER PEOPLE'S TROUBLES

JEAN woke to find the chill, wintry sunlight thrusting in long fingers through the space between the casements and the edges of the window-blinds. At first the unfamiliar look of a strange bedroom puzzled her, and she lay blinking drowsily at the wavering slits of light, wondering in vague, half-awake fashion where she was. Gradually, however, recollection returned to her, and with it a lively curiosity to view Staple by daylight. She jumped out of bed and, rattling up the blinds on their rollers, peered out of the window.

There was a hard frost abroad, and the stillness which reigned over the ice-bound country-side reminded her of the big Alpine silences. But here there was no snow—no dazzling sheet of whiteness spread, with cold, grey-blue shadows flung across it Green and shaven the lawns sloped gently down from a flagged terrace, running immediately beneath her window, to the very rim of the frozen lake that gleamed in the valley below. Beyond the valley, scattered woods and copses climbed the hillside opposite, leafless and bare save where a cluster of tall pines towered in evergreen defiance against the slate of the sky.

In the farther distance, beyond the confines of the manor park itself, Jean could catch glimpses of cultivated fields—the red Devon soil glowing jewel-like through filmy wisps of morning mist that still hung in the atmosphere, dispersing slowly as though loth to go. Here and there a little spiral of denser, blue-grey smoke wreathed its way upwards from the chimney of some thatched cottage or farmhouse. And back of it all, adumbrated in a dim, mysterious purple, the great tors of Dartmoor rose sentinel upon the horizon.

Jean's glance narrowed down to the sloping sward in front of the house. It was all just as her father had pictured it to her. On the left, a giant cedar broke the velvet smoothness of mown grass, its gnarled arms rimmed with hoar-frost, whilst to the right a tall yew hedge, clipped into huge, grotesque resemblances of birds and beasts, divided the lawns from a path which skirted a walled rose garden. By craning her neck and almost flattening her nose against the window-pane, she could just make out a sunk lawn in the rose garden, and in its centre the slender pillar of an ancient sundial.

It was all very English and old-fashioned, breathing the inalienable charm of places that have been well loved and tended by successive generations. And over all, hills and valleys, park and woodland, lay that faint, almost imperceptible humid veil wherewith, be it in scorching summer sunshine or iron frost, the West Country tenderly contrives to soften every harsh outline into something gracious, and melting, and alluring.

To Jean, familiarised from childhood with the piercing clarity of atmosphere, the brilliant colouring and the definiteness of silhouette of southern Europe and of Egypt, there was something inexpressibly restful and appealing in those blurred hues of grey and violet, in the warm red of the Devon earth, with its tender overtone of purple like the bloom on a grape, and the rounded breasts of green-clad hills curving suavely one into the other till they merged into the ultimate, rock-crowned slopes of the brooding moor.

"I'm going to love your England," she told Nick.

They were making their way down to the lake—alone together, since Blaise had curtly refused to join them—and as she spoke, Nick stopped and regarded her consideringly.

"I rather imagine England will love you," he replied, adding, with the whimsical impudence which was somehow always permitted Nick Brennan: "If it were not for a prior claim, I'm certain I should have loved you in about five minutes."

"I'm sorry I happened too late," retorted Jean.

"But I can still be a brother to you," he pursued, ignoring her interpolation. "I think," —reflectively—"I shall like being a brother to you."

"I should expect a brother to fetch and carry," cautioned Jean. "And to make himself generally useful."

"I haven't got the character from my last place about me at the moment, but I'll write it out for you when we get back. Meanwhile, I will perform the menial task of fastening on your skates."

They had reached the lake by now. It was a wide stretch of water several acres in extent, and rimmed about its banks with rush and alder. At the far end Jean could discern a boat-house.

"It must be an ideal place for boating in the summer," she said, taking in the size of the lake appreciatively as together they circled it with long, sweeping strokes, hands interlocked. It was much larger than it had appeared from her bedroom window, when it had been partially screened from her view by rising ground.

"It's all right just for paddling about," answered Nick. "But there's really jolly boating on our river. That's over on the west side of the park" — he pointed in the direction indicated. "It divides Staple from Willow Ferry — the property of our next-door neighbour, so to speak. You'd like the boating here," he added, "though I'm afraid our skating possibilities aren't likely to impress anyone coming straight from Switzerland."

"I'm sure I shall like skating—or anything else—here," said Jean Warmly. "It is all so beautiful. I suppose Devonshire is really quite the loveliest county in England? My father always declared it was."

"*We* think so," replied Nick modestly. "Though a Cornishman would probably want to knock me down for saying so! But I love it." he went on. "There's nowhere else I would care to live." His eyes softened, seeming almost to caress the surrounding fields and woods.

Jean nodded. "I can understand that," she said. "Although I've only been here a few hours, I'm beginning to love it, too. I don't know why it is—I can't explain it—but I feel as if I'd *come home*."

"So you have. The Petersons lived here for generations."

"Do you mean"—Jean stared at him in astonishment—"do you mean that they lived at Coombe Eavie?"

"Yes. Didn't you know? They used to own Charnwood—a place about a mile from here. It was sold after your grandfather's death. Did your father never tell you?"

She shook her head.

"He always avoided speaking of anything in connection with his life over here. I think he hated England. Is there anyone living at Charnwood now?" she asked, after a pause.

"Yes. It has changed hands several times, and now a friend of ours lives there—Lady Latimer."

"Then perhaps I shall be able to go there some day. I should like to see the place where my father's people lived"—eagerly.

Nick laughed.

"You've got the true Devonshire homing instinct," he declared. "Devon folk who've left the country always want to see the 'place where their people lived.' I remember, about a year ago, a Canadian girl and her brother turned up at Staple. They were descendants of a Tormarin who had emigrated two or three generations before, and they had come across to England for a visit. Their first trip was to Devonshire; they wanted to see 'the place where Dad's people had lived.' And, by Jove, they knew a lot more about it than we did! They were posted up in every detail, and insisted on a personally conducted tour over the whole place. They went back to Canada rejoicing, loaded with photographs of Staple."

Jean smiled.

"I think it was rather dear of them to come back like that," she said simply.

They swung round the head of the lake and, as they turned, Jean caught sight of a woman's figure emerging from the path which ran through the woods. Apparently the newcomer descried the skaters at the same moment, for she stopped and waved her hand in a friendly little gesture of greeting. Nick lifted his cap.

"That is Lady Latimer," he said.

Something in his voice, some indescribable deepening of quality, made Jean look at him quickly. She remembered on one occasion, in a jeweller's shop, noticing a very beautiful opal lying in its case; she had commented on it casually, and the man behind the counter had lifted it from its satiny bed and turned it so that the light should fall full upon it. In an instant the red fire slumbering in its heart had waked into glowing life, irradiating the whole stone with pulsing colour. It was some such vitalising change as this that she sensed in the suddenly eager face beside her.

Hastening their pace, she and Nick skated up to the edge of the lake where Lady Latimer awaited them, and as he introduced the two women to each other it seemed as though the eyes of the woman on the bank asked hastily, almost frightenedly: "Will you prove friend or foe?" And Jean's eyes, all soft and luminous like every real woman's in the presence of love, signalled back steadily: "Friend!"

"Claire!" said Nick. And Jean thought that no name could have suited her better.

She was the slenderest thing, with about her the pliant, delicate grace of a harebell. Ash-blonde hair, so fair that in some lights it looked silver rather than gold, framed the charming Greuze face. Only it was not quite a Greuze, Jean reflected. There was too much character in it—a certain gentle firmness, something curiously still and patient in the closing of the curved lips, and a deeper appeal than that of mere wondering youth in the gentian-blue eyes. They were woman's eyes, eyes out of which no weeping could quite wash the wistfulness of some past or present sorrow.

"So you are one of the Charnwood Petersons?" said Lady Latimer in her soft, pretty voice. "You won't like me, I'm afraid"—smiling—"I'm living in your old home."

"Oh, Jean won't quarrel with you over that," put in Nick. "She's got a splendacious castle all her own somewhere in the wilds of Europe."

"Yes. Beirnfels is really my home. I've never even seen Charnwood," smiled Jean. "But I should like to—some day, if you will ask me over."

"Oh, yes, certainly you must come," replied Lady Latimer a little breathlessly. But she seemed unaccountably flurried, as though Jean's suggestion in some way disquieted her. "But of course, Charnwood—now—isn't a bit like what it must have been when the Petersons had it. I think a place changes with the people who inhabit it, don't you? I mean, their influence impresses itself on it. If they are good and happy people, you can feel it in the atmosphere of the place, and if they are people with bad and wicked thoughts, you feel that, too. I know I do." And there was no doubt in the mind of either of her hearers that she was referring to the last-named set of influences.

"But I think Charnwood must be lovely, since it's your home now," said Jean sincerely.

"Oh, yes—of course—it is my home now." Lady Latimer looked troubled. "But other people live—have lived there. It's changed hands several times, hasn't it, Nick?"—turning to him for confirmation.

Nick was frowning. He, too, appeared troubled.

"Of course it's changed hands—heaps of times," he replied gruffly. "But I should think your influence would be enough to counteract that of—of everybody else. Look here, chuck discussing rotten, psychic influences, Claire, and come on the ice."

"No, I can't," she replied hastily. "I haven't my skates here."

"That doesn't matter. We've a dozen pairs up at the house. One of them is sure to fit you. I'll go and collect a few."

He wheeled as though to cross the lake on his proposed errand, but Claire Latimer laid her hand quickly on his arm.

"No, no," she said. "I can't skate this morning. I'm on my way home."

"Oh, change your mind!" begged Jean, noticing with friendly amusement Nick's expression of discontent.

"No, really I can't" Claire's face had whitened and her big eyes sought Nick's in a kind of pathetic appeal. "Adrian is not—very well to-day. My husband," she added explanatorily to Jean.

The latter was conscious of a sense of shock. She had quite imagined Lady Latimer to be a widow, and had been mentally engaged in weaving the most charming and happy-ever-after of romances since the moment she had seen that wonderful change come over Nick's face. Probably her impression was due to the manner of his first introduction of Claire's name, "A friend of ours lives there—Lady Latimer," without reference to any husband lurking in the background.

She observed that Nick made no further effort to persuade Claire to remain, and after exchanging a few commonplace remarks the latter continued her way back to Charnwood.

It was so nearly lunch time that it did not seem worth while resuming their skating. Besides, with Claire Latimer's refusal to join them, the occupation seemed to have lost some of its charm, and when Jean suggested a return to the house Nick assented readily.

"She is very sweet—young Lady Latimer," remarked

Jean, as they walked back over the frostily crisp turf. "But she looks rather sad. And she isn't the kind of person one associates with sadness. There's something so young and fresh about her; she makes one think of spring flowers."

Nick's face kindled.

"Yes, she's like that, isn't she?" he answered eagerly. "Like a pale golden narcissus."

They walked on in silence for a few minutes, the thoughts of each of them dwelling on the woman who had just left them. Then Jean said softly:

"So that's the 'prior claim?'"

"Yes," he acknowledged simply.

"You never mentioned that she had a husband concealed somewhere. I quite thought she was a widow till she suddenly mentioned him."

"I never think of him as her husband"—shortly. "You can't mate light and darkness."

"I suppose he's an invalid?" ventured Jean.

Rick's face darkened.

"He's a drug fiend," he said in a low, hard voice.

"Oh!"

After that one breathless exclamation of horror Jean remained silent. The swift picture conjured up before her eyes by Rick's terse speech was unspeakably revolting.

Years ago she had heard her father describing the effect of the drug habit upon a friend of his own who had yielded to it. He had been telling her mother about it, characteristically oblivious of the presence of a child of eleven in the room at the time, and some of Glyn Peterson's poignant, illuminating phrases, punctuated by little, stricken murmurs of pity from Jacqueline, had impressed a painfully accurate picture on the plastic mind of childhood. Ever since then, drug-mania had represented to Jean the uttermost abyss.

And now, the vision of that slender, gracious woman, Rick's "pale golden narcissus," tied for life to a man who must ultimately become that which Glyn Peterson's friend had become, filled her with compassionate dismay.

It was easy enough, now, to comprehend Claire Latimer's curious lack of warmth when Jean expressed the hope that she might go over to Charnwood some day. It sprang from the nervous shrinking of a woman at the prospect of being driven to unveil before fresh eyes the secret misery and degradation of her life.

Jean was still silent as she and Nick re-entered the hall at Staple. It was empty, and as, by common consent, they instinctively drew towards the fire Nick pulled forward one of the big easy-chairs for her. Then he stood gloomily staring down into the leaping flames, much as Tormarin had stood the previous evening.

Intuitively she knew that he wanted to give her his confidence.

"Tell me about it, Nick," she said quietly.

"May I?" The words jerked out like a sigh of relief. He dropped into a chair beside her.

"There isn't very much to tell you. Only, I'd like you to know — to be a pal to her, if you can, Jean." He paused, then went on quickly: "They married her to him when she was hardly more than a child — barely seventeen. She's only nineteen now. Sir Adrian is practically a millionaire, and Claire's father and mother were in low water — trying to cut a dash in society on nothing a year. So — they sold Claire. Sir Adrian paid their debts and agreed to make them a handsome allowance. And they let her go to him, knowing, then, that he had already begun to take drugs."

"*How could they?*" burst from Jean in a strangled whisper.

Nick nodded. His eyes, meeting hers, had lost their gay good humour and were dull and lack-lustre.

"Yes, you'd wonder how, wouldn't you?" he said. His voice rasped a little. "Still—they did it. Then, later on, the Latimers came to Charnwood, and Claire and I met. It didn't take long to love her—you can understand that, can't you?"

"Oh, Nick—yes! She is so altogether lovable."

"But understand this, too,"—and the sudden sternness that gripped his speech reminded her sharply of his brother—"we recognise that that is all there can ever be between us. Just the knowledge that we love each other. I think even that helps to make her life—more bearable."

He fell silent, and presently Jean stretched out a small, friendly hand.

"Thank you for telling me, Nick," she said. "Perhaps some day you'll be happy—together. You and Claire. It sounds a horrible thing to say—to count on—I know, but a man who takes drugs——"

Nick interrupted her with a short laugh.

"You needn't count on Latimer's snuffing out, if that's what you mean. He is an immensely strong man—like a piece of steel wire. It will take years for any drug to kill him. I sometimes think"—bitterly—"that it will kill Claire first."

CHAPTER XI
"THE SINS OF THE FATHERS"

A FEW days later, Jean, coming in from a long tramp across country in company with Nick and half a dozen dogs of various breeds, discovered Tormarin lounging in a chair by the fire. He was in riding kit, having just returned from visiting an outlying corner of the estates where his bailiff had suggested that a new plantation might be made, and Jean eyed his long supple figure with secret approval. Like most well-built Englishmen, he looked his best in kit that demanded the donning of breeches and leggings.

A fine rain was falling out of doors, and beads of moisture clung to Jean's clothes and sparkled in the blown tendrils of russet hair which had escaped from beneath the little turban hat she was wearing. Apparently, however, her appearance did not rouse Tormarin to any reciprocal appreciation, for, after bestowing the briefest of glances upon her as she entered, he averted his eyes, concentrating his attention upon the misty ribands of smoke that drifted upwards from his cigarette.

Jean knelt down on the hearth, and, pulling off her rain-soaked gloves, held out her hands to the fire's cheerful blaze.

"It's good-bye to all the skating, I'm afraid," she said regretfully. "Nick says we're not likely to have another hard frost like the last, now that the weather has broken so completely."

"No. It's April next month—supposedly springtime, you know," returned Blaise indifferently.

He seemed disinclined to talk, and Jean eyed him contemplatively. His attitude towards her baffled her as much as ever. He was unfailingly courteous and considerate, but he remained, nevertheless, unmistakably aloof, avoiding her whenever it was politely possible, and when it was not, treating her with a cool neutrality of manner that was as complete a contrast to his demeanour when they were together at Montavan as could well be imagined. Indeed, sometimes Jean almost wondered if the events of that day they spent amid the snows had really taken place—they seemed so far away, so entirely unrelated to her present life, notwithstanding the fact that she was in daily contact with the man who had shared them with her.

"It was rather uncomplimentary of you not to come skating with us a solitary *once*," she remarked at last, an accent of reproach in her voice. "Was my performance on the rink at Montavan so execrable that you felt you couldn't risk it again?"

He looked up, his glance meeting hers levelly.

"You've phrased it excellently," he replied briefly. "I felt I couldn't risk it."

A sudden flush mounted to Jean's face. There was no misunderstanding the significance that underlay the curt words, which, as she was vibrantly aware, bore no relation whatever to her skill, or absence of it, on the ice.

Blaise made no endeavour to relieve the awkward silence that ensued. Instead, his eyes rested upon her with a somewhat quizzical expression, as though he were rather entertained than otherwise by her evident confusion. Jean felt her indignation rising.

"It is fortunate that other people are not so—nervous," she said disdainfully. "Otherwise I should find myself as isolated as a fever hospital."

"It is fortunate indeed," he agreed politely.

In the course of the three weeks which had elapsed since her arrival at Staple, Jean had dared several similar passages-at-arms with her host. Woman-like, she was bent on getting behind his guard of reticence, on forcing him into an explanation of his altered attitude towards her—since no woman can be expected to endure that a man should completely change from ill-suppressed ardour to a cool, impersonal detachment of manner, without aching to know the reason why! But in every instance Tormarin had carried off the honours of war, parrying her small thrusts with a lazy insouciance which she found galling in the extreme.

Hitherto she had encountered little difficulty in getting pretty much her own way with the men of her acquaintance; she had sufficient of the temperament and charm of the red-haired type to compass that. But her efforts to elucidate the cause of the change in Blaise Tormarin were about as prolific of result as the efforts of a butterfly at stone-breaking.

Fortunately for the preservation of peace, at this juncture there came the sound of voices, and Lady Anne entered the room, accompanied by a visitor. Her clever, grey eyes flashed quickly from Jean's flushed face to that of her son, but, if she sensed the electricity in the atmosphere, she made no comment.

"Blaise, my dear, here is Judith," she said pleasantly. "I found her wandering forlornly in the lanes, so I drove her back here. She has just returned from town, and for some reason her car wasn't at the station to meet her."

"I wired home saying what time I should reach Coombe Eavie," explained the new-comer. "But as I was rather late reaching Waterloo, I rashly entrusted the wire to a small boy to send off for me, and I'm afraid he's played me false. I should have had to trudge the whole way back to Willow Ferry if Lady Anne hadn't happened along."

Lady Anne turned to Jean, and, laying an affectionate hand on her arm, drew her forward.

"Jean, let me introduce you to Mrs. Craig. My new acquisition, Judith, she went on contentedly. A daughter. I always told you I wanted one. Now I've borrowed someone else's."

Jean found herself shaking hands with a slender, distinctive-looking woman who moved with a slow, languorous grace that was almost snake-like in its peculiar suppleness.

She gave one the impression that she had no bones in her body, or that if she had, they had never hardened properly but still retained the pliability of cartilage.

She was somewhat sallow—the consequence, it transpired later, of long residence in India—with sullen, slate-coloured eyes, appearing almost purple in shadow, and a straight, thin-lipped mouth. Jean decided that she was not in the least pretty, though attractive in an odd, feline way, and that she must be about thirty-two. As a matter of fact, Judith Craig was forty, but no one would have guessed it—and she would certainly not have confided it.

Presently Nick, who had been personally supervising the feeding of his beloved dogs, joined the party, greeting Mrs. Craig with the easy informality of an old friend, and shortly afterwards Baines brought in the tea-things.

"And where is Burke?" enquired Blaise, of Mrs. Craig, as he handed her tea. "Didn't he come back with you?"

"Geoffrey? Oh, no. He's not coming down till the end of April. You know he detests Willow Ferry in the winter—'beastly wet swamp,' he calls it! He's dividing his time between London and Leicestershire—London, while that long frost stopped all hunting."

Mrs. Craig was evidently on a footing of long-established intimacy with the Staple household, and Jean, listening quietly to the interchange of news and of little personal happenings, regarded her with rather critical interest. She was not altogether sure that she liked her, but she was quite sure that, wherever her lot might be cast, Judith Craig would never occupy the position of a nonentity. She had considerable charm of manner, and there was a quite unexpected fascination about her smile—unexpected, because, when in repose, her thin lips lay folded together in a straight and somewhat forbidding line, whereas the moment they relaxed into a smile they assumed the most delightful curves, and two little lines, which should have been dimples but were not, cleft each cheek on either side of the mouth.

All at once Mrs. Craig turned to Jean as though she had made up her mind about something over which she had been hesitating.

"Have I seen you anywhere before?" she asked, her charming smile softening the abruptness of the question. "Your face is so extraordinarily familiar."

Jean shook her head.

"I don't think so," she answered. "I'm sure I should remember you if we had met anywhere. Besides, I've lived abroad all my life; this is only my first visit to England."

"I think I can explain," said Lady Anne. There was a deliberateness about her manner that suggested she was about to make a statement which she was aware would be of some special interest to at least one of the party. "Jean is Glyn Peterson's daughter; so of course you see a likeness, Judith."

Jean, glancing enquiringly across at Mrs. Craig, was startled at the sudden change in her face produced by Lady Anne's simple announcement. The sallow skin seemed to pale—almost wither, like a cut flower that needs water—and the lips that had been parted in a smile stiffened slowly into their accustomed straight line.

"Of course"—Mrs. Craig's voice sounded flat and she swallowed once or twice before she spoke—"that must be it. I—knew your father, Miss Peterson."

To Jean, always sensitive to the emotional quality of the atmosphere, it seemed as though some current of hostility, of malevolence, leapt at her through the innocent-sounding speech. "*I knew your father.*" It was quite ridiculous, of course, but the words sounded almost like a threat.

She had no answer ready, and a brief silence followed. Then Lady Anne bridged the awkward moment with some commonplace, adroitly steering the conversation into smoother waters, and a few minutes later Mrs. Craig rose to go.

"I'll see you across the park, Judith," volunteered Nick, and he and his mother accompanied her out of the room.

In the hall, Lady Anne detained her visitor an instant with a light hand on her arm, while Nick foraged for his own particular headgear, amongst the family assortment of hats and caps.

"Jean is a dear girl, Judith," she said earnestly. "I want you to be friends with her. Don't" — pleadingly — "visit the sins of the fathers on the children."

"Why, no, I shouldn't," replied Mrs. Craig, with apparent frankness. "It was only that, for the moment, it was rather a shock to learn that she was — that woman's — child."

"Of course it was," acquiesced Lady Anne. "Good-bye, dear Judith."

But notwithstanding Mrs. Craig's assurances, a troubled look lingered in Lady Anne's grey eyes long after her guest's departure.

CHAPTER XII
A SENSE OF DUTY

JEAN was immensely puzzled at the abrupt change which had occurred in Mrs. Craig's manner immediately upon hearing that she was the daughter of Glyn Peterson, and, as soon as the visitor had taken her departure, she sought an explanation.

"What on earth made Mrs. Craig freeze up the instant my father's name was mentioned? Did she hate him for any reason?"

Tormarin looked across at her.

"No," he answered quietly. "She didn't hate him. She loved him."

Jean stared at him in frank astonishment. She had never dreamed that there had been any other woman than Jacqueline in Glyn's life.

"Mrs. Craig—and my father?" she exclaimed incredulously.

"She wasn't Mrs. Craig in those days. She was Judith Burke."

"Well, but——" persisted Jean, determined to get to the bottom of the mystery. "I still don't see why."

"Why what?"—unwillingly.

"Why she looked as if she loathed the very sight of me. That's not"—drily—"quite the effect you would expect love to produce!"

There was a curiously abstracted look in Tormarin's eyes as he made answer.

"Love is productive of very curious effects on occasion. More particularly when it is without hope of fulfilment," he added in a lower tone.

"Well, I suppose my father couldn't help not falling in love with Mrs. Craig," protested Jean with some warmth. "Nor could he have prevented her caring for him. And it's certainly illogical of her to feel any resentment towards me on that score. *I* had nothing to do with it."

"Love and logic have precious little to say to each other, as a rule," replied Tormarin grimly. "To Judith, you're the child of the woman who stole her lover away from her, so you can hardly expect her to feel an overwhelming affection for you."

"The woman who stole her lover away from her?" repeated Jean slowly. "I don't understand. What do you mean, Blaise?"

He glanced at her in some surprise.

"Surely — — Don't you know the circumstances?"

She shook her head.

"No. I simply don't know in the least what you are talking about. Please tell me."

Tormarin made no response for a moment. He was standing with his back to the light, but as he lit a cigarette the flare of the match revealed a worried expression on his face, as though he deprecated the turn the conversation was taking.

"Oh, well," he said at last, evading the point at issue, "it's all ancient history now. Let it go. There's never anything gained by digging up the dry bones of the past." Jean's mouth set itself in a mutinous line of determination. "Please tell me, Blaise," she reiterated. "As it is something which concerns my father and a woman I shall probably be meeting fairly often in the future, I think I have a right to know about it."

He shrugged his shoulders resignedly.

"Very well—if you insist. But I don't think you'll be any happier for knowing." He paused. "Still inflexible?" She bent her head.

"Quite"—firmly—"whatever it is, I'd rather know it."

"On your own head be it, then." He seemed trying to infuse a lighter element into the conversation, as though hoping to minimise the effect of what he had to tell her. "It was just this—that your father and Judith Burke were engaged to be married at the time he met your mother, and that—well, to make a long story short, he ran away with Miss Mavory on the day fixed for his wedding with Judith."

A dead silence followed the disclosure. Then Jean uttered a low cry of dismay.

"My father did that? Are you sure?"

"Quite sure."

Tormarin could see that the story had distressed her. Her eyes showed hurt and bewildered like those of a child who has met with a totally unexpected rebuff.

"Don't take it like that!" he urged hastily. "After all, It was nothing so terrible. You look as though he had broken every one of the ten commandments"—smiling.

Jean smiled back rather wanly.

"I don't know that I should worry very much if he had—in some circumstances. But—don't you see?—it was so cruel, so horribly selfish!"

"You've got to remember two things in justification——"

"*Justification?*"—expressively. "There wasn't any. There couldn't be."

"Well, excuse, then, if you like. One thing is that Jacqueline Mavory was one of the most beautiful of women, and the other, that your father's engagement to Judith had really been more or less engineered by their respective parents—adjoining properties, friends of long standing, and so on. It was no love-match—on his side."

"But on her wedding-day!"—pitifully. "Oh! Poor Judith!"

Tormarin smiled a trifle cynically.

"That was the root of the trouble. It was Judith's pride that was hurt— as well as her heart. She married Major Craig not long after, and I believe they were really fond of one another and comparatively happy. But she has never forgiven Peterson from that day to this. And you, being Jacqueline Mavory's daughter, will come in for the residue of her bitterness. Unless"— ironically—"you can make friends with her."

"I shall try to," said Jean simply. "Is Major Craig living now?"

"No. He died out in India, and after his death Judith came back to England. She has lived at Willow Ferry with her brother, Geoffrey Burke, ever since."

There was a long silence, while Jean tried to fit in the new facts she had learned with her knowledge of her father's character. She was a little afraid that Tormarin might misunderstand her impulsive outburst of indignation.

"Don't think that I am sitting in judgment on my father," she said at last. "In a way, I can—even understand his doing such a thing. You know, for the last two years of my mother's life I was with them both constantly, and anyone living with them could understand their doing all kinds of things that ordinary people wouldn't do." She paused, as though seeking words that might make her meaning clearer. "They would never really mean to hurt anyone, but they were just like a couple of children together— gloriously irresponsible and happy. I always felt years older than either of them. Glyn used to say I was 'cursed with a damnable sense of duty'"— laughing rather ruefully. "I suppose I am. Probably I inherit it from our old Puritan ancestors on the Peterson side. I know I couldn't have cheerfully run off and taken my happiness at the cost of someone else's prior right."

A look of extreme bitterness crossed Tormarin's face.

"Wait till you're tempted," he said shortly. "Wait till *what you want* wars against what you ought to have—what you've the right to take."

For a moment she made no answer. Put bluntly like that, the matter suddenly presented itself to her as one of the poignant possibilities of life. Supposing—supposing such a choice should ever be demanded of her? She felt a vague fear catch at her heart, an indefinable dread.

When at last she spoke, the eyes she lifted to meet Tor-marin's were troubled. In them he could read the innate honesty which was prepared to face the question he had raised, and behind that—courage. A young, untried courage, not sure of itself, it is true, but still courage that only waited till some call should wake it into fighting actuality.

"I hope," she said with a wistful humility that was rather touching, "I hope I should stick it out One's ideals, and duty, and other people's rights— it would be horrible to scrap the lot—just for love."

"Worth it, perhaps. You"—his voice was the least bit uneven—"you haven't been up against love—yet."

Again she was conscious of that little catch at her heart—the same convulsive tightening of the muscles as one experiences when a telegram is put into one's hand which may, or may not, contain bad news.

"You haven't been up against love yet."

The words recalled her knowledge of the tragic episode that lay in Tormarin's own past. The whole history she did not know—only the odds and ends of gossip which one woman had confided to another. But here, in the man's curt brevity of speech, surely lay proof that he had suffered. And if he had suffered, it followed that he must have cared deeply for the woman who had thrown him aside for the sake of another man.

Jean's first generous impulse of pity as she realised this was strangely intermingled with a fleeting disquiet, a subconscious sense of loss. It was only momentary, and not definite enough for her to express in words, even to herself—hardly more than the slightly blank sensation produced upon anyone sitting in the sunshine when a cloud suddenly intervenes and drops a shadow where a moment before there has been warmth and light.

An instant later it was overborne by her spontaneous sympathy for the man beside her, and, recognising the rather painful similarity between her father's treatment of Judith Craig and the story she had heard of the unknown woman's treatment of Tormarin himself, she tactfully deflected the conversation to something that would touch him less closely, launching into a description of the life her parents had led at Beirnfels.

"They were wonderfully happy together there. Not in the least—as I suppose they ought to have been—an awful example of poetic justice!" she declared. "Glyn used to call Beirnfels his 'House of Dreams-Come-True'."

"Glyn?"—suddenly remarking her use of Peterson's Christian name.

She smiled.

"I never called them father and mother. They would have loathed it. Glyn used to say that anything which savoured so much of domesticity would kill romance!"

"That sounds like all that I have ever heard about him," said Tormarin, smiling too. "So does the 'House of Dreams-Come-True.' It's a charming idea."

"He took it from one of Jacqueline's songs. She had a glorious voice, you know."

"Yes, so I've heard. I suppose you have inherited it?"

She shook her head.

"No, I wish I had. But Jacqueline insisted on trying to teach me singing, all the same. Poor dear! I was a dreadful disappointment to her, I'm afraid."

"Couldn't you sing the 'House of Dreams' song? I'm rather curious to hear the remainder of it."

Jean rose and crossed to the piano.

"Oh, yes, I can sing you that. Jacqueline always used to say it was the only thing I sang as if I understood it, and Glyn declared it was because it agreed with my 'confounded principles'!"

She smiled up at him as her fingers slid into the prelude of the song, but her little joke against herself brought no answering smile to his lips. Instead, he stood waiting for the song to begin with an odd kind of expectancy on his face.

Jean had most certainly not inherited her mother's exquisite voice, but she had a quaint little pipe of her own, with a clouded, husky quality in it that was not without its appeal. It lent a wistful charm to the simple words of the song.

> "It's a strange road leads to the House of Dreams,
> To the House of Dreams-Come-True,
> Its Hills are steep and its valleys deep,
> And salt with tears the Wayfarers weep,
> The Wayfarers—I and you.

"But there's sure a way to the House of Dreams,
To the House of Dreams-Come-True.
We shall find it yet, ere the sun has set,
If we fare straight on, come fine, come wet,
Wayfarers—I and you."

The soft, husky voice ceased, and for a moment there was silence. Then Tormarin said quietly:

"Thank you. I don't think your mother need have felt any great disappointment concerning your voice. It has its own qualities, even if it is not suited to the concert hall."

"But the words of the song?" questioned Jean eagerly. "Don't you like them?"

"It's a pretty enough idea." He laid a faint, significant stress on the last word. "But for some of us the 'House of Dreams-Come-True' has never been built. Or, if it has, we've lost the way there."

There was a note of rigid acceptance in his voice, as though he no longer strove against the decisions of destiny, and Jean's eager sympathy leaped impulsively to her lips.

"Don't say that!" she began. Then checked herself, flushing a little. "I hate to hear you speak in that way," she went on more quietly. "It sounds as though there were nothing worth trying for—worth waiting for. I like to believe that everyone has a house of dreams which may 'come true' some day." She paused. "'If we fare straight on, come fine, come wet,'" she repeated softly.

Her eyes had a far-away look in them, as though they were envisioning that narrow, winding track which leads, somewhen, to the place where dreams even the most wonderful of them—shall become realities.

Glorious faith and optimism of youth! If we could only recapture it in those after years, when time has added tolerance and a little wisdom to our harvest's store, the houses where dreams come true might add themselves together until there were whole streets of them—glowing townships— instead of merely an isolated dwelling here or there.

As Tormarin listened to Jean's young, eager voice, his face softened and some of the tired lines in it seemed to smooth themselves out "Little Comrade," he said gently, and she felt her breath quicken as he called her again by the name which he had used at Montavan—and once since, when they had come suddenly face to face at Coombe Eavie Station. But that second time the words had escaped him unawares. Now he was using them deliberately, withholding no part of their significance. "Little comrade, I think the man who 'fares straight on' with you for fellow-traveller *will* find the House of Dreams-Come-True. But it isn't—just any man who may start that journey with you. It mustn't be"—his grave eyes held hers intently—"a man who has tried to find the road once before—and failed."

It seemed to Jean that, as he spoke, the wall which he had built up between them since she came to Staple crumbled away. This was the same man she had known at Montavan, whose hands reached out to hers across some fixed dividing line which neither he nor she might pass. She knew now what that dividing line must be—the shadow flung by a past love, his love for Nesta Freyne which had ended in hopeless tragedy.

There must always be a limit set to any friendship of theirs. So much he had implied at their first meeting. But, since then, he had taken even that friendship from her, substituting a deliberate indifference against which she had struggled in vain.

And now, without knowing quite how it had come about, the barrier was down. They were comrades once more—she and the Englishman from Montavan—and she was conscious of a great content that it should be so.

For the moment she asked nothing more, was unconscious of any further wish. The woman in her still slumbered, and, to the girl, this friendship seemed enough. She did not realise that something deeper, more imperative in its ultimate demands, was mingled with it—was, indeed, unrecognised by her, the very essence of it.

CHAPTER XIII
"WILL YOU WALK INTO MY PARLOUR?"

JEAN, sculling leisurely down the river which ran between Staple and Willow Eerry, looked around her with a little thrill of enjoyment—the sheer, physical thrill of youth unconsciously in harmony with the climbing sap in the trees, with the upward thrust of young green, with all the exquisite recreation of Nature in the spring of the year.

April had been, as it too commonly is in this northern clime of ours, the merest travesty of spring, a bleak, cold month of penetrating wind and sleet, but now May had stolen upon the world almost unawares, opening with tender, insistent fingers the sticky brown buds fast curled against the nipping winds, and misting all the woods with a shimmer of translucent green.

Overhead arched a sky of veiled, opalescent blue, and Jean, staring up at it with dreamy eyes, was reminded of the "great city" of the Book of Revelation whose "third foundation" was of chalcedony. This soft English sky must be the third foundation, she decided whimsically.

But the occupation of sky-gazing did not combine well with that of steering a straight course down a stream whose width hardly entitled it to its local designation of "the river," and a few minutes later the boat's nose cannoned abruptly against the bank.

As, however, to tie up somewhere under the trees which edged the water had been Jean's original intention, this did not trouble her overmuch, and discovering a gnarled stump convenient to her purpose, she looped the painter round it, collected the rug and a couple of cushions which she had brought with her, and established herself comfortably in the stern of the boat.

Everyone else at Staple having engagements of one sort or another, she had promised herself a lazy afternoon in company with the latest novel sent down from Mudie's. But she was in no immediate hurry to begin its pages. The mellow warmth of the afternoon tempted her to the more restful occupation of mere day-dreaming, and as she lay tucked up snugly amongst her cushions, enjoying the sweet-scented airs that played among the trees and over the surface of the water, she allowed her thoughts to drift idly back across the two months she had spent at Staple.

The time had slipped by so quickly that it was hard to believe that rather more than eight weeks had elapsed since that grey February evening when she had alighted on the little, deserted platform at Coombe Eavie Station. They had been quiet, happy weeks, filled with the pleasant building up of new friendships, and Jean reflected that she had already grown to look upon Staple almost as "home." She possessed in a large measure the capacity to adapt herself to her surroundings, and realising that Lady Anne had been perfectly sincere in her expressed desire to play at having a daughter, Jean had, at first a little tentatively, but afterwards, encouraged by Lady Anne's obvious delight, with more assurance, gradually assumed the duties that would naturally fall to the daughter of the house.

Day by day she had discovered an increasing pleasure and significance in their performance. They were like so many tiny links knitting her life into the lives of those around her, and already Lady Anne had begun to turn to her instinctively in the small difficulties and necessities which, one way or another, most days bring in their train. Jean appreciated this as only a girl who had counted for very little in the lives of those nearest her could do. It seemed to make her "belong" in a way in which she had never "belonged" at Beirnfels. There, Glyn and Jacqueline had turned to each other for counsel in the little daily vicissitudes of life equally as in its larger concerns, and Jean had learned to regard herself as more or less outside their lives.

She had had one letter from Peterson since her arrival at Staple, a brief, characteristic note in which he expressed the hope that she liked England "better than her father ever could" but suggested that if she were bored she should return to Beirnfels, and ask some woman friend to stay with her; he warned her not to expect further letters from him for some time to come as, according to his present plans—of which he volunteered no particulars— he expected to spend the next few months "as far from civilisation as the restricted size of this world permits."

With this letter it seemed to Jean as though the last link with her former life had snapped. She felt no regret. Beirnfels, and the unconventional, rather exotic life she had led there—dictated by her parents' whims and the practically unlimited wealth to gratify them which Peterson's flair for successful speculation had achieved—seemed very far away, and Staple, with its peaceful, even-flowing English life, very near and enfolding.

Her first visit to Charnwood had been a disappointment. Under changing ownerships, little now remained to remind her of the generations of Petersons who had lived there long ago. Such of the old pieces of furniture and china as Peterson had not considered worth transferring to Beirnfels at his father's death had been bought by the next owners of the place, and had been taken away by them when they, in their turn, disposed of the property. Only a great square stone remained, sunk into one of the walls and bearing the Peterson coat of arms and the family motto: *Omnia debeo Deo.*

Sir Adrian Latimer had translated the words to Jean, with a cynical gleam in his heavy-lidded eyes and accompanying the translation by a caustic reference to her father. The drug had not so far dulled his intellect. On the contrary, it seemed to have had the opposite effect of endowing him with an almost uncanny insight into people's minds, so that he could prick them on a sensitive spot with unerring accuracy and a diabolical enjoyment of the process.

Jean's sympathy for his wife was boundless. A great affection had sprung up between the two girls, and bit by bit Claire had drawn aside the veil of reticence, letting the other see into the arid, bitter places of her life.

Jean could understand, now, of what Claire had been thinking on the occasion of their first meeting, when she had spoken of the influences of the people who inhabit a house. The whole atmosphere of Charnwood seemed permeated with the influence of Adrian Latimer—a grey, sinister, unwholesome influence, like the miasma which rises from some poisonous swamp.

The hell upon earth which he contrived to make of life for his young wife had been a revelation to Jean, accustomed as she had been to the exquisite love and tenderness with which her father had surrounded Jacqueline.

Sir Adrian's chief pleasure in life seemed to be to thwart and humiliate his wife in every possible way, and once, in an access of indignation over some small refinement of cruelty of which he had been guilty, Jean had declared her intention of giving him her frank opinion of his behaviour. She had never forgotten the look of bitter amusement with which Claire had greeted the suggestion.

"Do you know what would happen? He would listen to you with the utmost politeness, and very likely let you think you had impressed him. But afterwards he would *make me pay*—for a day, or a week, or a month. Till his revenge was satisfied. And he would put an end to our friendship——"

"He couldn't!" Jean had interrupted impulsively.

"Couldn't he? You don't know Adrian.... And I can't afford to lose you, Jean. You're one of my few comforts in life. Promise me"—she caught Jean's hands in hers and held them tightly—"*promise me* that you will do nothing—

that you won't try to interfere? I can generally manage; him—more or less. And when I can't, why, I have to put up with the consequences of my own bad management"—with a smile that was more sad than tears.

With an effort of will Jean tried to banish the recollection of Sir Adrian from her thoughts. The picture of his thin, leaden-hued face, with its cruel mouth and furtive, suspicious eyes, was out of harmony with this soft day of spring. She wished she had not let the thought of him intrude upon her pleasant reverie at all. His sinister figure seemed to cast a shadow over the sunlit river, a shadow which grew bigger and bigger, blurring the green of the trees and the sky's faint blue, and even silencing the comfortable little chirrups of the birds, busy with their spring housekeeping. At least, Jean couldn't hear them any longer, and she took no notice even when one enterprising young cock-bird hopped near enough to filch a feather that was sticking out invitingly from the corner of the cushion behind her head.

The next thing she was conscious of was of sitting up with great suddenness, under the impression that she had overslept and that the housemaid was calling to her very loudly to waken her.

Someone *was* calling—shouting lustily, in fact, and collecting her sleep-bemused faculties, she realised that instead of being securely moored against the bank her boat was rocking gently in mid-stream, and that the occupant of another boat, coming from the opposite direction, was doing his indignant best to attract her attention, since just at that point the river was too narrow for them to pass one another unless each pulled well in towards the bank.

Jean reached hastily for her sculls, only to find, to her intense astonishment, that they had vanished as completely as though they had never existed. She cast a rapid glance of dismay around her, scanning the surface of the water in her vicinity for any trace of them. But there was none. She was floating serenely down the middle of the stream, perfectly helpless to pull out of the way of the oncoming boat.

Meanwhile its occupant was calling out instructions—tempering his wrath with an irritable kind of politeness as he perceived that the fool whose craft blocked the way was of the feminine persuasion.

"Pull in a bit, please. We can't pass here if you don't.... Pull in!" he yelled rather more irately as Jean's boat still remained in the middle of the river, drifting placidly towards him.

She flung up her hand.

" *I cant!* " she shouted back. "I've lost my sculls!"

"Lost your sculls?" The man's tones sufficiently implied what he thought of the proceeding.

A couple of strokes, and, gripping the gunwale of her boat as he drew level, he steadied it to a standstill alongside his own.

Jean's eyes travelled swiftly from the squarish, muscular-looking hand that gripped the boat's side to the face of its owner. He was decidedly an ugly man as far as features were concerned, with a dogged-looking chin and a conquering beak of a nose that jutted out arrogantly from his hatchet face. The sunlight glinted on a crop of reddish-brown hair, springing crisply from the scalp in a way that suggested immense vitality; Jean had an idea that it would give out tiny crackling sounds if it were brushed hard. His eyebrows, frowning in defence against the sun, were of the same warm hue as his hair and very thick; in later life they would probably develop into the bristling, pent-house variety. The eyes themselves, as Jean described them on a later occasion, were "too red to be brown"; an artist would have had to make extensive use of burnt sienna pigment in portraying them. Altogether, he was not a particularly attractive-looking individual—and just now the red-brown eyes were fixed on Jean in a rather uncompromising glare.

"How on earth did you lose your oars?" he demanded—as indignantly as though she had done it on purpose, she commented inwardly.

Her lips twitched in the endeavour to suppress a smile.

"I haven't the least idea," she confessed. "I tied up under some trees further up and—and I suppose I must have fallen asleep. But still that doesn't explain how I came to be adrift like this."

"A woman's knot, I expect," he vouchsafed rather scornfully. "A woman never ties up properly. Probably you just looped the painter round any old thing and trusted to Providence that it would stay looped."

She gave vent to a low laugh.

"I believe you've described the process quite accurately," she admitted. "But I've done the same thing before without any evil consequences. There's hardly any current here, you know. I don't believe"—with conviction—"that my loop could have unlooped itself. And anyway"—triumphantly—"the sculls couldn't have jumped out of the boat without assistance."

The man smiled, revealing strong white teeth.

"No, I suppose not. I fancy"—the smile broadening—"some small boy must have spotted you asleep in the boat and, finding the opportunity too good to be resisted, removed your tackle and set you adrift."

There was a sympathetic twinkle in his eyes, and Jean, suddenly sensing the "little boy" in him which lurks in every grown-up man, flashed back:

"I believe that's exactly what you would have done yourself in your urchin days!"

"I believe it is," he acknowledged, laughing outright. "Well, the only thing to do now is for me to tow you back. Where do you want to go—up or down the river?"

"Up, please. I want to get back to Staple."

He threw a quick glance at her.

"Surely you must be Miss Peterson?"

She nodded.

"Yes. How did you guess?"

"My sister, Mrs. Craig, told me a Miss Peterson was staying at Staple. It wasn't very difficult, after that, to put two and two together."

"Then you must be Geoffrey Burke?" returned Jean.

He nodded.

"That's right. So now that we know each other, will you come into my parlour?"—smiling. "If I'm going to take you back, there seems no reason why we shouldn't accomplish the journey together and tow your boat behind."

He held out his hand to steady her as she stepped lightly from one boat to the other, and soon they were gliding smoothly upstream, the empty craft tailing along in their wake.

For a while Burke sculled in silence, and Jean leant back, idly watching the effortless, rhythmic swing of his body as he bent to his oars. His shirt was open at the throat, revealing the strong, broad-based neck, and she noticed in a detached fashion that small, fine hairs covered his bared arms with a golden down, even encroaching on to the backs of the brown, muscular hands.

She found herself femininely conscious that the most dominant quality about the man was his sheer virility. Nor was it just a matter of appearances. It lay in something more fundamental than merely externals. She had known men of great physical strength to be not infrequently gifted with an almost feminine gentleness of nature, yet she was sure this latter element played but a small part in the make-up of Geoffrey Burke.

The absolute ease with which he sent the boat shearing through the water seemed to her in some way typical. It conveyed a sense of mastery that was unquestionable, even a little overpowering.

She felt certain that he was, above and before all other things, primeval male, forceful and conquering, of the type who in a different age would have cheerfully bludgeoned his way through any and every obstacle that stood between him and the woman he had chosen as his mate—and, afterwards, if necessary, bludgeoned the lady herself into submission.

"Here's where you tied up, then?"

Burke's voice broke suddenly across her thoughts, and she looked round, recognising the place where she had moored her boat earlier in the afternoon.

"How did you divine that?" she asked.

"It didn't require much divination! There are your sculls"—pointing—"stuck up against the trunk of a tree—and looking as though they might topple over at any moment. I fancy"—with a smile—"that my 'small boy' theory was correct. I believe I could even put a name to the particular limb of Satan responsible," he went on. "You moored your boat on the Willow Perry side of the stream, and our lodge-keeper's kids are a troop of young demons. They want a thorough good thrashing, and I'll see that they get it before they are much older."

He pulled in to the shore and rescuing the sculls from their precarious position, restored them to the empty boat.

"All the same," he added, as, a few minutes later, he helped Jean out on to the little wooden landing-place at Staple, "I think I'm rather grateful to the small boy—whoever he may be!"

She laughed and retorted impertinently:

"I'm sure I'm very grateful to the bigger boy who came to the rescue."

There was something quite unconsciously provocative about her as she stood there with one foot poised on the planking, her head thrown back a trifle to meet his glance, and a hint of gentle raillery tilting the corners of her mouth.

The cave-man woke suddenly in him. He was conscious of an almost irresistible impulse to take her in his arms and kiss her. But the conventions of the centuries held, and all Jean knew of that swift flare-up of desire in the man beside her was that the grip of his hand on hers suddenly tightened so that the pain of it almost made her cry out.

And because she was not given to regarding every unmarried man she met in the light of a potential lover—as some women are prone to do—and because, perhaps, her thoughts were subconsciously preoccupied by a lean, dark face, rather stern and weary-looking as though from some past discipline of pain, Jean never ascribed that fierce pressure of the hand to its rightful origin, but merely rubbed her bruised fingers surreptitiously and wished ruefully that men were not quite so muscular.

"I'll go with you up to the house," remarked Burke, without any elaboration of "by your leave."

She was privately of the opinion that her leave would have little or nothing to do with the matter. If this exceedingly autocratic and masculine individual had decided to accompany her through the park, accompany her he would, and she might as well make the best of it.

He was extraordinarily unlike his sister, she thought. Where Judith Craig would probably seek to attain her ends in a somewhat stealthy, cat-like fashion, Burke would employ the methods of the club and battering-ram. Of the two, perhaps these last were preferable, since they at least left you knowing what you were up against.

"Will you come in?" asked Jean, pausing as they reached the house. "Though I'm afraid everyone is out."

"So much the better," he replied promptly. "I'd much rather have tea alone with you."

"That's not very polite to the others"—smiling a little. "I thought the Staple people were old friends of yours?"

"So they are. That's exactly it. I feel the mood of the explorer on me this afternoon."

"You're one of the people with a penchant for new acquaintances, then?" she said indifferently, leading the way into the hall, where, in place of the great log fire of chillier days, a hank of growing tulips made a glory of gold and orange and red in the wide hearth.

"No, I'm not," he returned bluntly. "But I've every intention of making your acquaintance right now."

Jean rang the bell and ordered tea.

"I think perhaps I might be consulted in the matter," she returned lightly when Baines had left the room. "The settling of questions of that kind is usually considered a woman's prerogative. Supposing"—smiling—"I don't ask you to tea, after all?"

There was a smouldering fire in the glance he bestowed upon her vivid face.

"It wouldn't make a bit of difference—in the long run," he replied deliberately. "If a man makes up his mind he can usually get his own way—over most things."

"You can't force friendship," she said quickly. It was as though she were defying something that threatened.

Again that queer gleam showed for a moment in his eyes.

"Friendship? No, perhaps not," he conceded.

He said no more and an uncomfortable silence fell between them. Jean was suddenly conscious that it might be possible to be a little afraid of this man. She did not like that side of him—the self-willed, masterful side—of which, almost deliberately, he had just given her a glimpse.

With the appearance of tea the slight sense of tension vanished, and the conversation dropped into more ordinary channels. She discovered that he had travelled considerably and was familiar with many of the places to which, at different times, she had accompanied her father and mother, and over the interchange of recollections the little hint of discord—of challenge, almost—was forgotten.

They were still chatting amicably together half an hour later when Blaise returned. The latter's face darkened as he entered the hall and found them together, nor did it lighten when Jean recounted the afternoon's adventure.

"I suppose Miss Peterson has your lodge-keeper's boys to thank for this?" he demanded stormily of Burke.

"I'm afraid that's so," admitted the other.

"If you had any consideration for your neighbours, you'd sack the lot of them," returned Blaise sharply. "Or else see that they're kept under proper control. They've given trouble before, but it is a little too much of a good thing when they dare to play practical jokes of that description on a guest of ours."

Jean stared at him in astonishment. She had told the story as rather a good joke and in explanation of Burke's presence, and, instead of laughing at her dilemma, Tormarin appeared to be thoroughly angry over the matter.

Burke remained coolly unprovoked.

"I can't say I've any quarrel with the young ruffians," he said. "They afforded me a charming afternoon."

"Doubtless," retorted Blaise. "But that's hardly the point. Anyway"— heatedly—"I'll thank you to see that those lads are kept in hand for the future."

Jean glanced across at Burke with some apprehension, half fearing a responsive explosion of wrath on his part, but to her relief he was smiling—a twinkling, mirthful smile that redeemed the ugliness of his features.

"'Fraid I can't truthfully declare I'm sorry, Tormarin," he said good-humouredly. "You wouldn't, in my place."

The man was keeping his temper in the face of considerable provocation, and Jean liked him better at that moment than she had done throughout the entire afternoon. Tormarin's own attitude she quite failed to understand, and after Burke's departure she took him to task for his churlishness.

"It was really absurd of you, Blaise," she scolded, half-smiling, half in genuine vexation. "As if Mr. Burke could possibly be held responsible for the actions of a mischievous schoolboy! At least he did all he could to repair the damage; he brought me back, and recovered the missing pair of oars for me. You hadn't the least reason to flare up like that."

Blaise listened to her quietly. The anger had died out of his face and his eyes were somewhat sad.

"You're right," he said at last, "absolutely right. But there rarely is any reason for a Tormarin's temper. Do you know—it sounds ridiculous, but it's perfectly true—it was all I could do not to knock Burke down."

"My dear Blaise, you fill me with alarm! I'd no idea you were such a bloodthirsty individual! But seriously, what had the poor man done to incur your wrath? He's been most helpful."

There was an element of self-mockery in the brief smile which crossed his face.

"Perhaps that was just it. I've rather grown to look upon it as my own particular prerogative to help you out of difficulties."

"Well, naturally I'd rather it had been you," she allowed, twinkling.

"Do you mean that?"—swiftly.

"Of course I do"—lightly. She had failed to notice the eagerness of demand in his quick question. "I'm more used to it! Besides, I believe Mr. Burke rather frightens me. He's a trifle—overwhelming. Still"—shaking her head reprovingly—"I don't think that excuses you. You must have a shocking temper."

He laughed shortly.

"Most of the Tormarins have ruined their lives by their temper. I'm no exception to the rule."

Jean's thought flew back to the description she had overheard when in London: "*A Tormarin in a temper is like a devil with the bit between his teeth.*"

"Then it's true, escaped her lips.

"What's true?"—with some surprise. "That the Tormarins are a vile-tempered lot? Quite. If you want to know more about it, ask my mother. She'll tell you how I came by this white lock of hair—the mark of the beast."

Jean was trying to make the comments of the woman at the hotel and Blaise's own confession tally with her recollection of the latter's complete self-control on several occasions when he, or any other man, might have been pardoned for yielding to momentary anger.

"I believe you're exaggerating absurdly," she said at last. "As a matter of fact, I've often been surprised at your self-control, seeing that I know you have a temper concealed about you somewhere. I think that is why your anger this afternoon took me so aback. It seemed unlike you to be so fearfully annoyed over practically nothing at all. I don't believe"—half smiling—"that really you're anything like bad-tempered as a Tormarin ought to be—to support the family tradition!"

He was looking, not at her but beyond her, as she spoke, as though his thoughts dwelt with some past memory. His expression was inscrutable; she could not interpret it. Presently he turned back to her, and though he smiled there was a deep, unfathomable sadness in his eyes.

"I've had one unforgettable lesson," he said quietly. "The Tormarin temper—the cursed inheritance of every one of us—has ruined my life just as it has ruined others before me."

The words seemed to fall on Jean's ears with a numbing sense of calamity, not alone in that past to which they primarily had reference, but as though thrusting forward in some mysterious way into the future—*her* future.

She was conscious of a vague foreboding that that "cursed inheritance" of the Tormarins was destined, sooner or later, to impinge upon her own life.

At night, when she went to bed, her mind was still groping blindly in the dark places of dim premonition. Single sentences from the afternoon's conversation kept flitting through her brain, and when at last she slept it was to dream that she had lost her way and was wandering alone in a wild and desolate region. Presently she came to a solitary dwelling, set lonely in the midst of the interminable plain. Three wretched-looking scrubby little fir trees grew to one side of the house, all three of them bent in the same direction as though beaten and bowed forward by ceaseless winds. While she stood wondering whether she should venture to knock at the door of the house and ask her way, it opened and Geoffrey Burke came out.

"Ah! There you are!" he exclaimed, as though he had been expecting her. "I've been waiting for you. Will you come into my parlour?"

He smiled at her as he spoke—she could see the even flash of his white teeth—but there was something in the quality of the smile which terrified her, and without answering a word she turned to escape.

But he overtook her in a couple of strides, catching her by the hand in a grip so fierce that it seemed as though the bones of her fingers must crack under it.

"Come into my parlour," he repeated. "If you don't, you'll be stamped forever with the mark of the beast. It's too late to try and run away."

Jean woke in a cold perspiration of terror. The dream had been of such vividness that it was a full minute before she could realise that, actually, she was safely tucked up in her own bed at Staple. When she did, the relief was so immeasurable that she almost cried.

The next morning, with the May sunshine streaming in through the open window, it was easier to laugh at her nocturnal fears, and to trace the odd phrases which, snatched from the previous day's conversation with Burke and Tormarin and jumbled up together, had supplied the nightmare horror of her dream.

But, even so, it was many days before she could altogether shake off the disagreeable impression it had made on her.

—

CHAPTER XIV
A COMPACT

"YOU don't like Jean Peterson."

Burke made the announcement without preface. He and Judith were sitting together on the verandah at Willow Perry, where their coffee had been brought them after lunch. Judith inhaled a whiff of cigarette smoke before she answered. Then, without any change of expression, her eyes fixed on the glowing tip of her cigarette, she answered composedly:

"No. Did you expect I should?"

"Well, hang it all, you don't hold her accountable for her father's defection, do you?"

A dull red crept up under Mrs. Craig's sallow skin, but she did not lift her eyes. They were still intent on the little red star of light dulling slowly into grey ash.

"Not accountable," she replied coolly. "I look upon her as an unpleasant consequence." She bent forward suddenly. "Do you realise that she might have been—my child?" There was a sudden vibrating quality in her voice, and for an instant a rapt look came into her face, transforming its hard lines. "But she isn't. She happens to be the child of the man I loved—and another woman."

"You surely can't hate her for that?"

"Can't I? You don't know much about women, Geoff. Glyn Peterson stamped on my pride, and a woman never forgives that."

She leaned back in her chair again, her face once more an indifferent mask. Burke sat silent, staring broodingly in front of him. Presently her glance flickered curiously over his face.

"Why does it matter to you whether I like her or not?" she asked, breaking the silence which had fallen.

Burke shifted in his chair so that he faced her. His eyes looked far more red than brown at the moment, as though they glowed with some hot inner light.

"Because," he said deliberately, "I'm going to marry her."

Judith sat suddenly upright.

"So that's the meaning of your constant pilgrimages to Staple, is it?"

"Just that."

She laughed—a disagreeable little laugh like a douche of cold water.

"You're rather late in the field, aren't you?"

"You mean that Blaise Tormarin wants her?"

"Of course I do. It's evident enough, isn't it?"

Burke pulled at his pipe reflectively.

"I should have thought he'd had a sickener with Nesta Freyne."

"So he had. But not in the way you mean. He never—loved—Nesta."

"Then why on earth did he ask her to marry him?"

"Good heavens, Geoffrey! You're a man—and you ask me that! There are heaps of men who ask women to marry them on the strength of a temporary infatuation, and then regret it ever after. Luckily for Blaise, Nesta saved him the 'ever after' part. But"—eyeing him significantly—"Blaise's feeling for Jean isn't of the 'temporary' type. Of that I'm sure."

"All the same, I don't believe he means to ask her to marry him."

"No. I don't think he does—*mean* to. He's probably got some high-minded scruples about not asking a second woman to make a mess of her life as a result of the Tormarin temper. It would be just like Blaise to adopt that attitude. But he *will* ask her, all the same. The thing'll get too strong for him. And when he asks her, Jean will say yes."

"You may be right. I've always said you were no fool, Judy. But if it's as you think, then I must get in first, that's all. First or last, though"—with a grim laugh—"I'll back myself to beat Blaise Tormarin. *And you've got to help me.*"

Followed a silence while Judith threw away the stump of her cigarette and lit another. She did not hurry over the process, but went about it slowly and deliberately, holding the flame of the match to the tip of her cigarette for quite an unnecessarily long time.

At last:

"I don't mind if I do," she said slowly. "I don't think I—envy—your wife much, Geoffrey. She won't be a very happy woman, so I don't mind assisting Glyn Peterson's daughter to the position. It would make things so charming all round if he and I ever met again"—smiling ironically.

Burke looked at her with a mixture of admiration and disgust.

"What a thorough-going little beast you are, Judith," he observed tranquilly.

She shrugged her thin, supple shoulders with indifference.

"I didn't make myself. Glyn Peterson had a good share in kneading the dough; why shouldn't his daughter eat the bread? And anyhow, old thing"—her whole face suddenly softening—"I should like you to have what you want—even if you wanted the moon! So you can count on me. But I don't think you'll find it all plain sailing."

"No"—sardonically. "She'll likely be a little devil to break.... Well, start being a bit more friendly, will you? Ask her to lunch."

Accordingly, a day or two later, a charming little note found its way to Staple, inviting Jean to lunch with Mrs. Craig.

"I shall be quite alone," it ran, "as Geoffrey is going off for a day's fishing, so I hope Lady Anne will spare you to come over and keep me company for an hour or two."

Jean was delighted at this evidence that Judith was thawing towards her. She was genuinely anxious that they should become friends, feeling that it was up to her, as Glyn's daughter, to atone—in so far as friendliness and sympathy could be said to atone—for his treatment of her. Beyond this, she had a vague hope that later, if she and Judith ever became intimate enough to touch on the happenings of the past, she might be able to make the latter see her father in the same light in which she herself saw him—as a charming, lovable, irresponsible child, innocent of any intention to wound, but with all a child's unregarding pursuit of a desired object, irrespective of the consequences to others.

She felt that if only Judith could better comprehend Glyn's nature, she would not only be disposed to judge him less hardly, but, to a certain extent, would find healing for her own bitterness of resentment and hurt pride.

Judith was an unhappy woman, embittered by one of those blows in life which a woman finds hardest to bear. And Jean hated people to be unhappy.

So that it was with considerable satisfaction that she set out across the park towards Willow Perry, crossing the river by the footbridge which spanned it at a point about a quarter of a mile below the scene of her boating mishap.

Judith welcomed her with unaccustomed warmth, and after lunch completely won her heart by a candour seemingly akin to Jean's own.

"I've been quite hateful to you since you came to Staple," she said frankly. "Just because you were—who you were. I suppose"—turning her head a little aside—"you've heard—you know that old story?"

Then, as Jean murmured an affirmative, she went on quickly:

"Well, it was idiotic of me to feel unfriendly to you because you happened to be Glyn's daughter, and I'm honestly ashamed of myself. I should have loved you at once—you're rather a dear, you know!—if you had been anyone else. So will you let me love you now, please—if it isn't too late?"

It was charmingly done, and Jean received the friendly overture with all the enthusiasm dictated by a generous and spontaneous nature.

"Why, of course," she agreed gladly. "Let's begin over again"—smiling.

Judith smiled back.

"Yes, we'll make a fresh start."

After that, things progressed swimmingly. The slight gene which had attended the earlier stages of the visit vanished, and very soon, prompted by Judith's eager, interested questions, Jean found herself chatting away quite naturally and happily about her life before she came to Staple and confessing how much she was enjoying her first experience of England.

"It's all so soft, and pretty, and old," she said. "I feel as if Staple must always have been here—just where it is, looking across to the Moor, and nodding sometimes, as much as to say, 'I've been here so long that I know some of your secrets.' The Moor always seems to me to have secrets," she added dreamily. "Those great tors watch us all the time, just as they've watched for centuries. They remind me of the Egyptian Sphinx, they are so still, and silent, and—and eternal-looking."

"You've not been on to Dartmoor yet, have you?" asked Judith. "We have a bungalow up there—Three Fir Bungalow, it's called. You must come and spend a few days there with us when the weather gets warmer."

"I should love it," cried Jean, her eyes sparkling. "I'm aching to go to the Moor. I want to see it in all sorts of moods—when it's raining, and when the sun's shining, and when the wind blows. I'm sure it will be different each time—rather like a woman."

"I think it's loveliest of all by moonlight," said Judith, her eyes soft and shining with recollection. She loved all the beauty of the world as much as Jean herself did. "I remember being on the top of one of the tors at night. All the surrounding valleys were hidden in a mist like a silver sea, and I felt as if I had got right away from the everyday world, into a sort of holy of holies that God must have made for His spirits. One almost forgot that one was just an ordinary, plain-boiled human being tied up in a parcel of flesh and bone."

"Only people aren't really in the least plain-boiled or ordinary," observed Jean quaintly.

"You aren't, I verily believe." Judith regarded her curiously for a moment. "I think I wish you were," she said abruptly.

She was not finding the part assigned to her by her brother any too easy. It complicates matters, when you are deliberately planning a semblance of friendship towards someone, if that someone persists in inspiring you with little genuine impulses of liking and friendliness.

Jean herself was delighted with the result of her visit to Willow Perry. She was convinced that Judith was a much nicer woman than she had imagined, or than anyone else imagined her to be, and when she took her departure she carried these warmer sentiments with her, characteristically reproaching herself not a little for her first hasty judgment. People improved upon acquaintance enormously, she reflected.

She did not go straight back to Staple, but took her way towards Charnwood on the chance of finding Claire at home, and, Fate being in a benevolent mood, she discovered her in her garden, precariously mounted upon a ladder and occupied in nailing back a creeper.

Claire greeted her joyfully and proceeded to descend.

"I've been lunching at Willow Perry," explained Jean, "so I thought I might as well come on here and cadge my tea as well!"

"Of course you might Adrian has gone into Exeter to-day, so we shall be alone."

Jean was conscious of an immense relief. The knowledge that Sir Adrian was not anywhere on the premises seemed like the lifting of a blight.

Claire's blue eyes smiled at her understandingly.

"Yes, I know," she nodded, as though Jean had given voice to her thought. "It's just as if someone had opened a window and let the fresh air in, isn't it?"

She collected her tools, and slipping her arm within Jean's led her in the direction of the house.

"We'll have tea at once," she said, "and then I'll walk back with you part way."

"You're bent on getting rid of me quickly, then?"

"Yes" — seriously. "He" — there was little need to specify to whom the pronoun referred — "will be back by the afternoon train, and for some reason or other he is very unfriendly towards you just now."

"What have I done to offend?" queried Jean lightly. Somehow, with Sir Adrian actually away, it didn't seem a matter of much importance whether he was offended or not. Even the house had a different "feel" about it as they entered it.

"It's not anything you've done; it's what you are, I think, sometimes, that when a man is full of evil and cruel thoughts and knows he has given himself up to wickedness, he simply hates to see anyone young and — and *good*, like you are, Jean, with all your life before you to make a splendid thing of."

"And what about you?" asked Jean, her eyes resting affectionately on the other's delicate flower face with its pathetically curved lips and the look of trouble in the young blue eyes. "He sees you constantly."

"Oh, he's used to me. I'm only his wife, you see. Besides" — wearily — "he knows that he can effectually prevent me from making a splendid thing of my life."

The note of bitterness in her voice wrung Jean's heart.

"I don't know how you bear it!" she exclaimed.

"One can bear anything — a day at a time," answered Claire with an attempt at brightness. "But I never look forward," she added in a lower tone.

The words seemed to Jean to contain an epitome of tragedy. Not yet twenty, and Claire's whole philosophy of life was embodied in those four desolate words: "I never look forward!"

The world seemed built up of sadness and cross-purposes. Claire and Nick, Judith, and Blaise Tormarin — all had their own particular burdens to carry, burdens which had in a measure spoiled the lives of each one of them. It seemed as though no one was allowed to escape those "snuffers of Destiny" of which Blaise had spoken as he and Jean had climbed the mountain-side together. She felt a depressing conviction that her own turn would come and wondered whether it would be sooner or later.

"Don't look so blue!" Claire's voice broke in upon her gloomy trend of thought. She was laughing, and Jean was conscious of a sudden uprush of admiration for the young gay courage which could laugh even while it could not look forward. "After all, there are compensations in life. You're one of them, my Jean, as I've told you before! Now let's talk about something else."

Jean responded gladly enough, and presently Sir Adrian was temporarily forgotten in the little intimate half-hour of woman-talk which followed.

CHAPTER XV
LADY ANNE'S DISCLOSURE

"WELL, have you enjoyed yourself?" enquired Lady Anne when Jean returned. "I suppose so, as you stayed to tea" — smiling.

"Oh, I had tea with Claire. Sir Adrian was away" — with a small grimace — "so we had quite a nice little time together. But, yes, madonna" — Jean had fallen into the use of the gracious little name which Blaise and Nick kept for their mother — "I really enjoyed myself very much. Judith was ever so much nicer than I expected."

"So now, I suppose, we shall all be side-tracked in favour of Burke and his sister?" put in Blaise, who had been listening quietly. There was a sharpness in his tones, as though the prospect did not please.

Jean smiled at him engagingly.

"Of course you will," she replied. "I invariably sidetrack old friends when I get the chance."

"Oh, you'll get the chance right enough!" — rather sulkily. "Yes, I think I shall" — demurely. "Geoffrey has always been nice to me; and now Judith, too, has succumbed to my charms, and says she hopes we shall be good pals."

Tormarin rose, pushing back his chair with unnecessary violence.

"I don't think I see Judith Craig extending her friendship to Glyn Peterson's daughter," he commented cynically.

An instant later the door banged behind, and Lady Anne and Jean looked across at each other smiling, as women will when one of their menkind proceeds to behave exactly like a cross little boy.

But a quick sigh chased the smile from Lady Anne's lips.

"Poor old Blaise!" she murmured, as though to herself. Then, her grey eyes meeting Jean's squarely, she said quietly:

"Jean, you're so much one of us, now, that I should like you to know what lies at the back of things. You'd understand — some of us — better."

Jean turned impulsively.

"I don't need to understand you," she said quickly. "I love you."

"Thank you, my dear." Lady Anne's voice trembled slightly. "If I were not sure of that, I shouldn't tell you what I am going to. But I want you to understand Blaise—and to make allowances for him, if you can."

Jean pulled forward a stool and settled herself at Lady Anno's feet.

"Do you mean about the 'mark of the beast'?" she asked, smiling a little. "Blaise told me to ask you about it one day."

"Did he? He thinks far too much about it and what it stands for"—sadly. "It has come to be almost a symbol in his eyes. You see, he too has suffered from the family failing—the very failing that was responsible for that white lock of hair."

"Tell me about it."

Lady Anne looked down at her thoughtfully.

"Well, there's no need for me to tell you that the Tor-marins have hot tempers! You've seen evidences of it in Blaise—that sudden flaming up of anger. Though he has learnt through one most bitter experience to hold himself more or less in check." She paused a moment, as if her thoughts had reverted painfully to the past. Presently she resumed: "All the Tormarin men have had it—that blazing, uncontrollable kind of temper which simply cannot brook opposition. Blaise's father had it, and it was that which made our life together so unhappy."

So Destiny had been busy with her snuffers here, also!

"You—you, too!" whispered Jean.

"I. too?" Lady Anne questioned. "What does that mean?"

"Why, it seems to me as if *no one* is ever allowed to be really happy and to live their life in peace! There is Judith, whose life my father spoilt, and Claire, whose life Sir Adrian spoils—and that means Nick's life as well. And now—you!"

Some unconscious instinct of reticence deep within her forbade the mention of Blaise Tormarin's name.

"I expect we are not meant to be too joyful," said Lady Anne. "Though, after all, it's largely our own fault if we are not. We make or mar each other's happiness; it isn't all Fate.... But I've had my share of happiness, Jean—never think that I haven't. Afterwards, with Claude, I was utterly happy."

She fell silent for a space, ceasing on that quiet note of happiness. Presently, almost loth to disturb the reverie into which she had fallen, Jean questioned hesitantly:

"And the 'mark of the beast,' madonna? You were going to tell me about it."

"It came as a consequence of the Tormarin temper. That's why Blaise calls it the 'mark of the beast.' It was just before he was born—when I was waiting for the supreme joy of holding my first-born in my arms. Derrick—Blaise's father—was an extremely jealous-natured man. He hated to think that there had ever been anyone besides himself who cared for me. And there was one man, in particular, of whom he had always been foolishly jealous and suspicious. I can't imagine why, though"—with a little puzzled laugh. "You would think that the mere fact that I had married *him*, and not the other man, would have been sufficient proof that he had no cause for jealousy. But no! Men are queer creatures, and he always resented my friendship with John Lovett—which continued after my marriage. I had known John from childhood, and he was the truest friend a woman ever had!" She sighed: "And I needed friends in those days! For somehow, brooding over things to himself, my husband conceived the idea that the little son who was coming was not his own child—but the child of John Lovett. I think someone must have poisoned his mind. There was a certain woman of our acquaintance whom I always suspected; she hated me and was very much attached to Derrick—she had wanted to marry him, I believe. In any case, he came home one evening, from her house, like a madman; and there was a scene... a terrible scene... he hurling accusations at me.... I won't talk of it, because he was bitterly repentant afterwards. As soon as the fit of rage was past, he realised how utterly groundless his suspicions had been, and I don't think he ever ceased to reproach himself. But that has always been the way! The Tormarins have invariably brought the bitterest self-reproach upon themselves. One way or another, the same story of blind, reckless anger, and its consequences, has repeated itself generation after generation."

"And then? What happened then?" asked Jean in low, shocked tones.

"I was very ill—so ill that they thought I should not live. But I did live, and I brought my baby into the world. Only, he was born with that white lock of hair. And my own hair had turned perfectly white."

Jean was silent for a little. At last she said softly:

"I'm so glad, madonna, that you were happy afterwards. *Your* 'house of dreams' came true in the end!"

"Yes"—Lady Anne's grey eyes were very bright and luminous. "My house of dreams came true."

After a while, she went on quietly:

"But my poor Blaise's house of dreams fell in ruins. The foundation was rotten. You knew, didn't you, that there was a woman he once cared for?"

Jean nodded. Speech was difficult to her just at that moment.

"It was a miserable business altogether. The girl, Nesta Freyne was an Italian. Blaise met her when he was travelling in Italy, and—oh, well, it wasn't love! Not love as I know it, and as I think, one day, you too will know it. It blazed up, just one of those wild infatuations that sometimes spring into being between a man and a woman, and almost before he had time to think, Blaise had married her——"

"Married her!"

The words leapt from Jean's lips before she could check them. In the account of Tormarin's disastrous love affair which had been forced upon her hearing in London, there had been no mention of the word marriage, and she had always imagined that the woman, this Nesta Freyne, had simply jilted him in favour of another man. Moreover, since she had been at Staple, nothing had been said to correct this impression, as, very naturally, the subject was one avoided by general consent.

And now, without warning or preparation, she found herself face to face with the fact that Blaise had been married—that he had belonged to another woman! It seemed to set her suddenly very far apart from him, and a fierce, intolerable jealousy of that other woman leaped to life in her heart, racking her with an anguish that was almost physical. She was confused, bewildered, by the storm of emotion which suddenly swept her whole being.

"Married her?" she repeated with dry lips.

"Yes. Didn't you know that Blaise was a widower?"

Had Lady Anne divined the stress under which the girl was labouring that she so quickly interposed the knowledge that his wife was dead?

"No," answered Jean unsteadily. "I didn't even know that he had been married."

The fact of that other woman's being dead did not serve to allay the tumult within her. She had lived, and while she lived she had been *his wife!*

"Yes, he married her." Lady Anne went on speaking in level tones. "I think matters were hurried to a climax by the fact that Nesta's step-sister, Margherita Valdi, detested English people. She was much the elder of the two, and as their mother had died when Nesta was born, she had practically brought the girl up. She would never have countenanced the idea of her marrying an Englishman, but Nesta so contrived her meetings with Blaise that Margherita was unaware of his very existence, and eventually they married without her knowledge. From that day onward, Margherita declined to hold any communication with her sister."

"Why had she such a rooted antipathy to the English?" Jean had recovered her composure during the course of Lady Anne's narrative, and now put her question with a very good semblance of detachment. But, inside, her brain was dully hammering out the words "Married—married!"

"It seems that Margherita's step-father—Nesta's father, of course,— who was an Englishman, treated his wife extremely badly, and Margherita, who had adored her mother, never forgave him and hated all Englishmen in consequence. At least, that was what Nesta told Blaise, and it seems quite probable. Italians are a hot-blooded race, you know, and very vindictive and revengeful. Of course, these Valdis were of no particular family—that was where the trouble began. Nesta was just a rather second-rate, though extraordinarily beautiful girl, suddenly elevated to a position which she was not in the least fitted to fill. It didn't take a month for the glamour to wear off—and for Blaise to see her as I saw her. He came to his senses to find himself married to a bit of soulless, passionate flesh and blood. Oh, Jean! If I could only have been there—in Italy, to have saved him from it all!"

Jean hardly heeded that instinctive mother-cry. She was keyed up to know the end of the story. She felt as though she must scream if Lady Anne were long about the telling.

"Go on," she said, forcing herself to speak quietly. "Tell me the rest."

"The rest had the Tormarin temper for its corner-stone. Nesta was an utterly spoilt child, and a coquette to her very finger-tips. She tossed dignity to the winds, and there were everlasting scenes and quarrels. Then, one day, Blaise came in and found her entertaining a man whom he had forbidden the house. I don't know what he said to her—but I can guess, poor child! He horsewhipped the man, and he must have frightened Nesta half out of her mind. That evening she ran away from Staple—Nick and I, of course, were living at the Dower House then—and after months of fruitless enquiry I had a letter from Margherita Valdi telling me that she had been found drowned. She had evidently made her way back to Italy, hoping to reach her sister, and then, in a fit of despair, committed suicide."

"Oh, poor Blaise! How awful for him!" exclaimed Jean, horror-stricken. For the moment her own individual point of view was swept away in a flood of sympathy for Tormarin.

"Yes. It broke him up badly. Always, I think, he is brooding over the past. It colours his entire outlook on things. You see, he blamed himself—his ungovernable temper—for the whole tragedy.... If only he had been gentler with her, not terrified her into running away!... After all, she was a mere child—barely seventeen. But she was a heartless, conscienceless minx, nevertheless.... And Margherita Valdi did not let him down lightly. She wrote him a terrible letter, accusing him of her sister's death. I opened it—he was abroad at the time—but, of course, he had to see it ultimately. Tied up in a little separate packet was Nesta's wedding-ring, together with a newspaper report of the affair, and, to add a last stab of horror, she had folded the newspaper clipping and thrust it through the wedding-ring, labelling the packet 'Cause and effect.' It was a brutal thing to do."

They were both silent for a space, Jean painfully envisaging the tragedy that lay behind that stern, habitual gravity of Tormarin's, Lady Anne asking herself tremulously if she had been wise—if she had been wise in her disclosure? She wanted her son's happiness so immeasurably! She believed she knew wherein it might lie, and she had raked over the burning embers of the past that she might help to give it him.

She knew that he himself was very unlikely to confide in Jean the story of his unhappy marriage, or that if he ever did so, it would be but to shoulder all the blame himself, exonerating Nesta entirely. Nor, unless Jean understood the fiery furnace through which he had passed—that ordeal of impetuous, mistaken love, of disillusion, and, finally, of the most bitter self-reproach—could she possibly interpret aright Blaise's strange, churlish moods, his insistent efforts to stand always on one side, as though he were entitled to make no further claim on life, and, above all, the bitter quality which permeated his whole outlook.

All these things had been in Lady Anne's mind when she had decided to enlighten Jean. She had seen, just as Judith had seen, whither Blaise was tending, fight against it as he might, and she was determined to remove from his path whatever of stumbling-block and hindrance she could. And, in this instance, she felt instinctively that Jean's own attitude might constitute the greatest danger. Any woman, as sincere and positive as she, might easily be driven in upon herself, shrinkingly misunderstanding Blaise's deliberate aloofness, and thus unconsciously assist in strengthening that barrier against love which he was striving to hold in place between them—and which Lady Anne so yearned to see thrown down.

It was to this end that she had reopened the shadowed pages of the past—so that no foolish obstacle, born of sheer misunderstanding, might imperil her son's hope of happiness if the time should ever come—as she prayed it would come—when he would free himself from the shackles of a tragic memory and turn his face towards the light of a new dawn.

CHAPTER XVI
THE GIFT OF LOVE

THERE are some people to whom love comes in a single blinding flash; it is as though the heavens were opened and the vision and the glory theirs in a sudden, transcendant revelation. To others it comes gradually, their hearts opening diffidently to its warmth and light as a closed bud unfolds its petals, almost imperceptibly, to the sun.

With Jean, its coming partook in a measure of both of these. Love itself did not come to her suddenly. It had been secretly growing and deepening within her for months. But the recognition of it came upon her with an overwhelming suddenness.

Lady Anne, in recalling that bleak tragedy of the past, had accomplished more than she knew. She had shown Jean her own heart.

From those fierce, unexpected pangs of jealousy which had stabbed her as she realised the part played by another woman in Blaise's life—the woman who had been his wife—had sprung the knowledge that she loved him. Only love could explain the instant, clamorous rebellion of her whole being against that other woman's claim. And now, looking back upon the months which she had spent at Staple, she comprehended that the veiled figure of Love, face shrouded, had walked beside her all the way. That was why these even, uneventful weeks at Staple had seemed so wonderful!

The recognition of the great thing that had come into her life left her a little breathless and shaken. But she did not seek to evade or deny it. The absolute candour of her mind—candid even to itself—accepted the truth quite simply and frankly. No false shame that she had, as far as actual fact went, given her love unasked, tempted her to disguise from herself the reality of what had happened. For good or ill, whether Blaise returned her love or no, it was his.

But in her inmost heart she believed that he, too, cared—half-fearfully, half-joyfully recognising the pent-up force which surged behind the bars of his deliberate aloofness.

True, he had never definitely spoken of his love in so many words, hut Lady Anne had supplied the key to his silence. The past still bound him! Alive, Nesta had held him by her beauty; and dead, she still held him with the cords of remorse and unavailing self-reproach—cords which can bind almost as closely as the strands of love.

But for that— —

The hot colour surged into Jean's cheeks at the sweet, secret thought which lay behind that "but". Blaise cared! Cared for her, needed her, just as she cared for and needed him. To her woman's eyes, newly anointed with love's sacramental oil and given sight, it had become suddenly evident in a hundred ways, most of all evident in his sullen effort to conceal it from her.

So much that he had said, or had not said—those clipped sentences, bitten off short with a savage intensity that had often enough troubled and bewildered her, now found their right interpretation. He cared... but the bondage of the past still held.

And with that thought came reaction. The brief, quivering ecstacy, which had sent little fugitive thrills and currents racing through every nerve of her, died suddenly like a damped-out fire, as she realised all which that bondage implied.

It was possible he might never break the silence which he himself had decreed. From the very beginning he had recognised and insisted upon— the fact that they two were only "ships that pass," and though now, for a little space, Fate had directed the course of each into the same channel, a year, at most, would float them out again on to the big ocean of life where vessels signalled—and passed—each other. She must, in the ordinary course of events, return eventually to Beirnfels, while Blaise remained in England. And that would be the end of it.

She knew the man's dogged pertinacity; he would hold to an idea or belief immovably if he conceived it right, no matter what the temptation to break away. And in the flood of light vouchsafed by Lady Anne's disclosure, she felt convinced that he had somehow come to regard the tragic happenings of the past as standing betwixt him and any future happiness. Why, Jean could not altogether fathom, but she guessed that the dominant factor in the matter was probably an exaggerated consciousness of responsibility for his wife's death, and perhaps, too, a certain lingering tenderness, a subconscious feeling of loyalty to the dead woman, which urged him on to the sacrifice of his own personal happiness as some kind of atonement.

Unless—and a swift spasm of pain shot through her, searing its way like a tongue of flame—unless Lady Anne had been altogether mistaken in her fixed belief that Blaise had not really cared for his wife but had only been carried away on the swift tide of passion—that tide which runs so fiercely and untrammelled in hot youth.

Jean had her black hour then, when she faced the fact that although her love was given, and although she tremulously believed it was returned, she would probably never know the supreme joy of utter certainty, never hear the beloved's voice utter those words which hold all heaven for the woman who hears them.

But, through the darkness that closed about her, there gleamed a single thread of light—the light of her own bestowal of love. Even if she never knew, of a surety, that Blaise cared, even if—and here she shrank, but forced herself to face the possibility sincerely—even if she were utterly mistaken and he did not care for her in any other way save as a friend—his "little comrade"—still there would remain always the golden gleam of love that has been given. For no one who loves can be quite unhappy.

CHAPTER XVII
IN THE ROSE GARDEN

THE chalcedony of the spring skies had deepened into the glowing sapphire of early June—a deep, pulsating blue, tremulous with heat. On the sundial, the shadow's finger pointed to twelve o'clock, and the sleepy hush of noontide hung over the rose garden where Jean was gathering roses for the house.

"Can't I help?"

Burke's voice broke across the drowsy quiet so unexpectedly that she jumped, almost letting fall the scissors with which she was scientifically snipping the stems of the roses. She bestowed a small frown upon the head and shoulders appearing above the wooden gate on which he leant.

"It's not very helpful to begin by giving one an electric shock," she complained. "How long have you been there?" His attitude had a repose about it which suggested that he might have been standing there some time watching her.

"I don't know. But as I *am* here, may I come in?" Without waiting for her answer, he unlatched the gate and came striding across the velvet greenness of the lawn.

His visits to Staple had grown of late so much a matter of daily occurrence that they were no longer hedged about by any ceremony, and Jean had come to accept his appearance at any odd moment without surprise.

Since the day when she had lunched at Willow Eerry, and learned, as she believed, to understand and make allowances for the bitterness which had so warped Judith's nature, her acquaintance with both brother and sister had ripened rapidly into a friendly intimacy. But the fact that Burke's feeling towards her was something other, and much warmer than mere friendship, had failed to penetrate her consciousness.

It was patent enough to the lookers on, and probably Jean was the only one amongst the little coterie of intimate friends who had not realised what was impending.

It is not very often that a woman remains entirely oblivious of the small, unmistakable signs which go to indicate a man's attitude towards her. In Jean's case, however, her thoughts were so engrossed with the one man that, at the moment, all other men occupied but a very shadowy relationship towards the realities of life as far as she was concerned.

So that she scarcely troubled to look up as Burke halted beside her, but went on cutting her roses unconcernedly, merely observing:

"Idlers not allowed. You can make yourself useful by paring the thorns off the stems." She gestured towards a basket which stood on the ground at her side, already overflowing with its scented burden of pink and white and crimson roses.

He glanced at the russet head bent studiously above a bush rose and there was a gleam, half angry, half amused, in his eyes. His fingers went uncertainly to his pocket, where reposed a serviceable knife, then suddenly he drew his hand sharply away, empty.

"No," he said. "I didn't come over to be useful this morning. I came over"—he spoke slowly, as though endeavouring to gain her attention—"on a quite different errand." There was a vibration in his voice that might have warned her had she been less intent upon her task of wrestling with a refractory branch. As it was, she merely questioned absently:

"And what was the 'quite different' errand?"

The next moment she felt his hand close over both hers, gardening scissors and wash-leather gloves notwithstanding.

"Stop cutting those confounded flowers, and I'll tell you," he said roughly.

She looked up in astonishment, and, at last, a glimmering of what was coming dawned upon her. Even the blindest of women, the most preoccupied, must have read the expression of his eyes at that moment.

"Oh, no—no," she began hastily. "I must finish cutting the roses—really, Geoffrey."

She tried to release her hands, but he held them firmly.

"No," he said coolly. "You won't finish cutting your flowers—at least, not now. You're going to listen to me." He drew the scissors from her grasp, and they flashed like a fish in the sunshine as he tossed them down on to the rose-basket. Then, quite deliberately, he pulled off the loose gloves she was wearing and his big hands gripped themselves suddenly, closely, about her slight, bared ones.

"Geoffrey— —"

Her voice wavered uncertainly. The realisation of his intent had come upon her so unexpectedly, rousing her from her placid unconsciousness, that she felt stunned—nervously unready to deal with the situation. She struggled a little, instinctively, but he only laughed down at her, a ring of masterful triumph in his voice, holding her effortlessly, with all the ease of his immense strength.

"It's no good, Jean. You've got to hear me out. I've waited long enough." He paused, then drew a deep breath. "I love you!" he said slowly. "My God, how I love you!" There was an element of wonder in his tones, and she felt the strong hands gripping hers tremble a little. Then their clasp tightened and he drew her towards him.

"Say you love me," he demanded. "Say it!"

It was then Jean found her voice. The imperious demand, infringing on that secret, inner claim of which she alone knew, stung her into quick denial.

"But I don't! I don't love you!" Then, as she saw the blank look in his eyes, she went on hastily: "Oh, Geoffrey, I am so sorry. I never guessed—I never thought of your caring."

"You never guessed! Good God!"—with a harsh laugh—"I should have thought I'd made it plain enough. Why, even that first day, on the river—I wanted you then. What do you suppose has brought me to Staple every day? Affection for Blaise Tormarin?"—cynically.

"I thought—I thought— —" She cast about in her mind for an answer, then presented him with the simple truth. "I'm afraid I never thought about it at all. I just took your coming over for granted. I knew you and Judith were old friends and neighbours, so it seemed quite natural for you to be here often—just as Claire Latimer is."

Burke searched her face for a moment. He was thinking of the other women he had known—women who would never have remained blind to his meaning, who had, indeed, shown their willingness to come half-way— more than half-way—to meet him.

"I really believe that's true," he said at last, grudgingly. "But if it is, you're the most unselfconscious woman I've ever come across."

"Of course it's true," she replied simply. "I'm—I'm so sorry, Geoffrey. I like you far too much to have wished to hurt you."

"I don't want liking. I want your love. And I mean to have it. You may not have understood before, Jean, but you do now."

She drew herself away from him a little.

"That doesn't make any difference, Geoffrey. I have no love to give you," she said quietly.

He shook his head.

"I won't take no," he said doggedly. "You're the woman I want. And I mean to have you.... Don't you understand? It's no use fighting against me. You may say no, now; you may say no fifty times. But one day you'll say—yes."

Jean's slight frame tautened.

"You are mistaken," she said, in a chill, clear voice calculated to set immeasurable spaces between them. "I'm not a cave woman to be forced into marriage. Oh!"—the ludicrous side of this imperious kind of wooing striking her suddenly—"don't be so absurd, Geoffrey! You can't seize me by the hair and carry me off to your own particular hole in the rocks, you know." She began to laugh a little. "Let's just go on being good friends—and forget that this has ever happened."

She held out her hand, but he took no notice of the little friendly gesture. There was a red gleam in his eyes, a smouldering glow that needed but a breath to fan it into flame.

"You speak as if it were something that was over and done with," he said in a low, tense voice. "But it isn't; it never will be. I love you and want you, and I shall go on loving you and wanting you as long as I live. Jean—sweetest"—his voice suddenly softened incredibly—"I'll try to be more gentle. But when a man loves as I do, he doesn't stop to choose his words." He stepped closer to her. "Oh! You little, little thing! Why, I could pick you up and carry you off to my cave with two fingers. Jean, when will you marry me?"

His big frame towered beside her. He paid no more attention to her dismissal of him than if she had not spoken, and she was conscious of an odd feeling of impotence.

"You don't seem to have understood me," she said forcing herself to speak composedly. "If I loved you, you'd have no need to 'carry me off' to your cave. I'd come—gladly. But I don't love you, Geoffrey. And I shall never marry a man I don't love."

"You'll marry me," he returned stubbornly. "Do you think I'm going to give you up so easily? If you do, you mistaken. I love you, and I'll teach you to love me—when you're my wife."

The two pairs of eyes met, a challenging defiance flashing between them. Jean shrugged her shoulders.

"I think you must be mad," she said contemptuously, and turned to leave him.

In the same instant his hands gripped her shoulders and he swung her round facing him again.

"Mad!" he exclaimed hoarsely. "Yes, I am mad—mad for you. You little cold thing! Do you know what love is—man's love?"

She felt his arms close round her like a vice of steel, lifting her off her feet, so that she hung helpless in his embrace. For a moment his eyes burned down into hers—the hot flame of desire that blazed in them seeming almost to scorch her—the next, he had hidden his face against the warm white curve of her throat, where a little affrighted pulse throbbed tempestuously. Then, as though the touch of her snapped the last link of his self-control, his mouth sought hers, and he was kissing her savagely, crushing her soft, wincing lips beneath his own. Her slender body swayed helpless as a reed in his strong grip, while the tide of his passion, like some fierce, untamable flood, swept over her resistlessly.

When at last he released her, she stood back from him, staggering a little. Instinctively he stretched out his hand to steady her.

"Don't... touch me!" she panted.

The words came driven between clenched teeth, chokingly. Her face was milk-white and her eyes blazed at him out of its pallor. She felt as if her heart were beating in her throat, stifling her, and for a little space sheer physical stress held her silent But she fought it back, asserting her will against her weakness.

"How dare you?" There was bitter anger in her still tones. "How dare you touch me—like that?"

With a swift movement she passed her handkerchief across her lips and then let it fall on the ground as though it were something unclean. He winced at the gesture; for a moment the passion died out of his face and a rueful look, almost of schoolboy shame, took its place.

"Do you—feel like that about it?" he said, nodding towards the handkerchief.

"Just like that," she returned. "Do you think—if I had known—I would ever have risked being alone with you? But I thought we were friends—I never dreamed I couldn't trust you."

"Well, you can't," he said unsteadily. The sight of her slender, defiant figure and lovely, tilted face, with the scornful lips he had just kissed showing like a scarlet stain against its whiteness, sent the blood rioting through his veins once more. "You'll... you'll never be able to trust any man who loves you, Jean."

Her thoughts flew to Blaise. She would trust herself with him—now, at any time, always. But then, perhaps—the after thought came like a knife-thrust—perhaps he did not care!

"A man who—loved me," she said dully, "would not do what you've just done."

"He would—sooner or later. Unless his veins ran milk and water!" He drew a step nearer and stood staring down at her sombrely. "Do you know what you're like, I wonder? With your great golden eyes and your maddening mouth and that little cleft in your white chin.... You're angry because I kissed you. I wonder I didn't do it before! I've wanted to, dozens of times. But I wanted your love more than a passing kiss. I've waited for that—waited all these weeks. And now you refuse it—you've not even *understood* that you're all earth and heaven to me. God! How blind you must have been!"

She was silent. Her anger was waning, giving place to a certain distressful comprehension of the mighty force which had suddenly broken bondage in the man beside her. Dimly, from her own knowledge of the yearning bred of the loved one's nearness, she envisaged what these last weeks must have meant to a man of Burke's temperament. Was it any wonder, when suddenly made to realise that the woman he loved not only did not love him in return, but had failed even to sense his love for her, that his stormy spirit had rebelled—flung off its shackles? An element of self-reproach tinctured her thoughts. In a measure the fault had been hers; her self-absorption was to blame.

"Yes," she acknowledged. "I'm afraid I have been blind, Geoffrey. Indeed—indeed I would have prevented all this if I had known, if I had guessed. But, honestly, I just thought of you—you and Judith—as friends."

"I believe you really did," he said slowly, almost incredulously. Then, as though in swift corollary: "Jean, is there anyone else?"

The question drove at her with its sudden grasp of the truth. Her face grew slowly drawn and pinched-looking beneath his merciless gaze and her lips moved speechlessly.

"So it *is* that, is it? And does he—has he— —"

"Geoffrey, you are insufferable!" The words came wrung from her in quick, low protest. "You have no right—no right——"

"No, I suppose I haven't," he admitted, touched by the stricken look in her eyes. "I'd no business to ask that. For the moment, it's enough that you don't love me.... But I shall never give you up, Jean. You're mine—my woman!" The light of possession flared up once more in his eyes. "Do you remember I told you once that, if a man makes up his mind, he can get his own way over most things? Well, it's true."

He paused a moment, then abruptly swung round on his heel and without a word of farwell, strode away across the garden towards the gate by which he had entered.

As the latch clicked into its place behind him, Jean was conscious of a sudden tremor, of a curious, uncontrollable fear, as though his words held something of prophecy. The man's dominating personality seemed to swamp her, overwhelming her by its sheer physical force.

The remembrance of her sinister dream, and of the dream Burke's threat: *"It's too late to try and run away. If you don't come into my parlour, you'll be stamped with the mark of the beast forever,"* returned to her with a disagreeable sense of menace. She shivered a little and, picking up her basket, almost ran back to the house, as though seeking safety.

CHAPTER XVIII
CROSS-PURPOSES

IN the task of arranging her roses in the various bowls and vases Baines had set in readiness for her, Jean found a certain relief from the feeling of terror which had invaded her. Something in the homely everydayness of the occupation served to relax the tension of her mind, keyed up and overwrought by the stress of her interview with Burke, and it was with almost her usual composure of manner that she greeted Blaise when presently he joined her.

"I've raided the rose garden to-day," she said, smilingly indicating the mass of scented blossom that lay heaped up on the table. "I expect when Johns finds out he will proceed to meditate upon something for my benefit with boiling oil in it."

Johns was one of the gardeners to whom Jean's joyous and wholesale robbery of his first-fruits was a daily cross and affliction. Only chloroform would ever have reconciled him to the cutting off of a solitary bloom while still in its prime.

Blaise regarded the tangle of roses consideringly.

"I wonder you found time to gather so many. When I passed by the rose garden, you were—otherwise occupied." The quietly uttered comment sent the blood rushing up into Jean's face. When had he passed? What had he seen?

She kept her eyes lowered, seemingly intent upon the disposition of some exquisite La France roses in a black Wedge-wood bowl.

"What do you mean?" she asked negligently.

Tormarin was silent a moment.

Had she looked at him she would have surprised a restless pain in the keen eyes he bent upon her.

"Jean"—he spoke very gently—"have I—to congratulate you?"

It was difficult to preserve her poise of indifference when the man she loved put this question to her, but she contrived it somehow. Women become adepts in the art of hiding their feelings. The conventions demand it of them.

Jean's answer fluttered out with the airy lightness of a butterfly in the sunshine.

"I am sure I can't say, unless you tell me upon what grounds?"

"You know of none, then" —swiftly.

"None."

She nibbled the end of a stalk and surveyed the Wedge-wood bowl critically. Tormarin felt like shaking her.

"Then," he said gruffly, "let me suggest you revise your methods. The woman who plays with Geoffrey Burke might as safely play with an unexploded bomb."

His voice betrayed him, revealing the personal element behind the proffered counsel.

Jean glanced at him between her lashes. So that was it! He was jealous—jealous of Burke! At last something had happened to pierce the joints of his armour of assumed indifference! Her heart sang a little pæan of thanksgiving, and all that was woman in her rose bubbling to meet the situation. In an instant she had recaptured her aplomb.

"I think I rather enjoy playing with unexploded bombs," she returned meditatively. "There are always—possibilities—about them."

"There are" —grimly. "And it is precisely against those possibilities that I am warning you."

"Don't you think it's rather bad taste on your part to warn me against a man who is admittedly on terms of friendship with you all?"

"No, I don't" —steadily. "Nor should I care if it were. When it's a matter of you and your safety, the question of taste doesn't enter into the thing at all."

"My safety?" jeered Jean softly. (It was barely half an hour since Burke had inspired her with that sudden fear of him and of his compelling personality!)

"Well, if not your safety, at least your happiness," amended Blaise.

"It's very kind of you to interest yourself, but really my happiness has nothing whatever to do with Geoffrey Burke."

"Is that true?"

He flashed the question at her, and there was that in his tone which set her pulses athrill, quenching the light-hearted spirit of banter that had led her to torment him. It was the note of restrained passion which she had heard before in his voice, and which had always power to move her to the depths of her being.

"Perfectly true." She faltered a little. "But" — forcing herself to a defiance that was in reality a species of self-defence — "I fail to see that it concerns you, Blaise."

"It concerns me in so far as Burke is not the sort of man that a woman can make a friend of. It's all or nothing with him. And if you don't intend to give him all, you'd better give him — nothing."

His glance, grave and steady, met hers, and she knew then, of a certainty, that he had witnessed the scene which had taken place in the rose garden, when Burke had held her in his arms and the flood of his passion had risen and overwhelmed her. He had witnessed that — and had misunderstood it.

She was conscious of a fierce resentment against him. It mattered nothing to her that, in the light of her nonchalant answers to his questions, he was fully justified in the obvious conclusion he had drawn. She did not stop to think whether her anger was reasonable or unreasonable. She was simply furious with him for suspecting her of flirting — odious word! — with Geoffrey Burke. Well, if he chose to think thus of her, let him do so! She would not trouble to explain — to exculpate herself.

She regarded him with stormy eyes.

"Please understand, Blaise, that I want neither your advice nor your criticism. If I choose to make a friend of Geoffrey Burke — or of any other man — I shall do so without asking your permission or approval. What I do, or don't do, is no business of yours."

For a moment they faced each other, his eyes, stormy as her own, dark with anger. His hands clenched themselves.

"If I could," he said hoarsely, "I would *make* it my business."

He wheeled round and left the room without another word. Jean stood staring dazedly at the blank panels of the door which had closed behind him. She wanted to laugh... or to cry. To laugh, because with every sullen word he revealed the thing he was so sedulously intent on keeping from her. To cry, because he had taken her pretended indifference at its face value, and so another film of misunderstanding had risen to thicken the veil between them — the veil which he would not, and she, being a woman, could not, draw aside.

CHAPTER XIX
THE SPIDER

PROBABLY masculine obtuseness and the feminine faculty for dissimulation are together responsible for more than half the broken hearts with which the highways of life are littered.

The Recalcitrant Parent, the Other Woman—be she never so guileful—or the Other Man, as the case may be, are none of them as potent a menace to the ultimate happy issue of events as the mountain of small misunderstandings which a man and a maid in love are capable of piling up for themselves.

The man is prone to see only that which the woman intends he shall—and no self-respecting feminine thing is going to unveil the mysteries of her heart until she is very definitely assured that that is precisely what the man in the case is aching for her to do.

So she dissimulates with all the skill which Nature and a few odd thousand years or so of tradition have taught her and pretends that the Only Man in the World means rather less to her than her second-best shoe buckles. With the result that he probably goes silently and sadly away, convinced that he hasn't an outside chance, while all the time she is simply quivering to pour out at his feet the whole treasure of her love.

In this respect Blaise and Jean blundered as egregiously as any other love-befogged pair.

Following upon their quarrel over the matter of Jean's attitude towards Geoffrey Burke, Tormarin retreated once again into those fastnesses of aloof reserve which seemed to deny the whole memory of that "magic moment" at Montavan. And Jean, just because she was unhappy, flirted outrageously with the origin of the quarrel, finding a certain reckless enjoyment in the flavour of excitement lent to the proceedings by the fact that Burke was in deadly earnest.

Playing with an "unexploded bomb" at least sufficed to take her thoughts off other matters, and enabled her momentarily to forget everything for which forgetting seemed the only possible and sensible prescription.

But you can't forget things by yourself. Solitude is memory's closest friend. So Jean, heedless of consequences, encouraged Burke to help her.

Lady Anne sometimes sighed a little, as she watched the two go off together for a long morning on the river, or down to the tennis-court, accompanied, on occasion, by Claire Latimer and Nick to make up the set. But she held her peace. She was no believer in direct outside interference as a means towards the unravelment of a love tangle, and all that it was possible to do, indirectly, she had attempted when she revealed to Jean the history of Blaise's marriage.

She did, however, make a proposal which would have the effect of breaking through the present trend of affairs and of throwing Blaise and Jean more or less continuously into each other's company. She was worldly wise enough to give its due value to the power of propinquity, and her innocently proffered suggestion that she and her two sons and Jean should all run up to London for a week, before the season closed, was based on the knowledge of how much can be accomplished by the skilful handling of a *partie carrée*.

The suggestion was variously received. By Blaise, indifferently; by Jean, with her natural desire to know more of the great city she had glimpsed en route augmented by the knowledge that a constant round of sight-seeing and entertainment would be a further aid towards the process of forgetting; by Nick, the sun of whose existence rose and set at Charnwood, with open rebellion.

"Why go to be baked in London, madonna, when we might remain here in the comparative coolth of the country?" he murmured plaintively to his mother.

They were alone at the moment, and Lady Anne regarded him with twinkling eyes.

"Frankly, Nick, because I want Jean for my daughter-inlaw. No other reason in the world. Personally, as you know, I simply detest town during the season."

He laughed and kissed her.

"What a Machiavelli in petticoats! I'd never have believed it of you, madonna. S'elp me, I wouldn't!"

"Well, you may. And you've got to back me up, Nick. No philandering with Jean, mind! You'll leave her severely alone and content yourself with the company of your aged parent."

"Aged fiddlestick!" he jeered. "If it weren't for that white hair of yours, I'd tote you round as my youngest sister. 'And I don't believe"—severely—"that it *is* white, really. I believe your maid powders it for you every morning, just because you were born in sin and know that it's becoming."

So it was settled that the first week of July should witness a general exodus from Staple, and meanwhile the June days slipped away, and Tormarin sedulously occupied himself in adding fresh stones to the wall which he thought fit to interpose between himself and the woman he loved. While Jean grew restless and afraid, and flung herself into every kind of amusement that offered, wearing a little fine under the combined mental and physical strain.

Claire, perceiving the nervous tension at which the girl was living, was wistfully troubled on her friend's behalf, and confided her anxious bewilderment to Nick.

"I think Blaise must be crazy," she declared one day. "I'm perfectly convinced that he's in love with Jean, and yet he appears prepared to stand by while Geoffrey Burke completely monopolises her."

Nick nodded.

"Yes. I own I can't understand the fellow. He'll wake up one day to find that she's Burke's wife."

"Oh, I hope not!" cried Claire hastily.

They were pacing up and down one of the gravelled alleys that intersected the famous rhododendron shrubbery at Charnwood, and, as she spoke, Claire cast a half-frightened glance in the direction of the house. She knew that Sir Adrian was closeted with his lawyer, and that he was, therefore, not in the least likely to emerge from the obscurity of his study for some time to come. But as long as he was anywhere on the place, she was totally unable to rid herself of the hateful consciousness of his presence.

He reminded her of some horrible and loathsome species of spider, at times remote and motionless in the centre of his web—that web in which, body and soul, she had been inextricably caught—but always liable to wake into sudden activity, and then pounce mercilessly.

"Oh, I hope not!" she repeated, shivering a little. "If she only knew what marriage to the wrong man means!... And I'm certain Geoffrey is the wrong man. Why on earth does Blaise behave like this?"—impatiently. "Anyone might think—Jean herself might think—he didn't care! And I'm positive he does."

"If he does, he's a fool. Good Lord!"—moodily kicking a pebble out of his path—"imagine any sane man, with a clear road before him, *not taking it!!*" He swung round towards her suddenly. "Claire, if there were only a clear road—for us! If only I could take you away from all this!" his glance embracing the grey old house, so beautiful and yet so much a prison, which just showed above the tops of the tall-growing rhododendrons.

"Oh, hush! Hush!"

Claire glanced round her affrightedly, as though the very leaves and blossoms had ears to hear and tongues to repeat.

"One never knows"—she whispered the words barely above her breath—"where he is. He might easily be hidden in one of the alleys that run parallel with this."

"The skunk!" muttered Nick wrathfully.

"*What's that?*"

Claire drew suddenly closer to him, her face blanching. A sound—the light crunching of gravel beneath a footstep—had come to her strained ears.

"Nick! Did you hear?" she breathed.

A look of keen anxiety overspread his face. For himself, he did not care; Adrian Latimer could not hurt him. But Claire—his "golden narcissus"— what might he not inflict on her as punishment if he discovered them together?

The next moment it was all he could do to repress a shout of relief. The steps had quickened, rounded the corner of the alley, and revealed—Jean.

"We're mighty glad to see you," remarked Nick, as she joined them. "We thought you were—the devil himself"—with a grin.

"Oh, he's safe for half an hour yet," Jean reassured them, "I asked Tucker"—the Latimer's butler, who worshipped the ground Claire walked on—"and his solicitor is still with him. Otherwise I wouldn't have risked looking for you"—smiling. "I knew Nick was over here, and Sir Adrian might have followed me."

"You're sure he hasn't?" asked Claire nervously. "He is so cunning—so stealthy."

"Even if he had, you're doing nothing wrong," maintained Jean stoutly.

"*Everything* I do is wrong—in his eyes," returned Claire bitterly. "That's what makes the misery of it. If I were really wicked, really unfaithful, I should feel I deserved anything I got. But it's enough if I'm just happy for a few minutes with a friend for him to want to punish me, to—to suspect me of any evil. Sometimes I feel as if I couldn't bear it any longer!"

She flung out her arms in a piteous gesture of abandonment. There was something infinitely touching and forlorn about her as she stood there, as though appealing against the hideous injustice of it all, and, with a little cry Jean caught her outstretched hands and drew her into her embrace, folding her closely in her warm young arms.

Nick had turned aside abruptly, his face rather white, his mouth working. His powerlessness to help the woman he loved half maddened him.

Meanwhile Jean was crooning little, inarticulate, caressing sounds above Claire's bowed head, until at last the latter raised a rather white face from her shoulder and smiled the small, plucky smile with which she usually managed to confront outrageous fortune.

"Thank you so much," she said with a glint of humour in her tones. "You've been dears, both of you. It's awfully nice to—to let go, sometimes. But I'm quite all right again, now."

"Then, if you are," replied Jean cheerfully, "perhaps you can bear up against the shock of too much joy. We want you to have 'a day out.'"

"'A day out'?" repeated Claire. "What do you mean?"

"I mean we're organising a picnic to Dartmoor, and we want to fix it so that you can come too. Didn't you tell me that Sir Adrian was going to be away one day this week? Going away, and not returning till the next day?"

Claire nodded, her eyes dancing with excitement.

"Yes—oh, yes! He has to go up to London on business."

"Then that's the day we'll choose. Heaven send it be fine!"—piously.

"Oh, how I'd love it!" exclaimed Claire. "I haven't been on the Moor for such a long time."

"And I've never been there at all," supplemented Jean.

"Nick! Nick!" Claire turned to him excitedly. "Did you know of this plan? And why didn't you tell me about it before?"

He looked at her, a slow smile curving his lips.

"Why, I never thought of it," he admitted. "You see"—explanatorily—"when I'm with you, I can't think of anything else."

"Nick, I won't have you making barefaced love to a married woman under my very nose," protested Jean equably. And the shadow of tragedy that had lowered above them a few minutes earlier broke into a spray of cheery fun and banter.

"You seem very gay to-day."

The cold, sneering tones fell suddenly across the gay exchange of jokes and laughter that ensued, and the trio looked up to see the tall, lean, black-clad figure of Sir Adrian standing at the end of the path, awaiting their approach.

To Jean, as to Claire, occurred the analogy of a malevolent spider on the watch. Even the man's physical appearance seemed in some way to convey an unpleasant suggestion of resemblance—his long, thin, sharply-jointed arms and legs, his putty-coloured face, a livid mask lit only by a pair of snapping, venomous black eyes, half hidden between pouched lids that were hardly more than hanging folds of wrinkled skin, his long-lipped, predatory mouth with its slow, malicious smile. Jean repressed a little shudder of disgust as she responded to his sneering comment:

"We are—quite gay, Sir Adrian. It's a fine day, for one thing, and the sun's shining, and we're young. What more do we want?"

"What more, indeed? Except"—bowing mockingly—"the beauty with which a good Providence has already endowed you. You are a lucky woman, Miss Peterson; your cup is full. My wife is not, perhaps"—regarding her appraisingly—"quite so beneficently dowered by Providence, so it remains for me to fill her cup up to the brim."

He paused, and as the black, pin-point eyes beneath the flabby lids detected the slight stiffening of Claire's slender figure, his long, thin lips widened into a sardonic smile.

"Yes, to the brim," he repeated with satisfaction. "That's a husband's duty, isn't it, Mr. Brennan?"—addressing Nick with startling suddenness.

"You should know better than I, Sir Adrian," retorted Nick, "seeing that you have experience of matrimony, while I have none."

"But you have hopes—aspirations, isn't it so?" pursued Latimer suavely. There was an undercurrent of disagreeable suggestion in his tones.

Nick was acutely conscious that his keenest aspiration at the moment was to knock the creature down and jump on him.

"We must find you a wife, eh, Claire? Eh, Miss Peterson?" continued Sir Adrian, rubbing the palm of one bony hand slowly up and down over the back of the other. "I'm sure, Claire, you would like to see so—intimate—a friend as Mr. Brennan happily married, wouldn't you?"

"I should like to see him happy," answered Claire with tight lips.

"Just so—just so," agreed her husband in a queer cackling tone as though inwardly amused. "Well, get him a wife, my dear. You are such friends that you should know precisely the type of woman which appeals to him."

He nodded and turned to go, gliding away with an odd shuffling gait, and muttering to himself as he went: "Precisely the type—precisely."

As he disappeared from view down one of the branching paths of the shrubbery, an odious little laugh, half chuckle, half snigger, came to the ears of the three listeners.

Claire's face set itself in lines that made her look years older than her age.

"You'd better go," she whispered unevenly. "We shan't be able to talk any more now that he knows you are here. He'll be hovering round— *somewhere*."

Jean nodded.

"Yes, we'd better be going. Come along, Nick. And let us know, Claire"—dropping her voice—"as soon as you have found out for certain what day he goes away. You can telephone down to us, can't you?"

"Yes. I'll ring up when he's out of the house some time," she answered "Or send a message. Anyway, I'll manage to let you know somehow. Oh!"— stretching out her arms ecstatically—"imagine a day, of utter freedom! A whole day!"

CHAPTER XX
THE SHADOW OF THE FUTURE

GOLD of gorse and purple of heather, a shimmering haze of heat quivering above the undulating green of the moor, and somewhere, high up in the cloud-flecked blue above, the exultant, piercingly sweet carol of a lark.

"Oh! How utterly perfect this is!" sighed Jean.

She was lying at full length on the springy turf, her chin cupped in her hands, her elbows denting little cosy hollows of darkness in the close mesh of green moss.

Tormarin, equally prone, was beside her, his eyes absorbing, not the open vista of rolling moor, hummocked with jagged tors of brown-grey stone, but the sun as it rioted through a glory of red-brown hair and touched changeful gleams of gold into topaz eyes.

There was a queer little throb in Jean's voice, the low note of almost passionate delight which sheer beauty never failed to draw from her. It plucked at the chords of memory, and Tormarin's thoughts leaped back suddenly to that day they had spent together in the mountains, when, as they emerged from the pinewood's gloom to the revelation of the great white-pinacled Alps, she had turned to him with the rapt cry: "It's so beautiful that it makes one's heart ache!"

"Do you remember— —" he began involuntarily, then checked himself.

"'M—m?" she queried. The little interrogative murmur was tantalising in its soft note of intimacy.

The Jean of the last few days—the days immediately following their quarrel—had temporarily vanished. The beauty of the Moor had taken hold of her, and all the mockery and bitter-sweetness which she had latterly reserved for Tomarin's benefit was absent from her manner. She was just her natural sweet and wholesome self.

"'M—m? Do I remember—what?"

"I was thinking what a pagan little beauty-lover you are! You worshipped the Alps. Now you are worshipping Dartmoor."

She nodded.

"I don't see why you should call it 'pagan,' though. I should say it was equally Christian. I think we were *meant* to love beauty. Otherwise there wouldn't have been such a lot of it about. God didn't put it around just by accident."

"Quite probably you're right," agreed Blaise. "In which case you must be" — he smiled — "an excellent Christian."

"Positively I believe they're talking theology!"

Claire's voice, girlishly gay and free from the nervous restraint which normally dulled its cadence of youth, broke suddenly on their ears, as she and Nick, rounding the corner of a big granite boulder, discovered the two recumbent forms.

"You disgustingly lazy people!" she pursued indignantly. "Everybody's dashing wildly to and fro unpacking the lunch baskets, while you two are just lounging here in blissful idleness!"

"It's chronic with me," murmured Tormarin lazily. "And anyway, Claire, neither you nor Nick appear to be precisely overtaxing yourselves bearing nectar and ambrosia."

"I carried some of the drinks up this confounded hill," submitted Nick. "And damned heavy they were, too! I can't *think*" — plaintively — "why people should be so thirsty at a picnic. I'm sure Baines has shoved in enough liquid refreshment to float a ship."

"Praise be!" interpolated Blaise piously.

"Oh, we've done our share," supplemented Claire. "And now we're going to the gipsy who lives here to have our fortunes told."

"Before lunch," subjoined Nick, "so that in case they're depressingly bad you can stay us with flagons afterwards."

Jean sat up suddenly, her face alight with interest "Do you mean that there is a real gipsy who tells real fortunes?" she demanded.

"Yes — quite real. She's supposed to be extraordinarily good," replied Nick. "She is a lady of property, too, since she has acquired a few square yards of the Moor from the Duchy and built herself a little shanty there. She rejoices in the name of Keturah Stanley."

"I should like to have my fortune told," murmured Jean meditatively.

"I'll take you," volunteered Blaise.

There was a suddenly alert look in his face, as though he, too, would like to hear Jean's fortune told.

"We'll all go, then," said Claire. "You must let Keturah tell yours as well, Blaise."

He shook his head.

"Thanks, no," he answered briefly. "I know my fortune quite as well as I have any wish to."

Tormarin's curt refusal somewhat quenched the gaiety of the moment, and rather soberly they all four made their way down the slope to where, in a little sheltered hollow at the foot of the tor, the sunlight glinted on the corrugated iron roofing of a tiny two-roomed hut, built of wood.

Outside, sitting on an inverted pail and composedly puffing away at a clay pipe, they discovered a small, shrivelled old woman, sunning herself, like a cat, in the midday warmth.

She lifted her head as they approached, revealing an immensely old, delicately-featured face, which might have been carved out of yellow ivory. It was a network of wrinkles, colourless save for the piercing black eyes that sparkled beneath arched black brows, while the fine-cut nostrils and beautifully moulded mouth spoke unmistakably of race—of the old untainted blood which in some gipsy families has run clear, unmixed and undiluted, through countless generations.

There was an odd dignity about the shrunken, still upright figure as she rose from her seat—the freedom of one whose neck has never bowed to the yoke of established custom, whose kingdom is the sun and sea and earth and air as God gave them to Adam—and when the visitors had explained their errand, and she proceeded to answer them in the soft, slurred accents of the Devon dialect, the illiterate speech seemed to convey a strange sense of unfitness.

Claire and Nick were the first to dare the oracle. The old woman beckoned to them to follow her into the cottage, while Tormarin and Jean waited outside, and when they emerged once more, both were laughing, their faces eager and half excited like the faces of children promised some indefinite treat.

"She's given you luck, then?" asked Jean, smiling in sympathy.

The gipsy interposed quickly.

"Tezn't for me to give nor take away the luck. But I knaw that, back o' they gert black clouds the young lady's so mortal feared of, the zun's shinin' butivul. I tell 'ee, me dear"—nodding encouragingly to Claire, while her keen old eyes narrowed to mere pin-points of light—"you'll zee it, yourself—and afore another year's crep' by. 'Ess, fay! You'll knaw then as I tolled 'ee trew."

Then, with a gesture that summoned Jean to follow her, she disappeared once more into the interior of the hut.

Jean hesitated nervously in the doorway. For a moment she was conscious of an acute feeling of distaste for the impending interview—a dread of what this woman, whose eyes seemed the only live thing in her old, old face, might have to tell her.

"Come with me," she appealed to Blaise. And he nodded and followed her across the threshold.

The scent of a peat fire came warm and fragrant to her nostrils as she stepped out of the sunlight into the comparative dusk of the little shanty, mingling curiously with an aroma of savoury stew which issued from a black pot hung above the fire, bubbling and chuckling as it simmered.

The gipsy, as though by force of habit, gave a stir to its contents and then, settling herself on a three-legged stool, she took Jean's hand in her wrinkled, claw-like fingers and peered at its palm in silence.

"Your way baint so plain tu zee as t'other young lady's," she muttered at last, in an odd, sing-song tone. "There's life an' death an' fire an' flame afore yu zee the sun shinin' clear.... And if so be yu take the wrong turnin', you'll niver zee it. And there'll be no postes to guide 'ee. Tez your awn sawl must tell 'ee how to walk through the darkness. For there's darkness comin'... black darkness."

She paused, and the liquid in the black pot over the fire seethed up suddenly and filled the silence with its chuckling and gurgling, so that to Jean it seemed like the sound of some hidden malevolence chortling defiance at her.

The old woman clutched her hand a little tighter, turning the palm so that the light from the tiny window fell more directly upon it.

"There's a castle waitin' for 'ee, me dear," she resumed in the same sing-song voice as before. "I can zee it so plain as plain. But yu won't never live there wi' the one yu luve, though you'm hopin' tu. I see ruin and devastation all around it, and the sky so red as blid above it."

She released Jean's hand slowly, and her curiously bright eyes fastened upon Tormarin.

"Shall I tell the gentleman's hand?" she asked, stretching out her withered claw to take it.

But he drew it away hurriedly.

"No, no," he said, attempting to speak lightly. "This lady's fortune isn't sufficiently encouraging for me to venture."

The gipsy's eyes never left his face. She nodded slowly.

"That's as may be. For tez the zaim luck and zaim ill-lack will come to yu as comes to thikke maid. There's no ring given or taken, but you'm bound together so fast and firm as weddin'-ring could bind 'ee."

Jean felt her face flame scarlet in the dusk of the tiny room, and she turned and made her way hastily out into the sunshine once more, thankful for the eager queries of Nick and Claire, which served to bring back to normal the rather strained atmosphere induced by the gipsy's final comment.

As they climbed the side of the tor once more, Jean relapsed into silence. More than once, more than twice, since she had come to England, she had been vaguely conscious of some hidden menace to her happiness, and now the gipsy had suddenly given words to' her own indefinite premonition of evil.

"For there's darkness comin'... black darkness."

It was a relief to join the rest of the picnic party, who were clamouring loudly for their lunch, good-humouredly indignant with the wanderers for keeping them waiting.

"Another five minutes," announced Burke, "and we should have begun without you. Not even Lady Anne could have kept us under restraint a moment longer."

The party was quite a large one, augmented by a good many friends from round about the neighbourhood, and amid the riotous fun and ridiculous mishaps which almost invariably accompany an alfresco meal, Jean contrived to throw off the feeling of oppression generated by Keturah's prophecy.

Burke, having heaped her plate with lobster mayonnaise, established himself beside her, and proceeded to catechise her about her recent experience.

"Did the lady—what's her name, Keturah?—tell you when you were going to marry me?" he demanded in an undertone, his dare-devil eyes laughing down at her impudently.

"No, she did not. She only foresees things that are really going to happen," retorted Jean.

"Well, that is"—composedly. "She can't be much good at her job if she missed seeing it."

"Well," Jean affected to consider—"the nearest she got to it was that she saw 'darkness coming... black darkness.'"

Under cover of the general preoccupation in lunch and conversation, Burke's hand closed suddenly over hers.

"You little devil!" he said, half amused, half sulky. "I'll make you pay for that."

But out here, in the wind-swept, open spaces of the Moor, Jean felt no fear of him.

"First catch your hare——" she retaliated defiantly.

He regarded her tensely for a moment.

"I'll take your advice," he said briefly. Then he added: "Did you know that I'm driving you back in my cart this afternoon?"

Various cars and traps and saddle horses had brought the party together at the appointed rendezvous—a little village on the outskirts of the Moor, and Jean had driven up with Blaise in one of the Staple cars. She looked at Burke now, in astonishment.

"You certainly are not," she replied quickly. "I shall go back as I came—in the car."

"Quite impossible. It's broken down. They rashly brought on the lunch hampers in it, across that God-forsaken bit of moor road—with disastrous consequences to the car's internals. So that you and Tormarin have got to be sorted into other conveyances. And I've undertaken to get you home."

Jean's face fell a little. Throughout the drive up to the Moor Blaise had seemed less remote and more like his old self than at any time since their quarrel, and she could guess that this arrangement of Burke's was hardly likely to conduce towards the continuance of the new peace.

"How will Blaise get home?" she asked.

"They can squeeze him into her car, Judy says. It'll be a tight fit, but he can cling on by his eyelashes somehow."

"I think it would be a better arrangement if you drove Blaise and I went back in the car with your sister," suggested Jean.

"There's certainly not room for two extra in the car. There isn't really room for one."

"There wouldn't be two. You would drive Blaise."

"Pardon me. I should do nothing of the sort."

"Do you mean"—incredulously—"that you would refuse?"

"Oh, I should invent an armour-plated reason. A broken spring in the dog-cart or something. But I do mean that if I don't drive you, I drive no one."

Jean looked at him vexedly.

"Well," she said uncertainly, "we can't have a fuss at a picnic."

"No," agreed Burke. "So I'm afraid you'll have to give in."

Jean rather thought so, too. There didn't seem any way out of it. She knew that Burke was perfectly capable, under cover of some supposed mishap to his trap, of throwing the whole party into confusion and difficulty, rather than relinquish his intention.

"Oh, very well," she yielded at last, resignedly. "Have your own way, you obstinate man."

"I intend to," he replied coolly. "Now—-and always."

CHAPTER XXI
DIVERS HAPPENINGS

"I DON'T think I want any champagne," said Claire smilingly, as Nick filled a glass and handed it to her. "Being utterly free like this produces much the same effect. I feel drunk, Nick—drunk with happiness. Oh, why can't I be always free——"

She broke off abruptly in her speech, her face whitening, and stared past Nick with dilated eyes. Her lips remained parted, just as when she had ceased speaking, and the breath came between them unevenly.

Nick followed the direction of her glance. But he could see nothing to account for her suddenly stricken expression of dismay. A man in chauffeur's livery, vaguely familiar to him, was approaching, and it was upon him that Claire's eyes were fixed in a sick gaze of apprehension. It reminded Nick of the look of a wounded bird, incapable of flight, as it watches the approach of a hungry cat.

"What is it?" he asked quickly. "What's the matter? For God's sake don't look like that, Claire!"

Slowly, with difficulty, she wrenched her eyes away from that sleek, conventional figure in the dark green livery.

"Don't you see who it is?" she asked in a harsh, dry whisper.

Before Nick could answer, the man had made his way to Claire's side and paused respectfully.

"Beg pardon, my lady," he said, touching his hat, "Sir Adrian sent me to say that he's waiting for you in the car just along the road there." He pointed to where, on the white ribbon of road which crossed the Moor not far from the base of the tor, a stationary car was visible.

Claire, her face ashen, turned to Nick in mute appeal.

"Sir Adrian? I thought he left for London this morning?"

Nick shot the question fiercely at the chauffeur, but the man's face remained respectfully blank.

"No, sir. Sir Adrian drove as far as Exeter and then returned. Afterwards we drove on here, sir, and they told us in the village we should find you at Shelston Tors."

Meanwhile the other members of the party were becoming aware that some contretemps had occurred. Claire's white, stricken face was evidence enough that something was amiss, and simultaneously Lady Anne and Jean hurried forward, filled with apprehension.

"What is it, Claire?" asked Lady Anne, suspecting bad news of some kind. "What has happened?" Recognising the Charnwood livery, she turned to the chauffeur and continued quickly: "Has Sir Adrian met with an accident?" She could conceive of no other cause for the man's unexpected appearance.

"No, my lady. Sir Adrian is waiting in the car for her ladyship."

"Waiting in the car?" repeated Jean and Lady Anne in chorus.

The little group of friends drew closer together.

"Don't you see what it means?" broke out Claire in a low voice of intense anger. "It's been all a trick—a trick! He never meant to go to London at all. He only *pretended* to me that he was going, so that I should think that I was free and he could trap me." She looked at Nick and Jean significantly. "He must have overheard us—that day in the shrubbery at Charnwood— you remember?" They both nodded. "And then planned to humiliate me in front of half the county."

"But you won't go back with him?" exclaimed Nick hotly. He swung round and addressed the chauffeur stormily. "You can damn well tell your master that her ladyship will return this evening with the rest of the party." The man's face twitched. As far as it is possible for a well-drilled servant's face to express the human emotion of compassion, his did so.

"It would be no good, sir," he said in a low voice. "He means her ladyship to come. 'Go and fetch her away, Langton,' was his actual words to me. I didn't want the job, sir, as you may guess."

"Well, she's not coming, that's all," declared Nick determinedly.

"Oh, I must, Nick—I must go," cried Claire in distress. "I—I *daren't* stay."

Lady Anne nodded.

"Yes, I think she must go, Nick dear," she said persuasively. "It would be—wiser."

"But it's damnable!" ejaculated Nick furiously. "It's only done to insult her—to humiliate her!"

Claire smiled a little wistfully.

"I ought to be used to that by now," she said a trifle shakily. "But Lady Anne is right—I must go." She turned to the chauffeur, dismissing him with a little air of dignity that, in the circumstances, was not without its flavour of heroism. "You can go on ahead, Langton, and tell Sir Adrian that I am coming."

The man touched his hat and moved off obediently.

"Nick and I will walk down to the car with you," said Lady Anne. She was fully alive to the fact that her escort might contribute towards ameliorating the kind of reception Claire would obtain from her husband. "Jean dear, look after everybody for me for a few minutes, will you? And," raising her voice a little, "explain that Claire has been called home suddenly, as Sir Adrian was not well enough to make the journey to town, after all."

But Lady Anne's well-meant endeavour to throw dust in the eyes of the rest of the party was of comparatively little use. Although to many of them Claire was personally an entire stranger—since Sir Adrian intervened whenever possible to prevent her from forming new friendships—the story of her unhappy married life was practically public property in the neighbourhood, and it was quite evident that to all intents and purposes the detestable husband had actually insisted on her returning with him, exactly as a naughty child might be swept off home by an irate parent in the middle of a jolly party.

It was impossible to stem the flood of gossip, and though most of it was kindly enough, and wholeheartedly sympathetic to Lady Latimer, Jean's cheeks burned with indignation that Claire's dignity should be thus outraged.

The remainder of the afternoon was spoilt for her, and Nick's stormy face when he, together with Lady Anne, rejoined the rest of the party did not help to lighten her heart.

"I'm so sorry, Nick," she whispered compassionately, when presently the opportunity of a few words alone with him occurred.

He glared at her.

"Are you?" he said shortly. "I'm not. I think I'm glad. This ends it. No woman can be expected to put up with public humiliation of that sort."

"Nick!" There was a sharp note of fear in Jean's voice. "Nick, what do you mean? What are you going to do?"

There was an ugly expression on the handsome boyish-looking face.

"You'll know soon enough," was all he vouchsafed. And swung away from her.

Jean felt troubled. She had never seen Nick before with that set, still look on his face—a kind of bitter concentration which reminded her forcibly of his brother—and she rather dreaded what it might portend.

Her thoughts were still preoccupied with the afternoon's unpleasant episode, and with the possible consequences which might accrue, as she climbed into Burke's high dog-cart.

She had had a fleeting notion of claiming Claire's vacant seat for the homeward run, but had dismissed it since actually Claire's absence merely served to provide comfortable room for Blaise in the Willow Ferry car, which had held its full complement of passengers on the outward journey. Moreover, she reflected that any change of plan, now that she had agreed to drive back with Burke, might only lead to trouble. He was not in a mood to brook being thwarted.

A big, raking chestnut, on wires to be off, danced between the shafts of the dog-cart, irritably pawing the ground and jerking her handsome, satin-skinned head up and down with a restless jingle of bit and curb-chain. She showed considerable more of the white of a wicked-looking eye than was altogether reassuring as she fought impatiently against the compulsion of the steady hand which gripped the reins and kept her, against her will, at a standstill.

The instant she felt Jean's light foot on the step her excitement rose to fever heat. Surely this *must* mean that at last a start was imminent and that that firm, masterful pressure on the bit would be released!

But Burke had leaned forward to tuck the light dust-rug round Jean's knees, and regarding this further delay as beyond bearing the chestnut created a diversion by going straight up in the air and pirouetting gaily on her hind legs.

"Steady now!"

Burke's calm tones fell rebukingly on the quivering, sensitive ears, and down came two shining hoofs in response, as the mare condescended to resume a more normal pose. The next moment she was off at a swinging trot, breaking every now and again, out of pure exuberance of spirits, into a canter, sternly repressed by those dominating hands whose quiet mastery seemed conveyed along the reins as an electric current is carried by a wire.

"You needn't be afraid," remarked Burke. "She'll settle down in a few minutes. It's only a 'stable ahead' feeling she's suffering from. There's not an ounce of vice in her composition."

"I'm not afraid," replied Jean composedly.

She did not tell him why. But within herself she knew that no woman would ever be afraid with Geoffrey Burke. Afraid of him, possibly, but never afraid that he would not be entire master of any situation wherein physical strength and courage were the paramount necessities.

She reflected a little grimly to herself that it was this very forcefulness which gave the man his unquestionable power of attraction. There is always a certain fascination in sheer, ruthless strength—a savour of magnificence about it, something tentatively heroic, which appeals irresistibly to that primitive instinct somewhere hidden in the temperamental make-up of even the most ultra-twentieth-century feminine product.

And Jean was quite aware that she herself was not altogether proof against the attraction of Burke's dynamic virility.

There was another kind of strength which appealed to her far more. She knew this, too. The still, quiet force that was Tormarin's—deep, and unfathomable, and silent, of the spirit as well as of the body. Contrasted with the savage power she recognised in Burke, it was like the fine, tempered steel of a rapier compared with a heavy bludgeon.

"A penny for your thoughts!"

Jean came out of her reverie with a start. She smiled.

"Don't get conceited. I was thinking about you."

"Nice thoughts, I hope, then?" suggested Burke. "It's better"— audaciously—"to think well of your future husband."

The old gipsy's words flashed into Jean's mind: "You'm bound together so fast and firm as weddin-ring could bind 'ee," and her face flamed scarlet.

It was true—at least as far as she was concerned—that no wedding-ring could bind her more firmly to Blaise than her own heart had already bound her.

The instinct to flirt with Burke was in abeyance. It was an instinct only born of heartache and unhappiness, and now that Blaise's mood was so much less cool and distant than, it had been, the temptation to play with unexploded bombs had correspondingly lost much of its charm.

"Don't be tiresome, Geoffrey," she said vexedly. "If only you would make up your mind to be—just pals, I should think much better of you."

"Then I'm afraid you'll have to think worse," he retorted.

Just at that moment they encountered a flock of sheep, ambling leisurely along towards them and blocking up the narrow roadway, and Jean was spared the necessity of replying by the fact that Burke immediately found his hands full, manoeuvring a path for the mare between the broad, curly backs of the bleating multitude.

The drover of the flock was, of course, a hundred yards or more behind his charges, negligently occupied in relighting his pipe, so that no assistance was to be looked for in that direction, and as the sheep bumped against the mare's legs and crowded up against the wheels of the trap in their characteristically maddening fashion, it required all Burke's skill and dexterity to make a way through the four-footed crowd.

The chestnut's own idea of dealing with the difficulty was to charge full speed ahead, an idea which by no means facilitated matters, and she fought her bit and fairly danced with fury as Burke checked her at almost every yard.

They had nearly reached the open road again, and Jean, looking down on the sea of woolly backs, with the hovering cloud of hoof-driven dust above them, thought she could fully appreciate the probable feelings of the Israelites as they approached the further shore of the Red Sea. And it was just at this inauspicious moment that the drover, having lit his pipe to his satisfaction, looked up and grasped the situation.

Guilty conscience not only makes cowards, but is also prolific in the creation of fools, and the drover, stung into belated action by the consciousness of previous remissness, promptly did the most foolish thing he could.

He let off a yell that tore its way through every quivering nerve in the mare's body, and with a shout of, "Round 'em, lad!" sent his dog—a half-trained youngster—barking like a creature possessed, full tilt in pursuit of the sheep.

That settled it as far as the chestnut was concerned. With a bound she leapt forward, scattering the two or three remaining sheep that still blocked her path, and the next moment the light, high cart was rocking like a cockle-shell in a choppy sea, as she tore along, utterly out of hand.

Luckily, for a couple of miles the road ran straight as a dart, and after the first gasp of alarm Jean found herself curiously collected and able to calculate chances. At the end of the two miles, she knew, there came a steep declivity—a typical Devonshire hill, like the side of a house, which the British workman had repaired in his usual crude and inefficient manner, so that loose stones and inequalities of surface added to the dangers of negotiation. At the foot of this descent was a sharp double turn—a veritable death-trap. Could Burke possibly got the mare in hand before they reached the brow of the hill? Jean doubted it.

There was no sound now in all the world except the battering of the mare's hoofs upon the road and the screaming rush of the wind in their ears. The hedges flew past, a green, distorted blur. The strip of road fled away beneath them as though coiled up by some swift revolving cylinder; ahead, it ended sheer against a sky blue as a periwinkle, and into that blue they were rushing at thirty miles an hour. When they reached it, it would be the end. Jean could almost hear the crash that must follow, sense the sickening feeling of being flung headlong, hurled into space.... hurtling down into black nothingness.,..

Her glance sought Burke's face. His jaw was out-thrust, and she could guess at the clenched teeth behind the lips that shut like a rat-trap. His eyes gleamed beneath the penthouse brows, drawn together so that they almost met above his fighting beak of a nose.

In an oddly detached manner she found herself reflecting on the dogged brute strength of his set face. If anyone could check that flying, foam-flecked form, rocketing along between the shafts like a red-brown streak, he could.

She wondered how long he would be able to hold the beast—to hang on? She remembered having heard that, after a time, the strain of pulling against a runaway becomes too much for human nerves and muscles, and that a man's hands grow numb—and helpless! While the dead pull on the bit equally numbs the mouth of the horse, so that he, too, has no more any feeling to be played upon by the pressure of the hit.

Her eyes dropped to Burke's hands. With a little inward start of astonishment she realised that he was not attempting to pull against the chestnut. He was just holding... holding... steadying her, ever so little, in her mad gallop. Jean felt the mare swerve, then swing level again, still answering faintly to the reins.

Burke's hands were very still. She wondered vaguely why—now—he didn't pit his strength against that of the runaway. They must have covered a mile or more. A bare half-mile was all that still lay between them and disaster.

And then, as she watched Burke's hands, she saw them move, first one and then the other, sawing the bit against the tender corners of the mare's mouth. Jean was conscious of a faint difference in the mad pace of her.

Not enough to be accounted a check—but still *something*, some appreciable slackening of the whirlwind rush towards that blue blur of sky ahead.

It seemed as though Burke, too, sensed that infinitesimal yielding to the saw of the bit. For the first time, he gave a definite pull at the reins. Then he relaxed the pressure, and again there followed the same sawing motion and the fret of the steel bar against sensitive, velvet lips. Then another pull—the man's sheer strength against the mare's.... Jean watched, fascinated.

And gradually, almost imperceptibly at first, the frenzied beat of the iron-shod hoofs became more measured as the chestnut shortened her stride. It was no longer merely the thrashing, thunderous devil's tattoo of sheer, panic-driven speed.

Now and again Jean could hear Burke's voice, speaking to the frightened beast, chiding and reassuring in even, unhurried tones.

She was conscious of no fear, only of an absorbing interest and excitement as to whether Burke would be able to impose his will upon the animal before they reached that precipitous hill the descent of which must infallibly spell 'destruction'.

She sat very still, her hands locked together, watching... watching....

CHAPTER XXII
"WILLING OR UNWILLING!"

IT was over. A bare twenty yards from the brow of the bill the man had won, and now the mare was standing swaying between the shafts, shaking in every limb, her flanks heaving and the sweat streaming off her sodden coat in little rivulets.

Burke was beside her, patting her down and talking to her in a little intimate fashion much as though he were soothing a frightened child.

"You're all in, aren't you, old thing?" he murmured sympathetically. Then he glanced up at Jean, who was still sitting in the cart, feeling rather as though the end of the world had occurred and, in some surprising fashion, left her still cumbering the earth.

"She's pretty well run herself out," he remarked. "We shan't have any more trouble going home"—smiling briefly. "I hope not," answered Jean a trifle flatly.

"You all right?"

She nodded.

"Yes, thank you. You must be an excellent whip," she added. "I thought the mare would never stop."

Probably even Jean hardly realised the fineness of the horsemanship of which she had just been a witness—the judgment and coolness Burke had evinced in letting the mare spend the first freshness of her strength before he essayed to check her mad pace; the dexterity with which he had somehow contrived to keep her straight; and finally, the consummate skill with which, that last half-mile, he had played her mouth, rejecting the dead pull on the reins—the instinctive error of the mediocre driver—which so quickly numbs sensation and neutralises every effort to bring a runaway to a standstill.

"Yes. I rather thought our number was up," agreed Burke absently. He was passing his hands feelingly over the mare to see if she were all right, and suddenly, with a sharp exclamation, he lifted one of her feet from the ground and examined it.

"Cast a shoe and torn her foot rather badly," he announced. "I'm afraid we shall have to stop at the next village and get her shod. It's not a mile further on. You and I can have tea at the inn while she's at the blacksmith's."

With a final caress of the steaming chestnut neck, he came back to the side of the cart, reins in hand.

"Can you drive her with a torn foot?" queried Jean.

"Oh, yes. We'll have to go carefully down this hill, though. There are such a confounded lot of loose stones about."

He climbed into the dog-cart and very soon they had reached the village, where the chestnut, tired and subdued, was turned over to the blacksmith's ministrations while Burke and Jean made their way to the inn.

Tea was brought to them upstairs in a quaint, old-fashioned parlour fragrant of bygone times. Oaken beams, black with age, supported the ceiling, and on the high chimneypiece pewter dishes gleamed like silver, while at either end an amazingly hideous spotted dog, in genuine old Staffordshire, surveyed the scene with a satisfied smirk. Through the leaded diamond panes of the window was visible a glimpse of the Moor.

"What an enchanting place!" commented Jean, as, tea over, she made a tour of inspection, pausing at last in front of the window.

Burke had been watching her as she wandered about the room, his expression moody and dissatisfied.

"It's a famous resort for honeymooners," he answered. "Do you think" — enquiringly — "it would be a good place in which to spend a honeymoon?"

"That depends," replied Jean cautiously. "If the people were fond of the country, and the Moor, and so on — yes. But they might prefer something less remote from the world."

"Would you?"

"I?" — with detachment. "I'm not contemplating a honeymoon."

Suddenly Burke crossed the room to her side.

"We might as well settle that point now," he said quietly. "Jean, when will you marry me?"

She looked at him indignantly.

"I've answered that question before. It isn't fair of you to reopen the matter here — and now."

"No," he agreed. "It isn't fair. In fact, I'm not sure that it isn't rather a caddish thing for me to do, seeing that you can't get away from me just now. But all's fair in love and war. And it's both love and war between us two" —grimly.

"The two things don't sound very compatible," fenced Jean.

"It's only war till you give in—till you promise to marry me. Then"—a smouldering light glowed in his eyes—"then I'll show you what loves means."

She shook her head.

"I'm afraid," she said, attempting to speak coolly, "that it means war indefinitely then, Geoffrey. I can give you no different answer."

"You shall!" he exclaimed violently. "I tell you, Jean, it's useless your refusing me. I won't *take* no. I want you for my wife—and, by God, I'm going to have you!"

She drew away from him a little, backing into the embrasure of the window. The look in his eyes frightened her.

"Whether I will or no?" she asked, still endeavouring to speak lightly. "*My* feelings in the matter don't appear to concern you at all."

"I'd rather you came willingly—but, if you won't, I swear I'll marry you, willing or unwilling!"

He was standing close to her now, staring down at her with sombre, passion-lit eyes, and instinctively she made a movement as though to elude him and slip back again into the room. In the same instant his arms went round her and she was prisoned in a grip from which she was powerless to escape.

"Don't struggle," he said, as she strove impotently to release herself. "I could hold you from now till doomsday without an effort."

There was a curious thrill in his voice, the triumphant, arrogant leap of possession. He held her pressed against him, and she could feel his chest heave with his labouring breath.

"You're mine—mine! My woman—meant for me from the beginning of the world—and do you think I'll give you up?... Give you up? I tell you, if you were another man's wife I'd take you away from him! You're mine—every inch of you, body and soul. And I want you. Oh, my God, how I want you!"

"Let me go... Geoffrey..."

The words struggled from her lips. For answer his arms tightened round her, crushing her savagely, and she felt his kisses burning, scorching her face, his mouth on hers till it seemed as though he were draining her very soul.

When at last he released her, she leant helplessly against the woodwork of the window, panting and shaken. Her face was white as a magnolia petal and her eyes dark-rimmed with purple shadow.

A faint expression of compunction crossed Burke's face.

"I suppose—I shall never be forgiven now," he muttered roughly.

With an effort Jean forced her tongue to answer him.

"No," she said in a voice out of which every particle of feeling seemed to have departed. "You will never be forgiven."

A look of deviltry came into his eyes. He crossed the room and, locking the door, dropped the key into his pocket.

"I think," he remarked coolly, "in that case, I'd better keep you a prisoner here till you have promised to marry me. It's you I want. Your forgiveness can come after. I'll see to that."

The result of his action was unexpected. Jean turned to the window, unlatched it, and flung open the casement.

"If you don't unlock that door at once, Geoffrey," she said quietly, "I shall leave the room—this way"—with a gesture that sufficiently explained her meaning.

Her voice was very steady. Burke looked at her curiously.

"Do you mean—you'd jump out?" he asked, openly incredulous.

Her eyes answered him. They were feverishly bright, with an almost fanatical light in them, and suddenly Burke realised that she was at the end of her tether, that the emotional stress of the last quarter of an hour had taken its toll of her high-strung temperament and that she might even do what she had threatened. He had no conception of the motive behind the threat—of the imperative determination which had leaped to life within her to endure or suffer anything rather than stay locked in this room with Burke, rather than give Blaise, the man who held her heart between his two hands, ground for misunderstanding or mistrusting her anew.

Burke fitted the key into the lock of the door and turned it sulkily.

"You prim little thing! I was only teasing you," he said. "Do you mean you're really as frightened as all that of—*what people may say?* I thought you were above minding the gossip of ill-natured scandal-mongers."

Jean grasped eagerly at the excuse. It would serve to hide the real motive of her impulsive action.

"No woman can afford to ignore scandal," she answered quickly. "After all, a woman's happiness depends mostly on her reputation."

Burke's eyes narrowed suddenly. He looked at her speculatively, as though her words had suggested a new train of thought, but he made no comment. Somewhat abstractedly he opened the door and allowed her to pass out and down the stairs. Outside the door of the inn they found the mare and dog-cart in charge of an ostler.

"The mare's foot's rather badly torn, sir," volunteered the man, "but the blacksmith thinks she'll travel all right. Far to go, sir?"

"Nine or ten miles," responded Burke laconically.

He was curiously silent on the way home. It was as though the chain of reasoning started by Jean's comment on the relation scandal bears to a woman's happiness still absorbed him. His brows were knit together morosely.

Jean supposed he was probably reproaching himself for his conduct that afternoon. After all, she reflected, he was normally a man of decent instincts, and though the flood-tide of his passion had swept him into taking advantage of the circumstances which had flung them together in the solitude of the little inn, he would be the first to agree, when in a less lawless frame of mind, that his conduct had been unpardonable. Although, even from that, one could not promise that he would not be equally culpable another time!

Blaise had proved painfully correct in his estimate of the dangers attaching to unexploded bombs. Jean admitted it to herself ruefully. And she was honest enough also to admit that, with his warning ringing in her ears and with the memory of what had happened in the rose garden to illumine it, she herself was not altogether clear of blame for the incidents of the afternoon.

She *had* played with Burke, even encouraged him to a certain extent, allowing him to be in her company far more frequently than was altogether wise, considering the circumstance of his hot-headed love for her.

It was with somewhat of a mental start of surprise that she found herself seeking for excuses for his behaviour—actually trying to supply adequate reasons why she should overlook it!

His brooding, sulky silence as he drove along, mile after mile, was not without its appeal to the inherent femininity of her. He did not try to excuse or palliate his conduct, made no attempt to sue for forgiveness. He loved her and he had let her see it; manlike, he had taken what the opportunity offered. And she didn't suppose he regretted it.

The faintest smile twitched the comers of her lips. Burke was not the type of man to regret an unlawful kiss or two!

She was conscious that—as usual, where he was concerned—her virtuous indignation was oozing away in the most discreditable and hopeless fashion. There was an audacious charm about the man, an attractiveness that would not be denied in the hot-headed way he went, all out, for what he wanted.

Other women, besides Jean had found it equally difficult to resist. His sheer virility, with its splendid disregard for other people's claims and its conscienceless belief that the battle should assuredly be to the strong, earned him forgiveness where, for misdeeds not half so flagrant, a less imperious sinner would have been promptly shown the door.

But no woman—not even the women to whom he had made love without the excuse of loving—had ever shown Burke the door or given him the kind of treatment which he had thoroughly well merited twenty times over. And Jean was no exception to the rule.

At least he had some genuine claim on her forgiveness—the claim of a love which had swept through his very bung like a flame, the fierce passion of a man to whom love means adoration, worship—above all, possession.

And what woman can ever long remain righteously angry with a man who loves her—and whose very offence is the outcome of the overmastering quality of that love? Very few, and certainly none who was so very much a woman, so essentially feminine as Jean.

It was in a very small voice, which she endeavoured to make airily detached, that she at last broke the silence which had reigned for the last six miles or so.

"I suppose I shall have to forgive you—more or less. One can't exactly quarrel with one's next door neighbour." Burke smiled grimly.

"Can't one?"

"Well, there's Judith to be considered."

"A rather curious expression came into her eyes.

"Yes," he agreed. "There's Judith to be considered." There was a hint of irony in the dry tones.

"It would complicate matters if I were not on speaking terms with her brother," pursued Jean.

She waited for his answer, but none came. The threatened possibility contained in her speech appeared to have fallen on deaf ears, and the silence seemed likely to continue indefinitely.

Jean prompted him gently.

"You might, at least, say you are sorry for—for——"

"For kissing you?"—swiftly.

"Yes"—flushing a little.

"But I'm not. Kissing you"—with deliberation—"is One of the things I shall never regret. When I come to make my peace with Heaven and repent in sackcloth and ashes for my sins of omission and commission, I shan't include this afternoon in the list, I assure you. It was worth it—if I pay for it afterwards in hell."

He was silent for a moment. Then:

"But I'll promise you one thing. I'll never kiss you again till you give me your lips yourself."

Jean smiled at the characteristic speech. She supposed this was as near an apology as Burke would ever get.

"That's all right, then," she replied composedly. "Because I shall never do that."

He flicked the chestnut lightly with the whip.

"I think you will," he said. "I think"—he looked at her somewhat enigmatically—"that you will give me everything I want—some day."

CHAPTER XXIII
ON THE SIDE OF THE ANGELS

THROUGHOUT the day following that of the expedition to Dartmoor, Nick seemed determined to keep out of Jean's way. It was as though he feared she might force some confidence from him that he was loth to give, and, in consequence, deliberately avoided being alone with her.

On the second day, however, as luck would have it, she encountered him in the corridor just outside her own sitting-room. He was striding blindly along, obviously not heeding where he was going, and had almost collided with her before he realised that she was there.

He jerked himself backwards.

"I beg your pardon," he muttered, still without looking at her, and made as though to pass on.

Jean checked him with a hand on his sleeve. She had not watched the dogged sullenness of his face throughout yesterday to no purpose, and now, as her swift gaze searched it anew, she felt convinced that something fresh had occurred to stir him. It was impossible for Jean to see a friend in trouble without wanting to "stand by."

"Nick, old thing, what's wrong?" she asked.

He stared at her unseeingly. "Wrong?" he muttered. "Wrong?"

"Yes. Come in here and let's talk it out—whatever it is." With gentle insistence she drew him into her sitting-room. "How," she said, when she had established him in an easy-chair by the open window and herself in another, "what's gone wrong? Are you still boiling over about that trick Sir Adrian played on Claire the day of the picnic?"

She spoke lightly—more lightly than the occasion warranted—of set purpose, hoping to reduce the tension under which Nick was obviously labouring. His face hurt her. The familiar lazy insouciance which was half its charm was blotted out of it by some heavy cloud of tragic significance. He looked as though he had not slept for days, and his eyes, the gaiety burnt out of them by pain, seemed sunken in his head.

He stared at her blankly for a moment. Then he seemed to awaken to the meaning of her question.

"No," he said slowly. "No. The boiling over part is done with—finished.... I'm going to take her away from him."

He spoke with a curious precision. It frightened Jean far more than any impetuous outburst of anger could have done. She made no answer for a moment, but her mind worked rapidly. She did not doubt the absolute sincerity of his intention. This was no mere reckless boast of an angry lover, but the sane, considered aim and object of a man who has come, by way of some long agony of thwarting, to a set determination.

"Do you mean that, Nick?" she asked at last, to gain time.

"Do I mean it?" he laughed. Then his hands gripped the arms of the chair and he leaned forward. "I saw her—last evening after dinner.... Her shoulder was black."

A sharp cry broke from Jean's lips.

"Not—not—he hadn't——"

Nick nodded.

"He had struck her. There was one of the usual scenes when they got back from the Moor—and he struck her.... It's the first time he has ever actually laid hands on her. It's going to be the last"—grimly.

Jean was silent. Her whole soul was in revolt against the half-mad, drug-ridden creature who was making of Claire's life a devil martyrdom; the instinct to protect her, to succour her in some way, asserting itself with almost passionate force. And yet—— She knew that Nick's way was not the right way.

"Yes, it must be the last time," she agreed. "But—but, Nick, your plan won't do, you know."

Nick stiffened.

"Think not?" he said curtly. "Can you suggest a better?" Then, as Jean remained miserably silent: "Nor can I. And one thing I swear—I won't leave the woman I love in the hands of a man who is practically a maniac, to be tortured day after day, mentally and physically, just whenever he feels like it."

It struck Jean as curious that Nick had been able, more or less, to keep himself in hand whilst Sir Adrian inflicted upon Claire whatever of mental and spiritual torture seemed good in his distorted vision. It was the fact that he had hurt her physically, laid his hand upon her in actual violence, which had scattered Nick's self-control to the four winds of heaven. To Jean herself, it seemed conceivable that the mental anguish of Claire's married life had probably far outstripped any mere bodily pain. Half tentatively she gave expression to her thoughts.

Nick sprang to his feet.

"Good God!" he exclaimed. "If you were a man, you'd understand! I see red when I think of that damned brute striking the woman I love. It—it was sacrilege!"

"And won't it be—another kind of sacrilege—if you take her away with you, Nick?" asked Jean very quietly.

He flushed dully.

"He'll divorce her, and then we shall marry," he answered.

"Even so"—steadily—"it would be doing evil that good may come."

"Then we'll do it"—savagely. "It's easy enough for you to sit there moralising, perfectly placid and comfortable. Claire and I have borne all we can. It has been bad enough to care as we care for each other, and to live apart But when it means that Claire is to suffer unspeakable misery and humiliation while I stand by and look on—why, it's beyond human endurance. You're not tempted. You've no conception what you're talking about."

Jean sat very still and silent while Nick stormed out the bitterness of soul, recognising the truth of every word he littered—even of the gibes which, in the heedlessness of his own pain, he flung at herself.

Presently she got up and moved rather slowly across to his side.

"Nick," she said, and her eyes, looking into his, were very bright and clear and steady. Somehow for Nick they held the semblance of two flames, torches of pure light, burning unflickeringly in the darkness. "Nick, every word you say is true. I'm not tempted as you and Claire have been, and so it seems sheer cheek my interfering. But I'm only asking you to do what I pray I'd be strong enough to do myself in like circumstances. I don't believe any true happiness can ever come of running away from duty. And if ever I'm up against such a thing—a choice like this—I hope to God I'd be able to hang on... to run straight, even if it half killed me to do it."

The quick, impassioned utterance ceased, and half shrinkingly Jean realised that she had spoken out of the very depths of her soul, crystallising in so many words the uttermost ideal and *credo* of her being. In some strange, indefinable fashion it was borne in on her that she had reached an epoch of her life. It was as when a musician, arrived at the end of a musical period, strikes a chord which holds the keynote of the ensuing passage.

She faltered and looked at Nick beseechingly, suddenly self-conscious, as we most of us are when we find we have laid bare a bit of our inmost soul to the possibly mocking eyes of a fellow human being.

But Nick's eyes were not in the least mocking.

Instead of that, some of the hardness seemed to have gone out of them, and his voice was very gentle, as, taking Jean's two hands in his, he answered:

"I believe *you* would run straight, little Jean—even if it meant tearing your heart out of your body to do it. But, you know, you're always on the side of the angels—instinctively. I'm only a man—just an average earthy man"—smiling ruefully—"and my ideals all tumble down and sit on the ground in a heap when I think of what my girl's enduring as Latimer's wife. I believe I might stick my part of the business—but I can't stick it for her."

"And yet," urged Jean, "if you go away together, Nick, it's she who'll pay, you know. The woman always does. Supposing—supposing Sir Adrian *doesn't* divorce her—refuses to? It would be just like him to punish her that way. What about Claire—then?"

"He *would* divorce her," protested Nick harshly.

Jean shook her head.

"I don't think so. Honestly, I believe he would get undiluted satisfaction out of the fact that, as long as he lived, he could stand between Claire and everything that a normal woman wants—home, and a sheltered life, and the knowledge that no one can 'say things' about her. Oh, Nick, Nick! Between you—you and Sir Adrian—you'd make an outcast of Claire, make her life a worse hell with you than it is without you." She paused, then went on more quietly: "Have you said anything to her about this—told her what you want her to do?"

"No, not yet—not definitely."

Jean breathed a quick sigh of relief.

"Then don't! Promise me you won't, Nick?"

"She might refuse, after all," he suggested, evading a direct answer. "Refuse! You know her better than that. If you wanted Claire to make a burnt-offering of herself for your benefit to-morrow, you know she'd do it! And—and"—laughing a little hysterically—"pretend, too, that she enjoyed the process of being grilled! No, Nick, it's up to you to—to just go on helping to make her life bearable, as you have done for the last two years."

"It's asking too much of me, Jean."

Nick spoke a little thickly. He was up against one of man's most primitive instincts—the instinct to protect and comfort and cherish the woman he loved.

"I know. It's asking everything of you."

Jean waited. She felt that she had gained a certain amount of ground—that Nick's resolution had weakened a little in response to her pleading, but she feared to drive him too far. She fancied she could hear steps crossing the hall below. If someone should come upstairs and disturb them now, while things were still trembling in the balance— —

"See, Nick," she began to speak again hurriedly. "You believe I'm your pal—yours and Claire's?"

"I know it," he replied quietly.

"And—and you do care a bit about me?"—smiling a little.

"You're the third woman in my world, Jean. After Claire and my mother."

"Then, to please me—for nothing else in the world, if you like, but because I ask it—will you let things stay as they are for a few weeks longer? Just that little while, Nick? We're going to London next week. That'll make a break—bring us all back to a calmer, more everyday outlook on things. Will you wait? Sir Adrian may never strike Claire again. And it wouldn't be fair—just now, at a time when she is feeling horribly bitter and humiliated from that—that insult—to ask her to go away with you. Give her a fair chance to decide a big question like that when things are at their normal level—not when they are worse than usual. To ask her now would be to take advantage of the feeling she must have, just at this moment, that her life is unbearable. It wouldn't be playing the game."

He made no answer, and Jean waited with increasing trepidation. She was sure now that she could hear footsteps. Someone had mounted the stairs and was coming along the corridor towards her room.

"Nick!" The low, agitated whisper burst from her as the steps halted outside the door. "Promise me!"

It seemed an eternity before he answered.

"Very well. I promise. You've won for the moment—'Saint Jean'!"

He smiled at her, rather sadly. Before she could reply, Blaise's voice sounded outside the door, asking if he might come in, and with a feeling of intense relief that the battle was won for the moment, Jean gave the required permission. As his brother entered the room, Nick quitted it, brushing past him abruptly.

Tormarin's eyes questioned Jean's;

"We have been discussing Sir Adrian," she explained, as the door closed behind Nick. "And—and Claire."

He nodded comprehendingly.

"Poor old Nick!" he said. "It's damned rough on him. Latimer ought to be carefully and quickly chloroformed out of the way. He's as much a menace to society as a mad dog."

Jean sighed.

"I'm afraid they're very unhappy—Nick and Claire."

"I wonder Claire doesn't chuck her husband," said Blaise. "And take whatever of happiness she can get out of the world."

Jean shook her head.

"You know you don't mean that. You don't really believe in snatching happiness—at all costs."

"I'd let precious little stand in the way. If I were Nick I think I should do it."

"But being you?"

Jean did not know what unaccountable impulse induced her to give a personal and individual twist to what had been developing almost into an academic discussion. Perhaps it was the familiar, unsatisfied longing to hear Blaise himself define the thing which kept them apart—even though, since Lady Anne's disclosure, she could guess only too well what it was. Or perhaps it was the faint, tormenting hope that one day his determination would weaken and his love sweep away all barriers.

He looked at her contemplatively.

"Sometimes the past makes claims upon a man which forbid him to snatch at happiness. I don't believe in any man's shirking his just punishment for the evil he has done. What he has brought on himself, that he must bear. But Nick and Claire have had no part in bringing about their own tragedy. They are just the sport of chance—of an ill fate. They are morally free to take their happiness in a way in which I shall never be free to take mine, as long as I live." He regarded her steadily. "There are certain things for which I have proved myself unfitted—with which it is evident I am not to be trusted. And one of those is the safeguarding of any woman's happiness."

Jean felt her throat contract. It would always be the same, then! The long tentacles of the past would reach out eternally into the future. The woman who had been his wife—the woman who had destroyed herself, and, in so doing, hanged a millstone of remorse about his neck—would stand forever at the gateway of the garden of happiness, her dead lips silently denying him—and, with him, the woman who loved him—the right to enter.

With an effort Jean answered that part of his speech which had reference only to Claire and Nick.

"There are other ways, though, in which they have no moral right. I grant that Claire was persuaded, almost driven into marrying Sir Adrian by her parents, but, after all, we each have our individual free will. She *could* have refused to obey them. Or, if she felt there were reasons why she must marry him—the material advantage to her parents, and so on, why, she ought to have reckoned the cost I don't mean to be hard, Blaise— — — —-." She broke off wistfully.

"You—hard!" He laughed a little, as though amused.

"Only—only one must try to be fair all round—to look at things *straight*."

She leaned her chin on her palm and her eyes grew thoughtful.

"I don't know, but it seems to me that we weren't meant to run away from things—hard things. If a man and a woman marry, they must accept their responsibilities—not evade them."

So absorbed was she in her trend of thought that she never realised how directly this speech must strike at Blaise himself. His face changed slightly.

"You're right, of course," he said abruptly. "You—generally are. And if all women were like you, it would be easy enough."

His eyes dwelt with a curious intentness on the pure outline of her face; on the parted, tenderly curved lips, and the golden eyes with their momentary touch of the idealist and the dreamer.

It seemed as if the quiet intensity of his regard drew her, for slowly she turned her head and met his gaze, flushing suddenly and faltering under it. The consciousness of him, of his nearness, swept her from head to foot, and it seemed to her as though now, in this moment, they were in closer touch, nearer understanding, than they had ever been.

The dreamer and idealist vanished and it was all at once just sheer woman, passionate and wistful and tremulous, and infinitely alluring, that looked at him out of the golden eyes.

With a stifled exclamation he caught her hands in his.

"Beloved——"

And the whole of a man's forbidden, thwarted love vibrated in the word as he spoke it.

Then he bent his head, and for a moment his lips were against her soft palms....

She stood very still and quiet when he had gone, realising in every quivering nerve of her that whatsoever the future might bring—even though Blaise might choose to shut himself away from her again as in the past and the dividing wall between them rise as high as heaven—she knew now, without any shadow of doubt or questioning, that he loved her.

In the burning utterance of a single word, in the pressure of passionate, renouncing lips, the assurance had been given, and nothing could ever take it away again.

She spread out her hands, palms upward, and looked at them curiously.

CHAPTER XXIV
AN UNEXPECTED MEETING

"HAVE you been *very* bored, Nick?"

The week in London had nearly run its course, and Lady Anne's eyes begged charmingly for a negative. Nick accorded it with a smile.

"I'm never bored with you, madonna; you know that," he said. "And hotel life is always more or less amusing. One comes across such queer types. There's one here this evening has been intriguing me enormously. At a little table by herself—do you see her? A tall, rather gorgeous-looking being—kind of cross between the Queen of Sheba and Lucretia Borgia."

Lady Anne threw a veiled glance in the direction indicated.

"Yes, she's a very handsome woman, obviously not English." Her eyes travelled onwards towards the door. "I wish Blaise and Jean would hurry up," she added impatiently. "They're taking an unconscionable time to dress."

The two latter had come in late from a sight-seeing expedition undertaken on Jean's behalf, and had only returned to the hotel just as Lady Anne and Nick were preparing to make their way in to dinner.

"For such a deliberate matchmaker, you're a lot too impatient, madonna," commented Nick teasingly. "That they should have stayed out together until the very last moment ought to have pleased you immensely."

Lady Anne made a small grimace.

"So it does—theoretically. Only from a practical and purely material point of view, everything else sinks into insignificance beside the fact that I am literally starving. Oh!"—joyfully catching sight of Jean and Tormarin making their way up the room—"Here they are at last! Collect our waiter, Nick, and let's begin."

Neither of the late-comers appeared in the least embarrassed by the tardiness of their arrival, said they responded to tentative enquiries concerning their afternoon's amusement with a disappointing lack of self-consciousness.

Lady Anne experienced an inward qualm of misgiving. There seemed too calm and tranquil a camaraderie between the two to please her altogether. It was as though the last few days had brought about a silent understanding between them—a wordless compact.

She picked up the menu and assumed an absorption in its contents which she was far from feeling.

"What are we all going to eat?" she asked. "I think we must hurry a little, or we shall be late for the play. Then I shall lose the exquisite thrill of seeing the curtain go up." Tormarin looked entertained.

"Does it still thrill you, you absurdly youthful person?"

"Of course it does. I always consider that the quality of the thrill produced by the rise of the curtain is the measure of one's capacity for enjoyment. When it no longer thrills me, I shall know that I am getting old and bored, and that I only go to the theatre to kill time and because everyone else goes."

Dinner proceeded leisurely in spite of Lady Anne's admonition that they should hurry, and presently Nick, who had glanced across the room once or twice as though secretly amused, remarked confidentially:

"My Lucretia Borgia lady is taking a quite uncommon interest in someone of our party. I'm afraid I can't flatter myself that she's lost her heart to me, as I've only observed this development since Jean and Blaise joined us. Blaise, I believe it's you who have won her devoted—if, probably, somewhat violent—affections."

"Your Lucretia Borgia lady? Which is she?" enquired Jean.

"You can't see her, because you are sitting with your back to her," replied Nick importantly. "And it isn't manners to screw your head round in a public restaurant—even although the modern reincarnation of an unpleasantly vengeful lady may be sitting just behind you. But if you'll look into that glass opposite you—a little to the right side of it—you'll see who I mean. She's quite unmistakable."

Jean tilted her head a little and peered slantwise into the mirror which faced her. It was precisely at the same moment that Nick's "Lucretia Borgia lady" looked up for the second time from her *pêche* Melba, and Jean found herself gazing straight into the dense darkness of the eyes of Madame de Varigny.

"Why—why————" she stammered in astonishment. "It is the Comtesse de Varigny!" She turned to Lady Anne, adding explanatorily: "You remember, madonna, I told you about her? She chaperoned me at Montavan, after Glyn had departed."

The recognition had been mutual. Madame de Varigny had half-risen from her seat and was poised in an attitude of expectancy, smiling and gesturing with expressive hands an invitation to Jean to join her.

"I'll go across and speak to her," said Jean. "I can't imagine what she is doing in London."

"I suppose you, too, met this rather splendid-looking personage at Montavan?" enquired Nick of his brother, as Jean quitted the table.

Tormarin shook his head.

"I never spoke to her. I saw her once, on the night of a fancy-dress ball at the hotel, arrayed as Cleopatra."

"She'd look the part all right," commented Nick. "She gives me the impression of being one of those angel-and-devil-mixed kind of women— the latter flavour preponderating. I should rather feel the desirability of emulating Agag in any dealings I had with her. Good Lord!"—with a lively accession of interest—"Jean's bringing her over here. By Jove! She really is a beautiful person, isn't she. Like a sort of Eastern empress."

"Madame de Varigny wishes to be presented to you, Lady Anne," said Jean, and proceeded to effect introductions all round.

"I remember seeing you with Mees Peterson at Montavan," remarked the Countess, as she shook hands with Blaise, her dark eyes resting on him curiously.

"Join us and finish your dinner at our table," suggested Lady Anne hospitably.

But Madame de Varigny protested volubly that she had already finished her meal, though she would sit and talk with them a little if it was agreeable? It was—quite agreeable. She herself saw to that. No one could be more charming than she when she chose, and on this occasion she elected to make herself about as altogether charming as it is possible for a woman to be, entirely conquering the hearts of Lady Anne and Nick. Her simple, childlike warm-heartedness of manner was in such almost ludicrous contrast to her majestic, dark-browed type of beauty that it took them completely by storm.

"This is only just a flying visit that I pay to England," she explained artlessly. "It is a great good fortune that I should have chanced to encounter *ma chère Mees Peterson.*"

"It's certainly an odd chance brought you to the same hotel," agreed Nick.

"Is it not?"—delightedly.

And, from the frank wonder and satisfaction she evinced at the coincidence, no one could possibly have surmised that the sole cause and origin of her "flying visit" was a short paragraph contained in the *Morning Post*, a copy of which, by her express order, had been delivered daily at Chateau Varigny ever since her return thither from the Swiss Alps. The paragraph referred simply to the arrival at Claridge's of Lady Anne Brennan, accompanied by her two sons and Miss Jean Peterson.

"And are you making a long stay in London?" enquired Madame de Varigny.

Lady Anne shook her head.

"No. We go back to Staple to-morrow."

The other's face fell.

"But how unfortunate! I shall then see nothing of my dear Mees Peterson."

She seemed so distressed that Lady Anne's kind heart melted within her, albeit it accorded ill with her plans to increase the number of her party.

"We are going on to the theatre," she said impulsively. "If you have no other engagement, why not come with us? There will be plenty of room in our box."

Madame de Varigny professed herself enchanted. Curiously enough, she seemed to have no particular wish to draw Jean into anything in the nature of a private talk, but appeared quite content just to take part in the general conversation, while her eyes rested speculatively now upon Jean, now upon Tormarin, as though they afforded her an abstract interest of some kind.

Even at the theatre, where from her corner seat she was able to envisage the other occupants of the box, she seemed almost as much interested in them as in the play that was being performed on the stage. Once, as Tormarin leaned forward and made some comment to Jean, their two pairs of eyes meeting in a look of mutual understanding of some small joke or other, the quiet watcher smiled contentedly, as though the little byplay satisfied some inner questioning.

With the fall of the curtain at the end of the first act, she turned to Lady Anne, politely enthusiastic.

"But it is a charming play," she said. "It is no wonder the house is so full."

Her glance strayed carelessly over the body of the auditorium, then was suddenly caught and held. A minute later she touched Jean's arm.

"I think there is someone in the stalls trying to attract your attention," she observed quietly.

Even as she spoke, Nick, too, became aware of the same fact.

"Hullo!" he exclaimed. "There's Geoffrey Burke down below. I didn't know he was in town."

Madame de Varigny found the effect upon her companions of this apparently innocent announcement distinctly interesting. It was as though a thrill of disconcerting consciousness ran through the other occupants of the box. Jean flushed suddenly and uncomfortably, and the dark, keen eyes that were watching from behind the fringe of dusky lashes noted an almost imperceptible change of expression flit across the faces of both Lady Anne and Tormarin. In neither case was the change altogether indicative of pleasure. Then, following quickly upon a bow of mutual recognition, the music of the orchestra suddenly ceased and the curtain went up for the second act.

Once more the curtain had fallen, and, to the hum of conversation suddenly released, the lights flashed up into being again over the auditorium. Simultaneously the door of Lady Anne's box was opened from the corridor outside.

"May I come in?" said a voice—a pleasant voice with a gay inflection of laughter running through it as though its owner were quite sure of his welcome—and Burke, big and striking-looking in his immaculate evening kit, his ruddy hair flaming wickedly under the electric lights, strolled into the box.

He shook hands all round, his glance slightly quizzical as it met Jean's, and then Lady Anne presented him to the Comtesse de Varigny.

It almost seemed as though something, some mutual recognition of a kindred spirit, flashed from the warm southern-dark eyes to the fiery red-brown ones, and when, a minute or two later, Burke established himself in the seat next Jean, vacated by Nick, he murmured in a low tone:

"Where did you find that Eastern-looking charmer? I feel convinced I could lose my heart to her without any effort."

Jean could hardly refrain from smiling. This was her first meeting with Burke since the occasion of the scene which had occurred between them in the little parlour at the "honeymooners' inn," and now he met her with as much composure and arrogant assurance as though nothing in the world, other than of a mutually pleasing and amicable nature, had taken place. It was so exactly like Burke, she reflected helplessly.

"Then you had better go and make love to her," she suggested. "There happens to be a husband in the background—a little hypochondriac with quite charming manners—but I don't suppose you would consider that any obstacle."

"None," retorted Burke placidly. "I'm quite certain she can't be in love with him. Her taste would be more—robust, I should say. Where is she stopping?"

"At Claridge's. We met her there this evening. I knew her in Switzerland."

"Well, you shall all come out to supper with me to-morrow:—the Countess included."

Jean shook her head demurely.

"We shall all be back at Staple to-morrow—the Countess excepted. You can take her."

"Then the supper must be to-night," replied Burke serenely.

"What are you doing in town, anyway?" asked Jean. "Is Judith with you?"

"No. Came up to see my tailor"—laconically.

He crossed the box to arrange matters with Lady Anne, and before the curtain rose on the last act it was settled that they should all have supper together after the play.

Later, when Burke had once more resumed his seat next to Jean, Madame de Varigny, whose hearing, like her other senses, was preternaturally acute, caught a whispered plaint breathed into Nick's ear by Lady Anne.

"Now *isn't* that provoking, Nick, darling? Why on earth need Geoffrey Burke have turned up in town on our last evening? I was hoping, later on— if you and I were very discreet and effaced ourselves—that Blaise and Jean might settle things."

Madame de Varigny's eyes remained fixed upon the stage. There was no change in their expression to indicate that Lady Anne's plaintive murmur had at that moment supplied her with the key of the whole situation as it lay between Jean and the two men who were sitting one each side of her.

But the following evening, when, the Staple party having left town, she and Burke were dining alone together at a little restaurant in Soho, the knowledge she had gleaned bore fruit.

Burke never quite knew what impulse it was that had prompted him, as he made his farewells after the supper-party, to murmur in Madame de Varigny's ear, "Dine with me to-morrow night." It was as though the dark, mysterious eyes had spoken to him, compelling him to some sort of friendly overture which the shortness of his acquaintance with their owner would not normally have inspired.

It was not until the coffee and cigarette stage of the little dinner had been reached that Madame de Varigny suddenly shot her dart.

"So you come all the way up from this place, Coombe—Coombe Eavie?—to see Mees Peterson, and hey, presto! She vanish the next morning!"

Burke stared at her almost rudely. The woman's perspicacity annoyed him.

"I came up to see my tailor," he replied curtly.

"*Mais parfaitement!*" she laughed—low, melodious laughter, tinged with a frank friendliness of amusement which somehow smoothed away Burke's annoyance at her shrewd summing up of the situation. "To see your tailor. *Naturellement!* But you were not sorry to encounter Mees Peterson also, *hein?* You enjoyed that?"

Burke's eyes gleamed at her.

"Do you think a dog enjoys looking at the bone that's out of reach?" he said bluntly.

"And is Mees Peterson, then, out of your reach? Me, I do not think so."

Burke was moved to sudden candour.

"She might not be, if it were not that there is another man——"

"*Ce Monsieur Tor-ma-rin?*"

"Yes, confound him!"

"We-ell"—with a long-drawn inflection compact of gentle irony. "You should be able to win against this Monsieur Tor-ma-rin. I think"—regarding him intently—"I think you *will* win."

Burke shook his head gloomily.

"He had first innings. He met her abroad somewhere—rescued her in the snow or something. That rescuing stunt always pays with a woman. All *I* did"—with a short, harsh laugh—"was nearly to break her neck for her out driving one day recently!"

"Is she engaged to Monsieur Tormarin?" asked Madame do Varigny quickly.

"No. Luckily, there's some old affair in the past holds him back."

She nodded.

"You shall marry her," she declared with conviction. "See, Monsieur Bewrke—*aïe, aïe, quel nom!* I am *clairvoyante, prophétesse*, and I tell you that you weel marry zis leetle brown Jean."

Her foreign accent strengthened with her increasing emphasis.

Burke looked dubious.

"I'm afraid your clairvoyance will fail this journey madame. She'll probably marry Tormarin—unless"—his eyes glinting—"I carry her off by force."

Madame de Varigny shook her head emphatically.

"But *no!* I do not see it like that. *Eh bien!* If she become *fiancée*—engaged to him—you shall come to me, and I will tell you how to make sure that she shall not marry him."

"Tell me now!"

"*Non, non!* Win her your own way. Only, if you do not succeed, if Monsieur Tormarin wins her—why, then, come to visit me at Château Varigny."

That night a letter written in the Comtesse de Varigny's flowing foreign handwriting sped on its way to France.

"Matters work towards completion," it ran. "My visit here has chanced *bien à propos*. There is another would-be-lover besides Blaise Tormarin. I have urged him on to win her if he can, for if I have not wrongly estimated Monsieur Tormarin—and I do not think I have—he is of the type to become more deeply in love and less able to master his feelings if he realises that he –has a rival. At present he refrains from declaring himself. The opposition of a rival will probably drive him into a declaration very speedily. When the dog sees the bone about to be taken from him—he snaps! So I encourage this red-headed lion of a man, Monsieur Burke, to pursue his *affaire du cour* with vigour. For if Blaise Tormarin becomes actually betrothed to Mademoiselle Peterson, it will make his punishment the more complete. I pray the God of Justice that it may not now be long delayed!"

CHAPTER XXV
ARRANGED BY TELEPHONE

THE visit to London, if it had not been prolific in the results which Lady Anne had hoped for, had at least accomplished certain things.

It had acted as a brake upon the swiftly turning wheels of two lives precariously poised at the top of that steep hill of which no traveller can see the end, but which very surely leads to heartbreak and disaster, and had sufficed, as Jean had suggested that it might, to restore Nick to a more normal and temperate state of mind.

He and Claire had passed a long hour alone together the day after his return to Staple, and now that the first violent reaction, the first instinctive impulse of unbearable revolt from Sir Adrian's spying and brutality had spent itself they had agreed to shoulder once more the burden fate had laid upon them, to fight on again, just holding fast to the simple knowledge of their love for one another and leaving the ultimate issue to that great, unfathomable Player who "hither and thither moves, and mates, and slays," not with the shadowed vision of our finite eyes but with the insight of eternity.

Jean had seen them coming hand in hand through the cool green glades of the wood where the great decision had been taken, and something in the two young, stern-set faces brought a sudden lump into her throat. She turned swiftly aside, avoiding a meeting, feeling as though here was holy ground upon which not even so close a friend as she could tread without violation.

To Jean herself the week in London had brought a certain, new tranquillity of spirit. Quite ordinarily and without effort—thanks to Lady Anne's skilful stage-management—she and Blaise had been constantly in each other's company, and, with the word "Beloved" murmuring in her heart like some tender undertone of melody, the hours they had shared together were no longer a mingled ecstacy and pain, marred by torturing doubts and fears, but held once more the old magic of that wonder-day at Montavan.

Somehow, the dividing line did not seem to matter very much, now that she was sure that Blaise, on his side of it, was loving her just as she, on hers, loved him. Indeed, at this stage Jean made no very great demands on life. After the agony of uncertainty of the last few months, the calm surety that Blaise loved her seemed happiness enough.

Other sharp edges of existence, too, had smoothed themselves down—as sharp edges have a knack of doing if you wait long enough. Burke seemed to have accepted her last answer as final, and now spared her the effort of contending further with his tempestuous love-making, so that she felt able to continue her friendship with Judith, and her consequent visits to Willow Ferry, with as little *gêne* as though the episode at the "honeymooners' inn" had never taken place. She even began to believe that Burke was genuinely slightly remorseful for his behaviour on that particular occasion.

Apparently he had not made a confidant of his sister over the matter, for it was without the least indication of a back thought of any kind that she approached Jean on the subject of spending a few days with herself and Geoffrey at their bungalow on the Moor.

"Geoff and I are going for a week's blow on Dartmoor, just by way of a 'pick-me-up.' Come with us, Jean; it will do you good after stuffy old London—blow the cobwebs away!"

But here, at least, Jean felt that discretion was the better part of valour. It was true that Burke appeared fairly amenable to reason just at present, but in the informal companionship of daily life in a moorland bungalow it was more than probable that he would become less manageable. And she had no desire for a repetition of that scene in the inn parlour.

Therefore, although the Moor, with its great stretches of gold and purple, its fragrant, heatherly breath and its enfolding silences, appealed to her in a way in which nothing else on earth seemed quite to appeal, pulling at her heartstrings almost as the nostalgia for home and country pulls at the heartstrings of a wanderer, she returned a regretful negative to Judith's invitation. So Burke and Mrs. Craig packed up and departed to Three Fir Bungalow without her, and life at Staple resumed the even tenor of its way.

The weather was glorious, the long, hot summer days melting into balmy nights when the hills and dales amid which the old house was set were bathed in moonlight mystery—transmuted into a wonderland of phantasy, cavernous with shadow where undreamed-of dragons lurked, lambent with opalescent fields of splendour whence uprose the glimmer of half-visioned palaces or the battlemented walls of some ethereal fairy castle.

More than once Jean's thoughts turned wistfully towards the Moor which she had so longed to see by moonlight—Judith's "holy of holies that God must have made for His spirits"—and she felt disposed to blame herself for the robust attack of caution which had impelled her to refuse the invitation to the bungalow.

"One loses half the best things in life by being afraid," she told herself petulantly. "And a second chance to take them doesn't come!"

She felt almost tempted to write to Judith and propose that she should join her at the bungalow for a few days after all if she still had room for her. And then, as is often the way of things just when we are contemplating taking the management of affairs into our own hands, the second chance offered itself without any directing impulse on Jean's part.

The telephone bell rang, and Jean, who was expecting an answer to an important message she had 'phoned through on Lady Anne's behalf, hastened to answer it. Very much to her surprise she found that it was Burke who was speaking at the other end of the wire.

"Is that you, Geoffrey?" she exclaimed in astonishment. "I didn't know your bungalow was on the telephone. I thought you were miles from anywhere!"

"It isn't. And we are," came back Burke's voice. From a certain quality in it she knew that he was smiling. "I'm in Okehampton, 'phoning from a pal's house. I've a message for you from Judy."

"Ye-es?" intoned Jean enquiringly.

"She wants you to come up to-morrow, just for one night. It'll be a full moon and she says you have a hankering to see the Moor by moonlight. Have you?"

"Yes, oh yes!"—with enthusiasm.

"Thought so. It certainly does look topping. Quite worth seeing. Well, look here, Judy's got a party of friends, down from town, who are coming over to us from the South Devon side—going to drive up and stay the night, and the idea is to do a moonlight scramble up on to the top of one of the tors after supper. Are you game?"

"Oh! How heavenly!" This, ecstatically, from Jean.

"How what?"

"Heavenly! *Heavenly!*"—with increasing emphasis.

"Can't you hear?"

"Oh, 'heavenly'—yes, I hear. Yes, it would be rather—if you came."

Even through the 'phone Burke's voice conveyed something of that upsettingly fiery ardour of his.

"I won't come—unless you promise to behave," said Jean warningly.

Bubbling over with pleasure at the prospect unfolded by the invitation, she found it a little difficult to infuse a befitting sternness into her tones.

"Do I need to take fresh vows?" came back Burke's answer, spoken rather gravely. "I made you a promise that day—when we drove back from Dartmoor. I'll keep that."

"I'll never hiss you again till you give me your lips yourself."

The words of the promise rushed vividly into Jean's mind, and now that steady voice through the 'phone, uttering its quiet endorsement of the assurance given, made her feel suddenly ashamed of her suspicions.

"Very well, I'll come then," she said hastily. "How shall I get to you?"

"It's all planned, because we thought—at least we hoped—you'd come. If you'll come down to Okehampton by the three o'clock train from Coombe Eavie, I'll meet you there with the car and drive you up to the bungalow. Judy is going to drive into Newton Abbot early, to do some marketing, and afterwards she'll lunch with her London people—the Holfords. Then they'll all come up together in the afternoon."

"I see. Very well. I'll come to Okehampton by the three train to-morrow afternoon"—repeating his instructions carefully.

"Right. That's all fixed, then."

"Quite. *Mind* you also fix a fine day—or night, rather! Good-bye."

A murmured farewell came back along the wire, and then Jean, replacing the receiver in its clip, ran off to apprise Lady Anne of the arrangements made.

Lady Anne looked up from some village charity accounts which were puckering her smooth brow to smile approval.

"How nice, dear! Quite a charming plan—you'll enjoy it. Especially as there will be nothing to amuse you here to-morrow. I have two village committees to attend—I'm in the chair, so I must go. And Blaise, I know, is booked for a busy day with the estate agent, while Nick is going down to South Devon somewhere for a day's fishing. I think he goes down to-night. Really, it's quite unusually lucky that Judith should have fixed on to-morrow for her moonlight party."

CHAPTER XXVI
MOONLIGHT ON THE MOOR

THE moorland air, warm with its subtle fragrance of gorse—like the scent of peaches when the sun is shining on them—tonic with the faint tang of salt borne by clean winds that had swept across the Atlantic, came to Jean's nostrils crisp and sparkling as a draught of golden wine.

Before her, mile after mile, lay the white road—a sword of civilisation cleaving its way remorselessly across the green wilderness of mossy turf, and on either side rose the swelling hills and jagged peaks of the great tors, melting in the far distance into a vague, formless blur of purple that might be either cloud or tor as it merged at last into the dim haze of the horizon.

"Oh, blessed, blessed Moor!" exclaimed Jean. "How I love it! You know, half the people in the world haven't the least idea what Dartmoor is like. I was enthusing to a woman about it only the other day and she actually said, 'Oh, yes—Dartmoor. It's quite flat, I suppose, isn't it?' *Flat!*" with sweeping disgust.

Burke, his hand on the wheel of the big car which was eating up the miles with the facility of a boa-constrictor swallowing rabbits, smiled at the indignant little sniff with which the speech concluded.

"You don't like dead levels, then?" he suggested.

She shook her head.

"No, I like hills—something to look up to—to climb."

"Spiritual as well as temporal?"

She was silent a moment.

"Why, yes, I think I do."

He smiled sardonically.

"It's just that terrible angelic tendency of yours I complain of. It's too much for any mere material man to live up to. I wish you'd step down to my low level occasionally. You don't seem to be afflicted with human passions like the rest of us"—he added, a note of irritation in his voice.

"Indeed I am!"

Jean spoke impulsively, out of the depths of that inner, almost unconscious self-knowledge which lies within each one of us, dormant until some lance-like question pricks it into spontaneous affirmation. She had hardly heeded whither the conversation was tending, and she regretted her frank confession the instant it had left her lips.

Burke turned and looked at her with a curious speculation in his glance.

"I wonder if that's true?" he said consideringly. "If so, they're still asleep. I'd give something to be the one to rouse them."

There was the familiar, half-turbulent quality in his voice—the sound as of something held in leash. Jean sensed the danger in the atmosphere.

"You'll house one of them—the quite ordinary, commonplace one of bad temper, if you talk like that," she replied prosaically. "You've got to play fair, Geoffrey—keep the spirit of the law as well as the letter."

"All's fair in love and war—as I told you before," he retorted.

"Geoffrey"—indignantly.

"Jean!"—mimicking her. "Well, we won't quarrel about it now. Here we are at our journey's end. Behold the carriage drive!"

The car swung round a sharp bend and then bumped its way up a roughly-made track which served to link a species of cobbled yard, constructed at one side of the bungalow, to the road along which they had come.

The track cleaved its way, rather on the principle of a railway cutting, clean through the abrupt acclivity which flanked the road that side, and rising steeply between crumbling, overhanging banks, fringed with coarse grass and tufted with straggling patches of gorse and heather, debouched on to a broad plateau. Here the road below was completely hidden from view; on all sides there stretched only a limitless vista of wild moorland, devoid of any sign of habitation save for the bare, creeperless walls of the bungalow itself.

As the scene unfolded, Jean became suddenly conscious of a strange sense of familiarity. An inexplicable impress sion of having seen the place on some previous occasion, of familiarity with every detail of it—even to a recognition of its peculiar atmosphere of loneliness—took possession of her. For a moment she could not place the memory. Only she knew that it was associated in her mind with something disagreeable. Even now, as, at Burke's dictation, she waited in the car while he entered the bungalow from the back, passing through in order to admit his guest by way of the front door, which had been secured upon the inside, she was aware of a feeling of intense repugnance.

And then, in a flash, recollection returned to her. This was the house of her dream — of the nightmare vision which had obsessed her during the hours of darkness following her first meeting with Geoffrey Burke.

There stood the solitary dwelling, set amid a wild and desolate country, and to one side of it grew three wretched-looking, scrubby little fir trees, all of them bent in the same direction by the keen winds as they came sweeping across the Moor from the wide Atlantic. Three Fir Bungalow! Why, the very name itself might have prewarned her!

Her eyes fixed themselves on the green-painted door. She knew quite well what must happen next. The door would open and reveal Burke standing on the threshold. She watched it with fascinated eyes.

Presently came the sound of steps, then the grating noise of a key turning stiffly in the lock. The door was flung open and Burke strode across the threshold and came to the side of the car to help her out. Jean waited, half terrified, for his first words. Would they be the words of her dream? She felt that if he chanced to say jokingly, "Will you come into my parlour?" she should scream.

"Go straight in, will you?" said Burke. "I'll just run the car round to the garage and then we might as well get tea ready before the others come. I'm starving, aren't you?"

The spell was broken. The everyday, commonplace words brought with them a rush of overpowering relief, sweeping away the dreamlike sense of unreality and terror, and as Jean nodded and responded gaily, "Absolutely famished!" she could have laughed aloud at the ridiculous fears which had assailed her.

The inside of the bungalow was in charming contrast to its somewhat forbidding exterior. Its living-rooms, furnished very simply but with a shrewd eye to comfort, communicated one with the other by means of double doors which, usually left open, obviated the cramped feeling that the comparatively small size of the rooms might otherwise have produced, while the two lattice windows which each boasted were augmented by French windows opening out on to a verandah which ran the whole length of the building.

Jean, having delightedly explored the front portion of the bungalow, joined Burke in the kitchen, guided thither by the clinking of crockery and the cheerful crackle of a hearth fire wakened into fresh life by the scientific application of a pair of bellows.

"I had no idea you were such a domesticated individual," she remarked, as she watched him carefully warming the brown earthenware teapot as a preliminary to brewing the tea while she busied herself making hot buttered toast.

"Oh, Judy and I are quite independent up here, I assure you," he answered with pardonable pride. "We never bring any of the servants from Willow Ferry, but cook for ourselves. A woman comes over every morning to do the 'chores'—clean the place, and wash up the dishes from the day before, and so on. But beyond that we are self-sufficing."

"Where does your woman come from? I didn't see a house for miles round."

"No, you can't see the place, but there's a little farmstead, tucked away in a hollow about three miles from here, which provides us with cream and butter and eggs—-and with our char-lady."

Jean surveyed with satisfaction a rapidly mounting pile of delicately browned toast, creaming with golden butter.

"There, that's ready," she announced at last. "I do hope Judy and Co. will arrive soon. Hot buttered toast spoils with keeping; it gets all sodden and tastes like underdone shoe leather. Do you think they'll be long?"

Burke threw a glance at the grandfather's clock ticking solemnly away in a corner of the kitchen.

"It's half-past four," he said dubiously. "I don't think we'll risk that luscious-looking toast of yours by waiting for them. I'm going to brew the tea; the kettle's boiling."

"Won't Judith think it rather horrid of us not to wait?"

"Oh, Lord, no! Judy and I never stand on any ceremony with each other. Any old thing might happen to delay them a bit."

Jean, frankly hungry after her spin in the car through the invigorating moorland air, yielded without further protest, and tea resolved itself into a jolly little *tête-à-tête* affair, partaken of in the shelter of the verandah, with the glorious vista of the Moor spread out before her delighted eyes.

Burke was in one of those rare moods of his which never failed to inspire her with a genuine liking for him—when the unruly, turbulent devil within him, so hardly held in check, was temporarily replaced by a certain spontaneous boyishness of a distinctly endearing quality—that "little boy" quality which, in a grown man, always appeals so irresistibly to any woman.

The time slipped away quickly, and it was with a shock of astonishment that Jean realised, on glancing down at the watch on her wrist, that over an hour and a half had gone by while they had been sitting chatting on the verandah.

"Geoffrey! Do you know it's nearly six o'clock! I'm certain something must have happened. Judy and the Holfords would surely be here by now if they hadn't had an accident of some sort."

Burke looked at his own watch.

"Yes," he acquiesced slowly. "It is—getting late." A look of concern spread itself over Jean's face.

"I think we ought to get the car out again and go and see if anything has happened," she said decisively. "They may have had a spill. Were they coming by motor?"

"No. Judy drove down to Newton Abbot in the dog-cart, and the Holfords proposed hiring some sort of conveyance from a livery stable."

"Well, I expect they've had a smash of some kind. I'm sure we ought to go and find out! Was Judy driving that excitable chestnut of yours?"

He shook his head.

"No—a perfectly well-conducted pony, as meek as Moses. We'll give them a quarter of an hour more. If they don't turn up by then, I'll run the car out and we'll investigate."

The minutes crawled by on leaden feet. Jean felt restless and uneasy and more than a trifle astonished that Burke should manifest so little anxiety concerning his sister's whereabouts. Then, just before the quarter of an hour was up, there came the shrill tinkle of a bicycle bell, and a boy cycled up to the gate and, springing off his machine, advanced up the cobbled path with a telegram in his hand.

Jean's face blanched, and she waited in taut suspense while Burke ripped open the ominous orange-coloured envelope.

"What is it?" she asked nervously. "Have they—is it bad news?"

There was a pause before Burke answered. Then, he handed the flimsy sheet to her, remarking shortly:

"They're not coming."

Jean's eyes flew along the brief message.

> "*Returning to-morrow. Am staying the night with Holfords.*
> *Judy.*"

Her face fell.

"How horribly disappointing!" Her glance fluttered, regretfully to the faint disc of the moon showing like a pallid ghost of itself in a sky still luminous with the afternoon sunlight.

"I shan't see my moonlit Moor to-night after all!" she continued. "I wonder what has happened to make them change their plans?"

Burke volunteered no suggestion but stood staring moodily at the swiftly receding figure of the telegraph boy.

"Well," Jean braced herself to meet the disappointment, "there's nothing for it but for you to run me back home, Geoffrey. We ought to start at once."

"Very well. I'll go and get the car out," he answered. "I suppose it's the only thing to be done."

He moved off in the direction of the garage, Jean walking rather disconsolately beside him.

"I *am* disappointed!" she declared. "I just hate the sight of a telegraph boy! They always spoil things. I rather wonder you get your telegrams delivered at this outlandish spot," she added musingly.

"Oh, of course we have to pay mileage. There's no free delivery to the 'back o' beyond'!"

As he spoke, Burke vanished into the semi-dusk of the garage, and presently Jean heard sounds suggestive of ineffectual attempts to start the engine, accompanied by a muttered curse or two. A few minutes later Burke reappeared, looking Rather hot and dusty and with a black smear of oil across his cheek.

"You'd better go back to the bungalow," he said gruffly.

"There's something gone wrong with the works, and it will take me a few minutes to put matters right."

Jean nodded sympathetically and retreated towards the house, leaving him to tinker with the car's internals. It was growing chilly—the "cool of the evening" manifests itself early up on Dartmoor—and she was not at all sorry to find herself indoors. The wind had dropped, but a curious, still sort of coldness seemed to be permeating the atmosphere, faintly moist, and, as Jean stood at the window, gazing out half absently, she suddenly noticed a delicate blur of mist veiling the low-lying ground towards the right of the bungalow. Her eyes hurriedly swept the wide expanse in front of her. The valleys between the distant tors were hardly visible. They had become mere basins cupping wan lakes of wraithlike vapour which, even as she watched them, crept higher, inch by inch, as though responding to some impulse of a rising tide.

Jean had lived long enough in Devonshire by this time to know the risks of being caught in a mist on Dartmoor, and she sped out of the room, intending to go to the garage and warn Burke that he must hurry. He met her on the threshold of the bungalow, and she turned back with him into the room she had just quitted.

"Are you ready?" she asked eagerly. "There's a regular moor mist coming on. The sooner we start the better."

He looked at her oddly. He was rather pale and his eyes were curiously bright.

"The car won't budge," he said. "I've been tinkering at her all this time to no purpose."

Jean stared at him, a vague apprehension of disagreeable possibilities presenting itself to her mind. Their predicament would be an extremely awkward one if the car remained recalcitrant!

"Won't budge?" she repeated. "But you must make it budge, Geoffrey. We can't—we can't *stay* here! What's gone wrong with it?"

Burke launched out into a string of technicalities which left Jean with a confused feeling that the mechanism of a motor must be an invention of the devil designed expressly for the chastening of human nature, but from which she succeeded in gathering the bare skeleton fact that something had gone radically wrong with the car's running powers.

Her apprehensions quickened.

"What are we to do?" she asked blankly.

"Make the best of a bad job—and console each other," he suggested lightly.

She frowned a little. It did not seem to her quite the moment for jesting.

"Don't be ridiculous, Geoffrey," she said sharply. "We've got to get back *somehow*. What can you do?"

"I can't do anything more than I've done. Here we are and here we've got to stay."

"You know that's impossible," she said, in a quick, low voice.

He looked at her with a sudden devil-may-care glint in his eyes.

"You never can tell beforehand whether things are impossible or not. I know I used to think that heaven on earth was—impossible," he said slowly. "I'm not so sure now." He drew a step nearer her. "Would you mind so dreadfully if we had to stay here, little Miss Prunes-and-Prisms?"

Jean stared at him in amazement—in amazement which slowly turned to incredulous horror as a sudden almost unbelievable idea flashed into her mind, kindled into being by the leaping, half-exultant note in his tones.

"Geoffrey———" Her lips moved stiffly, even to herself, her voice sounded strange and hoarse. "Geoffrey, I don't believe there is anything wrong with the car at all!... Or if there is, you've tampered with it on purpose.... You're not being straight with me——"

She broke off, her startled gaze searching his face as though she would wring the truth from him. Her eyes were very wide and dilated, but back of the anger that blazed in them lurked fear—stark fear.

For a moment Burke was silent. Then he spoke, with a quiet deliberateness that held something ominous, inexorable, in its very calm.

"You're right," he said slowly. "I've not been straight with you. But I'll be frank with you now. The whole thing—asking you to come here to-day, the moonlight expedition for to-night—everything—was all fixed up, planned solely to get you here. The car won't run for the simple reason that I've put it out of action. I wasn't quite sure whether or no you could drive a car, you see!"

"I can't," said Jean. Her voice was quite expressionless.

"No? So much the better, then. But I wasn't going to leave any weak link in the chain by which I hold you."

"By which you hold me?" she repeated dully. She felt stunned, incapable of protest, only able to repeat, parrotlike, the words he had just used.

"Yes. Don't you understand the position? It's clear enough, I should think!" He laughed a little recklessly. "Either you promise to marry me, in which case I'll take you home at once—the car's not damaged beyond repair—or you stay here, here at the bungalow with me, until tomorrow morning."

With a sharp cry she retreated from him, her face ash-white.

"No—no! Not that!" The poignancy of that caught-back cry wrenched the words from his lips in hurrying, vehement disclaimer. "You'll be perfectly safe—as safe as though you were my sister. Don't look like that.... Jean! Jean! Could you imagine that I would hurt you—you when I worship—my little white love?" The words rushed out in a torrent, hoarse and shaken and passionately tender. "Before God, no! You'll be utterly safe, Jean, sweetest, beloved—I swear it!" His voice steadied and deepened. "Sacred as the purest love in the whole world could hold you." He was silent a moment; then, as the tension in her face gradually relaxed, he went on: "But the world won't know that!" The note of tenderness was gone now, swept away by the resurgence of a fierce relentlessness—triumphant, implacable—that meant winning at all costs. "The world won't know that," he repeated. "After tonight, for your own sake—because a woman's reputation cannot stand the breath of scandal, you'll be *compelled* to marry me. You'll have no choice."

Jean stood quite still, staring in front of her. Once her lips moved, but no sound came from them. Slowly, laboriously almost, she was realising exactly what had happened, her mind adjusting itself to the recognition of the trap in which she had been caught.

Her dream had come true, after all—horribly, inconceivably true.

The heavy silence which had fallen seemed suddenly filled with the dream-Burke's voice—mocking and exultant:

"... you'll be stamped with the mark of the beast for ever. It's too late to try and run away.... It's too late."

CHAPTER XXVII
INTO THE MIST

"THEN that telegram—that telegram from Judy—I suppose that was all part of the plan?"

Jean felt the futility of the question even while she asked it. The answer was so inevitable.

"Yes"—briefly. "I knew that Judy meant staying the night with her friends before she went away. She sent the wire—because I asked her to."

"Judy did that?"

There was such an immeasurable anguish of reproach in the low, quick-spoken whisper that Burke felt glad Judith was not there to hear it. Had it been otherwise, she might have regretted the share she had taken in the proceedings, small as it had been. She was not a man, half-crazed by love, in whose passion-blurred vision nothing counted save the winning of the one woman, nor had she known Burke's plan in its entirety.

"Yes, Judy sent the wire," he said.. "But give her so much credit, she didn't know that I intended—this. She only knew that I wanted another chance of seeing you alone—of asking you to be my wife, and I told her that you wouldn't come up to the bungalow unless you believed that she would be there too. I didn't think you'd trust yourself alone with me again—after that afternoon at the inn"—with blunt candour.

"No. I shouldn't have done."

"So you see I had to think of something—some way. And it was you yourself who suggested this method."

"I?"—incredulously.

"Yes. Don't you remember what you told me that day I drove you back from Dartmoor '*A woman's happiness depends upon her reputation.*'"

She looked at him quickly, recalling the scattered details of that afternoon—Burke's gibes at what he believed to be her fear of gossiping tongues and her own answer to his taunts: "No woman can afford to ignore scandal." And then, following upon that, his sudden, curious absorption in his own thoughts.

The remembrance of it all was like a torchlight flashed into a dark place, illuminating what had been hidden and inscrutable. She spoke swiftly.

"And it was then—that afternoon—you thought of this?"

He bent his head.

"Yes," he acknowledged.

Jean was silent. It was all clear now—penetratingly so.

"And the Holfords? Are there any such people?" she asked drearily.

She scarcely knew what prompted her to put so purposeless and unimportant a question. Actually, she felt no interest at all in the answer. It could not make the least difference to her present circumstances.

Perhaps it was a little the feeling that this trumpery process of question and answer served to postpone the inevitable moment when she must face the situation in which she found herself—face it in its simple crudeness, denuded of unessential whys and wherefores.

"Oh, yes, the Holfords are quite real," answered Burke. "And so is the plan for an expedition to one of the tors by moonlight. Only it will be carried out to-morrow night instead of to-night. To-night is for the settlement between you and me."

The strained expression of utter, shocked incredulity was gradually leaving Jean's face. The unreal was becoming real, and she knew now what she was up against; the hard, reckless quality of Burke's voice left her no illusions.

"Geoffrey," she said quietly, "you won't really do this thing?"

If she had hoped to move him by a simple, straightforward appeal to the best that might be in him, she failed completely. For the moment, all that was good in him, anything chivalrous which the helplessness of her womanhood might have invoked, was in abeyance. He was mere primitive man, who had succeeded in carrying off the woman he meant to mate and was prepared to hold her at all costs.

"I told you I would compel you," he said doggedly. "That I would let nothing in the world stand between you and me. And I meant every word I said. You've no way out now—except marriage with me."

The imperious decision of his tone roused her fighting spirit.

"Do you imagine," she broke out scornfully, "that—after this—I would ever marry you?... I wouldn't marry you if you were the last man on earth! I'd die sooner!"

"I daresay you would," he returned composedly. "You've too much grit to be afraid of death. Only, you see, that doesn't happen to be the alternative. The alternative is a smirched reputation. Tarnished a little—after to-night—even if you marry me; dragged utterly in the mire if you refuse. I'm putting it before you with brutal frankness, I know. But I want you to realise just what it means and to promise that you'll be my wife before it's too late—while I can still get you back to Staple during the hours of propriety"—smiling grimly.

She looked at him with a slow, measured glance of bitter contempt.

"Even a tarnished reputation might be preferable to marriage with you—more endurable," she added, with the sudden tormented impulse of a trapped thing to hurt back.

"You don't really believe that"—impetuously—"I know *I know* I could make you happy! You'd be the one woman in the world to me. And I don't think"—more quietly—"that you could endure a slurred name, Jean."

She made no answer. Every word he spoke only made it more saliently clear to her that she was caught—bound hand and foot in a web from which there was no escape. Yet, little as Burke guessed it, the actual question of "what people might say" did not trouble her to any great extent. She was too much her father's own daughter to permit a mere matter of reputation to force her into a distasteful marriage.

Not that she minimised the value of good repute. She was perfectly aware that if she refused to marry Burke, and he carried out his threat of detaining her at the bungalow until the following morning, she would have a heavy penalty to pay—the utmost penalty which a suspicious world exacts from a woman, even though she may be essentially innocent, in whose past there lurks a questionable episode.

But she had courage enough to face the consequences of that refusal, to stand up to the clatter of poisonous tongues that must ensue; and trust enough to bank on the loyalty of her real friends, knowing it would be the same splendid loyalty that she herself would have given to any one of them in like circumstances. For Jean was a woman who won more than mere lip-service from those who called themselves her friends.

Burke had never been more mistaken in his calculations than when he counted upon forcing her hand by the mere fear of scandal. But none the less he held her—and held her in the meshes of a far stronger and more binding net, had he but realised it.

Looking back upon the episode from which her present predicament had actually sprung, Jean could almost have found it in her heart to smile at the relative importance which, at the time, that same incident had assumed in her eyes.

It had seemed to her, then, that for Blaise ever to hear that she had been locked in a room with Burke, had spent an uncounted, hour or so with him at the "honeymooners' inn" would be the uttermost calamity that could befall her.

He would never believe that it had been by no will of hers—so she had thought at the time—and that fierce lover's jealousy which had been the origin of their quarrel, and of all the subsequent mutual misunderstandings and aloofness, would be roused to fresh life, and his distrust of her become something infinitely more difficult to combat.

But compared with the present situation which confronted her, the happenings of that past day faded into insignificance. She stood, now, face to face with a choice such as surely few women had been forced to make.

Whichever way she decided, whichever of the two alternatives she accepted, her happiness must pay the price. Nothing she could ever say or do, afterwards, would set her right in the eyes of the man whose belief in her meant everything. Whether she agreed to marry Burke, returning home in the odour of sanctity within the next hour or two, or whether she refused and returned the next morning—free, but with the incontrovertible fact of a night spent at Burke's bungalow, alone with him, behind her, Blaise would never trust or believe in her love for him again.

And if she promised to marry Burke and so save her reputation, it must automatically mean the end of everything between herself and the man she loved—the dropping of an iron curtain compared with which the wall built up out of their frequent misunderstandings in the past seemed something as trifling and as easily demolished as a card house.

On the other hand, if she risked her good name and kept her freedom, she would be equally as cut off from him. Not that she feared Blaise would take the blackest view of the affair—she was sure that he believed in her enough not to misjudge her as the world might do—but he would inevitably think that she had deliberately chosen to spend an afternoon on the Moor alone with Burke—"playing with fire" exactly as he had warned her not to, and getting her fingers burnt in consequence—and he would accept it as a sheer denial of the silent pledge of love understood which bound them together.

He would never trust her again—nor forgive her. No man could. Love's loyalty, rocked by the swift currents of jealousy and passion, is not of the same quality as the steady loyalty of friendship—that calm, unshakable confidence which may exist between man and man or woman and woman.

Moreover—and here alone was where the fear of gossip troubled her—even if the inconceivable happened and Blaise forgave and trusted her again, she could not go to him with a slurred name, give him herself—when the gift was outwardly tarnished. The Tormarin pride was unyielding as a rock—and Tormarin women had always been above suspicion. She could not break the tradition of an old name—do that disservice to the man she loved! No, if she could find no way out of the web in which she had been caught she was set as far apart from Blaise as though they had never met. Only the agony of meeting and remembrance would be with her for the rest of life!

Jean envisaged very clearly the possibilities that lay ahead—envisaged them with a breathless, torturing perception of their imminence. It was to be a fight—here and now—for the whole happiness that life might hold.

She turned to Burke, breaking at last the long silence which had descended between them.

"And what do you suppose I feel towards you, Geoffrey? Will you be content to have your wife think of you—as I must think?"

A faint shadow flitted across his face. The quiet scorn of her words—their underlying significance—flicked him on the raw.

"I'll be content to have you as my wife—at any price," he said stubbornly. "Jean"—a sudden urgency in his tones—"try to believe I hate all this as much as you do. When you're my wife, I'll spend my life in teaching you to forget it—in—wiping the very memory of to-day out of your mind."

"I shall never forgot it," she said slowly. Then, bitterly: "I wonder why you even offer me a choice—when you know; that it is really no choice."

"Why? Because I swore to you that you should give me what I want—that I wouldn't take even a kiss from you again by force. But"—unevenly—"I didn't know what it meant—the waiting!"

Outside, the mist had thickened into fog, curtaining the windows. The light had dimmed to a queer, glimmering dusk, changing the values of things, and out of the shifting shadows her white face, with its scarlet line of scornful mouth, gleamed at him—elusive, tantalising as a flower that sways out of reach. In the uncertain half-light which struggled in through the dulled window-panes there was something provocative, maddening—a kind of etherealised lure of the senses in the wavering, shadowed loveliness of her. The man's pulses leaped; something within him slipped its leash.

"Kiss me!" he demanded hoarsely. "Don't keep me waiting any longer. Give me your lips... now... now..."

She sprang aside from him, warding him off. Her eyes stormed at him out of her white face.

"You promised!" she cried, her voice sharp with fear. "You promised!"

The tension of the next moment strained her nerves to breaking-point.

Then he fell back. Slowly his arms dropped to his sides without touching her, his hands clenching with the effort that it cost him.

"You're right," he said, breathing quickly. "I promised. I'll keep my promise." Then, vehemently: "Jean, why won't you let me take you home? I could put the car right in ten minutes. Come home!"

There was unmistakable appeal in his tones. It was obvious he hated the task to which he had set himself, although he had no intention of yielding.

She stared at him doubtfully.

"Will you? Will you take me home, Geoffrey?... Or"—bitterly—"is this only another trap?"

"I'll take you home—at once, now—if you'll promise to be my wife. Jean, it's better than waiting till to-morrow—till circumstances force you into it!" he urged.

She was silent, thinking rapidly. That sudden break in Burke's control, when for a moment she had feared his promise would not hold him, had warned her to put an end to the scene—if only temporarily—as quickly as possible.

"You are very trusting," she said, forcing herself to speak lightly. "How do you know that I shall not give you the pledge you ask merely in order to get home—and then decline to keep it? I think"—reflectively—"I should be quite justified in the circumstances."

He smiled a little and shook his head.

"No," he said quietly. "I'm not afraid of that. If you give me your word, I know you'll keep it. You wouldn't be—you—if you could do otherwise."

For a moment, Jean was tempted, fiercely tempted to take his blind belief in her and use it to extricate herself from the position into which he had thrust her. As she herself had said, the circumstances were such as almost to justify her. Yet something within her, something that was an integral part of her whole nature, rebelled against the idea of giving a promise which, from the moment that she made it, she would have no smallest intention of keeping. It would be like the breaking of a prisoner's given parole—equally mean and dishonourable.

With a little mental shrug she dismissed the idea and the brief temptation. She must find some other way, some other road to safety. If only he would leave her alone, leave her just long enough for her to make a rush for it—out of the house into that wide wilderness of mist-wrapped moor!

It would be a virtually hopeless task to find her way to any village or to the farmstead, three miles away, of which Burke had spoken. She knew that. Even moorwise folk not infrequently entirely lost their bearings in a Dartmoor mist, and, as far as she herself was concerned, she had not the remotest idea in which direction the nearest habitation lay. It would be a hazardous experiment—fraught with danger. But danger was preferable to the dreadful safety of the bungalow.

In a brief space, stung to swift decision by that tense moment when Burke's self-mastery had given way, she had made up her mind to risk the open moor. But, for that she must somehow contrive to be left alone. She must gain time—time to allay Burke's suspicions by pretending to make the best of the matter, and then, on some pretext or other, get him out of the room. It was the sole way of escape she could devise.

"Well, which is it to be?" Burke's voice broke in harshly upon the wild turmoil of her thoughts. "Your promise—and Staple within an hour and a half? Or—the other alternative?"

"I don't think it can be either—yet," she said quietly. "What you're asking—it's too big a question for a woman to decide all in a minute. Don't you see"—with a rather shaky little laugh—"it means my whole life? I—I must have time, Geoffrey. I can't decide now. What time is it?"

He struck a match, holding the flame close to the dial of his watch.

"Seven o'clock."

"Only that?" The words escaped her involuntarily. It seemed hours, an eternity, since she had read those few brief words contained in Judith's telegram. And it was barely an hour ago!

"Then—then I can have a little time to think it over," she said after a moment. "We could get back to Staple by ten if we left here at eight-thirty?"

"There or thereabouts. We should have to go slow through this infernal mist Jean"—his voice took on a note of passionate entreaty—"sweetest, won't you give me your promise and let me take you home? You shall never regret it. I——"

"Oh, hush!" she checked him quickly. "I can't answer you now, Geoffrey. I must have time—time. Don't press me now."

"Very well." There was an unaccustomed gentleness in his manner. Perhaps something in the intense weariness of her tones appealed to him. "Are you very tired, Jean?"

"Do you know"—she spoke with some surprise, as though the idea had only just presented itself to her—"do you know, I believe I'm rather hungry! It sounds very material of me"—laughing a little. "A woman in my predicament ought to be quite above—or beyond—mere pangs of hunger."

"Hungry! By Jove, and well you might be by this hour of the day!" he exclaimed remorsefully. "Look here, we'll have supper. There are some chops in the larder. We'll cook them together—and then you'll see what a really domesticated husband I shall make."

He spoke with a new gaiety, as though he felt very sure of her ultimate decision and glad that the strain of the struggle of opposing wills was past.

"Chops! How heavenly! I'm afraid"—apologetically—"it's very unromantic of me, Geoffrey!"

He laughed and, striking a match, lit the lamp. "Disgustingly so! But there are moments for romance and moments for chops. And this is distinctly the moment for chops. Come along and help me cook 'em."

He flashed a keen glance at her face as the sudden lamplight dispelled the shadows of the room. But there was nothing in it to contradict the insouciance of her speech. Her cheeks were a little flushed and her eyes very bright, but her smile was quite natural and unforced. Burke reflected that women were queer, unfathomable creatures. They would fight you to the last ditch—and then suddenly surrender, probably liking you in secret all the better for having mastered them.

He had forgotten that he was dealing with a daughter of Jacqueline Mavory. All the actress that was Jean's mother came out in her now, called up from some hidden fount of inherited knowledge to meet the imperative need of the moment.

No one, watching Jean as she accompanied Burke to the kitchen premises and assisted him in the preparation of their supper, would have imagined that she was acting her part in any other capacity than that of willing playmate. She was wise enough not to exhibit any desire to leave him alone during the process of carrying the requisites for the meal from the kitchen into the living-room. She had noticed the sudden mistrust in his watchful eyes and the way in which he had instantly followed her when, at the commencement of the proceedings, she had unthinkingly started off down the passage from the kitchen, carrying a small tray of table silver in her hand, and thereafter she refrained from giving him the slightest ground for suspicion. Together they cooked the chops, together laid the table, and finally sat down to share the appetising results of their united efforts.

Throughout the little meal Jean preserved an attitude of detached friendliness, laughing at any small joke that cropped up in the course of conversation and responding gaily enough to Burke's efforts to entertain her. Now and again, as though unconsciously, she would fall into a brief reverie, apparently preoccupied with the choice that lay before her, and at these moments Burke would refrain from distracting her attention, but would watch intently, with those burning eyes of his, the charming face and sensitive mouth touched to a sudden new seriousness that appealed.

By the time the meal had drawn to an end, his earlier suspicions had been lulled into tranquillity, and over the making of the coffee he became once more the big, overgrown schoolboy and jolly comrade of his less tempestuous moments. It almost seemed as though, to please her, to atone in a measure for the mental suffering he had thrust on her, he was endeavouring to keep the vehement lover in the background and show her only that side of himself which would serve to reassure her.

"I rather fancy myself at coffee-making," he told her, as he dexterously manipulated the little coffee machine. "There!" — pouring out two brimming cups — "taste that, and then tell me if it isn't the best cup of coffee you ever met."

Jean sipped it obediently, then made a wry face.

"Ough!" she ejaculated in disgust. "You've forgotten the sugar!"

As she had herself slipped the sugar basin out of sight when he was collecting the necessary coffee paraphernalia on to a tray, the oversight was not surprising.

It was a simple little ruse, its very simplicity it's passport to success. The naturalness of it—Jean's small, screwed-up face of disgust and the hasty way in which she set her cup down after tasting its contents—might have thrown the most suspicious of mortals momentarily off his guard.

"By Jove, so I have!" Instinctively Burke sprang up to rectify the omission. "I never take it myself, so I forgot all about it. I'll get you some in a second."

He was gone, and before he was half-way down the passage leading to the kitchen, Jean, moving silently and swiftly as a shadow, was at the doors of the long French window, her fingers fumbling for the catch.

A draught of cold, mist-laden air rushed into the room, while a slender form stood poised for a brief instant on the threshold, silhouetted against the white curtain of the fog. Then followed a hurried rush of flying footsteps, a flitting shadow cleaving the thick pall of vapour, and a moment later the wreaths of pearly mist came filtering unhindered, into an empty room.

Blindly Jean plunged through the dense mist that hung outside, her feet sinking into the sodden earth as she fled across the wet grass. She had no idea where the gate might be, but sped desperately onwards till she rushed full tilt into the bank of mud and stones which fenced the bungalow against the moor. The sudden impact nearly knocked all the breath out of her body, but she dared not pause. She trusted that his search for the hidden sugar basin might delay Burke long enough to give her a few minutes' start, but she knew very well that he might chance upon it at any moment, and then, discovering her flight, come in pursuit.

Clawing wildly at the bank with hands and feet, slipping, sliding, bruised by sharp-angled stones and pricked by some unseen bushy growth of gorse, she scrambled over the bank and came sliding down upon her hands and knees into the hedge-trough dug upon its further side. And even as she picked herself up, shaken and gasping for breath, she heard a cry from the bungalow, and then the sound of running steps and Burke's voice calling her by name.

"Jean! Jean! You little fool!... Come back! Come back!" She heard him pause to listen for her whereabouts. Then he shouted again. "Come back! You'll kill yourself! Jean! Jean!...."

But she made no answer. Distraught by fear lest he should overtake her, she raced recklessly ahead into the fog, heedless of the fact that she could not see a yard in front of her—even glad of it, knowing that the mist hung like a shielding curtain betwixt her and her pursuer.

The strange silence of the mist-laden atmosphere hemmed her round like the silence of a tomb, broken only by the sucking sound of the oozy turf as it pulled at her feet, clogging her steps. Lance-sharp spikes of gorse stabbed at her ankles as she trod it underfoot, and the permeating moisture in the air soaked swiftly through her thin summer frock till it clung about her like a winding-sheet.

Her breath was coming in sobbing gasps of stress and terror; her heart pounded in her breast; her limbs, impeded by her clinging skirts, felt as though they were weighted down with lead.

Then, all at once, seeming close at hand in the misleading fog which plays odd tricks with sound as well as sight, she heard Burke's voice, cursing as he ran.

With the instinct of a hunted thing she swerved sharply, stumbled, and lurched forward in a vain effort to regain her balance. Then it seemed as though the ground wore suddenly cut from under her feet, and she fell... down, down through the mist, with a scattering of crumbling earth and rubble, and lay, at last, a crumpled, unconscious heap in the deep-cut track that linked the moor road to the bungalow.

CHAPTER XXVIII
THEY WHO WAITED

LADY ANNE sat gazing absently into the heart of the fire, watching the restless leap of the flames and the little scattered handfuls of sparks, like golden star dust, tossed upward into the dark hollow of the chimney by the blazing logs. The "warm and sunny south"—at least, that part of it within a twelve-mile radius of Dartmoor—is quite capable, on occasion, of belying its guide-book designation, particularly towards the latter end of summer, and there was a raw dampness in the atmosphere this evening which made welcome company of a fire.

It seemed a little lonely without Jean's cheery presence, and Lady Anne, conscious of a craving for human companionship, glanced impatiently at the clock. Blaise should surely have returned by now from his all-day conference with the estate agent.

She had not much longer to wait. The quick hoof-beats of a trotting horse sounded on the drive outside, and a few minutes later the door of the room was thrown open and Blaise himself strode in.

"Well, madonna?" He stooped and kissed her. "Been a lonely lady to-day without all your children?"

She smiled up at him.

"Just a little," she acknowledged. "When I came back from those stupid committees, which are merely an occasion for half the old tabbies in the village to indulge in a squabble with the other half, I couldn't help feeling it would have been nice to find Jean here to laugh over them with me. Jean's sense of humour is refreshing; it never lets one down. However, I suppose she's enjoying her beloved Moor by moonlight, so I mustn't grumble."

Blaise shook his head.

"Much moonlight they'll see!" he observed. "I rode through a thick mist coming back from Hedge Barton. It'll he a blanket fog on Dartmoor to-night."

"Oh, poor Jean! She'll he so disappointed."

Tormarin sat down on the opposite side of the hearth and lit a cigarette. The dancing firelight flickered across his face. He was thinner of late, his mother thought with a quick pang. The lines of the well-beloved face had deepened; it had a worn—almost ascetic—look, like that of a man who is constantly contending against something.

Lady Anne looked across at him almost beseechingly.

"Son," she said, "have you quite made up your mind to let happiness pass you by?"

He started, roused out of the reverie into which he had fallen.

"I don't think I've got any say in the matter," he replied quietly. "I've forfeited my rights in that respect. You know that."

"And Jean? Are you going to make her forfeit her rights, too?"

"She'll find happiness—somehow—elsewhere. It would be a very short-lived affair with me"—bitterly. "After what has happened, it's evident I'm not to be trusted with a woman's happiness."

There were sounds of arrival in the hall. Nick's voice could be heard issuing instructions about the bestowal of his fishing tackle. Lady Anne spoke quickly.

"I don't think so, Blaise. Not with the happiness of the woman you love." She laid her hand on his shoulder as she passed him on her way into the hall to welcome the wanderer returned. "Tell Jean," she advised, "and see what she says. I think you'll find she'd be willing to risk it."

When she had left the room Blaise remained staring impassively into the fire. His expression gave no indication as to whether or not Lady Anne's advice had stirred him to any fresh impulse of decision, and when, presently, his mother and Nick entered the room together, he addressed the latter as casually as though no emotional depths had been stirred by the recent conversation.

"Hullo, Nick! Had good sport?"

"Only so-so. We had a jolly time, though—out at Het-worthy Bridge. But I had the deuce of a business getting back from Exeter this evening. It was so misty in places we could hardly see to drive the car."

Blaise nodded.

"Yes, I know. I found the same. It's a surprising change in the weather."

"Poor Jean will have had a disappointing trip to Dartmoor," put in Lady Anne. "The mist is certain to be bad up there."

"Dartmoor? But she didn't go—surely?" And Nick glanced from one to the other questioningly.

"Oh, yes, she did. It was quite clear in the afternoon when she started— looked like being a lovely night."

"But—but——"

Nick stammered and came to a halt. There was a look of bewilderment in his eyes.

"But who's she gone with?" he demanded at last. "I thought she said she intended stopping the night with Judith and Burke at their bungalow?"

"So she did," replied Blaise. "Why? Have you any objection?"—smiling.

"No. Only"—Nick frowned—"I don't quite understand it Judith isn't *on* the Moor."

"Not on the Moor?" broke simultaneously from Lady Anne and Blaise.

"How do you know, Nick?" added the latter gravely.

"Why, because"—Nick's face wore an expression of puzzled concern— "because I saw Judith in Newton Abbot late this evening."

Blaise leaned forward, a sudden look of concentration on his face.

"You saw Judith?" he repeated. "What time?"

"It must have been nearly eight o'clock. I was buzzing along in Jim Cresswell's car to catch the seven forty-five up train, and I saw Judith with one of the Holfords—you know, those people from London—turning into the gateway of a house. I expect it was the place the Holfords are stopping at. They didn't see me."

"You're quite certain? You've made no mistake?" said Blaise sharply.

"Of course I've made no mistake. Think I don't know Judy when I see her? But what's the meaning of it, Blaise?"

Tormarin rose to his feet, tossing the stump of his cigarette into the fire.

"I'm not sure," he said slowly. "But I'm going to find out. Madonna"— turning to his mother—"did Jean tell you just exactly what Judith said when she rang her up on the'phone about this moonlight plan?"

"It wasn't Judith who rang up," replied Lady Anne, a faint misgiving showing itself in her face. "It was Geoffrey who gave the message."

Tormarin looked at her with a sudden awakened expression in his eyes. There was dread in them, too—keen dread. The expression of a man who, all at once, sees the thing he values more than anything in the whole world being torn from him—dragged forcibly away from the shelter he could give into some unspeakable darkness of disaster.

"That settles it." He pressed his finger against the bell-push and held it there, and when Baines came hurrying in response to the imperative summons, he said curtly: "Order me a fresh horse round at once—*at once*, mind—tell Harding to saddle Orion, and to look sharp about it."

"Blaise"—Lady Anne's obvious uneasiness had deepened to a sharp anxiety—"Blaise, what are you going to do? What—what are you afraid of?"

He looked her straight in the eyes.

"I'm afraid of just what you are afraid of, madonna—of the devil let loose in Geoffrey Burke."

"And—and you're going to look for her—for Jean?"

"I'm going to find her," he corrected quietly.

Gravity had set its seal on all three faces. Each was conscious of the same fear—the fear they could not put into words.

"But why do you take Orion?" asked Nick. "The little thoroughbred mare—Redwing—would do the journey quicker and he lighter of foot over any marshy ground on the Moor."

"Orion can go where he chooses," returned Tormarin. "And he'll choose to-night. Redwing is a little bit of a thing, though she's game as a pebble. But she couldn't carry—two."

The significance of Tormarin's choice of his big roan hunter, three-parts thoroughbred and standing sixteen hands, came home to Nick. He nodded without comment.

Silently he and Lady Anne accompanied Blaise into the hall. From the gravelled drive outside came the impatient stamping of Orion's iron-shod hoofs. Just at the last Lady Anne clung to her son's arm.

"You'll bring her back, Blaise?" she urged, a quiver in her voice.

"I'll bring her back, madonna," he answered quietly. "Don't worry."

A minute later he and the great roan horse were lost to sight in the mirk of the night. Only the beat of galloping hoofs was flung back to the two who were left to watch and wait, muffled and vague through the shrouding mist like the sound of a distant drum.

CHAPTER XXIX
THE GOLDEN HOUR

ORION had fully justified Blaise's opinion of his capabilities. As though the great horse had gathered that there was trouble abroad to which he must not add, he had needed neither whip nor spur as he carried his master with long, sweeping strides over the miles that lay betwixt Staple and the Moor. He was as fresh as paint, and the rush through the cool night, under a rider with hands as light as a woman's and who sat him with a flexible ease, akin to that of a Cossack, had not distressed him in the very least.

Now they were climbing the last long slope of the white road that approached the bungalow, the reins lying loosely on Orion's neck.

The mist had lifted a little in places, and a watery-looking moon peered through the clouds now and again, throwing a vague, uncertain light over the blurred and sombre moorland.

Tormarin had no very definite plan of campaign in his mind. He felt convinced that he should find Jean at the bungalow. If, contrary to his expectation, she were not there, nor anyone else to whom he could apply for information as to her whereabouts, he would have to consider what his next move must be.

Meanwhile, his thoughts were preoccupied with the main fact that she had failed to return home. If she had accepted Burke's invitation to the bungalow, believing that Judith and the Holfords would be of the party, how was it that she had not at once returned when she discovered that for some reason they were not there?

Some weeks ago—during the period when she was defiantly investigating the possibilities of an "unexploded bomb"—it was quite possible that the queer recklessness which sometimes tempts a woman to experiment in order to see just how far she may go—the mysterious delight that the feminine temperament appears to derive from dancing on the edge of a precipice—might have induced her to remain and have tea with Burke, chaperon or no chaperon. And then it was quite on the cards that Burke's lawless disregard of anything in the world except the fulfilment of his own desires might have engineered the rest, and he might have detained her at the bungalow against her will.

But Blaise could not believe that a *tête-à-tête* tea with Burke would hold any attraction for Jean now—not since that day, just before the visit to London, when he and she had been discussing the affairs of Nick and Claire and had found, quite suddenly, that their own hearts were open to each other and that with the spoken word, "Beloved," the misunderstandings of the past had faded away, to be replaced by a wordless trust and belief.

But if it *had* attracted her, if—knowing precisely how much the man she loved would condemn—she had still deliberately chosen to spend an afternoon with Burke, why, then, Blaise realised with a swift pang that she was no longer his Jean at all but some other, lesser woman. Never again the "little comrade" whose crystalline honesty of soul and sensitive response to all that was sweet and wholesome and true had come into his scarred life to jewel its arid places with a new blossoming of the rose of love.

He tried to thrust the thought away from him. It was just the kind of thing that Nesta would have done, playing off one man against the other with the innate instinct of the born coquette. But not Jean—not Jean of the candid eyes.

Presently, through the thinning mist, Tormarin discerned the sharp turn of the track which branched off from the road towards the bungalow, and quickening Orion's pace, he was soon riding up the steep ascent, the moonlight throwing strange, confusing lights and shadows on the mist-wet surface of the ground.

Suddenly, without the slightest warning, the roan snorted and wheeled around, shying violently away from the off-side bank. A less good horseman might have been unseated, but as the big horse swerved Tormarin's knees gripped against the saddle like a vice, and with a steadying word he faced him up the track again, then glanced keenly at the overhanging side of the roadway to discover what had frightened him.

A moment later he had jerked Orion to a sudden standstill, leapt to the ground and, with the reins over his arm, crossed the road swiftly to where, clad in some light-stuff that glimmered strangely in the moonlight, lay a slender figure, propped against the bank.

"Blaise!" Jean's voice came weakly to his ears, but with a glad note in it of immense relief that bore witness to some previous strain.

In an instant Tormarin was kneeling beside her, one arm behind her shoulders. He helped her to her feet and she leaned against him, shivering. Feeling in his pockets, he produced a brandy flask and held it to her lips.

"Drink some of that!" he said. "Don't try to tell me anything yet."

The raw spirit sent the chilled blood racing through her veins, putting new life into her. A faint tinge of colour crept into her face.

"Oh, Blaise! I'm so glad you've come—so glad!" she said shakily.

"So am I," he returned grimly. "See, drink a little more brandy. Then you shall tell me all about it."

At last, bit by bit, she managed to give him a somewhat disjointed account of what had occurred.

"I think I must have been stunned for a little when I fell," she said. "I can't remember anything after stepping right off into space, it seemed, till— oh, ages afterwards—- I found myself lying here. And when I tried to stand, I found I'd hurt my ankle and that I couldn't put my foot to the ground. So"—with a weak little attempt at laughter—"I—I just sat down again."

Blaise gave vent to a quick exclamation of concern. "Oh, it's nothing, really," she reassured him hastily. "Only a strain. But I can't walk on it." Then, suddenly clinging to him with a nervous dread: "Oh, take me away, Blaise—take me home!"

"I will. Don't be frightened—there's no need to be frightened any more, my Jean."

"No, I know. I'm not afraid—now."

But he could hear the sob of utter nerve stress and exhaustion back of the brave words.

"Well, I'll take you home at once," he said cheerfully. "But, look here, you've no coat on and you're wet with mist."

"I know. My coat's at the bungalow. I left in a hurry, you see"— whimsically. The irrepressible Peterson element, game to the core, was reasserting itself.

"Well, we must fetch it———"

"No! No!" Her voice rose in hasty protest. "I won't—I can't go back!"

"Then I'll go."

"No—don't! Geoffrey might be there——"

"So much the better"—grimly. "I'd like five minutes with him." Tormarin's hand tightened fiercely on the hunting-crop he carried. "But he's more likely lost his way in the mist and fetched up far enough away. Probably"—with a short laugh—"he's still searching Dartmoor for! you. You'd be on his mind a bit, you know! Wait here a minute while I ride up to the bungalow——"

But she clung to his arm.

"No, no! Don't go! I—I can't be left alone—again." The fear was coming back to her voice and Blaise, detecting it, abandoned the idea at once.

"All right, little Jean," he said reassuringly. "I won't leave you. Put my coat round you"—stripping it off. "There—like that." He helped her into it and fastened it with deft fingers. "And now I'm going to get you up on to Orion and we'll go home."

"I shall never get up there," she observed, with a glance at the roan's great shoulders looming through the mist. "I shan't be able to spring—I can only stand on one foot, remember."

Blaise laughed cheerily.

"Don't worry. Just remain quite still—standing on your one foot, you poor little lame duck!—and I'll do the rest."

She felt his arm release its clasp of her, and a moment later he had swung his leg across the horse and was back in the saddle again. With a word to the big beast he dropped the reins on to his neck and, turning towards Jean, where she stood like a slim, pale ghost in the moonlight, he leaned down to her from the saddle.

"Can you manage to come a step nearer?" he asked.

She hobbled forward painfully.

"Now!" he said.

Lower, lower still he stooped, his arms outheld, and at last she felt them close round her, lifting her with that same strength of steel which she remembered on the mountain-side at Montavan. Orion stood like a statue— motionless as if he knew and understood all about it, his head slewed round a bit as though watching until the little business should be satisfactorily accomplished, and blowing gently through his velvety nostrils meanwhile.

And then Jean found herself resting against the curve of Blaise's arm, with the roan's powerful shoulders, firm and solid as a rock, beneath her.

"All right?" queried Blaise, gathering up the reins in his left hand. "Lean well back against my shoulder. There, how's that?"

"It's like an arm-chair."

He laughed.

"I am afraid you won't say the same by the end of the journey," he commented ruefully.

But by the end of the journey Jean was fast asleep. She had "leant well back" as directed, conscious, as she felt the firm clasp of Blaise's arm, of a supreme sense of security and well-being. The reaction from the strain of the afternoon, the exhaustion consequent upon her flight through the mist and the fall which had so suddenly ended it, and the rhythmic beat of Orion's hoofs all combined to lull her into a state of delicious drowsiness. It was so good to feel that she need fight and scheme and plan no longer, to feel utterly safe... to know that Blaise was holding her...

Her head fell back against his shoulder, her eyes closed, and the next thing of which she was conscious was of being lifted down by a pair of strong arms and of a confused murmur of voices from amongst which she hazily distinguished Lady Anne's heartfelt: "Thank God you've found her!" And then, characteristically practical, "I'll have her in bed in five minutes. Blankets and hot-water bottles are all in readiness."

It was the evening of the following day. Jean, tucked up on a couch and with her strained ankle comfortably bandaged, had been reluctantly furnishing Blaise with the particulars of her experience at the bungalow. She had been very unwilling to confide the whole story to him, fearing the consequences of the Tormarin temper as applied to Burke. A violent quarrel between the two men could do no good, she reflected, and would only be fraught with unpleasant results to all concerned—probably, in the end, securing a painful publicity for the whole affair.

Fortunately Blaise had been out when Judith had rung up earlier in the day to inquire if Jean had returned to Staple, or he might have fired off a few candid expressions of opinion through the telephone. But now there was no evading his searching questions, and he had quietly but determinedly insisted upon hearing the entire story. Once or twice an ejaculation of intense anger broke from him as he listened, but, beyond that, he made little comment.

"And—and that was all," wound up Jean. "And, anyway, Blaise"—a little anxiously—"it's over now, and I'm none the worse except for the acquisition of a little more worldly wisdom and a strained ankle."

"Yes, it's over now," he said, standing looking down at her with a curious gleam in his eyes. "But that sort of thing shan't happen twice. You'll have to marry me—do you hear?"—imperiously. "You shall never run such a risk again. We'll get married at once!"

And Jean, with a quiver of amusement at the corners of her mouth, responded meekly:

"Yes, Blaise."

The next minute his arms were round her and their lips met in the first supreme kiss of love at last acknowledged—of love given and returned.

There is no gauge by which those first moments when two who love confess that they are lovers may be measured. It is the golden, timeless span when "unborn to-morrow and dead yesterday" cease to hem us round about and only love, and love's ecstasy, remain.

To Blaise and Jean it might have been an hour—a commonplace period ticked off by the little silver clock upon the chimneypiece—or half eternity before they came back to the recollection of things mundane. When they did, it was across the kindly bridge of humour.

Blaise laughed out suddenly and boyishly.

"It's preposterous!" he exclaimed. "I quite forgot to propose."

"So you did! Suppose"—smiling up at him impertinently—"suppose you do it now?"

"Not I! I won't waste my breath when I might put it to so much better use in calling you belovedest."

Jean was silent, but her eyes answered him. She had made room for him beside her, and now he was seated upon the edge of the Chesterfield, holding her in his arms. She did not want to talk much. That still, serene happiness which lies deep within the heart is not provocative of garrulity.

At last a question—the question that had tormented her through all the long months since she had first realised whither love was leading her, found its way to her lips.

"Why didn't you tell me before, Blaise?"

His face clouded.

"Because of all that had happened in the past. You know—you have been told about Nesta——"

"Ah, yes! Don't talk about it, Blaise," she broke in hastily, sensing his distasteful recoil from the topic.

"I think we must a little, dear," he responded gravely.

"You see, Nesta was not all to blame—nor even very much, as I'm sure"—with a little half-tender smile—"my mother tried hard to make you believe."

Jean nodded vigorously.

"She did. And I expect she was perfectly right"

He shook his head.

"No," he answered. "The fault was really mine. My initial mistake was in confusing the false fire with the true. It—was not love I had for Nesta. And I found it out when it was too late. We were poles apart in everything, and instead of trying to make it easier for her, trying to understand her and to lead her into our ways of looking at things. I only stormed at her. It roused all that was worst in me to see her trailing our name in the dust, throwing her dignity to the winds, craving for nothing other than amusement and excitement. I'm not trying to excuse myself. There *was* no excuse for me. In my way, I was as culpable and foolish as she. And when the crash came—when I found her deliberately entertaining in my house, against my express orders, a man who ought to have been kicked out of any decent society, why, I let go. The Tormarin temper had its way with me. I shall never forgive myself for that. I frightened her, terrified her. I think I must have been half mad. And then—well, you know what followed. She rushed away and, before anyone could find her or help her, she had killed herself—thrown herself into the Seine. Quite what happened between leaving here and her death we were never able to find out. Apparently since her marriage with me, her sister had gone to Paris, unknown to her, and had taken a situation as *dame de compagnie* to some Frenchwoman, and Nesta, though she followed from Italy to Paris, failed to find her there. At least that is what Margherita Valdi told me in the letter announcing Nesta's death. Then she must have lost heart. So you see, morally I am responsible for that poor, reckless child's death."

"Oh, no, no, Blaise! I don't see that"—pitifully.

"Don't you? I do—very clearly. And that was why, when I found myself growing to care for you, I tried to keep away."

He felt in his pocket and produced a plain gold wedding ring. On the inside were engraved the initials "B.T. and N.E.," and a date.

"That was my talisman. Alargherita sent it back to me when she wrote telling me of Nesta's death. Whenever I felt my resolution weakening, I used to take it out and have a look at it. It was always quite effective in thrusting me back into my proper place in the scheme of things—that is, outside any other woman's life." There was an inexpressible bitterness in his tones, and Jean drew a little nearer to him, her heart overflowing with compassion. He looked down at her, and smiled a thought ironically. "But now—you've beaten me." His lips brushed her hair. "I'm glad to be beaten, belovedest... I knew, that day at Montavan, what you might come to mean to me. And I intended never to see you again, but just to take that one day for remembrance. I felt that, having made such an utter hash of things, having spoiled one woman's life and been, indirectly, the cause of her death, I was not fit to hold another woman's happiness in my hands."

Jean rubbed her cheek against his shoulder.

"I'm glad you thought better of it? she observed.

"I don't know, even now, that I'm right in letting you love me——"

"You can't stop me," she objected.

He smiled.

"I don't think I would if I could—now."

Jean leaned up and, with a slender, dictatorial finger on the side of his face, turned his head towards her.

"*Quite* sure?" she demanded saucily. Then, without waiting for his answer: "Blaise, I do love your chin—it's such a nice, square, your-money-or-your-life sort of chin."

Something light as a butterfly, warm as a woman's lips, just brushed the feature in question.

He drew her into his arms, folding them closely about her.

"And I—I love every bit of you," he said hoarsely. "Body and soul, I love you! Oh! Heart's beloved! Nothing—no one in the whole world shall come between us two ever again!"

CHAPTER XXX
THE GATEWAY

AUGUST seemed determined to justify her claim to be numbered amongst the summer months before making her exit. Apparently she had repented her of having recently veiled the country in a mist that might have been regarded as a very creditable effort even on the part of November, for to-day the sun was blazing down out of a cloudless sky and scarcely a breath of wind swayed the nodding cornstalks, heavy with golden grain.

Jean, her strained ankle now practically recovered, was tramping along the narrow footpath through the cornfield, following in Blaise's footsteps, while Nick brought up the rear of the procession. She had not seen Claire since her engagement had become an actual fact, though a characteristically warm-hearted little note from the latter had found its way to Staple, and this morning Jean had declared her inability to exist another day "without a 'heart-to-heart' talk with Claire."

Hence the afternoon's pilgrimage across the cornfield which formed part of a short cut between Staple and Charnwood.

At first Jean had feared lest her new-found happiness might raise a barrier of sorts betwixt herself and Claire. The contrast between the respective hands that fate had dealt them was so glaring, and the rose and gold with which love had suddenly decked Jean's own life seemed to make the bleak tragedy which enveloped Claire's appear ever darker than before.

But Claire's letter, full of a quiet, unselfish rejoicing in the happiness which had fallen to the lot of her friend, had somehow smoothed away the little uncomfortable feeling which, to anyone as sensitive as Jean, had been a very real embarrassment. Nick's felicitations, too, had been tendered with frank cordiality and affection, and with a delicate perception that had successfully concealed the sting of individual pain which the contrast could hardly fail to have induced.

So that it was with a considerably lightened heart that Jean, with her escort of two, passed between the great gates of Charnwood and, avoiding the lengthy walk entailed by following the windings of the drive, struck off across the velvety lawns—smooth stretches of close-cropped sward which, broken only by branching trees and shrubbery, and undefaced by the dreadful formality of symmetrical flower-beds, swept right up to the gravelled terrace fronting the windows of the house itself.

The two men loitered to discuss the points of a couple of young spaniels rollicking together on the grass, but Jean, eager to see Claire, smilingly declined to wait for them, and, speeding on ahead, she mounted the short flight of steps leading to the terrace from the lower level of the lawns.

Facing her, as she reached the topmost step was a glass door, giving entrance to Claire's own particular sanctum, which usually, in summer, stood wide open to admit the soft, warm air and the fragrant scents breathed out from a border of old-fashioned flowers, sweet and prim and quaint, which encircled the base of the house.

But to-day the door was shut and forbidding-looking, and Jean experienced a sudden sense of misgiving. Supposing Claire chanced to be out just when she had arrived brimming over with the hundred little feminine confidences that were to have formed part of the "heart-to-heart" talk! It would be too aggravating!

Her eager glance flew ahead, searching the room's interior, clearly visible through the wide glass panel of the door. Then, with a startled cry, she halted, her hand clapped against her lips to stifle the involuntary exclamation of dismay and terror that had leapt to them.

The afternoon sunshine slanted in upon a picture of grotesque horror—--a nightmare conception that could only have sprung from the macabre imagination of a madman.

In the middle of the room Claire sat bound to a high-backed chair, secured by cords which cut cruelly across her slender body. Her face had assumed a curious ashen shade, and her eyes were fixed in a numbed look of fascinated terror upon the tall, angular figure of her husband, which pranced in front of her jerkily, like a marionette, while he threatened her with a revolver, his thin lips, smiling cruelly, drawn back from his teeth like those of a snarling animal.

He was addressing her in queer, high-pitched tones that had something inhuman about them—the echoing, empty sound of a voice no longer controlled by a reasoning brain.

"And you needn't worry that Mr. Brennan will be overwhelmed with grief at your early demise. He won't—te-he-he!"—he gave a foolish, cackling laugh—"he won't have time to miss you much! I'll attend to that—I'll attend to that! There'll be a second bullet for your dear friend, Mr. Brennan." ...

Crack! The sharp report of a revolver shattered the summer silence as Jean sprang forward and wrenched at the handle of the door. But it refused to yield. It had been locked upon the inside!

Then, as the smoke cleared away, she saw that Claire was Unhurt. Sir Adrian had deliberately fired above her head and was now rocking his long, lean body to and fro in a paroxysm of horrible, noiseless mirth. Evidently he purposed to amuse himself by inflicting the torture of suspense upon his victim before he actually murdered her, for Latimer had been at one time an expert revolver shot, and, even drug-ridden as he had since become, he could not well have missed his helpless target by accident.

Claire's head had fallen back, but no merciful oblivion of unconsciousness had come to her relief. Her mouth was a little open and the breath came in short, quick gasps between her grey lips. Her face looked like a mask, set in a blank stupor of horror.

The sound of the shot brought Blaise and Nick racing to Jean's side. One glance through the glass door sufficed them.

"God in heaven! He's gone mad!" Nick's voice was quick with fear for the woman he loved.

"Get Tucker here at once!"

Blaise's swift command, flung at her as he and Nick leaped forward, sent Jean flying along the terrace as fast as feet winged with unutterable terror could carry her. As she ran, she heard the crash of splintering glass as the two men she had left behind smashed in the panel of the locked door, and, almost simultaneously, Sir Adrian's pistol barked again—another shot, and then a third in quick succession.

The sound seemed to wring every nerve in her body... had that madman shot him?

With sobbing breath she rushed blindly on into the house and met the butler, running too, white faced and horror-stricken.

"My God, miss! Sir Adrian's murdering her ladyship—and the room door's locked!"

The man almost babbled out the words in his extremity of fear.

"The terrace door... Quick, Tucker!"—Jean gasped out the order. "Mr. Brennan's there they've broken in the glass..."

Not waiting to hear the end of the sentence, Tucker bolted out of the hall and along the terrace, while Jean leaned up against the doorway drawing long, shuddering breaths that seemed actually to tear their way through her throat and yet brought no relief to the agonised thudding of her heart. For the moment she was physically unable to run another yard.

But her mind was working with abnormal clarity and swiftness. This was her doing—hers! If she had not dissuaded Nick that day when he had proposed taking Claire away with him, all this would never have happened.... Claire would have been safe—safe! But she had interfered, clinging to her belief that no real good ever came by doing wrong, and now her creed had failed her utterly. Nick's resistance of temptation was culminating in a ghastly tragedy that might have been avoided. To Jean it seemed in that moment as if her world were falling in ruins about her.

Sick with apprehension, she almost reeled out again into the mocking summer sunlight, and, running as fast as the convulsive throbbing of her heart would let her, regained the far end of the terrace and peered through the door that led into Claire's room.

Its great panes were shattered. Jagged teeth and spites of glass stuck out from the wooden framework, while here and there, dependent from them, were bits of cloth tom from the men's coats as they had scrambled through.

Within the room Jean could discern a confused hurly-burly of swaying, writhing figures—Blaise and Nick and the butler struggling to overpower Sir Adrian, who was fighting them with all the cunning and the amazing strength of madness. From beyond came the clamour of people battering uselessly at the door, the shrill, excited voices of the frightened servants who had collected in the hall outside the room.

For a few breathless seconds Jean was in doubt—wondered wildly whether Sir Adrian would succeed in breaking away from his captors. Then she saw Nick's foot shoot out suddenly like the piston-rod of an engine, and Sir Adrian staggered and came crashing down on to his knees. The other two closed in upon him swiftly, and a minute later he was lying prone on his back with the three men holding him down by main force.

With difficulty avoiding the protruding pieces of glass, Jean stepped into the room. Her first thought was for Claire, who now hung helpless and unconscious against the bonds that held her. But Blaise very speedily directed her attention to something of more urgent importance for the moment.

"Unlock that door," he called to her. "Quick!" He was still panting from the exertion of the recent struggle. "Get a rope of some sort!"

Jean turned the key and tore open the door leading into the hall. The little flock of servants gathered outside it overflowed into the room, frightened and excitedly inquisitive.

"Get some cord, one of you," commanded Jean authoratively. "Anything will do if it's strong."

Two or three of the servants broke away from the main body and ran frantically in search of the required cord, glad to be of use, and very soon Sir Adrian, bound as humanely as his struggles rendered possible, was borne to his own room and laid upon his bed.

"Ring up the doctor," ordered Blaise, as he assisted in the rather difficult process of conveying Sir Adrian upstairs. "Tell him to come to Charnwood as quickly as he can get here." And another eager little detachment of domestics flew off to carry out his bidding. The under-footman won the race for the telephone by a good half-yard, and, in a voice which fairly twittered with the agitating and amazing news he had to impart, transmitted the message to the doctor's parlour-maid at the other end of the wire, adding a few picturesque and stimulating details concerning the struggle which had just taken place—and which, apparently, he had perceived with the eye of faith through the wooden panels of the locked door.

Meanwhile Nick and Jean had turned their attention towards releasing Claire, who, as the last of her bonds was cut, toppled forward in a dead faint into the former's arms.

A second procession wended its way upstairs, Nick bearing the slight, unconscious figure in his arms while Jean and a kindly-faced housemaid followed.

"Her ladyship's maid is out, miss," volunteered the girl. "But perhaps I can help?"

Jean smiled at her, the frank, friendly smile that always won for her the eager, willing service of man and maid alike.

"I'm sure you can," she said gently. "As soon as we can bring her ladyship round, you shall help me undress her and put her to bed."

In a few minutes Claire recovered consciousness, but she was horribly shaken and distraught, crying and clinging to Jean or to the housemaid— who was almost crying, too, out of sympathy—like a child frightened by the dark.

Jean, understanding just what was needed, shepherded Nick to the door of the room, where he lingered unhappily, his anxious gaze still fixed on the slender, shrinking figure upon the couch.

"Don't worry, Nick," she said reassuringly. "She'll he all right; it's only reaction. But I know what she wants—she wants a real mother-person. Go down and ring up Lady Anne, will you, and ask her to come over in the car as quickly as she can."

Nick nodded; the idea commended itself to him. His "pale golden narcissus," so nearly broken, would be safe indeed with the kind, comforting arms of his mother about her.

It was an intense relief to Jean when Lady Anne arrived and quietly and efficiently took command of affairs. And there was sore need for her unruffled poise and capability throughout the night that followed.

Claire, nervous and utterly unstrung, slept but little, waking constantly with a cry of terror as in imagination she relived the ordeal of the afternoon, while in the big bedroom across the landing, where her husband lay, the grim shadow of death itself was drawing momentarily closer.

By the time the doctor had arrived in answer to the summons sent, there seemed small need for the strong cords with which Sir Adrian's limbs were bound. The wild fury of the afternoon's struggle had thoroughly exhausted him, and he lay, propped up with pillows, apparently in a state of stupor, breathing very feebly.

"Heart," the doctor told Tormarin after he had made a swift examination. "I've known for months that Sir Adrian might go out at any moment. His heart was already impaired, and, of course, he's drugged for years. He may recover a little, but if, as I think is highly probable, there's any recurrence of the brain disturbance—why, he'll not live out a second paroxysm. The heart won't stand it."

Tormarin endeavoured to look appropriately shocked. But the doctor was a man and an honest one, and not even professional etiquette prevented his adding, with a jerk of his head in the direction of Claire's bedroom:

"It would be a merciful deliverance for that poor little woman. There's a strain of madness in the Latimer's you know. And"—with a shrug—"naturally Sir Adrian's habits have accentuated it in his own case."

But the doctor was mistaken in his calculations. Sir Adrian's constitution was stronger than he estimated. As Nick had once bitterly commented to Jean, the man was like a piece of steel wire, and two dreadful outbreaks of maniacal fury had to be endured before the wire began to weaken.

During the course of the first paroxysm it was all the four men could do to restrain him from leaping from the bed and rushing out of the room, since, during the period of quiescence which had preceded the doctor's arrival, a mistaken feeling of humanity had dictated the loosening of the cords which bound him.

He fought and screamed, uttering the most horrible imprecations, and his evil intent towards the woman who was his wife was unmistakable.

With her husband free to work his will, Claire's life would not have been worth a moment's purchase.

In the period of coma that succeeded this outbreak Sir Adrian, was again secured, as mercifully as possible, from any possibility of doing his wife a mischief, and the second paroxysm which convulsed the bound and shackled madman was very terrible to witness.

Like its predecessor, this attack was followed by a stupor, during which Sir Adrian appeared more dead than alive.

He was palpably weaker, restoratives failing to produce any appreciable effect, and towards morning, in those chill, small hours when the powers of the body languish and fail, the crazed and self-tormented spirit of Adrian Latimer quitted a world in which he had been able to perceive none of those things that are just and pure and lovely and of good report, but only distrust and malice and, finally, black hatred.

A fortnight had come and gone. Sir Adrian's body had been laid to rest in Coombe Eavie churchyard, and Claire, in the simplest of widow's weeds, went about once more, looking rather frail and worn-out but with a fugitive light of happiness on her face that was a source of rejoicing to those who loved her.

She made no pretence at mourning the man who had turned her life into a living hell for nearly three years and who stood like a gaoler betwixt her and the happiness which might have been hers had she been free. But the conventions, as well as her own feelings, dictated that a decent interval must elapse before she and Nick could be married, and this would be for her a quiet period dedicated to the readjustment of her whole attitude towards life.

The length of that period was the subject of considerable discussion. Nick protested that six months was amply long enough to wait—too long indeed!—but Claire herself seemed disposed to prolong her widowhood into a year.

"It isn't in the least because I feel I owe it to Adrian," she said in answer to Nick's protest. "I don't consider that I owe him anything at all. But I feel so battered, Nick, so utterly tired and weary after the perpetual struggle of the last three years that I don't want to plunge suddenly into the new duties of a new life—not even into new happiness. It's difficult to make you understand, but I feel just like a sponge which has soaked up all it can and simply can't absorb any more of *anything*. You must let me have time for the past to evaporate a bit."

But it required the addition of a few common-sense observations on the part of Lady Anne to drive the nail home.

"Claire is quite right, Nick," she told him. "She is temporarily worn out—mentally, physically and spiritually spent. Her nerves have been kept at their utmost stretch off and on for years, and now that release has come they've collapsed like a fiddle-string when the peg that holds it taut is loosened. You must give her time to recover, to key herself up to normal pitch again. At present she isn't fit to face even the demands that big happiness brings in its train."

So Nick had perforce to bow to Claire's decision, and it was settled that for the first month of two, at least, of her widowhood Jean should remove herself and her belongings from Staple and bear her company at Charnwood. And meanwhile Nick and Claire would spend many peaceful hours together of quiet happiness and companionship, while Claire, as she herself expressed it, "rebuilt her soul."

To Jean the issue of events had brought nothing but pure joy. Her belief had been justified, and the grim gateway of death had become for these two friends of hers the gateway to happiness.

She had neither seen nor heard anything from Burke since the day she had fled from him on the Moor, although indirectly she had discovered that he had quitted the bungalow the day following that of her flight from it and had gone to London.

Judith sent her a brief, rather formal letter of congratulation upon her engagement, but in it she made no reference to him nor did she endeavour to explain away or palliate her own share in his scheme to force Jean's hand. Probably an odd kind of loyalty to her brother prevented her from clearing herself at his expense, added to a certain dogged pride which refused to let her extenuate any action of hers; to the daughter of Glyn Peterson.

But none of these things had any power to hurt Jean now. In her new-born happiness she felt that she could find it in her heart to forgive anybody anything! She was even conscious of a certain tentative understanding and indulgence for Burke himself. He had only used the "primitive man" methods his temperament dictated in his effort to win the woman he wanted for his wife. And he had failed. Just now, Jean could not help sympathising with anybody who had failed to find the happiness that love bestows.

She reflected that the old gipsy on the Moor had been wonderfully correct in her prophecy concerning Nick and Claire. The sun was "shin' butivul" for them at last, just as she had assured them that it would.

And, with the same, came a sudden little clutch of fear at Jean's heart, like the touch of a strange hand. The gipsy had had other words for her— harsher, less sweet-sounding.

"For there's darkness comin'... black darkness."

She shivered a little. She felt as though a breath of cold air had passed over her, chilling the warm blood that ran so joyously in her veins.

CHAPTER XXXI
AN UNWELCOME VISITOR

BLAISE was seated at his study table, regarding somewhat dubiously a letter which lay open in front of him.

It was written in a flowing, foreign hand and expressed with a quaintly stilted, un-English turn of phrase. The heading of the notepaper upon which it was inscribed was that of a hotel in Exeter.

> *"Dear Mr. Tormarin," it ran. "You will, without doubt, be*
> *surprised to receive a letter from me, since we have met*
> *only once. But I have something of the most great importance*
> *to confide in you, and I therefore beg that you will accord*
> *me an interview. When I add to this that the matter*
> *approaches very closely the future of your fiancée, Miss*
> *Peterson, I do not doubt to myself that you will appoint a*
> *time when I may call to see you."*

The letter was signed *M. de Varigny.*

Blaise had received this thought-provoking epistle two days previously, and had been impressed by an uncomfortable consciousness that it foreboded something unpleasant. He could not imagine in what manner the affairs of Madame de Varigny impinged upon his own, or rather, as she seemed to imply, upon those of his future wife, and this very uncertainty had impelled him to fix the interview the Countess had demanded at as early a moment as possible. Disagreeables were best met and faced without delay. So now he was momentarily awaiting her arrival, still unable to rid himself of the impression that something of an unpleasant nature impended.

He glanced through the open window, facing him. Afterwards, he was always able to recall every little detail of the picture upon which his eyes rested; it was etched upon his mind as ineffaceably as though cut upon steel with a graver's tool.

Although the mellow sunlight of September flooded the lawns and terraces, that indescribable change which heralds autumn had already begun to manifest itself. Not that any hint of chill as yet edged the balmy atmosphere or tint of russet reddened the gently waving foliage of the trees. It was something less definite—a suggestion of maturity, of completed ripening, conveyed by the deep, rich green of the grass, the strong, woody growth of the trees, the full-blown glory of the roses nodding on their stems.

To the left, in the shade of a stately cedar, Lady Anne and Jean were encamped with their sewing and writing materials at hand, and the rays of sunshine, filtering between the widespread branches above them, woke fugitive gold and silver lights in the down-bent auburn and white-crowned heads. Further away, in the valley below, the brown smudge of a wide-bottomed boat broke the smooth expanse of the lake whence the mingled laughter of Nick and Claire came floating up on the breeze.

It was a peaceful scene, full of intimate happiness and tender promises, and Blaise watched it with contented eyes. The voice of Baines, formal and urbane, roused him from a pleasant reverie.

"Madame de Varigny," announced that functionary, throwing open the door and standing aside for the visitor to enter.

Blaise rose courteously to greet her, holding out his hand. But the Countess shook her head.

"No, I will not shake hands," she said abruptly. "When you know why I am come, you will not want to shake hands with me."

There was something not unattractive about the outspoken refusal to sail under false colours, more especially softened, as it was, by the charm of the faintly foreign accent and intonation.

Madame de Varigny had paused a moment in the middle of the room and was regarding her host with curiously appraising eyes, and as Blaise returned her gaze he was conscious, as once before at the fancy-dress ball at Montavan, of the strange sense of familiarity this woman had for him.

"I am sorry for that," he said, answering her refusal to shake hands. "Won't you, at least, sit down?" pulling forward a chair.

"Yes, I will sit."

She sank into the chair with the quick, graceful motion of the South, and continued to regard Blaise watchfully between the thick fringes of her lashes. Had Jean been present, she would have been struck anew by the expression of implacability which hardened the dark-brown eyes. By that, and by something else as well—a look of unmistakable triumph.

"I have much—much to say to you, Monsieur Tor-ma-rin," she began at last. "I will commence by telling you a little about myself. I am"—here she looked away for an instant, then shot a swift, penetrating glance at him—"an Italian by birth."

A brief silence followed this announcement. Blaise was thinking concentratedly. So Madame de Varigny, despite her French name and her French mannerisms, was an Italian! He might have guessed it had the possibility ever definitely presented itself to him—guessed it from those broad, high cheek bones, those liquid, southern-dark eyes, and the coarse, blue-black hair. Yet, except for one fleeting moment at Montavan, the idea had never occurred to him, and it had then been swiftly dissipated by Jean's explanation that the impressive-looking Cleopatra was the Comtesse de Varigny and her chaperon for the time being.

Italian! Blaise felt more convinced than ever now that Madame de Varigny's visit portended unpleasant developments. Something, a voice from the past, was about to break stridently on the peaceful present. He braced himself to meet and counter whatever might be coming. Vaguely he foresaw some kind of blackmail, and he thanked Heaven for Jean's absolute understanding and complete knowledge of the past and of all that appertained to his first unhappy marriage. There would be little foothold here for an attempt at blackmail, however skilfully worked, he reflected grimly.

He therefore responded civilly to Madame de Varigny's statement, apparently accepting it at its mere face value.

"I am surprised," he told her. "You have altogether the air of a Parisian."

The Countess smiled.

"Oh, I had a French grandmother," she returned carelessly. "Also, I have lived much in Paris."

"Ah! that explains it," replied Tormarin, leaning back in his chair as though satisfied. "It's the influence of environment and heredity, I expect."

He was fencing carefully, waiting for the woman to show her hand.

"I have also Corsican blood in my veins," pursued Madame de Varigny. Then, as Tormarin made no answer, she leaned forward and said intently: "Do you know the characteristic of the Corsicans, Monsieur Tor-ma-rin? They never forget—*nevaire*"—her foreign accent increasing, as usual, with emotion of any kind. "The Corsican always repays."

"Yes? And you have something to repay? Is that it?"

"Yes. I have something to repay."

"A revenge, in fact?"

"She shook her head.

"No. I do not call it revenge. It is punishment—the just punishment earned by the man who married Nesta Freyne and brought her in return nothing but misery." Tormarin rose abruptly.

"What have the affairs of Nesta Freyne to do with you?" he asked sternly. "As you are obviously aware, she was my wife. And I do not propose to discuss private personal matters with an entire stranger." He moved towards the door. "I think our interview can very well terminate at that. I do not wish to forget that I am your host."

"You are more than that," said Madame de Varigny suavely. "You are my brother-in-law."

"*What?*" Tormarin swung 'round and faced her.

"Yes." The suavity was gone now, replaced by a curious deadly precision of utterance, enhanced by the foreign rendering of syllabic values. "I am—or was, until my marriage—Margherita Valdi. I am Nesta's sister."

Tormarin regarded her steadily.

"In that case," he said, "I will hear what you have to say. Though I don't think," he added, "that any good can come of raking up the past. It is better—forgotten."

"Forgotten?" Madame de Varigny seized upon the unlucky word. "Yes—it may be easy enough for you to forget—you who took Nesta's young, beautiful life and crushed it; you who came like a thief and stole from me the one creature in the whole world whom I loved—my *bambina*, my little sister. Oh, yes"—her voice rose passionately—"easy enough when there is another woman—a new love—with whom you think to start your life all over again! But I tell you, you *shall not!* There shall be no new beginning for you—no marriage with this Jean Peterson to whom you are now *fiancé*. I forbid it—I——"

Blaise stemmed the torrent of her speech with an authoritative gesture.

"May I ask how the news of my engagement reached you?" he asked, his cool, dispassionate question falling like a hailstone dropped into some molten stream of lava.

"Oh, I have kept watch. I have the means of knowing. There is very little that has happened to you since—since I wrote to you of Nesta's death"—she stumbled a little over the words, and Blaise, despite his anger, was conscious of a sudden flash of sympathy for her—"very little that I have not known. And this—your engagement, I knew of that when it was barely a week old."

"I'm really curious to know why my affairs should be of such surpassing interest to you. My engagement, for instance—how did you hear of it?"

"Oh, that was easy"—contemptuously. "There was another man who loved your Mees Peterson—this Monsieur Burke. I used him. I knew he was afraid that you might win her, and I told him that if ever you became engaged he must come and tell me, and I would show him how to make sure that you should never marry her. Oh! That was *vairy* simple!"

"I'm afraid you promised him more than you can hope to perform. I grant that you have every reason to dislike me—hate me, if you will. I acknowledge, too, that I was to blame, miserably to blame, for Nesta's unhappiness—as much in fault as she herself. But there is nothing gained at this late hour by apportioning the blame. We each made bad mistakes—and we have each had to pay the price."

"Yours has been a very light price—comparatively," she commented with intense bitterness.

"Do you think so?"

Something in the quiet, still utterance of the brief question brought her glance swiftly, curiously, back to his face. It was as though, behind those four short words, she could feel the intolerable pressure of years of endurance. For a moment she seemed to waver, then, as though she had deliberately pushed the impression aside, she laughed disagreeably.

"Too light to satisfy her sister, at any rate."

Tormarin froze.

"It is fortunate, then, that my ultimate fate does not lie in your hands," he observed.

"But that is just where it does lie—in the palm of my hand—there!"

She flung out one shapely hand, palm, upward, and pointed to it with the other.

"And now—see—I close my hand—so!... And this beautiful marriage of which you have dreamed, your marriage with Mees Peterson—*it does not take place!*"

"Are you mad?" asked Blaise contemptuously, experiencing all an Englishman's distaste for this display of unforced drama.

She shook her head.

"No," she said quietly. "I am not mad."

The air of theatricality seemed to fall suddenly away from her, leaving her a stern and sombre figure, invested with an intrinsic atmosphere of tragedy, filled with one sentiment only—the thirst for vengeance.

"No. I am not mad. I am telling you the truth. You can never marry Jean Peterson, because Nesta—your wife—still lives."

Tormarin fell back a pace. For one moment he believed the woman had gone genuinely mad—that by dint of long brooding upon how she might most hurt and punish the Englishman whom she had never forgiven for marrying her sister, she had evolved from a half-crazed mind the belief that Nesta still lived and that thus she would be able to prevent his marriage with any other woman.

And then, looking into those seeming soft brown eyes with the granite hardness in their depths, he could see the light of reason burning steadily within them.

Madame de Varigny was quite sane, as sane as he was himself. And if so...

A great fear came upon him—the fear of a man who dimly senses the approach of some appalling danger and knows that it will find him utterly defenceless.

"Do you know what you are saying?" he demanded, his voice roughened and uneven.

"Yes, I know. Nesta is alive," she repeated simply.

"*Alive?*"

The word was wrung from him, hardly more than a hoarse whisper of sound. He swung round upon her violently.

"But you yourself wrote and told me of her death?" She nodded placidly.

"Yes. I wrote a lie."

"But the official information? We had that, too, later, from the French police, confirming your account. You had better be careful about what you are telling me," he added sternly. "Lies won't answer, now."

"The need for lying is past," she answered with the most absolute candour. "The French police wrote quite truthfully all they knew. They had found the body of a suicide, whom I identified as my sister. To strengthen matters I bribed someone I knew also to identify the dead girl as Nesta. She was a married woman, too, the poor little dead, one! So it was quite simple. And I took Nesta home—home to Château Varigny. I had married by then. But she had heard of my marriage through friends in Italy and wrote to me from there, telling me of her misery with you and begging me to succour her. So I went to Italy and brought her back with me to Varigny. Then I planned that you should believe her dead. It was all very simple," she repeated complacently.

"But what was your object in all this? Why did you scheme to keep me in ignorance? What was your purpose?"

"Why?" Her voice deepened suddenly, the placid satisfaction with which she had narrated the carrying out of her plan disappearing from it completely. "Why? I did it to punish you—first for stealing my Nesta from me and then because, after you had stolen her, you brought her nothing but misery and heart-break. She was so young—so young! And you, with your hideous temper and cold, formal English ways—you broke her heart, cowed her, crushed her!"

"She was old enough to coquette with every man she met," came grimly between Tormarin's teeth. "No husband—English or Italian, least of all Italian—would have endured her conduct."

"She would not have played with other men if you had loved her. She was all fire. And you—you were like a wet log that will not burn!" She gestured fiercely. "You *never* loved her! It was in a moment of passion—of desire that you married her!... But you were sure, eventually, to meet some other woman and learn what love—real love—is. So I waited. And when I saw you at Montavan with Jean—I knew that the day I had waited for so long would come at last. I knew that your punishment was ready to my hand."

"Do you mean"—Blaise spoke in curiously measured accents—"do you mean that you deliberately concealed the fact that Nesta still lived so that——"

"So that you should not marry the woman that you loved when the time came! Yes, I planned it all! I kept Nesta safely hidden at Varigny, and I made little changes in her appearance—a woman can, you know"—mockingly—"the colour of her hair, the way of dressing it. Oh, just little changes, so that if by chance she was seen in the street by anyone who had known her as your wife she would not easily be recognised." Oh once more with that exasperating complacence at her own skill in deception—"I thought of every little detail."

Tormarin stood listening to her silently, like a man in a trance. His face had grown drawn and haggard, and his eyes burned in their sockets. Once, as she poured out her story of trickery and deception, she heard him mutter dazedly: "Jean... Jean," and the anguish in his voice might have moved any woman to pity save only one who was utterly and entirely obsessed with the desire for vengeance.

But the intolerable suffering which had suddenly lined his face and rimmed his mouth with tiny beads of sweat was meat and drink to her. She gloried in it. This was her hour of triumph after long years of waiting.

She smiled at him blandly.

"I think I have behaved very well," she pursued. "I might have waited till you were actually married. But I have no wish to punish the little Jean. She, at least, is 'on the square,' as you say—though it would have revenged my Nesta well had I waited. You ruined Nesta's life; I could have ruined the life of the woman you love. I did think of it. Ah! You would have suffered then, knowing that the Jean you worshipped was neither wife, nor maid, but a——"

"Be silent, woman!"

Tortured beyond bearing, this final taunt, levelled at the woman he held more dear than anything in life, snapped his last thread of self-control.

He flung himself forward and his hands were gripping, gripping at the soft ivory throat from which the taunt had sprung. He felt the woman writhe, struggling to pull his hands from her neck. But it meant nothing to him. He did not think of her any longer as a woman. She was something vile—leprous to the very core of her being—a thing to be destroyed. The thing which had made of all Jean's promised happiness a black and bitter mockery.

The mad Tormarin rage surged through his veins like a consuming fire. He would break her—break her and utterly destroy her just as one destroyed a deadly snake.

And then across the thunderous roar that beat in his ears came the beloved voice, the voice that would have power to call him out of the depths of hell itself—Jean's voice.

"Blaise! Blaise! What are you doing? Stop!"

CHAPTER XXXII
THE DIVIDING SWORD

SLOWLY, reluctantly, Tormarin's hands loosened their clasp of Madame de Varigny's throat, and with a swift, flexible twist of the body she slipped aside and stood a few paces away from him.

Jean looked from one to the other with horrified eyes. "Madame de Varigny?—Blaise?" she stammered. "What is it?... Why, you—you might have killed her, Blaise!"

He stared at her blankly. His release of the Italian woman had been in mere blind response to Jean's first imperative appeal that he should desist But the mists of ungovernable anger had hardly yet cleared from his brain; the blood still drummed in his ears like the roar of the sea.

"Blaise"—Jean spoke imploringly. "What were you doing? Tell me——"

With an effort he seemed to recover himself.

"It's a pity you didn't let me finish it, Jean," he said harshly. "Such women are better dead."

Madame de Varigny was fingering her neck delicately where the pressure of Blaise's grip had scored red marks on the cream-like flesh. She seemed quite composed. Her smile still held its quiet triumph and her long dark eyes gleamed with the same mockery that had brought her within measureable distance of quick death.

"As Monsieur Tor-ma-rin seems to find a difficulty in explaining—permit me," she said at last "He was angry with me because I bring him the good news that his wife is still alive, that he need mourn no longer."

While she spoke her eyes, resting on Blaise's mask-like face, held an expression of malicious satisfaction.

"His wife... alive?" repeated Jean dazedly. "Blaise, is she mad? Nesta has been dead years—years." Then, as he made no answer, she continued rapidly, a faint note of fear vibrating in her voice: "Isn't it so? Blaise—speak! Quickly, tell her—Nesta has been dead some years!"

"He cannot tell me anything about her which I do not know already, Mees Peterson, seeing that she is my sister and has been living with me ever since her husband's cruelty drove her from his home."

"Is it true, Blaise?" whispered Jean.

Belief that some substance of terrible truth lay behind the Italian's coolly uttered statements was beginning to lay hold of her.

"Blaise, Blaise"—her voice rising a little—"say it isn't true—tell her it isn't true."

He looked at her speechlessly, but the measureless pain in his eyes answered her more fully, more convincingly than any words.

"You see?" broke in Madame de Varigny triumphantly. "He cannot deny it! It was I who told him of her death and I who now tell him that she still lives. Listen to me, mademoiselle, and I will recount you how— —"

"No!" interrupted Jean proudly. "Whatever there may be for me to hear, I will hear it from Blaise—not from you."

She turned again to Tormarin.

"Tell me everything, Blaise," she said simply.

He took her outstretched hands and drew her slowly towards him. No one, reading now the calm sadness, the stern imprint of endurance on his face, could have imagined it was that of the same man who, a few moments earlier, had been swept by such a tempest of uncontrollable anger.

"Jean," he said very gently and pitifully. "I'm afraid that what Madame de Varigny says may be true. I have no proof that it is not— —"

"Nor have you any proof that it is," broke in Jean swiftly. She swung round on Madame de Varigny. "Where is your proof—where is your proof?"

The Italian smiled.

"Monsieur Tor-ma-rin will find his wife in my car. I bade the chauffeur wait with it at the lodge gate."

"Do you mean you have brought Nesta—here?" cried Blaise.

"Why not?" replied Madame do Varigny, with a return to the same exasperating complacency with which she had originally described her whole scheme of revenge. "And—here? Surely her husband's house is the proper place to which to bring his wife?"

"She cannot remain here," said Blaise with decision.

"No? For the moment that was not my idea. I brought her with me because I thought there could be no more convincing proof."

Blaise looked at her searchingly. He fancied he detected a false note in her voluble speech, and a new idea presented itself to him. Was the woman simply putting up a gigantic bluff? Or was it really Nesta, his wife, waiting in the car at the lodge gates? It occurred to him as perfectly feasible that it might be merely some woman whose remarkable resemblance to the dead girl had suggested to the Countess's fertile brain the scheme that she should impersonate her.

His mind seized eagerly upon the idea, bolstering it up with Madame de Varigny's own admissions. "*I made little changes in her appearance,*" she had said. "*The colour of her hair, the way of dressing it.*" Probably she was relying on those "little changes," and on the blurred recollection resulting from the length of time which had elapsed since Nesta's death, to aid her in her plan of introducing as his wife a woman who closely resembled her. He felt morally sure of it, and the light of hope suddenly shone bravely.

"I believe you are deceiving me," he said quietly. "Lying—as you have lied all through the piece. I'll come and see this 'wife' you have waiting in the car for me"—grimly. He turned to Jean. "Keep up your courage, sweetheart" he said in a low voice full of infinite solicitude. "I believe the whole thing is a put-up job to separate us."

Jean smiled at him radiantly. She felt all at once very confident. In a few minutes this nightmarish story of a Nesta still alive and claiming her rights as Blaise's wife would be proved a lie.

Tormarin crossed the room and opened the door.

"Now, Madame de Varigny—will you come with me?"

The woman hesitated a moment.

"Come," insisted Blaise firmly. "Or—are you afraid, after all, to bring me face to face with my wife?"

She shook her head.

"No," she said. "I am not afraid. It is only that I am so sorry—so sorry for the little Jean."

Her eyes, soft and dark and liquid as the eyes of a deer, sought Jean's beseechingly.

"I am so sorry," she repeated. And passed, slowly,—almost unwillingly, it seemed, out of the room, followed by Tormarin.

Jean raised her head from Blaise's shoulder and pushed back her hair, damp with perspiration, from her forehead. It seemed to her as though she had been down, down into some awful, limitless abyss of darkness from which she was now feebly struggling back to a painful consciousness of material things. A great sea had surged over her head, blotting out everything, and remained poised above her like a huge black arch, imprisoning her in the vast, deserted chaos in which she found herself wandering. Then—after a long time, it seemed—it had surged away again and she could distinguish Blaise's face bent above her.

"Then—then it's true?" she said stupidly. Her voice sounded tiny, even to herself—a mere thread of sound.

Blaise made no answer. He only held her a little closer in his arms. She supposed he hadn't heard that thin little thread of voice. She must try again.

"Is it true, Blaise? Is Nesta——" But somehow the last word wouldn't come.

She felt his arm jerk against her side.

"Yes," he said baldly. "It's true. Nesta is alive. I've seen her."

Jean said nothing. She knew it—had known it all the time the arched wall of sea had kept her down in that awful black waste where there had been neither warmth nor sunshine but only bitter, freezing cold and lightless space. She clung a little closer to Blaise, like a frightened, exhausted child.

"Heart's beloved... little *dearest* Jean..." She heard the wrung murmur of his voice above her head. Then suddenly, his arms tightening round her: "*My soul!*"

The sunlight still slanted in through the windows, mellow and golden. A gay shout of laughter came up from the boat on the lake. The clock on the chimney-piece struck the hour—twelve slow, maddening strokes.

Jean stared at its blank, foolish face. The hands had pointed to half-past eleven when the door of the room had closed behind Blaise and Madame de Varigny. It had taken just a brief half-hour to smash up her whole world—to rob her of everything that mattered.

"I must think—I must think," she muttered.

"Belovedest"—Blaise's voice was wonderfully tender—not with the passionate tenderness of a lover but with a solicitude that was almost maternal. "Belovedest, don't try to think now. Try to rest a little, won't you?"

And at that Jean came right back to an understanding of all that had happened, as the needle of a compass swings back to the frozen north.

"Rest?" she said. "*Rest?* Do you realise that I shall have all the remainder of life to—rest in? There'll he nothing else to do."

She released herself very gently from Tormarin's arms and, crossing the room to the window, stood looking out.

"How funny!" she said in a rather high-pitched, uncertain voice. "It all looks just the same—although everything in the world is changed."

He came and stood beside her.

"No," he said quietly. "Nothing is changed, dear. Our love is the same as it was before. Always remember that."

"But we can't every marry now."

"No. We can't marry—now. You'll never have the Tormarin temper to bear with, after all!"

She laid her hand swiftly across his lips.

"Oh, it was dreadful!" she said, recalling the terrible scene which she had interrupted. "It—it hardly seemed—*you*, Blaise."

"For the moment it wasn't. It was the Tormarin devil—the curse of every generation. But I think that Varigny woman could turn a saint into a devil if she tried! She said something about you—and I couldn't stand it."

"Was that it? Then I suppose I shall have to forgive you"—with a pale little attempt at a smile.

But the half-hearted smile faded again almost instantly.

"Oh, Blaise, what would your temper matter if we could still be together?" she cried passionately. "Nothing in the wide world would matter then!"

Presently she spoke again.

"But it's worse for you than for me. I wish it were more equal."

"How worse for me? I don't understand. Unless"—with a brief, sad smile—"you love me less?"

"Ah, you know I don't mean that! But I've only the separation to face. I'm not tied to somebody I don't love. You've got Nesta to consider."

"Nesta?" He gave a short, grim laugh. "Nesta can go back to where she came from."

There was a long silence. At last Jean broke it.

"Blaise, you can't do that—you can't send her away again," she said in quick, low tones. "She's your wife."

"My wife! She seems to have been oblivious of the fact—and to have wished me to be equally oblivious of it—for the last few years."

"Yes, of course she's been wrong, wickedly wrong. But that doesn't alter the fact that she's your responsibility, Blaise. You must take her back."

"Take her back?"—violently. "I'll be shot if I do! She's chosen to live her life without me for the last few years—she can continue to do so."

Jean laid her hand on his arm. She was smiling wistfully. "Dear, you'll have to take her back," she persisted gently. "Don't you see—she's not wholly to blame? You've admitted that. You've blamed yourself in a large measure for her running away. It's up to you now to put things straight, to—to give her the chance she didn't have before."

"You're discounting these last few years," he returned gravely. "These years in which she has lived a lie, allowing me to believe her dead—cheating and deceiving me as no man was ever cheated before. She's cheated me out of my happiness"—heavily—"taken *you* from me!"

"Yes, I know." Jean's voice quivered, but she steadied it again. "But even in that, she was not solely to blame. You've told me how—how weak she is and easily led astray. And she's very young. What chance would Nesta have of asserting her will against her sister's, even had she wished to return to you? She ran away from Staple in a fit of temper and because you had frightened her. After that—you can see for yourself—Madame de Varigny is responsible for everything that has happened since."

Tormarin remained silent. The quiet justice of Jean's summing up of the situation struck at him hard.

She waited a moment, then added quietly:

"You must take her back, Blaise."

He wheeled round on her violently.

"And you?" he exclaimed. "You? Did you ever love me, Jean, that you can talk so coolly about turning me over to another woman?"

She whitened at the bitter accusation in his tones, but she did not flinch.

"It's just *because* I love you, Blaise, that I want you to do this thing—to do the only thing that is worthy of you. Oh, my dear, my dear"—her hands went out to him in sudden, helpless pleading—"do you think it's *easy* for me to ask it?" The desolate cry pierced him. He caught her in his arms, kissing her fiercely, adoringly.

"Sweetheart!... Forgive me! I'm half mad, I think. Beloved, say that you forgive me!"

She leaned against him, glad to feel the straining clasp of his arms about her—to rest once more in her place against his heart.

"Dearest of all," she said tremulously, "there is no question of forgiveness between us two. There never will be. We're just—both of us—struggling in the dark, and there's only duty"—brokenly—"only duty to hold to."

They stood together in silence, comforted just a little by the mere human touch of each other in this communion of sorrow which had so suddenly come upon them, yet knowing in their hearts that this was the very comfort that must for ever be denied them in the lonely future.

At last Jean raised her head from its resting-place and her eyes searched Blaise's face, asking the question she could no longer bring herself to put in words. He met their gaze. "Jean, is it your wish I do this thing—take Nesta back?" He felt a shudder run through her frame. Twice she tried ineffectually to answer. At last she forced her dry lips to utter an affirmative.

"So be it."

His answer sounded in her ears like the knell to the whole meaning of life. The future was settled. Henceforth their lives must lie apart.

"So be it," said Blaise. "She shall come back and take her place again at Staple."

Jean clung to him a little closer.

"Blaise, beloved—I know the harder part will be yours. But mine won't be easy, dear. I shall go to Charnwood to be with Claire at once—to-morrow—and it won't be easy, when I see in an evening the lights twinkle up at Staple, to know that you two are within, shut in from the world together, while I'm outside—always outside your life and your love."

"You'll never be outside my love," he said swiftly. "That's yours, now and forever. And no other woman shall rob you of one jot or tittle of it, were she my wife twenty times over. I will bring Nesta back to Staple, and she shall bear my name and live as my wife in the eyes of the world. But my love—that is yours, utterly and entirely. Yours and no other's."

She lifted her face to his, and their lips met in a kiss that was the seal of love and all love's faithfulness.

"So is mine yours," she said. "How and forever, in this world and the next. Oh, Blaise—beloved!"—she clung to him in a passion of love and anguish and straining belief—"Some day, surely, in that other world, God will give us freedom to take our happiness!"

CHAPTER XXXIII
THE RETURNING TIDE

TWO months had elapsed since Fate's dividing sword had fallen, forever separating Jean from the man she loved, and the subsequent march of events, with the many changes involved and the bitter loneliness of soul entailed, had made the two months seem to her more like two years.

She had left Staple for Charnwood on the day following that of Madame de Varigny's visit. It was no longer possible for her to remain under the same roof with Blaise, where the enforced strain of meeting each other daily, and of endeavouring to behave as though nothing more than mere commonplace friendship linked them together, would have been too great for either of them to endure even for the few remaining days which still intervened before the date originally planned for her departure.

Lady Anne, with her usual sympathetic insight, had made no effort to dissuade her, reluctant though she had been to part with her. For herself, the fact that Nesta was alive had come upon her in the light of an almost overwhelming blow. She had never liked the girl, whereas she had grown to look upon Jean as a beloved daughter, and no one had rejoiced more sincerely than his mother when Blaise had confided to her the news of his engagement. At last she would see that grey page in his life turned down for ever and the beginning of a newer, fairer page, illuminated with happiness! And instead, like a tide that has receded far out and then rushes in again with redoubled energy, the whole misery and sorrow of the past had returned upon him, a thousand times accentuated by reason of his love for Jean.

It was with a heavy heart, therefore, that Lady Anne, together with Nick, quitted Staple and established herself for the second time at the Dower House, retiring thither in favour of Nesta who was now installed once more at the Manor. And the thought of how gladly she would have effected the same change, had it been Jean whom Blaise was bringing home as his bride, added but a keener pang to her sorrow.

She watched with anxious eyes the progress of events at Staple. At the commencement of the new régime Nesta had appeared genuinely repentant and ashamed of her conduct in the past, and there was something disarming in the little, half-apologetic air with which she had at first reassumed her position of châtelaine of Staple, deferring eagerly to Blaise on every point and trying her utmost to please him and conform to his wishes. It held something of the appeal of a forgiven child who tries to atone for former naughtiness by an almost alarming access of virtue.

She accepted with meek docility Blaise's decision regarding the purely formal relations upon which their married life was henceforth to be based, apparently humbly thankful to be reinstated as his wife on any terms whatsoever that he chose to dictate..

"I know I have been bad—*bad*," she declared, "to run away and leave you like that. I can't" —forlornly—"hope for you to love me again——"

And Tormarin had replied with unmistakable decision:

"No, you can't hope for that. And I'm glad you understand and recognise the fact. Still, we can try to be good friends, Nesta, at least."

But this tranquil state of things only lasted for a comparatively short time. Very soon, as the novelty and satisfaction of her reinstatement began to wear off, Nesta became more self-assured and, apparently, considerably less frequently visited by spasms of repentance and remorse.

Her butterfly nature could retain no very deep impression for any length of time, and gradually the characteristics of the old Nesta—the pettish, self-willed, pleasure-loving woman of former times—began to reassert themselves.

Blaise tried hard to exercise forbearance with her and to treat her, at least with justice and with a certain meed of kindliness. But she did not second his efforts. Instead, she became more exigent and difficult as time passed on.

She was no longer satisfied by the fact that she was once more installed as the mistress of Staple. She demanded a husband who would surround her with all the little observances that only love itself can dictate, whom she could alternately scold and cajole as the fancy took her, but who would always come back to her, after a tiff, ready anew to play the adoring lover.

She found Blaise's cool, measured, elder-brotherly kindness unendurable, and she exhausted herself beating continually against the rock of his determination, without producing any effect other than to make his manner even more austere, less friendly than it had been before.

Then when she recognised her total inability to move him to any sort of responsive emotion, and that her beauty—which was undeniable—made no more impression upon him than if he had been blind, she resorted to the old, painfully, familiar weapons of tears and fits of temper, in the course of which she would upbraid him bitterly, pouring forth streams of reproaches which more often than not culminated in an attack of hysterics.

All of which Blaise bore with a curious, stoical self-control. It seemed as though the Tormarin temper had been exorcised, as if that fierce storm of anger provoked by Madame de Varigny's taunts, and which had so nearly resulted in a tragedy, had shocked Blaise into realisation of the terrible latent possibilities of the family failing and the absolute necessity for an iron self-government.

For weeks he supported Nesta's petty gibes and ebullitions of temper with illimitable patience, and it was only when, trading on his unaccustomed forbearance, she ventured too far, that she was brought very suddenly to understand that there was a limit beyond which she might not go.

"I know why you no longer love me," she told him at last, on an occasion when she had been vainly endeavouring, by every feminine blandishment and wile of which she was mistress, to evoke from him some sign of an awakening *tendresse*. "I know!"

She nodded her dark head significantly, while pin-points of jealous anger flickered in her long, narrow eyes, black as midnight.

"Then, if you know," replied Tormarin patiently, "it is surely most foolish of you to keep asking why I do not. Why can't you content yourself with things as they are, Nesta? We can only try to make the best of a bad job. You don't help me much in the matter."

"I don't want to help you," she retorted viciously. "I want you to love me. And you won't, because of that washed-out-looking, carroty-haired woman who is living with Lady Latimer. And she's in love with you, too!... No! I *won't* be quiet! Oh!"—her voice rising hysterically—"you think I don't notice things, but I do. I do, I tell you!"

She sprang up from the couch, where she had been lolling indolently amid a heap of cushions, and crossed the room to his side.

"Do you hear me?" she cried violently, shaking him by the arm. "You think I'm a blind fool! But I'm not! I'm not! I've seen that Peterson woman looking at you like a cat looking through the larder window——"

Suddenly she felt Blaise's hand clapped against her lips, stemming the torrent of vulgar recrimination and abuse that poured from them. He held it there quite gently, so as not to hurt her, but immovably, and she had perforce to hear what he wished to say in rebellious silence.

"Listen to me," he said gently. "It is quite true what you say—that I love Jean Peterson and that she loves me. But we have given up our love, and with it our hope of happiness in this world, for you. In return, you will give up something for us. You will give up the infinite pleasure you appear to derive from vilifying and belittling a woman who is as much above you as the heavens are above the earth, whose conception of love is as fine and pure as yours is mean and commonplace and jealous. You will never again speak to Miss Peterson with anything but respect, nor will you ever again refer to the love which you now know for a fact exists between us. Your lips soil such love as ours. If you do, if you disobey my commands in either of these respects, you go out of my house that same day. *And you don't return.*"

He released her and had the satisfaction, for once, of perceiving that she believed he meant what he said. Presumably she came to the conclusion that, in the circumstances, discretion was the better part of valour, for she made no attempt to challenge his determination in the matter.

At the same time, unknown to him, she compelled Jean to pay for the silence enforced upon her at home. With a species of venom, absurdly childish in its manifestation, she essayed to excite Jean's envy by constantly enlarging to her upon the subject of Blaise's perfections as a husband, drawing entirely imaginary descriptions of the attention he paid her and of his constant solicitude for her welfare, and vaunting her happiness at being his wife.

"I am so proud to have won so fine and splendid a husband," she would declare fervently. "Would you not feel the same, Miss Peterson, if you were me?"

And Jean would make answer, outwardly unmoved:

"Indeed I should. You ought to be a happy woman, Mrs. Tormarin."

The quiet composure which Jean invariably opposed to these knat-like attacks annoyed Nesta intensely. Endowed with all the petty jealousy of a small nature, she herself, had the situation been reversed, would have found this pinprick kind of warfare insupportable, and it made her furious that her best thought-out and most spiteful efforts failed to goad Jean into any expression of either anger or distress. The "cold Englishwoman's" armour of indifference and reserve seemed impervious to no matter what poison-tipped dart she loosed against her.

Nesta felt that, as the woman in possession, she was missing half the satisfaction in life by reason of her inability to triumph openly over the other woman—the woman without the gate. Finally, at the end of her resources of innuendo and allusion, she tried the effect of open warfare.

She had driven over to Charnwood to call and, as Claire was away, spending the afternoon with friends, Jean had perforce to entertain her undesired visitor alone. It was just as she was preparing to take her departure that Nesta launched her attack.

"You look so ill, Miss Peterson," she remarked commiseratingly. "So pale and worn! It does not suit you, I am sure, for of course you must have been very pretty at one time for my husband to have wished to marry you."

Jean stared at her without reply. The outrageous speech almost took her breath away, by its sheer, impudent bravado.

"There!" Nesta feigned dismay. "Now I have offended you! And I so want us to be good friends. But of course"—quickly—"it is difficult for you to feel friendly towards the wife of Blaise. I can understand that. I suppose"—her head a little tilted to one side like that of an enquiring robin and her eyes fastened on the other's white face with a merciless, gimlet gaze that filled Jean with helpless rage—"I suppose you loved him *very* much?"

Jean felt the blood rush into her cheeks and caught a responsive gleam of satisfaction in the other's half-closed eyes.

"I think that is hardly a subject which can be discussed between us," she said, with a supreme effort at self-control.

And then, to her unbounded thankfulness, Tucker threw open the door and announced that Mrs. Tormarin's car was waiting.

This open declaration of hostility on Nesta's part gave Jean food for reflection. Briefly she recounted the incident to Claire, adding:

"It means I must not go to Staple again. If she intends to adopt that attitude, it would make a situation which is already quite difficult enough hopelessly impossible."

The two girls were pacing up and down the terrace at Charnwood together when Jean indicated the consequences of Nesta's visit, and Claire, sensing the pain in her friend's voice, pressed her arm sympathetically. But she said nothing. What was there to say? Within herself, she felt that Jean's determination to eschew the Tormarin menage altogether was the only wise one.

"Poor Blaise!" pursued Jean, a slight tremor in her voice. "He has the hardest part to bear. She must make life hideously difficult for him."

Claire nodded.

"Yes. He is looking very fagged and strained. Horrid little beast!" she added with unusual vehemence. "Why on earth couldn't she have *stayed* dead?"

Jean laughed joylessly.

"Why indeed?—Only she never really died, you see."

"Jean"—Claire's hand crept further along the other's arm and the kind little fingers sought and clasped Jean's own—"if you knew how miserable I am about you! It makes me feel wicked—disgustingly selfish and wicked!— to be so happy myself when you have so much to bear."

There were tears in her voice, and Jean squeezed her hand reassuringly.

"My dear," she said earnestly, "you had your black years if anyone ever had! If a woman ever deserved her happiness at last, you do.... I suppose we all get our share of trouble in this world," she went on thoughtfully. "I remember the first time I ever met Blaise—that day at Montavan, you know—he said that Destiny, with her snuffers, came to most of us sooner or later and snuffed out our light of happiness. Well"—rather drearily—"I suppose it's my turn now and she's come to me. That's all."

A little wind blew up from the valley, chill and complaining. Autumn had the world at her mercy now, and a grey mist was rising from the sodden fields, soaked by the continual rains of the preceding fortnight.

Claire shivered.

"Let's go in," she said. "It's growing too cold to stay out any longer. Besides, it's depressing. Grey skies, bare branches—Oh! How I detest the autumn!" They turned and retraced their steps to the house. As they entered by way of the front door, they caught a glimpse of the postman making his way briskly down the drive. A solitary letter lay upon the hall table, addressed to Jean in a rather flourishy copper-plate style of writing.

"A bill, I suppose!" she commented indifferently.

She picked it up carelessly, carrying it unopened to her room. Nor did she open it immediately upon arriving there, stopping first to remove her hat and coat.

When at last she slit the envelope she found that it was no tradesman's bill, as she had imagined, but a letter from Glyn Peterson's family solicitor, announcing, in the stiff phraseology without which no lawyer seems able to express himself, the sudden death of her father.

Jean sat down abruptly, her legs seeming all at once to give way under her. She could not grasp it—could not realise that the witty, charming personality which, after all, in spite of Peterson's lack of the more conventional paternal attributes, had meant a great deal to her, had been swept without warning out of her life for ever.

Glyn Peterson had, it seemed, died very suddenly, in a remote corner of Africa whither his restless wanderings had led him, and it had been some weeks before the news of his death had reached his lawyer, who had immediately communicated it to Jean.

By his will, everything he possessed, except for a certain sum set aside to cover a few legacies to old and valued servants, was left to Jean, and with the quaint whimsicality which was characteristic of him he had particularly mentioned: "*Beirnfels, the House of Dreams-Come-True.*"

The little phrase, with its suggestion of joyous consummation, stabbed her with a sharp thrill of pain. Greeting her, as it did, at the moment when all her hopes of happiness were lying trampled beneath the iron heel of hostile destiny, it seemed to add a last touch of irony to the bitterness of the burden she had to bear.

The House of Dreams-Come-True! In the solicitude and silence of her room Jean laughed out loud at the mockery of it! But her breath caught in her throat, sobbingly, and then quite suddenly the merciful, healing tears began to fall, and, laying her head down on her arms, she cried unrestrainedly.

CHAPTER XXXIV
THE TEST

NEW YEAR'S EYE found Jean sitting alone in Claire's special sanctum — the room which had witnessed that frightful scene when Sir Adrian had suddenly gone mad.

It was a cosy enough little room in winter-time. A cheery fire crackled in the open grate, while a heavy velvet curtain was drawn across the door that gave egress to the terrace, effectually screening out the ubiquitous draught which invariably seeks entry through crack and hinge-space.

Claire was at the Dower House this evening, where a New Year's dinner-party was in progress, but Jean had no heart for festivities of any kind even had she not been precluded from taking part in them by reason of her father's death.

The grief and strain of the last four months had set their mark upon her. She was much thinner than formerly — her extreme slenderness accentuated by the clinging black of the dress she was wearing — while faint purple shadows lay beneath her eyes, giving her a look of frailty and fatigue.

She and Claire led a very sober and uneventful existence at Charnwood, the one absorbed in her quiet happiness, the other in her quiet grief. But the bond of their friendship had held true throughout the differing fortunes which had fallen to the lot of each, and although for Jean there was inevitable additional pain involved in still remaining within the neighbourhood of Staple, it was counterbalanced by the comfort she drew from Clare's companionship.

Besides, as she reflected dispiritedly, where else had she to go? The Dower House would have been open to her, of course, at any time, but there she would be certain to encounter Blaise more frequently, and of late her principal preoccupation had been to avoid such meeting whenever possible. And she could not face Beirnfels yet — alone! Some day, when Claire was married, she knew that she must brace herself to return there — to a house of dreams that would never come true now. But at present she shrank intolerably from the idea. She craved companionship—above all, the consoling, tender understanding which Claire, who had herself suffered, was so well able to give her.

The book that she had been reading earlier in the evening lay open on her knee, and her thoughts were with Claire now. She pictured her sitting next to Nick at dinner, her flower-like face radiant with unclouded happiness, and Jean was thankful to the very bottom of her heart that she was able to feel glad—glad of that happiness. At least her own sorrow had not yet taught her the grudging envy which cannot endure another's joy.

With a quickly repressed sigh, she turned again to her book. Its pages fluttered faintly, as though stirred by some passing current of air, and Jean, coming suddenly out of her reverie, was conscious of a cool draught wafting towards her from the direction of the terrace door.

Vaguely surprised, she glanced up, and a startled cry broke from her lips. The door was open, the folds of the curtain had been drawn aside, and in the aperture stood Blaise Tormarin.

Jean sprang up from her chair and stood staring at him with dilated eyes, one hand gripping the edge of the chimney-piece.

"Blaise!... You!" The words issued stammeringly from her lips.

"Yes," he returned shortly. "May I come in?"

Without waiting for an answer he closed the door behind him, letting the curtain fall back into its place, and crossed the room to her side.

Jean felt her heart contract as her eyes marked the changes wrought in him by the few weeks which had elapsed since she had seen him. His face was haggard as though from lack of sleep, and the lines on either side the mouth were scored deep into the flesh. The mouth itself closed in a tense line of savage misery and the stark bitterness of his eyes filled her with grief and pity, knowing how utterly powerless she was to help or comfort him.

Distrusting her self-control, she snatched at the first conventional remark that suggested itself.

"I thought—I thought you and Nesta were both dining at the Dower House," she said confusedly.

"Nesta is there. I made an excuse. I came here instead."

Something in the curt, clipped sentences sounded a note of warning in her ears.

"But you ought not to have come here," she replied quickly—defensively almost. "Why have you come, Blaise?"

"I came," he said slowly, "because I can't bear my life without you a day longer. Because— — Oh, Jean! Jean!... *Beloved!* Do you need to ask me why I came?"

With a swift, irresistible movement he swept her up into his arms, holding her crushed against his breast, his mouth on hers, kissing her as a man kisses when love that has been long thwarted and denied at last bursts asunder the shackles which constrained it.

And Jean, starved for four long months of the touch of the beloved arms, the pressure of the beloved lips upon her own, had yielded to him almost before she was aware of her surrender.

Then the remembrance of the woman who stood between them rushed across her and she tore herself free from his embrace, white and trembling in every limb.

"Blaise!... Blaise!... What are you thinking of? Oh! We're mad—mad!"

She covered her face with her shaking hands but he drew them away, gazing down at her with eyes that worshipped.

"No, beloved, we're not mad," lie cried triumphantly. "We're sane— sane at last. We were mad to think we could live apart, mad to dream we could starve love like ours. That was when we were mad! But we'll never be parted again; sweet— —"

"Blaise," she whispered, staring at him with horrified, dilated eyes. "You don't know what you are saying! You're forgetting Nesta—your wife. Oh, go—go quickly! You must not stay here and talk like this to me!"

"No," he returned. "I won't go, Jean. I've come to take you away with me." Once more his arms went round her. "Belovedest, I can't live without you any longer. I've tried—and I can't do it. Jean, you'll come? You love me enough—enough to come away with me to the ends of the earth where we'll find happiness at last?"

She sought to free herself from his, clasp, pressing with straining hands against his chest.

"No! No!" she cried breathlessly. "I can't go with you... you know I can't! Ah! Don't ask me, Blaise!" There was an agony of supplication in her voice.

"But I do ask you. And if you love me"—his eyes holding hers—"you'll come, Jean."

"I do love you," she answered earnestly. "But it isn't the you I love asking me this, Blaise. It's some other man—a stranger— —" "If you love me, you'll come," he reiterated doggedly. "I can't live without you, Jean. I want you—oh, heart's beloved, if you knew—" And the burning, passionate words, the pent-up love and longing of months of separation and despair, came pouring from his lips—beseeching and demanding, wringing her heart, pulling at the love within her that ached to give him the answer which he craved.

"Oh, Blaise, dearest of all—hush! Hush!" She checked him brokenly, with quivering lips. "I can't go with you. It wouldn't bring us happiness. Ah, listen to me, dear!" She came close to him and laid her hands imploringly on his arm, lifting her white, stricken face to his. "It would only spoil our love—to take it like that when we have no right to. It would smirch and soil it, make it something different. I think—I think, in the end, Blaise, it would kill it."

"Nothing would ever kill my love for you," he exclaimed passionately. "Jean, little Jean, think of what our life together might be—the glory and beauty of it—just you and I in our House of Dreams!"

She caught her breath. Oh! Why did he make it so hard for her? With every fibre of her being yearning towards him she must refuse, deny him, drive him away from her.

"No, no!" she cried tremulously. "We could never reach our House of Dreams that way—Oh, I know it! At least, not the sort of House of Dreams that would be worth anything to you or me, Blaise. It would only be a sham, a make-believe. You can't build true on a rotten foundation.... Don't ask me any more, dear. It's so hard—so hard to keep on saying no when everything in me wants to say yes. But I must say it. And you... you must go back to Nesta."

Her voice almost failed her. She could feel her strength ebbing with every moment that he stayed beside her. She knew that she would not be able to resist his pleading much longer. Her own heart was fighting against her—fighting on his side!

He saw her weakness and caught at it eagerly.

"Do you know what you're asking?" he demanded hoarsely. "Do you know what you are sending me back to? Our life together—Nesta's and mine—has been simple hell upon earth. I obeyed you—and I took her back. But I have done no good by it. She is as weak and worthless as she ever was. Our days are one continual round of bickering and quarrels." His face darkened. "And she is not satisfied! Her nominal position as my wife does not con tent her. Do you understand what that must mean—if I go back?"

He paused, his eyes bent steadily upon her. "Jean"—very low—"now that you know—will you still send me back to Nesta? Or will you come with me and let us find our happiness together?"

He watched the scarlet flood surge into her face and then retreat, leaving it a pallid white.

"Answer me!" he persisted, as she remained silent.

"Wait... wait a little..." she muttered helplessly.

She turned away from him and, leaning her elbows on the chimney-piece, buried her face in her hands.

The supreme test had come at last. She realised, now, that her renunciation—that renunciation which had cost her so much pain and bitterness—had been, after all, only something superficial and incomplete. She had not made the full sacrifice that duty and honour demanded of her. Though she had outwardly renounced her lover—bade him return to Nesta—she still held him hers by the utter faithfulness of his love for her. Nesta had had but the husk, the shell—a husband in name only, every hour of their life together an insult to her pride and womanhood.

Jean's thoughts lashed her. Her shoulders bent and cowered a little as though beneath a physical blow.

There had been a time—oh! very long ago, it seemed, before Destiny had come with her snuffers and quenched the twin flames and love and happiness—a time when dimly, as in some exquisite dream, she had heard the sound of little voices, felt the helpless touch of tiny hands. Perhaps Nesta, too, had heard those voices, felt those clinging hands, while her soul quickened to the vision of a future which might hold some deeper meaning, some more sacred trust and purpose, than her empty, wayward past.

And she, Jean, had stood between Nesta and the fulfilment of that dream, forever forbidding her entrance to her woman's kingdom.

She saw it all now with a terrible clarity of vision, understood to the full the two alternatives which faced her—to go with Blaise, as he implored, or to send him—her man, the man she loved—back to Nesta. There was no longer any middle course.

A voice sounded in her ears.

"*No true happiness ever came of running away from duty. And if ever I'm up against such a thing—a choice like this—I hope to God I'd be able to hang on, to run straight, even if it half-killed me to do it!*"

The words sounded so clear and distinct that Jean half raised her head to see who spoke them. And then, in an overwhelming rush of memory, she recognised that it was no actual voice she heard but the mental echo of her own words to Nick—to Nick at the time when he had been passing through a like fire of fierce temptation.

How easily, in her young, untried ignorance, the words had fallen from her lips as she had urged Nick to renounce his fixed resolve! Such eminently wise and excellent counsel! And how little—how crassly little had she realised at the time the huge demand that she was making!

She had spoken as though it were comparatively easy to reject the wrong and choose the right—to follow the stern and narrow path of Duty, through the mists and utter darkness that enshrouded it, up to those shining heights which lie beyond human sight—the outposts of Eternal Heaven itself.

Easy!.... Oh, God!....

When at last Jean uncovered her face and lifted it to meet the set gaze of the man beside her, it was wan and ravaged "the face of one who has come through some fierce purgatory of torment."

"Well?" he demanded, his voice roughened because he found himself unable to steady it with that strained and altered face upturned to his. "Well? Are you going to send me back to Nesta?"

She did not answer his question. Instead, she put another.

"Do you think she—loves you?"

He stared.

"Nesta? Yes. As far as her sort can love, I believe she does."

Jean nodded, as though it were the answer she had expected.

"Blaise... I'm going to send you back to her. I'm sure now. I *know*. It's the only thing we can do... We must say good-bye—altogether—never see each other again."

"Never?" The word came draggingly.

"Never. It—it would be too hard for us, Blaise, to see each other."

"Yes," he answered slowly. "It would be too hard."

They were both silent. The minutes ticked away unregarded. Time had ceased to count. This farewell was till the end of time.

"Blaise—" All the resonance had gone out of her voice. It sounded flat and tired. "You—you will go back to her?"

"Yes, I will go back."

She stretched out her hands flutteringly.

"Then go.... go soon, Blaise! I—I can't bear very much more."

He opened his arms, then, and she went to him, and for a space they clung together in silence. For the last time he set his lips to hers, held her once more against his heart. Then slowly they drew apart, stricken eyes gazing lingeringly into other eyes as stricken, and presently the closing of the terrace door told her that he had gone, and that she must turn her feet to the solitary path of those who have said farewell to love.

Henceforth, she would be alone—living or dying, quite alone.

It was long past midnight when Claire returned from the Dower House.

She found Jean sitting beside the grey embers of a burnt-out fire, her hands lying folded upon her knee, her eyes staring stonily in front of her in a fixed, unseeing gaze.

Claire called to her softly, as when one wakes a sleeper.

"Jean!"

Jean turned her head.

"So you have got back?" she said dully. She stood up stiffly, as though her limbs were cramped. "Claire, I am going away—right away from here—to Beirnfels."

"Why?" asked Claire.

She waited tensely for the answer.

"Blaise has been here. He asked me to go away with him. I've sent him back to Nesta."

The short, stilted sentences fell mechanically from her lips. She spoke exactly like a child repeating a lesson learned by rote.

Claire's eyes grew very pitiful.

"And must you go to Beirnfels alone?" she asked quietly. "Won't you take me with you?"

"*Will you come?*"—incredulously.

"Of course I'll come. I shouldn't dream of letting you go by yourself."

And then, all at once, Jean's tired body, exhausted by the soul's long conflict, gave way, and she slipped to the ground in a dead faint.

CHAPTER XXXV
THE EVE OF DEPARTURE

A WEEK later Jean sat at the foot of the stairs and surveyed with faint amusement the motley collection of trunks and suit-cases which thronged the hall.

She was still looking pale and worn, strung up to face her self-imposed exile from the country which now held everything that was dear to her, but no enormity of sorrow, would ever blind Jean for long to the whimsical aspect that attends so many of the little things of daily life.

"What a lot of useless lumber we women carry about with us wherever we go!" she commented. "Five—six—*seven* packages to supply the needs of two solitary females—and Heaven only knows how many brown paper parcels will be required at the last moment for all the things we shall find we have forgotten when the time actually comes to start." Claire, standing on the flight of stairs above and viewing the assemblage in the hall from over the top of the banister rail, giggled helplessly.

"Yes, they do look a lot," she admitted. "However"—hopefully— "there'll be plenty of room for them all when we actually get to Beirnfels."

"Oh, plenty," agreed Jean. "But we've got to convey them half across Europe first—two lone women and one miserable maid who will probably combine train-sickness and home-sickness to an extent that will totally incapacitate her for the performance of her duties."

At this moment the front-door bell clanged violently through the house, as though pulled by someone in a tremendous hurry. Claire hastily withdrew her head from over the banister rail and disappeared upstairs, while Jean relinquished the accommodation offered by the bottommost step and sought refuge in the nearest of the sitting-rooms, closing the door stealthily behind her.

A moment later Tucker, who had caught sight of her hurriedly retreating figure, reopened it and announced imperturbably:

"Mr. Burke."

Jean greeted him with surprise, but without any feeling of embarrassment. So much had happened since the day she had eluded him on the Moor, events of such intimate and tragic import had swept her path, that the unexpected meeting failed to rouse any feeling either of anger or dismay. Burke, and everything connected with him, belonged to another period of her existence altogether—to that glorious care-free time when it had seemed as though life were a deep, inexhaustible well bubbling over with wonderful possibilities. Burke was merely a ghost—a *revenant* from that far distant epoch.

"I'm in time, then?" he said, when he had shaken hands. "In time? In time for what?"

"In time to see you before you go."

"Oh, yes." Jean spoke lightly. "You're in time for that. But who told you I was going away? I didn't know you were in England, even."

"I came back a fortnight ago—to London. Judith wired me from home that you were leaving Coombe Eavie."

"I don't see the necessity for her wiring you," remarked Jean a little coldly. "There was no need for you to see me."

"There was—every need."

She glanced at him keenly, detecting a new note in his voice, an unexpected gravity and restraint.

"Every need," he repeated. He paused, then went on quickly, with a nervousness that was foreign to him. "Jean, I know everything that has happened—that your engagement to Tormarin is at an end—and I have come to ask you if you will be my wife. No—hear me out!"—as she would have interrupted him. "I'm not asking you now as—as I did before. If you will marry me, I swear I will ask for nothing that you are not willing to give. I'm making no demands. I've learned now"—with a faint weary smile—"that you cannot force love. It can only be given. And I want nothing but just the right to take care of you, to shield you—to keep the sharp corners of life away from you." Then, as he read her incredulous face, he went on gravely: "If I had wanted more than that, Jean, if I had not learned something—just from loving you, I should not have waited until now. I should have come at once—as soon as I learned from Madame de Varigny that Tormarin's wife was still alive."

She looked at him curiously.

"Why didn't you come then, Geoffrey? I sometimes wondered—you being you!"—with a faint smile. "Because, of course, I knew why you had rushed off to France. Madame de Varigny explained that."

A dull flush mounted to his face.

"Did she? I expect she told you merely what was the truth. I went to see her because she had assured me that she could stop your marriage with Tormarin—could interfere in some way to prevent it. That was why I went to France.... But when she told me her blackguardly scheme—how she had planned and plotted to conceal the fact that Tormarin's wife was alive—*and why* she had done it, I would have no hand in anything that followed. I'm no saint"—a brief, ironical smile flitted across his face—"but there are some methods at which even I draw the line."

"So—that was why you stayed away?"

"That was why. I wanted you, Jean—God only knows how I wanted you!—but I couldn't try to force your hand at such a time. I couldn't profit by a damnable scheme like that."

Jean's eyes grew soft as she realised that beneath all the impetuous arrogance and dominant demands of the man's temperament there yet lay something fine and clean and straight—difficult to get at, perhaps, but which could yet rise, in answer to a sense of honour and fairness with which she had not credited him, and take command of his whole nature.

"I'm glad—glad you didn't come, Geoffrey," she said gently. "Glad you—couldn't."

"I don't know that I'm glad about it," he returned with a grim candour. "I simply couldn't do it, and that's all there is to it. But I've come now, Jean. I've come because I want you to give me just the right to look after you. I'm not asking for anything. I only want to serve you—if you'll let me—just to be near you. If Tormarin were free, I would not have come to you again. I know I should have no chance. But he's not free. Does that give me a chance, Jean? If it doesn't, I'll take myself off—I'll never bother you again. I'll try Africa—big game shooting"—with a short laugh. "But if it does——"

He paused and waited for her answer. The intensity of longing in his eyes was the sole indication of the emotion that stirred within him—an emotion held in check by a stern self-control that seemed to Jean to be part of this new, changed lover of hers. Surely, in the months which had elapsed since she had fled from him on Dartmoor, he had fought with his devils and cast them out!

She held out her hands to him.

"Geoffrey, I'm so sorry—but I'm afraid it doesn't. I wish—I wish I could give you any other answer. But, you see, it isn't marrying—it's love that matters. And all my love is given."

He took her hands in his and held them gently with that strange, new restraint he seemed to have learned.

"I see," he said slowly. Then for a moment his calm wavered. The underlying passion, so strongly held in leash, shook the even tones of his voice. "Tormarin is a lucky man—in spite of everything! I'd give my soul to have what he has—your love, Jean."

His big hands closed round her slight ones and he lifted them to his lips. Then, without another word, he went away, and Jean was left wondering sorrowfully why the love that she did not want was offered her in such full measure, hers to take at will, while the love for which she craved, the love which would have meant the glory and fulfilment of life itself, was denied her—shut away by all the laws of God and Man.

CHAPTER XXXVI
REUNION

JEAN leaned idly against the ancient wall which bounded the stone-paved court at Beirnfels and looked down towards the valley below.

Spring was in the air—late comer to this eastern corner of Europe—but, at last, even here the fragrance of fresh growing things was permeating the atmosphere, strips of vivid blue rent the grey skies, and splashes of golden sunshine lay dappled over the shining roofs of the village that nestled in the valley.

But no responsive light had lit itself in Jean's wistful eyes. She was out of tune with the season. Spring and hope go hand in hand, the one symbolical of the other, and the promise of spring-time, the blossom of hope, was dead within her heart—withered almost before it had had time to bud.

The months since she had quitted England had sufficed to blunt the keen edge of her pain, but always she was conscious of a dull, unending ache—a corroding sense of the uselessness and emptiness of life.

Yet she had learned to be thankful for even this much respite from the piercing agony of the first few weeks which she had spent at Beirnfels. Whatever the coming years might bring her of relief from pain, or even of some modicum of joy, those weeks when she had suffered the torments of the damned would remain stamped indelibly upon her memory.

During the last days at Charnwood she had been keyed up to a high pitch of endurance by the very magnitude of the renunciation she had made. It seems as though, when the soul strains upwards to the accomplishment of some deed that is almost beyond the power of weak human nature to achieve, there is vouchsafed, for the time being, a merciful oblivion to the immensity of pain involved. A transport of spiritual fervour lifts the martyr beyond any ordinary recognition of the physical fire that burns and chars his flesh, and some such ecstasy of sacrifice had supported Jean through the act of abnegation by which she had surrendered her love, and with it her life's happiness, at the foot of the stern altar of Duty.

Afterwards had followed the preparations and bustle of departure, the necessary arrangements to be made and telegraphed to Beirnfels, and finally the long journey across Europe and the hundred and one small details that required settlement before she and Claire were fully installed at Beirnfels and the wheels of the household machinery running smoothly.

But when all this was accomplished, when the need to arrange and plan and make decisions had gone by and her mind was free to concern itself again with her own affairs, then Jean realised the full price of her renunciation.

And she paid it. In days that were an endless procession of anguished hours; in sleepless nights that were a mental and physical torment of unbearable longing such as she had never dreamed of; in tears and in dumb, helpless silences, she paid it. And at last, out of those racked and tortured weeks she emerged into a numbed, listless capacity to pick up once more the torn and mutilated threads of life.

Looking backward, she marvelled at the wonderful patience with which Claire had borne with her, at the selfless way in which she had devoted all her energies to ministering to one who was suffering from heart-sickness — that most wearying of all complaints to the sufferer's friends because so difficult of comprehension by those not similarly afflicted.

Nick's "pale golden narcissus!" To Jean, who had clung to her, helped inexpressibly by her tranquil, steadfast, unswerving faith and loving-kindness, it seemed as though the staunch and sturdy oak were a more appropriate metaphor in which to express the soul of Claire.

She heard her now, coming with light steps across the court. She rarely left Jean brooding long alone these days, exercising all her tact and ingenuity to devise some means by which she might distract her thoughts when she could see they had slipped back into the past.

Jean turned to greet her with a faint smile.

"Well, my good angel? Come to rout me out? I suppose" — teasingly — "you want me to ride down to the village and bring back two lemons urgently demanded by the cook?"

Claire laughed a little. Many had been the transparent little devices she had employed to beguile Jean into the saddle, knowing well that once she was on the back of her favourite mare the errand which was the ostensible purpose of the occasion would quite probably be entirely forgotten. But Jean would return from a long ride over the beloved hills and valleys that had been familiar to her from childhood with a faint colour in her pale cheeks, and with the shadow in her eyes a little lightened. There is no cure for sickness of the soul like the big, open spaces of the earth and God's clean winds and sunlight.

"No," said Claire, "it's not lemons this time."

"Then what is it?" demanded Jean. "You didn't come out here just to look at the view. There's an air of importance about you."

It was true. Claire wore a little fluttering aspect of excitement. The colour came and went swiftly in her cheeks, and her eyes had a bright, almost dazzled look, while a small anxious frown kept appearing between her pretty brows. She regarded Jean uncertainly.

"Well—yes, it is something," she acknowledged. "I had a letter from Lady Anne this morning."

Both girls had their *premiers déjeuners* served to them in their rooms, so that each one's morning mail was an unknown quantity to the other until they met downstairs.

"From Lady Anne?" Jean looked interested. "What does she say?"

"She says—she writes———" Here Claire floundered and came to a stop as though uncertain how to proceed, the little puzzled frown deepening between her brows. "Oh, Jean, she had a special reason for writing—some news——"

Jean's arm, hanging slackly at her side, jerked suddenly. Something in Claire's half-frightened, deprecating air sent a thrill of foreboding through her. Her heart turned to ice within her.

"News?" she said in a harsh, strangled voice. "Tell me quick—what is it?... Blaise? He's not—dead?" Her face, drained of every drop of colour, her suddenly pinched nostrils and eyes stricken with quick fear drew a swift cry from Claire.

"No—no!" she exclaimed in hasty reassurance. "It's *good* news! Good—-not bad!"

Jean's taut muscles relaxed and she leaned against the wall as though seeking support.

"You frightened me," she said dully. "Good news? Then it can't be for me. What is it, Claire? Is Nick"—forcing a smile—"coming out here to see you?"

Claire nodded.

"Yes, Nick—and Blaise with him."

Jean stared at her.

"Blaise—coming here? Oh, but he must not—he mustn't come!"—in sudden panic. "I couldn't go through it all again! I couldn't!"

Claire slipped an arm round her.

"You won't have to," she answered. "Because, Jean-Jean! Blaise has the right to come now. He's free!"

"Free? *Free?*" repeated Jean. "What do you mean! How can he be free?"

"Nesta is dead," said Claire simply.

"Dead?" Jean began to laugh a trifle hysterically.

"Oh, yes, she's been 'dead' before. But— —"

"She is really dead this time," said Claire. "That is why Lady Anne has written—to tell us."

"I can't believe it!" muttered Jean. "I can't believe it."

"You *must* believe it," insisted Claire quietly. "It is all quite true. She was buried last week in the little churchyard at Coombe Eavie, and Lady Anne writes that Nick and Blaise will be here almost as soon as her letter. They're on their way now—*now*, Jean! Do you understand?" Her eyes filling with tears, Claire watched the gradual realisation of the amazing truth dawn in Jean's face. That face so tragically worn, so fined and spiritualised by suffering, glowed with a new light; a glory of unimaginable hope lit itself in the tired golden eyes, and on the half-parted lips there seemed to quiver those kisses which still waited to be claimed.

Jean passed her hand across her eyes like one who has seen some bright light of surpassing radiance.

"Tell me, Claire," she said at last, tremulously. "Tell me..." She broke off, unable to manage her voice.

"I'll read you what Lady Anne says," replied Claire quickly. "After writing that Nesta is dead and Nick and Blaise are coming here, she goes on: 'Poor Nesta! One cannot help feeling sorry for her—killed so suddenly and so tragically. And yet such a death seems quite in the picture with her lawless, wayward nature! She was shot, Claire, shot in the Boundary Woods by a Frenchman who had apparently followed her to England for the express purpose. It appears he met her at Château Varigny, in the days when she was posing as Madame de Varigny's niece, and fell violently in love with her. Of course Nesta could not marry him, and equally of course the Frenchman—he was the Vicomte de Chassaigne—did not know that she had a husband already. So, naturally, he hoped eventually to win her, and Nesta, (who, as you know, would flirt with the butcher's boy if there were no one else handy) encouraged him and allowed him to make love to her to his heart's content. Then, after her return to Staple, he learned of her marriage, and, furious at having been so utterly deceived, he followed. He must have watched her very carefully for some days, as he apparently knew her favourite walks, and waylaid her one afternoon in the woods. What passed between them we shall never know, for Chassaigne killed her and then immediately turned the revolver on himself. Blaise and Nick heard the shots and rushed down to the Boundary Woods where the shots had sounded—you'll know where I mean, the woods that lie along the border between Willow Ferry and Staple. There they found them. Nesta was dead, and de Chassaigne dying. He had just strength enough to confide in Blaise all that I have written. I am writing to you, because I think it might come as too great a shock to Jean as you say she is still so far from strong. You must tell her——"

Jean interrupted the reading with a shout of laughter.

"Oh, Claire! Claire! You blessed infant! I suppose all those preliminary remarks of yours about 'a letter from Lady Anne' and the 'news' it contained were by way of preparing me for the shock—'breaking the news' in fact?"

"Yes," admitted Claire, flushing a little.

Jean rocked with laughter—gay, spontaneous laughter such as Claire had not heard issue from her lips since the day when Madame de Varigny had come to Staple.

"And you just about succeeded in frightening me to death!" continued Jean. "Oh, Claire, Claire, you adorable little goose, didn't you know that good news never kills?"

"I didn't feel at all sure," returned Claire, laughing a little, too, in spite of herself. "You've looked lately as though it wouldn't take very much of anything—good or bad—to kill you."

"Well, it would now," Jean assured her solemnly. "Not all the powers of darkness would prevail against me, I verily believe." She paused, frowning a little. "How beastly it is though, to feel outrageously happy because someone is dead! It's indecent. Poor little Nesta! Oh, Claire! Is it hateful of me to feel like this? Do say it isn't, because—because I can't help it!"

"Of course it isn't," protested Claire. "It's only natural."

"I suppose it is. And I really *am* sorry for Nesta—though I'm so happy myself that it sort of swamps it. Oh, Claire darling"—the shadow passing and sheer gladness of soul bubbling up again into her voice—"I'm bound to kiss someone—at once. It'll have to be you! And look! Those two may be here any moment—Lady Anne said so. I'm going to make myself beautiful—if I can. I wish I hadn't grown so thin! The most ravishing frock in the world would look a failure draped on a clothes-horse. Still, I'll do what I can to conceal from Blaise the hideous ravages of time. And I'm not going to wear black—I won't welcome him back in sackcloth and ashes! I won't! I won't! I've got the darlingest frock upstairs—a filmy grey thing like moonlight. I'm going to wear that. I know—I know"—softly—"that Glyn would understand."

And if he knew anything at all about it—and one would like to think he did—it is quite certain Peterson would have approved his daughter's decision. For to his incurably romantic spirit, the idea of a woman going to meet the lover of whom a malign fate had so nearly robbed her altogether, clad in the sable habiliments with which she had paid filial tribute to her father's death, would have appeared of all things the most incongruous and irreconcilable.

So that when at last a prehistoric vehicle, chartered from the inn of the Green Dragon in the village below, toiled slowly up the hill to Peirnfels and Blaise and Nick climbed down from its musty interior, a slender, moon-grey figure, which might have been observed standing within the shadow of a tall stone pillar and following with straining eyes the snail-like progress of the old-fashioned carriage up the steep white road, flitted swiftly back into the shelter of the house. Claire, dimpling and smiling at the great gateway of the castle, alone received the travellers.

"Go along that corridor," she said to Blaise, when they had exchanged greetings. "To the end door of all. That's the sun-parlour. You'll find Jean there. She thought it appropriate"—smiling at him.

Then, as Blaise strode down the corridor indicated, she turned to Nick and asked him with an adorable coquetry why he, too, had come to Beirnfels?

"I've heard it is the House of Dreams-Come-True," replied Nick promptly. "It seemed a likely place in which to find you, most beautiful."

Claire beamed at him.

"Oh, am I that—really, Nick?"

"Of course you are. The most beautiful in all the world. Claire"—tucking his arm into hers—"tell me, how is the 'soul-rebuilding' process getting on? That's why I came, really, you know, to find out if you had completely finished redecorating your interior?—I can vouch for the outer woman myself"—with an adoring glance at the fluffy ash-blonde hair and pure little Greuze profile.

Claire rubbed her cheek against his sleeve. To a woman who has been for four months limited almost exclusively to the society of one other woman—even though that other woman be her chosen friend—the rough 'feel' of a man's coat-sleeve (more particularly if he should happen to be *the* man) and the faint fragrance of tobacco which pervades it form an almost delirious combination.

Claire hauled down her flag precipitately.

"I'm ready to go back to England any time now, Nick," she murmured.

"Are you? Darling! How soon can you be ready? In a week? To-morrow? Next day?"

"Quite soon. And meanwhile, mightn't you—you and Blaise—stay for a bit at the Green Dragon?"

"We might," replied Nick solemnly, quite omitting to mention that something of the sort had been precisely their intention when leaving England.

Meanwhile Blaise had made his way to the door at the end of the corridor. Outside it he paused, overwhelmed by the sudden realisation that beyond that wooden barrier lay holy ground—Paradise! And the Angel with the Flaming Sword stood at the gate no longer....

She was waiting for him over by the window, straight and slim and tall in her moon-grey, her hands hanging in front of her tight-clasped like those of a child. But her eyes were woman's eyes.

With a little inarticulate cry she ran to him—to the place that was hers, now and for all time, against his heart—and his arms, that had been so long empty, held her as though he would never let her go.

"Beloved of my heart!" he murmured. "Oh, my sweet—my sweet!"

They spoke but little. Only those foolish, tender words that seem so meaningless to those who are not lovers, but which are pearls strung on a thread of gold to those who love—a rosary of memory which will be theirs to keep and tell again when the beloved voice that uttered them shall sound no more.

CHAPTER XXXVII
"AN HOUSE NOT MADE WITH HANDS"

THE landlord of the inn of the Green Dragon watched his two English visitors ride away up the steep road that led to Beirnfels with unquestionable regret.

They had been lodging at the Green Dragon for the past fortnight, and he had discovered that English milords, whatever else they might be, were not niggardly with their money. They required a good deal of attention, it is true, and had a strange, outlandish predilection for innumerable baths, demanding a quite unheard-of quantity of water for the same. And at all unlikely hours of the day, too—when returning from a ride or before going up to the castle to dine, mark you!

Still, they made no difficulty about paying—and paying handsomely—for all they wanted, and if a man chooses to spend his money upon the superfluous scrubbing of his epidermis, it is, after all, his own affair!

And now the two English milords were taking their departure from the Green Dragon and, so the landlord understood, proposed to stay at the castle itself until their return to England.

It appeared that their lady-mother—who, it was rumoured in the village, was the daughter of an English archduke, no less!—was coming to Beirnfels and there was much talk amongst the village girls of weddings and the like. Apparently the Green Dragon's two eccentric visitors, not withstanding their altogether abnormal liking for soap and water, were much as most men in other respects and had lost their hearts to the two pretty English ladies living at the castle.

So, no doubt, the "daughter of an English archduke, no less" was coming from England post haste to enquire into the suitability of the brides-elect—and also into the important point of the amount of the dowry each might be expected to bring her future husband.

There was no question that Lady Anne was certainly coming post haste—in reply to a series of joyful and imperative telegrams demanding that she should pack up and come to Beirnfels immediately—"for we are all enjoying ourselves far too much to return to England at present," as Nick wired her with an iniquitous disregard for the cost per word of foreign telegrams. And Lady Anne, who always considered money well-spent if it purchased happiness, proceeded to wire back with equal extravagance that she was delighted to hear it and that she and her maid would start at once.

It was a very happy party that gathered round the table in the great dining-hall at Beirnfels on the night of Lady Anne's arrival, and beneath all the surface laughter and gaiety lay the deep, quiet thanksgiving that only comes to those who have emerged out of the night of darkness and sorrow into a glorious sunlight of happiness and hope.

After dinner, in the soft, candle-lit dusk—for Peterson had never introduced the garish anomaly of electric light into the ancient castle—Jean sang to them in that quaintly appealing, husky voice of hers, simple tender folk-songs of the country-side, and finally, at a murmured request from Blaise, she gave them *The House of Dreams*.

"It's a strange road leads to the House of Dreams,
To the House of Dreams-Come-True,
Its hills are steep and its valleys deep,
And salt with tears the Wayfarers weep,
The Wayfarers—I and you.

"But there's sure a way to the House of Dreams,
To the House of Dreams-Come-True.
We shall find it yet, ere the sun has set,
If we fare straight on, come fine, come wet,
Wayfarers—I and you."

As the last words died away into silence, she looked up and met Blaise's eyes. He was leaning against the piano, looking down at her with a tranquil happiness in his gaze.

"*Our* House of Dreams-Come-True, Jean, at last," he said softly.

She met his glance with one of utter trust.

"And we needn't ever fear, now, that it will tumble down. But oh! Blaise, if we had built on a rotten foundation, we should never have felt safe—not safe like this!"

"No. You were right, belovedest—as you always have been, always will be." Then, very low, so that none but she should hear: "Thank God for you, my sweet!"

The House Of Dreams-Come-True | 263

It was ultimately settled that the whole party should remain at Beirnfels until the latter end of June, when they would all return to England together and the two weddings should take place as soon as possible afterwards.

"But we won't have a double wedding," declared Jean. "It's always supposed to be unlucky."

"Do you believe in good and bad luck, then?" asked Lady Anne, smiling.

"I don't know," Jean answered seriously. "But it's always just as well to be on the safe side. Anyway, we won't tempt Fate by running unnecessary risks!"

"Besides, madonna," added Nick, "in the excitement of the moment we might get mixed and the parson hitch us up to the wrong people. The average nerve-strain attendant upon the rôle of bridegroom will be quite sufficient for me, thank you, without the added uncertainty as to whether I'm getting tied up to the right woman or not."

So spring lengthened out into summer, and, as the heat increased, boating and swimming on the big lake that nestled in a basin of the hills were added to the long rides and excursions with which they whiled away the pleasant, sunshiny days.

Ever afterwards, the memory of those tranquil months at Beirnfels would linger in the minds of those who shared them as something rare and precious. It was as though for this little span of time, passed so far away from the noise and bustle of the big world, they had pulled their barque out of the busy fairway of the river and moored it in some quiet, shady backwater. Then, when they were rested and refreshed, they would be ready to face anew, with fresh strength and courage, the difficulties and dangers of midstream.

"I'm sorry it's so nearly over—this long, long holiday of ours," said Jean regretfully. "The only thing that reconciles me to the fact is that after we're married Blaise and I propose to spend at least six months out of every year at Beirnfels."

She was lying on her back in the shady wood whither they had ridden out to lunch that day, staring up at the bits of blue sky overhead which showed between the interlacing branches of the trees. The remainder of the party were grouped around her, reclining in various attitudes of a *dolce far niente* nature, while from a little distance away, where the horses were picketed in charge of a groom, came the drowsy, rhythmic sound of the munching of corn, punctuated by an occasional stamp of an impatient hoof.

"Yes, it's been good," agreed Lady Anne. "I shall never settle down again properly as a dowager at the Dower House!" And she laughed gleefully.

To her, it had been almost like a return to the days of her youth, for "her four children" — as she called them — had insisted on her sharing in all their active pursuits, and Lady Anne, who in her girlhood and early married life had been a first-class horsewoman and a magnificent swimmer, had consented *con amore*.

Blaise pulled himself lazily up into a sitting posture and glanced toward the crimson glow of westering sun where it struck athwart the tall trunks of the trees.

"You'll none of you live to go back to England. Instead, you'll be dying of pneumonia and a few other complaints — if we don't get a move on soon," he observed. "It's almost sunset, and after that it grows abominably chilly in this eastern paradise of Jean's. Besides, I fancy it's going to blow great guns before long."

It was true. Already a little chill whisper of wind was shaking the tops of the trees, and before the party was fairly mounted and away, the whisper had changed to a shrill whistling, heralding the big gale which drove along behind the innocent seeming breeze which at first had barely rocked the topmost branches.

It was a longish ride back to Beirnfels, and the sun had dipped below the horizon in a sullen splendour of purple and red before the shoulder of the hill, upon the further side of which the castle stood, came into sight.

Now and again the moon peered out between the racing, wind-driven clouds, clearly limning the bold, black curve of the hill against a background of lowering sky.

Jean and Blaise were riding abreast, a little in advance of the rest, engrossed by the difficulties of carrying on an animated conversation in a high wind. As they swung round the bend in the road which brought the hill's great shoulder into view, Jean threw back her head and stared at the sky above it with a puzzled frown on her face.

"Why... how queer!" she ejaculated. "The sun set nearly half an hour ago and yet there's still quite a brilliant red glow in the sky. Look, Blaise — just above where Beirnfels stands."

Blaise glanced up casually in the direction indicated, then suddenly reigned in his horse and half-rose in the stirrups, staring at the red glow deepening in the sky ahead.

"That's no sunset!" he exclaimed sharply. "It's—Great heavens, Jean! Beirnfels is *on fire!*"

Even as he spoke a tongue of flame, mocking the dull glow with its gleaming blaze, shot up like a thin red knife into the sky and sank again.

A shout came from behind. The others had seen it, also, and recognised its deadly import. The next moment the clatter of galloping hoofs echoed along the road as the whole party urged their horses on towards home as fast as they could cover the ground.

Soon they struck off from the road, taking a bridle-path which slanted through the woods clothing the base of the hill, and as they emerged on to the broad plateau where Beirnfels had stood sentinel through wind and weather for so many years, the whole extent of the catastrophe was revealed.

By this time the angry glow in the sky had turned dusk into day, while from the doors and windows of the castle fire vomited forth as from a furnace—upward in long, sinuous tongues of flame, licking the blackened walls, downward in spangled showers of sparks that drifted towards the earth like flights of golden butterflies.

Little groups of men and women, helpless as ants to stay the fire, rushed futilely hither and thither with hosepipe and engine, while on the smooth sward which fronted the castle lay piled enormous quantities of household stuff a medley of fine old furniture, torn tapestry wrenched from its place against the walls, pictures, mirrors—anything and everything that could be dragged out into the open by eager hands and willing arms.

The major-domo, an elderly, grey-haired man who had been born and reared upon the estate and who had taken service with Glyn Peterson on the day when he had first brought Jacqueline, a bride, to Beirnfels, caught sight of the riding-party returned and came hurrying to Jean's side.

The tears were running down his wrinkled face as he recounted the discovery of the fire, which must have started either just before or during the servants' dinner-hour, when few people, of course, were about the castle, and which had obtained a firm hold before it was detected.

The household staff, practised to a limited extent,—a fire drill had been held once a month in Peterson's time—had done their hest to cope with the flames, but vainly. The high wind which had arisen had thwarted their utmost efforts, and finally giving up all hope of saving the interior from being gutted, they had confined themselves to rescuing such valuables as could be easily removed.

There was the usual mystery as to how the fire had originated, and several stories circulated amongst the chattering throng which hurried hither and thither, momentarily augmented by the peasants who, at sight of the castle in flames, had come trooping up the hill from the village below.

The most likely story, and the one to which Blaise inclined to give most credence, was that the child of a woman who worked daily at the castle, escaping from its mother's care and launched on an independent voyage of discovery through the rooms, had knocked over a burning lamp. Then, terrified at the immediate consequences—the sudden flaring of some ancient tapestry, dry as tinder with the summer heat, near which the lamp had fallen—he had bolted away, out of the castle and so home, too scared to tell anyone of the accident.

But, as Jean commented mournfully, what did it matter how it happened? Except from the prosaic viewpoint of the fire insurance company, who would probably desire to know: all kinds of details that it was impossible to supply!

For her, nothing mattered except that Beirnfels, her home from childhood and the place where she and Blaise had proposed to spend a great part of their married life, was a furnace of flames.

It was a splendid but very terrible sight The great, grim walls of the castle stood four-square against the sky, charred and blackened but defiantly impervious to the flames that were licking covetously against the solid stone which fashioned them. Sentinel to the very end, they reared themselves unvanquished, guardians still, though all that they had sheltered through their centuries of watch and ward lay consumed within their very heart.

Jean, standing beside Blaise and watching the upward tossing flames and the crimson banner of the lowering heavens, spoke suddenly:

"'And the sky as red as blood above it.' Blaise, the last of Keturah Stanley's prophecies has come true!"

An hour later help was forthcoming from the distant town to which a messenger had been despatched post haste as soon as it was realised that the household staff, even with assistance from the village, was hopelessly inadequate to cope with a fire of such magnitude. But it was already too late to accomplish very much in the way of salvage. All that remained possible was to quench that inferno of fire as soon as might be and so, perhaps, save some of the outbuildings.

Hour after hour through the night, human endeavour fought with the flames—subduing them again and again only to find them kindling into fresh life at the gusty bidding of the wind, leaping redly from the lambent heart of the conflagration, which glowed and pulsed and heaved like some living monster intent upon destruction.

It was not until dawn was breaking that, with the dying down of the wind, the flickering crimson light faded finally from the sky; and half an hour later, when the fire had been at last extinguished, the village folk, gathered about the scene of the catastrophe, had dispersed to their homes.

Lady Anne, accompanied by Nick and Claire, started for the inn of the Green Dragon, whither the landlord had hurried on ahead to prepare temporary quarters for the now homeless little company from the castle. But Jean and Blaise still lingered by the deserted ruins, loth to say farewell to the place that had meant so much to them.

Beneath the misty azure of the summer morning sky, fanned by little vagrant zephyrs—rearguard of the hurricane which had passed—stood all that remained of Beirnfels—blackened, naked walls, stark against that tender blue, brooding above a mass of cooling wreckage.

Jean's mouth quivered a little as her glance took in the scene of utter desolation.

"My House of Dreams," she whispered brokenly.

She was silent for a few moments, her eyes embracing all that had once been Beirnfels in a gaze which held both farewell and retrospect. And something more—some vision of the future. In the dawn-light pearling the sky above she recognised the eternal promise of Him Who "commanded the light to shine out of darkness."

Her House of Dreams! The inner meaning of the song had grown suddenly clear to her.

When she turned again to Blaise, her expression was serene and tranquil. Touched with regret perhaps, but bravely confident.

"I don't think it matters, Blaise," she said simply. "Beirnfels was only a symbol, after all. My House of Dreams-Come-True isn't built of stones and mortar. No one's is. It's just—where love is."